Chalice

Erik Dolson

"Chalice" is a work of fiction. Some will see characters they think they recognize, or scenes they think are real. This is not the case. I may use the color green from the juniper tree outside my window in this painting, but that does not mean I paint that tree, or any other tree — only that I thought that color green conveyed what I wanted to convey.

"Chalice" is a fictional aggregation of traits, insecurities, wishes, aspirations, hopes, fears, dreams and nightmares bound together by my imagination. Any resemblance of any entity in "Chalice" to an actual juniper tree, business, or any individual, living or dead, is coincidental.

PO Box 1450
Sisters, Oregon 97759
erik@erikdolson.com

ISBN 978-0-9897479-1-2

Dedication

In memory of R.i.p

Frances Marie Gignoux.

+ Nia Georgiva

I wish we'd had a chance
to know each other.

Dear Nia,
This book sounds cooll + im
going to annotate this book
for you.. bestay
from, Megan

Thank you.

Many deserve mention, but only a few will receive it. My sincere apologies to anyone I leave out, due to lapse of memory or simple thoughtlessness.

First, Jim Cornelius and Paul Lipscomb: Without Jim's encouragement, from the beginning, "Chalice" would never have been written. His belief in the artist, and that "character is fate," proved to be a constant beacon. Thank you.

Paul gave crucial support. While at times I wanted to resist his advice about language and concept, he was always right. If the book succeeds, his insights were essential. Thank you.

Before this book was even an idea, Samantha Grace Taylor said, "You have to write." Thank you. Jo Ellen Zucker, whose love of language and the written word were inspirational — thank you. Geniece Shirts Brown lived through the writing with incredible courage and patience. Thank you.

To readers who provided feedback on various drafts of "Chalice:" It was an amazing process to watch the book evolve, become something other than what it started out to be, what I thought it would be, under your guidance. You gave "Chalice" a life of its own. Thank you.

Steven Pressfield & Co., for pioneering new directions in publishing, talking about what it takes, and showing how faith in The Muse allows art to transcend the artist, thank you.

Finally, to those about to begin "Chalice": I hope you find something of value. Thank you for being willing to find out.

Erik Dolson
July, 2013

Spring

Hot Chocolate

From: Debra Shapiro <debrashapiro4@gmail.com>
Date: Wed, Mar x, 20XX at 10:18 AM
Subject: your suit
To: Peter Hamilton <peterhamilton06@gmail.com>

Mr. Hamilton, I have to say again how sorry I am about your suit!

Are you absolutely sure I can't get it cleaned? I am on a first-name basis with the best dry cleaner in Seattle. If it would be easier I will even pick it up from your home or office and deliver!

My children have since heard plenty about appropriate behavior on the ferry! It was a lesson I thought they already knew. I had no idea they would be so rambunctious or I would have tied them to their seats with books in their hands!

If the chocolate won't come out, I insist on being able to replace the suit with one of comparable quality. Please let me take care of this so I can at least assuage my guilt. You would be doing me a favor!

— Debra Shapiro

From: Peter Hamilton <peterhamilton06@gmail.com>
Date: Wed, Mar x, 20XX at 10:45 AM
Subject: Re: your suit
To: Debra Shapiro <debrashapiro4@gmail.com>

Ms. Shapiro, I've already had the suit cleaned, which was past due in any case, and it was undamaged. So no expense incurred and no harm done, besides a somewhat sticky ferry ride home.

Please tell your kids everything is fine. The expression of horror on your daughter's face when the cup landed in my lap is something I will not forget for some time, nor the sight of you bent at the waist to be at her level, nose-to-nose and eye-to-eye, making your point with a matching mane of curls. dang

It's obvious you have high expectations for your children, in addition to mutual respect. I appreciate your parenting style.

Thank you for being so concerned, but there is no need.

I'm just glad the hot chocolate had already cooled, and that I was reading *The Seattle Times* instead of working on my laptop. That could have been a little more catastrophic.

~Peter Hamilton

on the Shapiro's email she used a dash & hes using this squiggly thing hes already flirting

Nose-to-nose? I can only hope she grows up less self-conscious about her profile than I am.

same

Yes, my children and I do have mutual respect. Certainly, in that instance, I had Hannah's attention, though I suspect Jacob was equally at fault despite his denials. Sometimes the peer relationship is strong and rewarding, other times I worry about drawbacks.

She has just met this man & is already telling him personal things...

May I at least buy you a coffee at Martha's Cafe one of these days to make up for the discomfort?

—Debra

Coffee would be great, but only for its own sake. I don't have a firm schedule next week, but perhaps if we are headed to the mainland on the same ferry, we could meet early at Martha's and take a cup on board.

Self-conscious? I was speaking only of emotional proximity. Jacob's crime was his inability to hide a smile when he saw the wet spot on my pants, which he shared with my daughter, who sniggered when I got home, "Oooh Dada, did you have an 'aaaccideeent?' "

I will shoot you an email when I know what my work schedule looks like.

~Peter

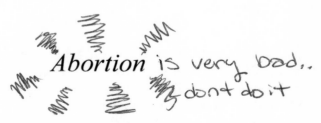

Abortion

Mr. Hamilton; Just a note to tell you how much I enjoyed your op-ed in The Seattle Times *re: those trying to capitalize on the tragic murder of a pregnant woman to push a political anti-abortion agenda by classifying the crime as a double-homicide.*

I assume the piece was written by you. There can only be one "Peter Hamilton, Port Cedar, Washington," right?

If that was what you would have been working on when Hannah's hot (luke-warm? Or were you just being nice?) chocolate landed in your lap but missed your laptop, I am quite glad.

Since we are "neighbors" in a manner of speaking, both having chosen to "hide out" here in rural Port Cedar, perhaps we will meet at a school board meeting.

Of course, I still owe you that cup of coffee.

—Debra Shapiro.

So if I were opposing abortion, the laptop would have been a worthwhile sacrifice?

Thank you for your note. It is a good thing I am so "calloused to the suffering of others," according to my hate mail.

~Peter Hamilton.

I was trying to make a joke.

But you nailed their attempt at a back-door "laying the bricks" (wasn't that your phrase?) toward criminalizing abortion. (In law school the classic metaphor was "heading down the slippery slope." You must be Liberal, capital "L."

By the way, how is it that you wear suits and write op-eds in The Times? That all seems so far removed from quaint Port Cedar on Vincente Island.

—Debra

I once heard my hero Ken Kesey say of abortion even in cases of rape, "God doesn't care whose shovel plants the corn." I was about to say he was Liberal, but maybe he was just an outlaw.

The op-ed was the result of a friendly argument with the editor of The Times, who was a classmate in college.

~Peter

Well, I don't believe in heros. Nor in God. And it's just too easy for White men in particular to dictate how others should live. You shouldn't oppose abortion if you don't have a womb.

I didn't realize you had access to The Times *for dissemination of your personal opinions. I'm* less *impressed but hope we continue to agree.*

–Debra Shapiro

I don't understand why the nature of my access changes your opinion of the content.

Women don't own the abortion debate. You don't get to invalidate an argument because of who is making it. Ad hominem? Even White men get to have opinions.

It might be more fun to have this discussion over at Martha's if you are still willing. ~Peter Hamilton.

Ad hominem? Men are not as affected by the abortion debate as their wives or girlfriends. Prima facie.

Can't do Martha's. I'm off to take my son for an X-ray; he may have broken his second digit in 4 months on our trampoline. Then I need to pick up some books they are holding for me at the library.

We are off to Phoenix at the end of the week so my husband Robert can pay an obligatory visit to his parents. He's a commercial pilot and we'll fly nearly free. That is, if I can find a house-sitter to take care of the 3 dogs, 7 cats and 3 horses.

–Debra Shapiro

I hope the finger is sprained and not broken.

The library is closed for eight more weeks until they finish the renovation.

~Peter

Yes, I know the library "building" is undergoing renovation. But they set up a temporary drop/pickup, a "library" in a spare room in the county offices. I have some books on order that came over from the mainland.

The finger is fine, thank you, the doctor could not find a thing wrong on the X-ray. My son is a bit of a hypochondriac.

Running

Touching base about ~~coffee~~. How was Phoenix? Did you all swim? Was the weather warm?

~Peter Hamilton.

Phoenix weather was so-so, but it was a mercy-mission-accomplished and we got in two days of swimming, and I had what might be the most beautiful run of my life on a truly brilliant day.

– Debra Shapiro

Mercy mission? I hope there isn't a family tragedy.

Tell me about your run in the sun. Weather in Port Cedar has been so dismal even the harbor seals are looking for some place to dry out.

~Peter

No tragedy, other than old age. Robert's folks are in adjoining rooms in a care facility. They don't recognize any of us. They ask 4 times in 10 minutes "Who are you?" which makes my kids uncomfortable.

The run was spectacular. I drove to the Salt River, parked my car and ran up an arroyo in the Tonto National Forest. Forest being a misnomer, of course, to those of us from the Northwest.

oooo sounds cool

The desert was at its most lush (this year's near-record rainfall breaking a drought); purples and yellows everywhere.

I found a network of trails and ran among towering saguaros and spider-like cacti bearing orange blossoms on the tips of their tentacles. Nothing but the sound of birds and a view of the salt.

–Debra

hes getting to confortable

Do you run for a reason or just for the joy? ~P P

I'm training for a marathon in Seattle next month. But yes, I run for the joy. And to relieve stress. And because I love the desert. And because I love dessert, with food issues stemming from genetic obesity and a passion for sweets and big portions (both of which I indulge daily).

same sis

You are tiny. How ~~big~~ can the portions be? ~P

dmcccc

Huge. But more horrifying than the size of the slice of cake I eat each night is the fact that it's usually from Safeway, or some other working-class bakery. I have no interest in fine-quality dessert. Even the fresh-baked offerings of Martha's are too upscale. I like sickeningly sweet, lardy, synthetic frosting atop old-fashioned cake.

gurl stop ur makeing me hungrey :(

My addiction is for vanilla bean ice cream stuffed into a coffee cup and laced with layers of cheap Hershey's syrup. Especially with real, fresh-picked blackberries.

I used to run on the deer trails above my home. Then about eight or nine years ago it was below zero for about a week. It was hard to breathe in the cold but I ran anyway. I got a cough. We went to Mexico and stayed in a cheap run-down place along the Baja coast.

The cough got worse. When we got back I was diagnosed with pneumonia. They gave me antibiotics that had no effect. Eventually they said I had asthma.

I couldn't run after that, so I went back to lifting weights, which I can do without getting aerobic. Or anaerobic. Or whatever they call it. If I don't breath too hard I don't get an asthma attack.

We were living in Seattle during that freeze! Pipes bursting everywhere! Robert was off flying or training pilots somewhere and I was home alone with a six-year-old and a four-year-old. I had to get an entire hardwood floor replaced along with sheet rock in the master bedroom. What a nightmare!

I think if I could not exercise I would go insane. Running, climbing mountains, riding my bike. I didn't really start until I was in law school, but I don't think a week has gone by since when I haven't run or worked out at least four days a week. It didn't matter where Robert was flying... Australia, Athens, Istanbul... if I went along, I ran.

We went to Panama with friends a few years ago and we stayed on their boat. I made our hosts take me to the beach every day so I could run back and forth on the sand for an hour. It was a small beach, probably not 200 yards long. Back and forth. Back and forth. They thought I was crazy. They didn't know I did it for their benefit as much as my own.

I do miss the high I used to get after running for about an hour. There would come a point when the fact that I was running just disappeared. It became effortless and I was just flowing over the ground.

Did you mean flowing or flying?

this question makes me mad for no reason

I actually meant flowing. I was never fast even at my best. But there were times when I felt like a drop of water in a creek flowing along the trails.

oop poetic

I don't get that feeling much anymore except at the end of really long runs, or during an especially rigorous bike ride. That was one of the wonderful things about the run in the Tonto Forest. I don't know if it was the different setting or if I was just in a different mood, but that "disappearing" was nearly miraculous.

More often, when I run I become absorbed in my own world where I know just how to handle my kids. I know exactly the right words for my friend Kym about that new boyfriend of hers. I know what to say to my mother who is always asking when I'm going to leave "the sticks" of Port Cedar and move back to Seattle. these people are old

I run and I talk it all through with each of them and I run and rephrase and I run and rehearse and I run and I think and then I am done with my run.

That's a lot of heavy to carry on a run.

I cant tell if hes trying to be funny

It's almost as bad as my insomnia. I am probably a candidate for Prozac. lol they are old

Prozac has its place, I'm sure, but I'm not convinced medicating always solves the issues.

Then you don't have the same issues.

—D. dang shes kind cold

Texting

Peter, as a parent, what do you think about the debate here in Port Cedar about class size versus instructional days? I know we haven't lived here very long, but am I so off-base in thinking that instructional days are of limited efficacy when there are 30-plus students in the class? Aaaagh!

You have kids in school. Want to join in a protest to the school board?

The discussion over school days versus class size is moot. There are no funds to improve either. Water taken from one end of the beach does little good when put back at the other end of the beach. All parents can do is build rafts for our children and then trust the tides. ~Peter

Nicely put, though I don't know that I agree. As my kids plough through the schools (Hannah is in seventh grade, Jacob in ninth) I keep exploring, in a vague way and usually during a runner's high, ways to add teacher accountability to the system without marginalizing the "have-nots."

Of course politically it'd never sell. What about using your access to The Times *to get in an editorial advocating for adequate school funding?*

Writing about school funding isn't of much interest to me, nor would I suggest to the editor what he should promote.

My twins, Sam and Abby, are a year ahead of your Jacob. I agree schools are not creating excitement for learning. But it's a social problem as much as one of education. When my wife Molly is gone to care for her terminally ill mother over in Seattle, I teach my twins to cook and we have conversations at dinner about the constant area ratio of circles drawn inside of squares and whether there is space enough in space.

So you only do what is "of interest" to you, regardless of potential benefit? That seems a little... self-focused?

What odd dinner conversation! We talk about my kids' friends and what they did in the lunch room. And about their teachers, most of whom they don't like.

My Jacob says he has seen your children on the soccer field, they often play before or after he does. He said they seem very good.

I did not know they were twins. Do they have the same friends? Do they socialize together? That would be heaven. It seems that most of my days are spent shuttling my kids around Port Cedar to games or social engagements on opposite sides of Vincente Island. Sometimes I go to the library to read, it's often in-between the stops. Other times I just read in my car while I wait for the soccer practice or play-date to end, otherwise I would spend all my days wasting the world's petroleum reserves and polluting the air.

I focus my contributions, meager as they are, where I feel the effort might have the most impact.

My kids don't socialize that much, actually. Abby spends a lot of time reading or drawing and listening to music, Sam is usually doing sports or helps me on projects around the house.

When my kids aren't in school they always want to be with other kids, and on weekends they always get together with friends. I've raised them mostly alone, with Robert flying and gone for a week or two at a time, or working four days a week in Seattle where he has an apartment close to the airfield and main office.

I do worry there isn't that much for them to do in provincial Port Cedar. I can't expect them to paint the play room or work on the lawn.

Painting and mowing is exactly what I want my twins to do. Though sometimes I feel the job would go faster if I didn't have their help. I don't know how to teach that doing an unpleasant task more quickly gets it over with even sooner.

I wouldn't have Jacob or Hannah paint or mow, they have their own interests, things they want to do. I don't see any reason why they should have to do work like that. I can do it just as easily.

dang i wish my parents treated me like this.

But we don't always get to do what we want to do. Life is in session, right? It's good for them to learn how to work.

It's good for them to mow a lawn? How is that good for them? I'm sure they could learn to mow a lawn any time they actually needed to mow a lawn. Which is unlikely in any case. They work all week in school. And they are excellent students.

Shane

I don't think learning to mow a lawn is really all that educational. If they are home, they can be on their phone or texting. If they go out, I take them to meet with friends, maybe go to the mall on the mainland and meet with other kids, go to a movie. You know, what kids do.

These kids have the perfect life ♡

Texting is better than mowing the lawn? It just seems that all of you working outside together would be healthy.

So now it's about family, or health? They would rather be around their friends and I would rather they be socializing, communicating. They are learning to interact.

No they're not. They are inside, looking at a tiny screen, their attention someplace else. I see kids texting all the time. They walk and text. They sit in restaurants and text. They don't look out the windows of cars, they sit in the back seat and text. It's like that's all they do, they don't see anything except words on a little screen.

dang chill man

Why is that bad? That's the way the world is now.

kinda true tho

Just because that's the way the world is doesn't mean that's the way it should be.

well karen if every one jumped off a cliffe would you?

Who appointed you judge of how things should be?

oop they mad now...

Nobody. It just seems like so many kids are acting like addicts, needing their phone fix all the time. I think they should be looking outside, doing things with their brains or their hands.

like wat

kp biteing emoji*

They are *using their brains, and they are learning social rules, interacting, multitasking. What does mowing the lawn give them?* same sister or broth...

Fresh air? Learning to work?

They get plenty of fresh air doing sports at school. I already told you they know how to work.

It just seems like they are not in the moment.

Of course they are. They are in a moment with their friends, and their friends are in that moment. It just doesn't happen to be the moment you think they should be in.

gurl this person is getting canceled

Library

I am dropping the kids off at school this morning, then headed to the library. Shall we try for ~~coffee~~?

~~Coffee~~ would be great but I should probably stay near my office this morning. I'm waiting on a few phone calls.

You read a lot. You don't download to a Kindle or an iPad or your phone?

Yes, I read voraciously. The ~~library~~ is my salvation, especially since moving here. I could not afford all the books and reading isn't the same on my computer or worse, on my phone. I love how words look and feel on the paper page. It's not just about absorbing information.

Do you mind if I ask what it is you "do" in your office, besides write pithy opinion pieces for newspapers and correspond with bored housewives?

Let me guess: You were an early employee of Microsoft, made a small fortune with stock options, retired at 45 and built a home out here on Vincente Island to pursue philanthropic endeavors.

Nice scenario. But no. I buy and renovate old buildings into office spaces.

So is that why you know the library is undergoing renovation? Are you the contractor doing the work?

kinda like me

No, I'm not a contractor. I'm a developer, which is an ugly word in Port Cedar. I have been involved in the project, but only by contributing to the public interest.

I just looked online at the list of contributors and your name was not on it. Are you one of those anonymous benefactors?

big word that i dont understand

Two years ago the county announced they wanted to sell the historic county seat to a developer and use the money to build a new library on land they owned next to the Safeway. I was approached but pushed to instead sell the land to Safeway and use that money to renovate the historic county building for the library.

Safeway got to expand instead of move, which would have left one more empty, ugly big box behind, the library is about twice the size it would have been and the historic building was saved. I helped shepherd the process.

So everyone came out ahead? It really is a very nice addition to downtown. And generous of you to turn down the opportunity. You must be very successful to be able to do that.

Thank you. It's a lovely building and an important part of Port Cedar history. I doubt we will ever again see that kind of investment in public architecture.

sorry this page was boring

I'm not big-time. I make enough to feed my family and follow some interests. And I don't know how big the opportunity would have been. There is always risk and I don't do residential.

Not everyone came out ahead. The realtor who was going to list the county building was pretty angry with me, along with a group he put together to buy it. They were going to turn it into some nice condos and he was going to be able to sell those, too. random comment but my dad lived in a condo once

I have a reputation for being a bit abrasive at times, and I believed pretty passionately that the building should remain in the public domain. I'm sure I ruffled some feathers.

This ~~[illegible]~~ ~~metafor~~ metaphor is dumb.
Just saying

Zen

May I buy you a coffee as a personal thank you for your contribution to our new library? I prefer mine with non-fat milk and stevia. I'd guess you'd prefer a double shot of straight espresso, or an Americano?

Stevia after all that cake? Have to raincheck on coffee. I'm pushing deadlines to catch the 2:15 ferry, heading to Seattle on business and to get a car worked on for a day or two.

Why do you get your car worked on in Seattle? I've been told Tim's Garage can fix anything, from trawler diesels to Porsches. Or is your fine machinery only trusted to dealerships?

The mechanic is a specialist. It's a race car.

As much as I enjoy the isolation of Port Cedar, in downtown Seattle there is a seafood restaurant not far from the University Club that is supposed to be superb.

Oh god! A race car? Do you have sponsors? Aren't race cars all sponsored by chewing tobacco or lite beers? Does it have a gun rack? That just doesn't seem like you! Do you own a driver? Does he speak with a drawl? This is such a surprise! Another rabbit out of your hat!

You are quite misinformed. I drive the car myself. It's a hobby, a passion. There are no sponsors. I think a deeper explanation would be wasted.

Ooooh, is someone being defensive? Please forgive my insensitivity. I'm headed to Seattle for a half-marathon tomorrow; I wish I didn't have to spend 4 hrs in the car, particularly after waking at 4 a.m. Damn insomnia! As soon as it's over I have to jump in the car and drive like hell to catch the last ferry back to Port Cedar! Let's get together when I get back.

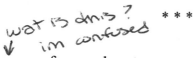

* * *

I'm sorry for my abrupt response the other day. I won't dilute the apology with an explanation. Please accept.

Did you do well in your marathon? Are you well? Sane?

Accepted. There was some truth in your pique. Accept mine in turn?

Well: Yes. Sane: Never. No, the half-marathon was aborted (don't start) because I did not have a "less-than-3/8" wrench in order to remove the damn battery from my rig so I could replace it with the new damn battery that I spent the afternoon procuring.

That battery weighs 2/3s what you weigh! Not that I doubt for a minute your determination. Batteries also take a small Crescent wrench and a flat-blade screw driver… use the driver to pry the two halves of the clamp apart.

The loathsome battery wasn't heavy at all, but the corrosion and stripped hex-nut that clamps the cable on the battery left me grounded (so to speak), Hannah sobbing because we couldn't make it to Seattle, and both my parents crushed. And I was all carbed out with no place to go.

But after a 30-minute jump the car was finally running and I'll bring the old/new battery into Tim's Garage on Monday.

I will never understand your love of cars. Or driving, which for me is just a chore.

Beautiful cars are works of art. Driving well is to dance, emotion in motion, especially hanging it out on the edge of traction, in competition. I will come back from a race of 30 or so minutes wet but not knowing what happened when. Memory is compressed into still-frame snap shots, moments of Zen.

So "Zen" is of coughs and splutters and roars of engines? The smell of rubber and grease and gas, all those worldly distractions draw your concentration further inward to the hub and heart of your being?

Perhaps your half-hour of "forgetting" is really a half-hour of immersion in your own essence, devoid of pretensions and expectations and abstract thought. No time to think, only time to react.

Spiritualism rarely rocks the core of my cynical soul and I could never let down the barriers between myself and my essence among people, or with noise, or the smell of fresh-baked cookies or just about any other distraction.

It's most familiar to me when I am on a mountain, well above timberline, and the air is thin and the sound of a rock ricocheting off the walls of a cirque bowl echoes and echoes. I've found it (cliche as it may be) while lost in the hypnotic power of ocean waves. I've known it on a sparkling winter day, standing amidst fresh snow: blinding, brilliant diamond dust.

Yah, nature provides direct access. But I also love the forgetting that comes with driving well and the eagerness of 600 horsepower spinning from a snarl to a howl that you don't hear as much as feel deep in your chest and the base of your skull.

Finding the brakes at 160 mph about to dive down into a sharp right turn then a hairpin left, things happen too fast to be decided. When the car starts to slide in oil from an engine blown into fragments in the car just ahead, my hands move and my feet dance on pedals before my mind knows the sheen on the track is not just the setting sun.

That forgetting, the Zen time, that half-hour of running at the absolute edge, is near the center of my being.

You are trying to bedazzle me with metaphors so that even I (with less than no inherent interest in those monstrous metal necessities and who has spent the evening glaring at my Ford) could glean the beauty of cars.

I wish I could climb mountains and run marathons like you, but my asthma is worse from breathing all that auto exhaust. Sorry about your car and your missed trip to Seattle. You should have called. I could have helped get you there.

Missed Coffee

Maybe coffee on this less dismal afternoon? Or are you going to take advantage of the weather break and go for a run?

Too late to run anywhere, but I have work to do around the house. My Mom had been listening to Nabokov's Lolita on CD and I insisted on borrowing it... I'm in a blissful, drowsy rapture. What a man he must have been.

A man on the most exquisite of opiates. I'm taking Sam to guitar practice at 2:30.

No, I don't think he was on any opiates at all, unless you mean those produced by vibrancy, brilliance and passion.

I'll probably ride my bike tomorrow morning (it'll have to be something gruesome as penance for today's lapse). Coffee in afternoon would work best.

Yes, those opiates. And those derived from obsession.

Maybe coffee is not such a good idea. It would not take much to set tongues wagging in "provincial Port Cedar," did you call it?

Oh let them wag. Or what about a walk along the river? We could meet at Lumberman's Park, have you ever been? It's lovely, and there's a trail that heads along the cliff. No one ever goes there.

Why don't I see you there about noon? I will do chores today and do my bike ride tomorrow, the weather is supposed to get better anyway.

* * *

Sorry I missed you at the river.

Didn't you get my text?!

I did, but not until I got back to a place where there was reception. Not good service at the bridge.

I thought I had caught you before you left for the park! I'm so sorry! Jacob forgot his lunch, again, and by the time I got it to him at school I was behind in my errands and the day was half gone!

If he forgot his lunch "again," why did you take it to him? Aren't you encouraging him to forget if you make up for the consequences?

Today was pizza at school, which is nothing but congealed white flour soaked in fat. And I didn't know if he had any money. It wasn't a big deal, I just got behind, is all.

Maybe an afternoon being a bit hungry might sharpen his memory.

I really doubt that you would let your son go hungry because he forgot his lunch.

I don't worry about my son's lunch. It's his responsibility. He wouldn't call me to bring it if he forgot, which he doesn't.

Look, I'm sorry I blew you off. I didn't mean to do it. We'll reschedule, okay?

No big deal. The river was beautiful there at the bridge, and I needed a break from the office.

Recent rains are washing the island clean. Leaves and even some branches were carried by the river as it rushed around the rocks toward the sea. It was really very nice. Thank you for sharing a special place.

Do me a favor? Don't tell anyone about it, okay? It really is special to me and if I started running into half of Port Cedar there it would just be ruined.

Absolutely. Though I may go back myself if that's okay. I didn't know there was a place that nice so close to town. Reschedule for tomorrow?

Can't. We are having a party this weekend, and I think my sister is coming from Seattle. My parents are coming separately (divorced, they don't get along), and Robert and I are taking the kids to Mexico over Spring Break. I have packing to do, and I think my passport is expired.

I have too much to do!

Chameleon

I went to "your" bridge again this morning on my way to Henery's Hardware. Even in the pouring rain, that spot in the river casts a spell. Was your party over the weekend a success?

We had our party last night, and my sister and her 5-yr.-old son are staying until tomorrow. The party was great, but I realize how I dislike large groups and snippets of small talk. I am a chameleon, the person that the person I am talking to wants to see. It's exhausting.

You need to be who you really are, not a chameleon you parade for people you don't care about.

I tentatively disagree. At some level, for some reasons, all a bit blurry, I think the "casual human contact" is good for me. It keeps me in tune with the world.

Also, for the most part these were lovely people I like having in my distant orbit. They're intelligent, interesting and we have many things in common. But they aren't my folk, my kin.

If you were just you, the "you" that I speak with, you might be able to enjoy them more. But I suffer the same self-consciousness, wanting to please, and should have at least three more cups of coffee before I indulge in pop psychology.

I'm just trying to imagine where you drink your coffee. I'll write later; I'm eagerly helping my sister and nephew out the door.

I drink my coffee on the deck of an old hand-scribed log house near the end of the road on a meadow where I can watch my kids play in the creek; where I can look out over Port Cedar harbor and on clear days see other islands; where Steller's Jays scold in the morning's delightful contradiction of warm sun pushing through chill air that drifts down from higher elevations. In the front yard is a giant gnarled cedar once struck by lightning, twisted and made majestic by the experience.

Steller's Jays do scold and the morning is filled with pleasant contradictions... very nice. And I'm glad you don't live in a mausoleum. Creekside... I envy you!

Like the opening day of a road trip, the morning is potent with promise. Another contradiction: I'm a control freak who likes to know just what she is getting into, but I greet the morning with eagerness and expectation and leap into the day's unknown...

I didn't have the heart to send Hannah to drama school in Seattle without me, and I couldn't find a house-sitter, so she and I will be here w/o the boys all week (Jacob has all-stars in Everett) beginning tomorrow afternoon.

Do you know any agate beaches?

There's Agate Beach on Guemas Island.

I'm on my way over to the mainland on the 5 p.m. ferry. I got a call from a business associate who wants to meet as soon as each of us can find the time. Tomorrow is the only day open. Plus, there's a race in two weeks, and I need to get the car finished up. I'm trying to be efficient.

I've been very efficient these past few days, accomplished much, and am now hosting my dad (on the heels of my mom, on the heels of my sister, oh my), but I'm not seeing the world the way I usually do... using my imagination. I guess I'm also lapsing into fake punctuation and run-on sentences. Hmmmm...

Glad you wrote. Don't worry about the gray mood, it will pass. Time of year, allergies of the soul.

Robert caught the 2 p.m. ferry back from the mainland in time to go to Jacob's baseball practice and brought him home. I told him he MUST spend some time with Hannah (he never does, NEVER) and if nothing else he could help her with her homework.

I'm listening to Jacob practice guitar. I had a glass of wine with dinner, and was sleepy to begin with (my dad brought his two retrievers and the five dogs were a cacophony last night);

You also seem distracted.

Am not distracted. I'm intensely annoyed. Robert bribed Jacob to continue baseball and I have to go to his games. Baseball bores me to tears. Jacob doesn't mind playing (although he certainly doesn't enjoy it) but he doesn't like the coach who is a right-wing fanatic.

And now $20 later Jacob knows he can be bought. When describing it he actually asked me if I would pay him $20 each time he won his soccer games next Fall. Agh!

Best of luck this weekend. Prepared for your race? You leave Thurs?

The race isn't this weekend but the one after. The car is at the mechanic's still for a final check. I leave next Wednesday a.m., stash the car at the track and will look at boats, too.

Boats? LITTLE boats? Those things that bob around uncomfortably on cold water? I see those people living on their boats down at the Port Cedar Marina. I don't care HOW much money they have, all I can think of is a floating trailer park.

Yes, boats. And I'm not going to try to explain my ancestral Viking urges.

Well, I'm always open to a conversation about urges. I imagine I would be very curious about yours.

We are nearly ready for Mexico. I am actually looking forward to this. Despite some recent rocky patches, Robert and I and the kids mostly enjoy vacations together.

Cars

This is one of the times I lament the limitations of "cybersations." If we were orally conversing, the flow of our discourse would twist and skip and meander, while naturally and ineluctably leading to the next topic.

Cars... did your interest stem from boyhood summers tinkering under the hood? I know your current love is for driving, or maybe racing, rather than mechanics.

No no no... I was trying to draw YOU out.

I'm so bored of me.

I was in my 40s when I rediscovered this sport from my 20s when I ran a BMW 2002 at Seattle International Raceway on track days. Others noticed a skill I never knew I had. I got some great help from some great drivers, amateur and professional: Gordon Jones, Cindi Lux, Gary Bockman, Don Kitch. I asked questions, they were generous with time and knowledge. It is now my passion.

I am what is known as a "checkbook mechanic." I write checks to mechanics who do wrench work. I do much of my own research, develop the "whys," and depend on others for their often-more-relevant experience of "how" to get things done.

That embarrassed me for the first couple of years, then I saw the guys from Microsoft with chefs at the track and I became a reverse snob. I take pride in changing my own calipers, and though I could rebuild them, it would take me four times as long as someone who knew what they were doing.

I leave the track after a day of racing. When other drivers go have Chinese or to a strip club, I disappear into the heart of my beloved Seattle to show up 12 hours later at the track refreshed and ready to drive.

What's a caliper? No, don't answer that. So, how much of successful auto racing is attributable to the "fitness" of the car, itself, vs the talents of the driver? What ARE the talents of a driver: racing tactics, raw nerve or a combo? Do your wife and your children watch you race? Does it make them nervous? Is racing as dangerous as it looks? If you crash (is that even a distinct possibility?) will you be killed, maimed or merely bruised?

Auto racing is not as dangerous as it looks. We wear fire-proof suits and helmets and tethers to keep us inside the car in case of rolling over or hitting something hard. I have been hit by other drivers and spun, but damage was minimal. I suppose my day is coming for something more serious. Drivers have been maimed, some have died.

My kids have not watched me race in several years. Molly has no interest.

A great car will not cover for a lousy driver. A great driver can be limited by his car. A good driver has a visceral sense of physics.

Raw nerve? Maybe a little. But it is technique that really matters. At 150 mph things go by too fast to think about, so I have trained to use braking points and turn-in points, I study the course and my tach and my times and I'm always looking for the next 1/10th of a second.

Tactics are important. I love being behind the car I want to beat, I love spotting his weakness, riding his bumper, letting him know he can't get away, making him "drive his mirrors" instead of the track, exploiting his uncertainty about when I will make my move. I love taking the position away from him, owning the corner, forcing him to race my choice of his line until I can snake by and shake him loose somewhere on the last two laps.

Becoming balanced with the car, putting it on the very edge of traction, four tires wailing that I'm asking "too much — too much!" as they melt from the heat, monster motor howling aggression as it claws us through time, all of it just barely harnessed and attacking and owning the course, the afternoon…

OK, I'll come clean: before reading this my view of your "sport" was tinged with more than a bit of condescension. I had an athlete's arrogance toward driving cars and calling it a sport. And car racing, in particular, summoned visions of Nascar and Southern White males (Right-wing voting/gun toting/...) waving Confederate flags.

So much for being a broad-minded liberal, huh?

But you've conveyed the beauty, the harmony, the thrill, the challenge. I'm not very competitive at sports, but lately I've been placing highly in running races. When I'm up there jockeying for first, second or third I could easily substitute some version of the phrases you use to describe racing cars. As I re-read your words, I really FELT what driving might be like.

There are many race cars of all shapes and sizes and some wonderfully exotic. As for racers, most of us are not athletes of your caliber, but racing is a sport. Having lost 30 lb. and spending hours in the gym lifting weights, I'm a better racer being fit.

Really, Peter, thanks for sharing. You've awakened curiosity and piqued my interest. And, of course, it adds quite a dimension to you. There is so much of you hidden from the citizens of Port Cedar.

It's not that I hide these things in Port Cedar. It's more that I let people see what they want to see, believe what they want to believe. I make no effort to correct misperceptions.

Finding a Line

So where do you disappear after the race? Frankly, I don't see you spending hours drinking beer and debating baseball stats with your mechanics. What is your Seattle routine? Where do you stay? Why do you love Seattle so much?

At night when the boys go back to their rooms or clubs I have dinner at Ruth's or the Red Star or Pazzos or Sammy's or one of the boutique restaurants.

I pretend to be somebody dressed in slacks and shirts of fine cloth and shoes I wear only there and I review strategy for the next day of the race I intend to win.

I stay at the Vintage or the Marriott or the Governor or the Courtyard Marriott near the track. I love the smooth cool crispness of white motel sheets and pillow cases, the roughness of industrial towels.

When I go, I begin to covet. And I long for things that aren't even very important to me: civility, refinement, luxuries. I hate Baily's Food Mart for not being Whole Foods. I want to dress female chic instead of androgynous hayseed. I yearn for ethnic food and I ain't talkin' Rancho Grande. Does this happen to you?

At Trader Joe's in Northwest Seattle I buy interesting cheeses and bottles of olives; there is a Zupan's Market near the track. I picnic in my truck and wait for the moment when I slide into my black and yellow suit and climb into my black and yellow monster and become not somebody else, but who I really am.

Tell me, who do you entertain as you wear your fine clothes in the city? With whom do you review your tactics for the next day? Because I do not see you sitting alone in those restaurants. Food is not companion enough to dress up for the town.

Do not discount the allure of spinach sautéed in light olive oil with garlic, a "Brie and Regiano stuffed chicken" or chocolate sin cake with a raspberry purée.

Brie is soft white skin in a room with a sloped wall of skylight windows open to bright-night neon-lit sky, shadows not concealing, perhaps we are visible to rooms in the hotel across the street, a man keeps coming to his window, can he see?

Rich chocolate on the tongue is staring into brown eyes which widen slightly with surprise and desire as she accepts the tease of fingertips tracking curves and soft hollows, overwhelming separateness, willing and vulnerable.

That is chocolate, that is Brie.

You are indeed a man of large appetites. Are the courses of your meals professionally prepared? I doubt we frequent the same restaurants, or for that matter, if we enjoy the same cuisine.

oops… did I find the line?

Well ... no. But it is rather disconcerting: for the first time in a long time I would feel more comfortable if there were lines. Heavily outweighing my discomfort, however, is the desire to know you. I can't both know you and ask you to remain within the confines of social convention in our "conversations."

Your comfort is important. We will respect the conventions. Please accept my apologies. ~P

No! What's the point? I don't know about you, but I have plenty of conventional relationships.

If we merely skim the surface I might as well meet my sweet and boring friend Brenda for coffee. Don't you think?

I have never had coffee with Brenda and though I'm sure she is quite nice I don't think she and I speak the same language. I don't know, Debra. I obviously strayed into territory that was not as safe as I thought.

Peter, you asked me whether you had "found the line"; I assumed you were asking me if your words had made me uncomfortable. It would have been easy for me to toughly brush it aside, and say "no, of course not," avoiding the even greater discomfort of telling you that those intimate words had, indeed, disquieted me. But in the spirit of the candor which has distinguished our "conversations," I told you the simple truth.

I was hoping to stir you with my prose, not just the sensuality of Seattle, because you seem to enjoy how I relate to the world. I should have had more awareness of your possible discomfort.

It doesn't matter whether, objectively, your words "should" have made me uncomfortable. (In law school we learned of the "reasonable man" standard: would your words have made a "reasonable man" uncomfortable?) They did. But that isn't necessarily a bad thing.

As I told you, a beautiful aria makes me uncomfortable. An emotional novel makes me uncomfortable. I need more uncomfortable in my life.

Be careful what you wish for. You did not answer the question about which it was that made you uncomfortable and why.

Maybe I am treating you differently because of your gender? If you were a woman, would I have been uncomfortable with tongues and curves and hollows? Maybe. Maybe not. Why should I distinguish between the sensual passions of driving cars or eating or the feel of crisp laundered sheets and those of sex, itself? I don't know, but apparently I do. I apologize for my 19th century prudery; I wasn't aware I had an ounce of it.

Perhaps I need to rein in my over-stylized prose.

But now I ask, why do you want to know me at all? I'm invisible in most ways. It is not necessary to lift a corner of the curtain. Perhaps it is not wise. The illusion of safety given by the exchange of electrons rather than oxygen may not serve us. I will slide back into my shell.

Transformational Totems

Come out of that shell! I haven't heard from you forever! Shells are for hiding secrets or protecting vulnerabilities. Which?

Tell me something about where you came from, where you grew up. If you could choose a single object from your childhood that describes who you are today, or how you became who you are today, what would it be?

Not to spotlight the obvious, but wouldn't telling you disclose the secrets or make me vulnerable? I think we should stick to safe topics like religion and politics and not go to "transformational totems of childhood." ~P

My "transformational totem" was a green dress.

I was a tomboy, born in San Francisco but raised in Seattle, in some ways my father's "son."

My father was a New York Jew who grew up poor, insecure, angry and with a love of opera.

He had a variety of jobs but not a "career." I think he got fired a lot. He always needed to "prove" himself by telling stories of what he had done in the war, what was wrong with government, how things could be made better, as if he were some sort of expert. Which he was not.

This was hard on my very intelligent but somewhat unattractive mother, who had come from an upper-class Jewish family of some privilege. She resented the marriage. She felt trapped by a man who was obviously not her equal, plus she had a tendency to carp and find fault.

She wasn't a feminine creature. She was overweight and her low self-esteem (her sister was beautiful and glamorous) prevented her from buying herself clothes or make-up.

I played outside a lot. I was usually the fastest, sometimes the smartest and always the instigator. I was extremely headstrong and learned to get my way by throwing tantrums that I would not tolerate in my own children.

My mom finished law school and worked for the Dept. of Justice, driving from our home in Northwest Seattle to catch her 7 am bus at the Safeway, returning at 6 and stopping at the Safeway bakery (!!) to get bags of discounted donuts which she put in the freezer and I stole regularly in lieu of meals. She left in the dark and returned in the dark.

She was not at all a sexual creature, so I was quite confused and thought there was nobility of some kind in denying femininity. I wasn't very good-looking either during adolescence and didn't have a feminine guide into a very unfamiliar territory.

To be frugal, she made me a dress with her nearly non-existent sewing skills that I wore to my first dance in high school. It was green. It might as well have been made from burlap. But I was this Jewish girl tomboy who didn't know any better.

At first I was so excited to be there. My first dance! AT HIGH SCHOOL! But nobody asked me to dance. Then I started to really look around and saw all those pretty blond girls in pretty dresses. And it wasn't just that they were nice dresses. They weren't all the same but they were alike, you know what I mean? And then the worst part: I saw them looking at me. Laughing at me.

I was humiliated. I went outside and waited for my mother to come pick me up. She asked me how it was. I told her it was wonderful and made up stories for her and didn't really start crying until after we got home and I was in my room with my stuffed kitty. Kitty is another story.

I never went to another dance, though I had a boyfriend who had ultra-cool parents. I took German (from an anti-Semite) and Russian, took classes at the local community college and finished high school in three years, went to college, finished that in three years.

I lived in New York for a year with my cousin, my mother's sister's daughter. She is as glamorous as it is possible to be, with men falling at her feet just to see her smile. She used them terribly and she taught me that "Girls make the rules."

I came back to Seattle, went to law school where I was the "It Girl." Practiced law for a while, public defender's office mostly, some family law, got married, got pregnant despite my vow not to have kids, moved to Port Cedar to raise my two lovely children away from the grime and the crime.

But even now if I am "caught out" wearing something I don't feel is appropriate for the occasion or think I'm being judged, my reaction is a toxic mix of anger and humiliation. Robert has suffered the consequences on more than one occasion.

What a poignant portrait.

Okay. I would have to say my totem is a "sock monkey," one of those silly sock dolls where the smile on the monkey's face is the same on its ass?

I was raised in Northern California redwood country by drunks of high intelligence and major dysfunction in a financially comfortable household.

My father was an abusive alcoholic and head of the math department at the college. He had a reputation for humiliating students in the classroom and thought he should be teaching at Stanford.

My mother was a writer and a poet with a few things published. She had known Ginsberg and Kerouac in San Francisco and those who knew her said she was the brightest person they had ever met. That was when she was sober, a rare event even before I entered kindergarten. She may have had drug problems too, but not much was known about that in those days. It was also whispered at family functions she had an active libido my father could not match.

For the most part my two sisters and I hid from the fights and the ugliness and the affairs and the inconsistencies. We had each other. During the day we played outdoors, made forts in the woods out of fir boughs, came in for meals.

In the summer we would be outside until dark. In the winter we loved school; we were really good at it and the adults there gave us pats on the head, so different than at home.

In the evening, we played with these sock monkeys. We would invent elaborate situations and play them out. We held monkeys face to face and had conversations in monkey voices. We made each other laugh until we couldn't breathe, until someone nearly peed or someone actually did.

When I was 10, my mother's sister came up from San Francisco. We always loved Aunt Ruth's big laugh, she didn't have any children of her own but loved us like we were hers. I came home from fourth grade one day to find that my aunt had left and taken my two sisters back with her. Everyone had decided that my mother was too disabled by booze to raise girls going into junior high and puberty.

They had not told us and did not allow us to communicate.

"You have to grasp a thistle firmly," was all my father said. I did not know at the time why they left me behind. Before she died my aunt told me everyone felt that as the boy, I could manage on my own and she could not take on another.

I made up stories that I believed about how my sisters were happy with Aunt Ruth and living a much better life and I felt sorry for myself being exposed to the raging ugliness of my household.

One night my father was in a particularly vile mood and had already driven my mother into vulgar screams of obscenities and tears. He heard me talking in my room. He slammed through the door and asked what I was doing. I told him I was just playing with my sock monkey. He came across the room and held out his hand.

I handed Monkey over to him. He said I was too old to play "make believe" and boys don't play with dolls. I told him Monkey was not a doll and told him to give it back. He laughed and walked out of the room. I followed him, trying to jump up to grab Monkey, but my father was 6' 2" and held Monkey over his head. So I kicked him as hard as I could and I bit him as hard as I could.

He knocked me to the floor in anger and pain and threw Monkey into the fireplace that was burning in the living room. Apparently I went crazy with rage. At some point he called the police. They took me to a "hospital" for a while. I know I missed the rest of that school year, but I was so far ahead of my class that I started with them again in the fall.

My god. I can't imagine the sense of loss. And then what? How did you get from there to here?

Children are pretty resilient.

I don't remember much of the next several years except that I got in trouble a lot. I took a lot of drugs: LSD and pot and alcohol, mostly. I left home at 16, returned when my mother was institutionalized, and graduated from high school. Somehow, I got into Berkeley.

I worked summers in Alaska at a salmon cannery and spent my last terms of college in France trying to study the Existentialists in their own language. After I finished up with school I traveled the world for a couple of years, working in Israel during one of their many wars, avoiding Turkish troops on Cyprus, trekking the Himalayas of Pakistan among the opium fields. Looking for God, I said at the time.

I fell in love with a woman from New Jersey while in India. We returned to the states for my mother's funeral. Wendy left me for her former love and broke my heart. I came to Seattle and worked as a waiter and tried to write and took a lot of drugs: cocaine, pot and alcohol, mostly.

I met Molly and we got married and I stopped taking drugs and alcohol 20 years ago. It wasn't hard because I told myself it was just another adventure, trying life sober and on its own terms. I did not want to recreate the environment I grew up in.

It stuck, and instead of living in bars and taverns I began buying and redeveloping old buildings, learned to race cars, we had two wonderful children, we moved to Port Cedar.

Now, that's enough personal info. You have me feeling quite exposed.

This is just like having a new girlfriend!

Don't take offense, I mean it in a really, really good way. We have so much in common. Is it okay, Girlfriend?

It's okay. I'm just not at all used to this kind of openness, but I do kind of like it. Girlfriend.

Mexico Aborted

It doesn't look like we're going to Mexico. My passport isn't going to be here, and when I was at the gym Robert realized he couldn't deal with the kids. He had a complete tantrum, and has said categorically that he isn't going to Mexico no matter what. Is this the height of dysfunction?

Debra, can you fix this? Can I help?

No, I don't think I can. Thank you for the kindness, but I can't think of anything you could do.

Want a phone call?

I'm barely holding it together and a sympathetic ear would melt every ounce of resolve I've mustered.

Robert is his own captain. But you all have enjoyed vacations. Not going will change things irrevocably. Give him a chance. Let him reach out.

I think the best thing for all of us will be to postpone. I'm not angry with Robert, not a bit. I'm just shocked. He told the kids they were "bad kids" tonight. That is how he sees it: black and white. It must be very frightening for him. He is so impaired.

I defused the situation an hour ago, telling everyone to discuss it in the morning, seeing that Robert had backed himself into a corner. But I don't think anything will have changed.

Enough. For once my resolve is to NOT do anything.

This morning started at 4 a.m. with first the cat and then the dog wanting outside. By 5:30 sleep was a lost hope and I flopped out in my Sorrels and sleep clothes to get *The Times.*

I'm thinking with sadness of Robert not wanting to go to Mexico with his children. The fear of loss he must have as he looks forward, seeing life's momentum as too large. But then I wonder if I am cloaking him in my emotions.

My own kids are still suspended in sleep in their rooms down the hall.

The rising sun paints clouds on the eastern horizon iridescent pink, then orange, over the bay that lays so still and steel blue. Tiny boats in the distance do not float on water. They are set into space and time that congealed sometime during the night.

Thank you for sharing that.

Robert is back on board. Found my old passport. It hasn't expired, unless the new one has been processed. Cross your fingers.

I'm making little packs for the kids for the Mexico trip: pencils, journals, books, snacks. No matter how old (or, like my kids, how unartistic) there is nothing like a brand-new box of sharpened pencils. Even those words "brand-new" evoke sharpened crayons and "school shoes," don't they?

I'm dying to know what got Robert back on board. Support that, Debra, whatever it is.

I pointed out to Robert that we had already purchased non-refundable slots at an all-inclusive hotel. That he could sit on the patio and work on whatever technical specifications for whatever airplane all day and night without interruption.

And that the kids and I were going to Mexico whether or not he chose to join us.

We leave the island on the 4:15 ferry, spend the night near SeaTac and fly out tomorrow morning at 7 a.m. I think I have nearly everything together. We'll see.

Deflated in Mexico

I hope you and Robert and the kids are having a wonderful time, that you made all your connections. Sometimes living on Vincente Island adds a full day to do anything.

Robert chose the same "Park 'n Leave" hotel he stayed at last week. The decrepit building smelled of smoke and commercial-grade air freshener.

There were no fitted sheets on the bed, merely a thin, gray flat sheet which wasn't large enough to cover the dirty, blue mattress beneath. "Gross" said my Hannah. "Disgusting" I concurred. Somehow the kids managed to get to sleep, despite the tremendous rattle of the fan, which produced far more noise than heat.

Despite my sleeping pill half, then another, I was wide awake. My head lay on Hannah's coat so I wouldn't have to touch the pillowcase. I was furious at Robert for — for what? For thinking that this dump was habitable? For not having any sense of "grace"?

I snatched Robert's car keys (why do all you superannuated hippie wanna-bes drive stick-shifts?) and drove to my mom's at 10:30, returning at 3.

But all's well that ends well. Jacob just dined on Il Fornaio pizza; I allowed the kids to run gleefully up and down the escalator (airport is deserted) while I munched a pumpkin muffin. Oh, yeah, The NY Times, *what a treat.*

I still haven't gotten out my pajamas (Pit Bull weightlifting pants and Hammerhead Gym sweatshirt). But first, a reply.

We annuated hippies (not super yet, please?) drive stick-shifts and ignore the sleaziness of hotels because they give us utilitarian value, feel less detached. To know that from a certain hotel the shuttle does run to the terminal and it's not just a promise, that is worth something to us. That the car will shift is security.

One of my favorite mornings is an espresso with a copy of *The NY Times.* I can imagine fighting with you over the paper. You assail corporate greed, and I defend sweatshops in Asia where children make shoes because their alternative is starvation.

The Marriott here in Mexico compensates generously for the deprivations of Robert's "Park 'n Leave." Lush gardens, a vast and flowing network of waterfalls and koi ponds, bougainvillea and stately palms... no, no, palms aren't stately, they're too playful, like exploding fireworks, their fronds burst out and up and then arc gracefully downward. Oooooh, phallic.

Only the beach volleyball net disturbs the illusion created by the infinity-edge pool, which melds seamlessly into the mountain-ringed bay. The resort is empty. We always used to go Christmas week, which is bedlam.

I allow myself to slip into the quicksand luxury of middle age, readily sacrificing the perfect tan I used to hold most dear for a 180 view of my children in the pool. I no longer notice, much, whether men's eyes flicker behind the protection of sunglasses as I walk by, whether their heads tilt, barely conspicuously, or their gaze seems to linger.

And while sitting upright in a pool chair I see that my belly roll has escaped the upper rim of my bikini bottom, patently exposed. There it is, encapsulated: middle age. In my youth I would have been vigilant, now it is secondary, and one day it will be irrelevant. Vanity ebbs.

With that said (and here I smile at you playfully through my little cat mouth), I single-handedly put a halt to construction at the unfinished hotel down the beach. I loved the security of the catcalls and wolf whistles, though I walked demurely and seemingly obliviously onward in traditional Catholic Mexican style.

Do we ever lose vanity altogether? I remember the last days of my beautiful grandmother's life, and her shame at finally having to remove her painful false teeth. And I'm vain and secretive, too, hiding my breasts which droop and splay slightly outward beneath my bathing suit camouflage (can never spell that damn word).

Phallic palms, very nice, Nature is a bawdy girl, isn't she?

Vanity: God's own practical joke. Enjoy the catcalls, for sure the eyes follow you behind the shades.

One of my greatest flaws is to long for permanence. I build a house without the stairs my children would love because I fear needing a wheelchair ramp in my old age — in a house I will sell long before the ramp was used. A foolishness of excessive planning.

I enjoy these snapshots, but don't hover near a computer.

I took the kids to a panaderia yesterday. We each picked a round, aluminum tray and a pair of tongs and proceeded around the room plucking crisp and puffy cookies, not-too-sweet sweetbread and little cakes with sprinkles.

Everything here resembles a loaf of peasant bread: rough and crude and open and generous. Americans... their contemporary cuisine, their fashion, their love... so much more austere, guarded, almost stingy.

There's Internet right in the hotel, so I'll check despite your order to not hover around the computer.

When we were down in Zijuateneo a few years back I took the car back to the airport, we didn't need it, and I took the bus, an overfilled mini of a minivan, back to town on back roads with people with baskets and bags. I love that kind of travel. I prefer that to playing golf among the shanties with fat Americans demanding American beer in voices that make me cringe at their insults for the local brew.

My favorite experiences, too, are taking the Mexican buses. You might have appreciated today's adventure. I dragged us all about 40 miles north to a town I've been eyeing for a few years: Sayulita. Quite a few American expats, but mostly still Mexican. Very rough, very raw. I don't think the kids or Robert "got it," but the surf was awesome and I ate the best food I've had in ages, a paella without the chorizo.

I would have loved to be on that bus with you and the kids and with my kids, I think they would have got it, the sheer intensity of life, the differentness. Molly hates that kind of travel, the uncertainties, the smells, the dangers she fears at every turn.

Peter, if you were here we could tell stories about all the other guests and laugh about the phallic palms.

The game is called "Biography." I used to play it when on the road in India, I don't play it with the twins, they are too literal.

Pick a guest, give me a snapshot and I will weave you a tale.

Biography

We're staying at the hotel today, by the pool and in the giant "C" waves near the shore, in which Jacob and I will boogie, as in board. Hannah is creating sand forms for each of her cats: "Mt. Oreo," "Fenny Lake." She'll be busy all day.

There is a woman too old for the bikini she is wearing and hair dyed platinum blond sitting a few chairs over. What is her story?

The woman with the diamonds, way too many, and the pink bikini, way too small, with the constant supply of gin and tonic? The one who looks like she was built in an L.A. clinic, her breasts too large, her legs too thin, and of course, the cigarette?

She thinks she is forty, looks fifty and I bet you a dollar she is well into her sixties with the best plastic surgeon money can buy.

What is it the towel boy is doing over there, I ask you, if he puts even one more coat of sun screen on her back I think she will come right out of that lounge chair.

"Or come right in it," you shoot back.

The towel boy is the sixth child of the family that lives in that shanty we saw on the hill with the chickens in the village we passed on our way back in the minibus, you say.

He is very handsome and she has tipped him lavishly. And kissed him nearly too long on the cheek, brushing the plastic globe of her right breast against him as she got up to get another drink from the bar.

She also slipped him a five dollar bill, but the real currency was the room key she had folded inside.

What a treat! And I think you are right about the room key! I swear I saw her do it! Thank you!

A blossom picked just for you.

This morning it dropped below freezing. Just a few degrees, but that many are an order of magnitude. The cold seeps under the door to lick at my ankles with an icicle tongue. At least there is no wind to carry a wet salty sting off the harbor. I'm tired of holding my shoulders up around my ears against its assault on my collar.

Didn't sleep well. I've been up for hours, drinking coffee in the lobby. I'm reading a particularly bad book my adored uncle sent me as one of his favorites.

My brilliant uncle loves those nouveau 40s film noir detective novels, with ultra-macho males who use a never-ending string of quips and witticisms.

Not sure what we're doing today. Jacob and I are happy to play in the waves (well, he plays and I join him here and there, retreating regularly to the pool chair I've dragged to the beach's edge) and Hannah and her imagination are content in the sand.

I bring my legs up on the couch and huddle under a blanket and think about Mexico, drawing designs in the sun, sketching with words the beach, how the waves slingshot you and Jacob to shore, with Hannah telling you to draw her a house in the sand with a room just for her and a place for the cats.

I ran into the "real" part of PV yesterday afternoon; it felt a little like Zijuatenejo, middle-class Mexican. It's prettier, though, b/c the streets are cobblestoned and built into hillsides weaving in and out of the jungle. I ended up along the river, which I could only hear but not see b/c of the dense vegetation.

I remember running along the other side of the river 17 years ago when I first came, and not much had changed. The smells were redolently organic: feces, decaying animal, a trace of flower, omnipresent palms.

I don't think I'd enjoy traveling half as much if I couldn't run. It's the best way I can imagine to really experience a place. I often just go and get lost, I can always walk back if I really bite off more than I can chew.

When I hike/mountaineer it usually only takes a few miles to bring me to a place where there are very, very few people. It's the same way with running. No tour bus would bring me to these neighborhoods, these country roads, these wide and dusty paths.

I'm sorry you are in the cold. Hope everything else is going well.

A family arrived yesterday from the states. Father has his newspaper, his two sons, very athletic, play in the pool. His wife draws. Who are they? Will you go pluck me a portrait?

Paul Williams sells Real Estate in Southern California. Gloria is an artist; she paints in oil and works part-time doing interior design out of a lovely little decorating store in Pasadena, owned by a friend, so she can get her own expensive furnishings at cost. It's a hobby but allows her (and Paul) the fiction of a career.

Their son Jamie brought along his friend Clayton. They are on the swim team at Cal State. It is not a championship team and the two boys, both seniors, are not stars even of that mediocrity, but they train and compete, they are now in the pool.

Paul is proud; he will have a place at the firm for Jamie when he gets out of school. Oh, Jamie will have to work for it; he won't just be given wealth. Oh no, he will have to perform just like anybody else, and just because his last name is Williams and he works at Williams Real Estate, that doesn't mean it will be easy. Everybody will know the boy made it on his own.

Gloria has been taking pictures of sunsets behind the palms, which she sketches onto a large piece of paper. Later she will use the photo to bring the colors to life. She debates for a moment whether to include the lovely woman playing with her two children on the beach. She includes them for now and will decide later whether to leave them in the painting.

Gloria looks with pride at Jamie, his strength and broad shoulders, and she smiles; she is glad that so many years ago she made the right decision not to tell Paul that Jamie was not his son.

She loved Jamie's biological father, but it was the right decision for her beautiful boy. His "real" father was a beautiful man but lost, unable to produce the income that allowed her to paint and Jamie to swim on the college team; she was glad when he finally moved away from La Cañada and she didn't have to run into him any more.

He didn't know he had a son, Gloria didn't tell him, either.

Jamie sees his mother sketching by the pool, and his father reading the newspaper, a four-day-old copy of *The L.A. Times* brought into the hotel by another guest from the plane. Every day he can remember, his father had read the newspaper.

"I have some news for you, dear Dad," Jamie smiles to himself, thinking of how it will feel on the flight home when he can finally tell his parents that he and Clayton intend to get married in June.

You satisfy me. I go to my screen with only a grumbling of hunger but leave each time licking my chops, smiling. And you put us in the story!

I'm beginning to think it is beyond hope that Hannah will have a relationship with Robert. And it's my fault. For years I have ignored him, raising my little family in my house with my animals and my art and my schedules and my food and my plans and my, always my decisions. I have rendered him irrelevant, and Hannah has done the same.

What else could she have done? Oh, my guilt.

She would adore you, you know. She would thrive. Or maybe I'm just projecting (there: in my Jewish mother's tradition I got Freudian).

More later, I just needed a nibble.

You take my breath away.

Find a couple at the pool and spin me a tale. Your turn.

Yikes. Performance anxiety.

"No fair," I whine, "you're choosing all the beautiful women, getting off as I describe them in sumptuous detail. I demand some diversity!"

So this time you choose a Mexican man of your own age, though he hasn't resisted the physical manifestations of age as successfully as you have. In fact, I describe, Professor Guzman of Mexico City is quite thick through his middle, though he's small-boned underneath his bulging stomach. His large glasses rest below his bushy eyebrows, and the dark hair on his chest also furs his arms and back.

Senora Guzman has treated herself to a facial at the hotel spa this morning. (Professor Guzman wanders around the pool, not knowing how to amuse himself without his vivacious wife.) Lately Senora Guzman has spent a good deal of time at the health club at home and it shows. Always prone to chubbiness, she's slimmed to voluptuous.

"She's screwing the personal trainer at the health club," you interject.

I roll my eyes. "NOT," I respond in a tone you're used to hearing from your daughter. "That would be too obvious. Give me some credit, I'm going for the O'Henry twist ending." You grin, and put your hand on my wrist in mock apology. I slap it away in mock indignation. (We're very mock today.) "Hands off the biographer."

Then, many seconds later, I teasingly finger the back of your hand, and your own wrist, and your arm up to your elbow.

And that's enough Biography.

I watched the sun set over the Pacific, a glowing orb falling into the ocean through a terrace of rich, pink bougainvillea. Of course the world is flat.

Carmen

Let me try:

Professor Guzman smiled as Carmen walked toward his lounge chair by the pool. She was so beautiful with her high cheekbones, hair thick and black with highlights of copper.

She'd lost weight in the last year, she seemed younger. He smiled about that, too, knowing why. He pulled her lounge chair close to his before she had walked past the end of the pool.

"I'm not having an affair with my trainer," she had laughed at him, when he suggested last fall that she had fallen in love with someone at her health club.

Carlos knew Carmen was not having an affair with her trainer. He had known that since December 2nd, when a Mexico City Police detective moonlighting on city time dropped an envelope on his desk at work.

Carlos had wanted to know where Carmen went for those many hours nearly every Tuesday and Friday when he could not find her on her phone, when he could not find her at the club, or at their house. Shopping she said, and yet, she never seemed to bring anything home from the stores.

The envelope showed she was having an affair with a young lawyer who had come to their house in Mexico City to help with their estate. Hector Mendoza-Martinez. An ambitious young man. Carlos could hardly blame him. Carmen was beautiful, charming.

"Carmen, you do know how much I love you?" Carlos asked. She was startled by the question, even though for the last several weeks he had been so much more attentive and affectionate.

She put down her bag and grabbed the rough blue-striped towel from her chair, shaking it, she aligned the stripes of the towel and moved her chair as if to align it with the sun but really to be not quite so close to his large belly, his sweating in the sun by the pool.

She sat and watched two young men in the pool, they were here for the holidays from California, they had beautiful bodies, they laughed and seemed close, very close. Carmen knew there were a lot of young men like that in California. Their bodies were nicer than her Hector's but he was beautiful, too, not so wide in the shoulders but lean, smooth.

Hector had asked her not to come on this trip with Carlos, Hector was jealous, nearly crazy with it. "Hector, it is what it is. I must go. He will not touch me, I shall tell him I am ill if he tries. It won't be long, and I will not enjoy it. I promise." Hector sulked, until she laughed at him and pulled him to her in his large soft bed.

Carlos looked over at his wife as she fussed with the towel, and then down at the beach, where the thin, muscular American woman played with her children in the waves. He liked watching her, watching them.

The American woman's husband had been on the veranda when Carlos came to lie in the sun, reading the newspaper. A few minutes ago the man got up but did not join his family on the sand, instead headed back to the lobby of the hotel, perhaps to their room. The relationship was odd, Carlos wondered if those were his children, or if the man had married into the family.

He and Carmen had no children. She never wanted any; not common in Mexico, but he understood. Her own mother and father had only her as their one child, they had been living on old money that was nearly gone when he met Carmen in what would have been her last year of university, they could not afford another year of tuition.

Carmen had the thin nose and lips of aristocracy, Carlos knew he looked more like a peasant, with his bushy mustaches and thick features. Carmen would have been the right woman to bear his children, she would have brought some elegance to the Guzmans of Mexico City. Carlos wondered if there was still time.

Carlos thought he should not have bought Carmen the Doberman, Max. As he intended, it provided her companionship in the large empty house, but perhaps without the dog she might have been more inclined to have children.

But Max did protect Carmen, to the point that it never left her side and would even growl at Carlos if he walked in certain ways toward his wife. She loved Max and took him wherever she went.

"Carmen, you know I would do anything for you," Carlos said, and Carmen tried not to flinch. The affection was becoming suffocating. She knew that at some time today Carlos would want to touch her, have sex with her. Perhaps she could satisfy him with her mouth, that seemed less intimate somehow, she would not have to look at his face looking at her, as if they were lovers.

Since Hector had come into her life, when she felt herself falling in love with him, having sex with Carlos had moved from enjoyable to routine to distasteful, and not just because Hector could not accept it.

The waiter came up and started to hand Carlos a large, fat, brown envelope. Carlos just waved it toward the table. Carmen thought that was odd, normally Carlos would open these immediately, his work always seemed to follow him, even here, for a week's vacation on the Pacific, he would work for a few hours each day.

Hector would stare into her eyes when they made love. She loved looking at his sensual mouth; she loved the way his faced changed as he came close to climax, how his features softened, how he became not a younger man, but an essence of all men.

Carlos was saying something and she was letting herself become aroused on the deck in the sun watching the two young men in the pool. One pulled at the swimsuit of the other, yanking it down to his knees, they both laughed, it was disconcerting, they sounded like girls.

Hector was her age, 17 years younger than Carlos, she was grateful for all Carlos had done for her, for her parents, finding for them a facility when they could not afford to keep the family home on the broad street with the old trees where she had grown up in Mexico City.

Carlos complained only mildly at the time, but he could afford it and was gracious about it now, paying the bills without complaint or even comment. She could not remember if she had loved Carlos once.

But Hector was her age, he liked the same music, he liked her dog Max, and Max liked him, unlike the wariness the dog had for Carlos.

One afternoon they went to the Dali exhibit in Mexico city, Hector had insisted, Carmen worried they would run into one of Carlos' friends or associates but Hector had said, "I don't care. If he finds out, perhaps we can be together."

And they had laughed and talked about art and life and whether Dali could see into other dimensions, if he was *from* other dimensions.

But Carmen did care if Carlos found out, she cared because Hector did not know Carlos, that he could be a dangerous man despite his position in Mexico City or because of it, she cared because of her parents, she cared because she had 17 years with Carlos, since she was 20, and because she did not know if Hector would achieve at age 50 what Carlos had today.

"I have not given you the attention you deserve," Carlos was saying, now. Carmen looked over at him, she could not see his eyes behind the dark glasses but he was looking right at her, she could tell there was intensity there, and a smile, it was an odd smile, it frightened her a little, like the smile she saw in Mexico City earlier this month when the man came to the house and walked into Carlos' study, it was the smile Carlos gave her when he looked at her just before he closed the door.

"Carlos, I know you love me, and I love you." She tried to make it sound as if she meant it, but it was coming out all wrong, flat, like something she had memorized, and she saw the pain that it caused as he quickly looked away. He reached over to the table and picked up the envelope the waiter had left there.

"I think you need to see this."

"Carlos, you know I don't understand your work." Long before, she had given up trying to understand the intricate contracts he prepared, the legal decisions he rendered, and he had stopped trying to educate her.

"There is something there you need to see."

She opened the envelope, and pulled out a stack of large photos. The first was of her parents in their pension. Sitting in the garden. It was a nice enough photo, but appeared to have been taken from a distance, perhaps from across the street.

"Carlos…" she started to say, but he just shook his head, and pointed at the stack of photos in her hand.

She could hear the doves working their way around the pool, cooing, cleaning up the crumbs from muffins and toast tourists ate while luxuriating in the sun.

The next photo was of her and Hector at a small restaurant, they had dined there just a week ago. In the photo they were both laughing.

"Carlos…" she started to explain about legal matters and the estate, she had rehearsed an explanation if she and Hector were ever seen together, but this time Carlos hushed her with a finger tip on his own lips, then, oddly, reached over and placed that finger on her lips, a gesture more intimate than he ever used, more gentle than he ever was.

The next photo was of Carmen and Hector in Hector's immaculate garden in Mexico City, she and Hector had been in that garden just before coming on this trip, and they had been dressed in those very clothes. Max, her loyal Doberman, was sitting in the shade under the table, its head on its paws.

Carmen could not speak now, she was afraid, afraid to look, but did and yes, the next photo showed her with her blouse nearly off in that same garden.

"Oh no..." was all she could say, her voice very soft, almost hidden under the lap of waves drifting across the patio.

She looked off at a white ship in the bay, beyond those waves. As far away as it was moored, its whiteness nearly hurt her eyes. There was something in the light, the darkness of the water and the blueness of the sky, that made it seem too bright.

The next photo showed her in bed with Hector, in his room, top sheet on the floor where it often ended up, white-washed plaster, the vibrant scene of a village in the painting over his bed. The photo was quite clear, and showed the passion on her face.

"How did you…" But Carlos again hushed her, and pointed at the stack of photos in her lap.

The next one was just a picture of Hector, sitting in that chair that was in his bedroom, his face very odd, his hands out of sight, then she realized that his hands were probably tied behind him.

She often sat in that chair, pulling on her shoes. Sometimes she moved it to the window where it overlooked the garden. She would sit in that chair and wonder what life would be like if she woke in this room every day.

The next photo was of Hector in the same chair, at least his torso, his head was missing, the white shirt crimson with his blood. Carmen froze.

Carlos reached over and pulled that photo off the stack. The next photo was just Hector's head sitting in his bathroom sink, a sink where she had often stood, brushing her long dark hair after an afternoon of making love. The fear and pain in Hector's eyes seared into Carmen's brain.

Carlos reached over and pulled that photo off the stack. The next photo was Hector's torso again in the chair with the neck and head of Max, her beloved Doberman, jammed down onto the shoulders in the white shirt, the fierce dog's eyes open and mouth open and tongue and long white teeth almost a grin making the man-dog in the photo into a monster.

In an instant Carmen knew she would see those images forever, that not five minutes would go by for the rest of her life when she would not see the pain and fear in Hector's eyes… the dog-man monster, she would see those pictures every day in everything she did forever until she died her Hector the blood his head that sink her Max the chair the room the garden the bed…

Carmen was able to release only half a scream. Carlos smoothly gathered up the photos and put them back into his envelope. Carmen threw up, violently, loudly, then moans were mixed with sobs and with retching. By the time hotel staff arrived Carlos had Carmen's hands in his and refused suggestions that she be taken immediately to a doctor, asking that they instead assist her to their room, saying that his lovely wife had simply spent too much time in the sun.

Oh, my god. How fun! It reminds me (now don't be offended) of the detective novel of my uncle's I just read: the uni-dimensionality of the characters, their cliche, though artistically rendered. A genre piece. Running out of computer time, will comment much more later. It is so lovely you are here in Mexico with me, Peter.

Debra, you are with me here in the cold. I'm losing my boundaries, crossing the line.

Good. Boundaries are artificial limitations. There are no lines.

Stutter

The ship was on its way to Cuba, via the Yucatan, where we would conveniently misplace our passports and travel as Canadians.

We spent a few long, thirsty days in our Yucatan, wandering the ruins outside of Merida. We've read the guidebook to each other along the bumpy roads. You love to listen to me read aloud, marveling at my voice's inflections and intonations, yet you aren't distracted. You absorb every fact.

I tend to drift, and forget half of what has interested me just moments before. You say, tenderly chiding, that I'm intellectually lazy, which is probably true, yet my time has not been wasted. I'm absorbing, I'm feeling, I'm trying to detach and capture moments.

We're empty at the end of the day. Your skin is tight and burned behind your knees where you forgot to put sunscreen. I'm driven nearly mad by a bug bite near my ankle. We're stingy and have retreated into our discomfort when we reach the casita.

We indulge in American amenities: hot shower, thick towels, aqua purificada y frio that tastes better than champagne.

Oh, God. I had written this whole spiel about a massage but realize it probably sounds more like soft porn than literature, or anything else you'd like to hear. I hate it when I feel something, then write it, then look at it mere hours later self-consciously, embarrassed. I'll spare you.

Boundaries. Why? Be careful, Girlfriend.

By pulling back you set your own boundaries. Didn't you just say "there are no lines?" Why?

Because, because I guess I justify our, our, our, whateverthisis by thinking that it is on a semi-literary plane, a higher thing than just, just, just

and if I descend into something with little literary merit and a lot of, of, of, it, it it it

I'm stammering and and and you're laughing and

Maybe the me who cautioned you, cautioned Girlfriend, was afraid to dance.

trust me, please.

I know not what to make of "trust me, please," and "*Maybe the me who cautioned you, cautioned Girlfriend, was afraid to dance.*"

Are they the same, are they contradictions? Never mind. Back to safety, Girlfriend.

It has warmed up to 34 degrees, which is a vast improvement over 28 degrees, the temperature that greeted us yesterday. Feels odd to say, "Wow, it's up to 34 degrees this morning. Wonder if I should grab a coat…"

Abby and Sam are tired, it has been a long week, I'm tired.

I hope the four of you will find a laugh together before lunch.

Now it is you who takes cover under broad leaves of the banana tree, under the dappled shade of the palms, who has gone into hiding.

Thirty-four degrees? How frigid. We fly out in three days and transition from hot and vibrant Mexico to dreary Seattle, then take the ferry to lovely-yet-sodden, gray and green Port Cedar on Vincente Island. When we come back, it always seems like I have left something important behind but don't know what it is.

I know exactly what you mean. It happens to me after race weekends. The time away that seems so real, when lived, becomes unreal and so vague so quickly when I return to blueprints and phone calls and lawyers. It is as if the context is necessary for "me" to be real, and when the context changes, the reality of "before" fades away.

It's like that optical illusion of a chalice defined by two faces. I can see the chalice, or the faces, but not both at the same time.

Fever

Hannah woke with a burning fever, then threw up. I've been with her, of course.

I don't think Robert said anything more than "How do you feel?" when he woke up. He hasn't said a word to her, hasn't stroked her hot forehead, hasn't placed a cold washcloth over the bridge of her nose. He is so hopeless and empty, sometimes I just hate him.

What's the fear? The fear is that Hannah and I have already abandoned him, even as he has abandoned us, and I feel the heavy guilt, and one day she will, too.

I'm tired, too, drained. I will offer you this, though: I thrive in your garden among the patch of iris just within the gate.

Keep an eye on Hannah's temperature. Give her Tylenol to break the fever. Strip her and look all over for rashes and bites, especially near soft skin. Give her 7-up, water, lemon water. And then more. Keep her hydrated. If she pees, check the color of her urine. Dark tea color is bad, apple juice color is okay.

Now, it is probably just too much sun.

The fear behind the anger at Robert is that you and Hannah are trapped, and Jacob too.

You're very cruel for pointing out your beautiful engagement as a father. Almost painful, the contrast is so starkly drawn.

We arrive SeaTac Monday night. Kids and I will spend the night at Mom's and return home the next day, with Mom.

Robert will go directly to his hovel and not come back to Port Cedar for a full week, thank God.

Oh, Peter, it's awful. We sleep in separate beds, the kids bidding on who gets to sleep with mommy. I don't think Robert and I have even touched, literally, in months.

I'll stop complaining. (Then you'll wonder who I am.)

Girlfriend, I did not mean to be cruel. Mexico has hazards.

You come home from Seattle on Tuesday, and I will be going. I wonder if I will be getting on the ferry you will be getting off.

Where are you going in Seattle?

I have a business meeting first thing Wednesday morning, which is why I need to head to the mainland Tuesday afternoon. I will grab the race car and head to a "test-and-tune" session on Thursday, and will do some shopping for Molly on Friday, her birthday is coming up.

I'm glad you are coming home and hope Hannah is recovered before you get on the plane.

Hannah's much better today, thank you, just sniffles. I'd like to coax everyone to Sayulita again. The surf is amazing, though you have to paddle quite a way out to ride the waves to shore; it makes me a bit nervous to supposedly be Jacob's supervising adult. I'm not much of a swimmer, though Robert certainly is.

Oooh, I stepped in something. Why the formality?

Formality btwn us: OK, I admit: I felt this intense intimacy, and then I'm brought back to life with the realization that you have much more of an intimacy with someone else.

Everyone wants to be the Only, the Best. I know it doesn't make any sense. I guess I just got greedy or something. Forgive?

Our relationship seems to have taken a turn. What did we do, drop the outer ring of our defenses? Nothing to apologize for, but something to be wary of.

Peter, (now that's formality, a real heading, a salutation, forebodes trouble...) I need a break. I've lost my objectivity, my Girlfriendness. I can't be a reliable Girlfriend to you right now. Let's try again this summer.

She tells me to back off, that she is not REALLY there, she won't necessarily be there, try again this summer? Try what in the summer, Girlfriend? Biography? Communicating? Did you just say goodbye? Bringing you flowers, did I chase you away?

Of course I am really here. Too much here. Here in ways I did not intend. Here in ways that will not work right now. But now it's passed. Just a mood swing. Not enough sleep. No big deal.

Washing a Cat

We are home. Was up most of the night with poor Hannah, she has a fever and threw up repeatedly.

The first vomit splash was comprised of cake and pizza and sugared root beer, and landed squarely on unsuspecting Oreo, who was curled up next to her.

So in addition to washing comforter covers and sheets at 1 a.m., I was washing her cat.

If you've ever tried to wash a cat, you'll know it's virtually impossible. But I persevered, and eventually most of the puke ended up on the bathroom mirror, floor, counter, etc., but off the fluffy, long-haired cat-cum-struggling-vicious-beast.

However, more optimistically, it's a great excuse for my dad NOT to come for a visit. We brought my mom back from Seattle, and after she goes back, I could really use a break from 24/7 family.

I don't know which is more disturbing: washing a cat at 1 a.m. or the fact that all that crap was in her stomach in the first place. But I'm glad you are back and glad you wrote.

Please check Hannah's temperature and the whites of her eyes for color. They need to be white and not yellow. Check for rashes ALL over. Did she come into contact with any animals in Mexico? ANY animals? Ask her. Half a Tylenol for fever.

If fever doesn't come down or any more vomiting… it is time to call a nurse's hotline or take her in to the doctor.

You're a godsend. Mild fever, no more vomiting. Just gave her 1/2 dose of Tylenol for the fever... she didn't want it earlier, afraid even the little pill wouldn't stay down. I concurred.

The one weird thing is that yesterday she hurt the heel of her foot jumping off a chair. I didn't think much of it, but she really complained of pain, which isn't like her unless it's real (the opposite of her brother, the hypochondriac).

When I looked, she had a blood blister about the size of a nickel, and a dime-sized blister right next to it. I don't see how it could be connected, but it is odd.

Unless Hannah is really sick and/or needy for me I'm leaving her with Mom and heading to the gym for a quick workout.

Sorry I'll miss you. Sorry you'll miss me: I've still got a pretty nice tan. Last night Mom actually said that she thought I was flushed from the wine I drank at dinner, my inch in a small glass! I don't think there's a single Jewish alcoholic in the world.

Hannah: Check the fever at noon. It needs to be better. And she needs those liquids, Debra, even if she is afraid of them not staying down. Fear of vomiting can't be allowed to keep her from getting enough fluids.

No milk unless to settle the stomach and make the next barf softer on the gullet. Any blood in barf or urine, get her to doctor asap.

Rinsing the mouth with baking soda (you DO bake, I just know it) will prevent stomach acid from damaging teeth.

Thank you. I will keep my eye on her but I think she is going to be fine. My mother is here to back-stop me so I can get to the gym. I also promised to bring something for the ribbon-cutting at the new library tonight. And no, I don't bake, it will be a salad, not cookies. Will you be there?

I haven't decided if I am going to go. I'm not a big fan of crowds.

Ribbon Cutting

Well, Mr. Hamilton, you've pulled another rabbit out of your hat. What lovely accolades for you at the ribbon cutting for the library! I owe you a personal debt of gratitude along with that offered by the community. How can I thank you?

I saw you, too, but when I was able to break free of the conversation, you'd disappeared. Nice tan. Even though it was just a glimpse. How is Hannah doing?

Hannah seems to be better, but she is still pretty listless. Robert tells me to stop worrying, for whatever that's worth.

Nice tan? That's it? You're going to have to do better.

She had her back to him while unloading the car. He paused, watching her sort through detritus in the back seat, reach for a huge bowl of salad, close the back door and then the front. He liked watching her, athleticism obvious even in the mundane.

But it was when she turned he caught his breath. Her skin showed weeks of sun, a smile crinkled in her eyes. He wasn't sure, but she did not seem unhappy to see him. Her cat mouth seemed to offer a welcome.

"Nice tan," he said.

"Thank you," she said. "Nice weather. Two days ago I had sun, sand and sangria and now..." She nodded at the dirty sheet of water that slopped the parking lot.

"Carry you across the puddle?" he asked.

"You don't have that much money," she tossed back with a smile.

"I was offering a service, not looking to purchase one."

She laughed and looked at him. He wished she would say more so he would have one more excuse to look into her eyes and make her smile again.

She turned toward the gathering at the new library as he locked his truck and followed. He wondered if she saw, reflected in the glass door, that he watched her every step of the way.

He liked watching her move. He liked making her smile.

Yes, this was MUCH better, thank you. And you can't imagine what it means being seen by you. Really seen, on many levels.

It's a lot of fun. But the more we play Biography, the more dangerous the game.

Who was the brunette woman standing beside you at the ribbon cutting? She was very beautiful. Was that your wife?

No, Molly was home with our kids. I was introduced to the brunette after the dedication but didn't catch her name. She may have been from the mainland, maybe one of the live-aboards in the marina. I don't know who she was with but she had "danger" written all over.

Danger? You don't seem like the type of man easily tempted by worldly distractions.

It's raining so hard again this morning. This is a winter like we used to get every year, a flood from Thanksgiving to St. Patrick's Day. Normally I enjoy the rain, certainly don't mind it. But it's been oppressive this year.

You changed the subject! How am I supposed to get to know you if you avoid my only slightly intrusive forays?

I don't talk about myself. There are more interesting topics.

Maybe. Well, Port Cedar Society enjoyed what you were saying at the library. I hung at the periphery for a while.

I didn't know Port Cedar had "Society."

Society, in Port Cedar or elsewhere, can be so... I don't know what word I'm looking for... constraining? Boring doesn't capture it. Empty? Stultifying?

It's like we put on costumes and speak lines we've rehearsed but that have no internal meaning. I used to enjoy going out and rubbing elbows, and I suppose I'm still good at it. But I'm afraid I'm becoming a misanthrope.

Do you have a more optimistic view? What do you think of society and one's place in it?

"Society" is an organism of information made up of other organisms that are always changing, reinventing themselves, modifying boundaries, overlapping but with different dynamics. We have simultaneous membership in many of these sets.

You examine a topic by defining it, thus avoid having to share your response to it.

You asked what I thought of society and our place in it. I thought I answered what was asked.

Our "conversation" again feels like that optical illusion of a chalice and two faces. I can see the chalice, or the two faces, but not both at the same time.

Given that there is no chalice nor faces, just ink on a page or pixels on a screen, perhaps there is nothing but optical illusion.

But you're right. I did change the questions mid-stream. And only subtly, so it was confusing. Don't give up on me; I usually am far more clear-thinking. I'm distracted. But I'm the one who should apologize.

A waiter can be fired from the local restaurant, a Catholic priest may change parish. They occupy different "places" in society, and this might have no affect on restaurant or parish at a certain scale of measurement such as profits or donations.

Or it might, if the waiter is the illegitimate child of the parish priest. It depends on the tools you use for observation.

One does not have a single "place" in society.

Of course one cannot have a "place" in society, so the greater humanity's folly for pursuing it. Yet we do. As you say, we join organizations that do take tangible form. And we write books which will sit on a shelf, spine facing outward, our names indelibly announcing our place in the world. We run races and play sports and serve on school boards and bring home medals or certificates, evidence of both our participation and our "place" in the pecking order. We go to church and worship the flag.

We beg for significance. Religion or patriotism helps individuals identify their "mortal small self" (organism) with the "immortal large organism" (Church, America)" and a sense of worth otherwise impossible to achieve. That's society. You misanthropes may be correct: Mankind may be a melanoma on the face of the Earth.

You go to a library ribbon cutting because you save old buildings. But why do you chat with half of Port Cedar beforehand? Are you maintaining your place in society, or does it provide you with inherent satisfaction?

And you're not allowed to explain that man is a social creature by nature. That's another definition. I seek your personal response to whether you generally enjoy the company of man. And, since your answer won't be a categorical "yes" or "no," what is it about a person that captures your imagination? And, as a husband, father, esteemed community member at the prime of his life, how important are those titles to how you define yourself?

No, I do not particularly enjoy the "company" of other people. I'm socially inept, caustic when I don't mean to be, intolerant when I should be gracious, am considered abrasive, nearly incapable of small-talk. I have a facetiousness in my phrasing when I'm trying to be funny, think everyone shares my joke when I often give offense.

Because I cannot skate well on the surface I quickly go to places where many are uncomfortable.

Titles mean nothing. I love being in strange places where I can disappear. Or did you mean responsibilities? The responsibilities of father are immense and I castigate myself regularly over my failings while recognizing that I do better than most. I have responsibilities to make my community "better when I leave than when I arrived." A Boy Scout credo.

I'm not surprised you don't enjoy the company of other people. Yet I would be surprised if they didn't enjoy the company of you. From what I saw the other night, you definitely have a style all your own, and it's not glib and groovy. But it does have charm and graciousness and, inevitably, resonates your depth of character.

I am a man of impatience, intelligence, faith, strength in some ways but bent or broken in so many others, of passion, who knows the difference between right and wrong, but who struggles with doing right and avoiding wrong in a universe that may not care.

Is that what you want to know?

I want to know you, Peter.

I'm one of the silly multitude, searching for my "place" in life. I see similarities between you and me, like not skating well on the surface and not "suffering fools gladly," and was only trying to learn whether you successfully strike the balance between being yourself and being a part of provincial Port Cedar.

Backgammon

Hannah in St. Claire Hospital in Everett;

Toxic shock; infection from something in foot picked up in Mexico... probably no surgery... she's much better after antibiotics and fluids, Robert telling me I was being hysterical and refusing even to drive up from Seattle.

Mom going to stay until Hannah better, then I will take Mom back to Seattle. Depending on Robert's flying schedule, I may be able to stay at Mom's for a couple of days, see friends and run in the hills where I grew up... if it's not raining.

I'm so glad Hannah is okay. You did what you knew was right in the face of pretty severe peer pressure. Good for you. Let me know if your dogs need out.

You grew up in Seattle, and I came of age here. My old haunts were along 1st and 3rd in the Belltown District before it was desirable, and I worked as a waiter downtown in some of the finest restaurants at the time.

Belltown... my high school boyfriend lived there (with his liberal, ultra-hip parents) on 4th and Vine. My only extracurricular activities in high school, playing backgammon *and screwing, took place at that venue. (By the way, I also did my share of car racing on the Alaskan Viaduct in the dead of night.)*

But the neighborhood really became mine during law school. I lived in a top-floor studio between 2nd and 3rd. I loved that place. The neighborhood had not yet gentrified. New York-style pizza was a new thing. There was still no place to buy a bagel, and not even a hint of Starbucks (to this day I go to Coffee People instead).

It was a little grimy, with the wispiest aura of hip. Even though I was dead broke, I'd spend $3.45 each night buying a massive cake slice at The Rainier Bakery. They called me "The Hazelnut Torte Lady." And long live Pike Place Theater and Cinema 5!

Hazelnut tort at The Rainier!? When I worked at First Street Steak House, we served an elegant hazelnut tort, but nothing like the small mountain of sugar and fatty frosting served at The Rainier. That was one of my favorites. And the carrot cake.

When I first moved to that area of Seattle, it felt like I'd discovered something I'd missed since San Francisco urban living. There were drug dealers who sold luxury cars on Jefferson Street between 32nd and 33rd.

There must have been something about Belltown that caused backgammon and screwing. I learned one there and tried my best to refine the other. Mary the bartender broke my friend Roger with cocaine and outrageous sex just up the street.

OK, I'll bite: which one did you learn, how well did you learn it, and did you succeed in refining the other?

There are similarities. Each requires attentiveness, a willingness to be vulnerable at one moment and assertive the next, there is delight in surprise. One may move from either side of the board and it's much more enjoyable when played between equals.

Touché. For once I'm speechless.

I hope my love of wordplay and metaphor crossed no lines. If so, please forgive me.

There are no lines. Isn't possible to have a conversation without them?

Of course. If I've not ruined the chance for an afternoon of backgammon.

You speak the game between "equals." What about the balance of power?

"balance of power?" Explain, please.

You're the second man to whom I've used this phrase in the past couple of weeks, and the second to be unfamiliar with it. It seems so obvious to me, yet neither of you recognize it. Maybe it's another example of my assuming the way I see the world is universal.

It goes back to my Darwinian view of the world: one person, and at various times during the relationship it may be one or the other, is more invested in the relationship than the other... usually the person who, for whatever reason or combination of reasons, is more insecure.

The "weaker" of the two is the one who cares more. I know you'll urge that the person with the strength to show vulnerability is the stronger, but that's a different phenomenon.

I'm incoherent (more than usual). Tired. The trip home was long. Hannah's scare. Barn repairs and heavy lifting and baseball practice and track workouts and play-dates and and and...

I would like to respond to this specifically, but are you sure you don't have any lines I mustn't cross? I wait for your assent.

I hereby assume the risks associated with a "lines-free" relationship. Tell all. I spend too much of my life "watching" myself and not enough of it "being" myself. All those lines contribute to the former.

The lines are a corral we struggle to get out of, or if out, find our way back in. Laughter and passion take us outside the lines, as does being in love, being vulnerable, emotionally and physically. A place of giving and receiving, accepting and being.

Passion sets one free of the lines, love can set one free. There is nothing more beautiful than a woman in the throes of passion. Bathed in forgetting, the lines disappear if she trusts her lover, as she offers herself, knowing he will care for her as he carries her past the lines that define who is watching and who is "being," as she watches her body respond without intention as she comes to release, there is pure passion and freedom.

There is no "balance of power," there.

I see a "balance of power" in most every relationship, but especially and almost invariably in sexual relationships. I never see a relationship between equals, or however you referred (how many "r's" does that have?) to it.

In emotional terms it translates into a four-step formula, and one which isn't very flattering to me.

Step 1: I am "attracted" to someone. B/c I don't know them well, and have probably seen them "on stage" and at their best (particularly when the attraction is mutual), I subconsciously assume that this sketch of a person, when filled in by the artistry of time, will reveal a full painting of the depth and quality of the sketch. I immortalize them.

Step 2: It gets worse. I find my huge ego gratified that the god returns my adoration, and I bask in the heady glow of being loved by a god. The huntress is also sated, having caught a desirable and elusive prey.

Step 3: Mutual basking in chemicals and mutual adoration and sex.

Step 4: The remainder of the sketch is completed, and the original bold, daring lines that seemed to form the essence are now squiggles and smears. The hunt rendered meaningless b/c the prey was mortal, obtainable, perhaps not even all that desirable. Return to romantic ennui.

My favorite love scene was from "Rob Roy" with Liam Neeson and Jessica Lange. He is a warrior, she is every bit his partner.

She takes him up to a ridge above the lake where they have their home, hikes her skirt and his kilt and sits in his lap facing him. Nothing is seen but their fully clothed torsos. He has his arms around her waist, she has hers around his neck. They are looking at each other, swaying with passion, building to climax, all very strong and at the same time very gentle. Intertwined.

That giving between the lovers, the equal sharing of that moment between them, the simultaneity of their passion, the patience each had for the other within the quickening of their bodies, deeply aroused by each other's desire, her hot passion for him bringing him closer, knowing of his closeness fanning her flames, it glows hotter and hotter until it bursts with sparks like a fire at night on the beach when a stacked log falls.

I'm intimidated by your nimbleness of word. I'm sorry you have to struggle through my byzantine ramblings to get to the core.

I'm soon off to the track, which has far different connotations for me than you! I dread speed (if you can call my pitiful huffing "speed").

You never have to be intimidated by me. I found your comment about lines to be open and honest.

Darwinist

What about a lover who wanted nothing more than to turn you inside out with desire and exhaust you with pleasure, not as an exercise of power but an act of the truly erotic, and when you are limp, wants to hold you close, envelop you, allow you to nap and to dream?

"Power" and "weakness" interfere with sharing. Weakness is different than making oneself vulnerable to one you trust. We either have a different view of this, or are using the same words but not communicating.

No, no, we do have the same view. But what you're describing is an ideal, or a brief and transient affair, rather than an on-going relationship. It never lasts.

I don't know where love goes, or the erotic. Perhaps it is taken from us by design, so we hunt for it and create greater possible combinations for preservation of the species.

See, I can be Darwinist, too.

Or perhaps we are just too lazy to invest the on-going effort. Or perhaps the thousand cuts that one lives through in a long-term relationship build up scar tissue that prevents us from feeling a caress. The intensity of a brief affair freshens the skin, but what abrades the leather of knowing this is all the life we have?

Transient or not, passion is what makes life worth living if the alternative is all form and lines and power and approval.

A thousand cuts would be pleasure bittersweet compared to the hollow pain of their absence. Where does the passion go? Affection can grow, as can respect, and the closeness born of shared experience. Why does passion inevitably fade?

I can't help but think part of the answer lies in the dark side of passion. With the newness, strangeness and novelty of a new lover comes the daring thrill of uncertainty; trusting and making oneself vulnerable becomes part of the excitement.

"The game is so much more enjoyable for being a play between equals..." There are no equals. There are only fragments of ephemeral moments in which a person is distilled to their pure, raw being. Maybe that's one reason why sex, especially for men loath to unveil themselves, is so important. Orgasm is the only moment in which passion is simple.

I admit I was fondling my metaphor, but I was thinking of a long afternoon … if one player always wins at backgammon the game is not fun for either.

Such an afternoon is best spent between equals. Where each partner is more concerned for the other's physical pleasure and emotional well-being than being defensive of their own.

What about the time before and the time after? Intimacy fills those hours with anticipation, then warmth. I think "men loath to unveil" treasure those moments because of intimacy, being able to let someone inside to places normally out of bounds.

Interesting, but in your discussions of intimacy you invariably refer to the intimacy between lovers… heady and giddy and immersed in their own and each other's passion. But I'm speaking more globally, of the intimacy between friends, acquaintances in which intimacy is often sought.

Isn't intimacy the essence of a real relationship with anyone, whether a friendship or a love relationship?

I guess I always seek an idealized relationship. The foundation would be like a mother's love: as deep and real as the earth's core, unconditional, unwavering. That foundation would give me the courage to ignore the lines, cross the lines, obliterate the lines. I would like to live in an ideal world of simple candor, rather than our world of artifice and social convention and driven by fear of being exposed, of showing weakness. Even intimacy is bound up in Darwinian constraints.

This is another "Chalice" discussion. Wasn't it you who brought up "balance of power" in sexual relationships?

Intimacy, as I define it, is not the essence of a "real relationship with anyone," friendship or love. Unless you are defining "real" as intimate, then it becomes a tautology.

There are those whom I love but with whom I am not intimate even in spirit. There are those lines, again, not only for self-preservation but necessary for preservation of the relationship. And where is "trust" in your equation?

Trust is an essential ingredient, a necessary underpinning of intimacy, but not the definition. I'll tell you what "intimacy" means to me: it means laying oneself bare, naked rather than nude, it means guilelessness, it means mutual understanding.

Ideally it would be the relinquishment of judgment.

Intimacy and "balance of power" can co-exist. The (im)balance of power occurs when one person is more invested in the relationship than the other. This is a fact, a condition, a quantity. Rarely does either party even know it is there, except on a subliminal level.

But it exists, turning equals not into competitors but into... non-equals! And if intimacy is the absence of judgment, then I wonder if it can be achieved... Isn't there always judgment, and never freedom? Is what I observe part of the human condition, or my own neurotic insecurity?

No. Emphatically no. Trust does not evolve from an imbalance of power. Intimacy comes from trust.

The extent to which there is judgment is the extent that there is no trust, no intimacy, no freedom. It takes work for those who at times would rather eat the menu than the meal.

Perhaps this is why my passions, fathomless and primed, are for those things which are unquestionably more powerful than myself, allowing me to submit myself fully. Those moments I perch upon a rock on the beach and the ocean surges and roils around me in its hypnotic, insistent omnipotence.

Or hunkered down alongside a rock and sheltered from the wind on a mountain summit, suffused in the chill of hazy, high-altitude sunshine, enveloped in a soundless universe which is at once stark and full. There are no lines in this purity.

The more I think about it, though, even these moments are contaminated by power, strength and dominance. Isn't part of your racing your sense of control? And part of my mountain the fact that I have conquered it? Humans remain slaves to their instincts.

Look, Mr. Philosophy Degree from Berkeley, I'm out of my league here and not thinking very clearly. But I do think we have a strange dichotomy going: we observe the world in much the same way, our souls in tandem, but my perception of human nature (perception being distinct from observation) is a cynical version of your far more romantic and optimistic view. Make sense?

Chemicals

I've finally come up for air. Just a gasp of breath, but I'd like to spend it on you.

I'm troubled by my own misanthropy. I have always valued time alone, but wonder if the degree to which I choose to be alone is "healthy."

I'm bedeviled by The Shoulds: Should I have more "let's have coffee" relationships? Should I have running partners instead of heading into the forest with my dog? Should I invite other couples to dinner more often?

Should I seek the company of my spouse? Regardless of whether I Should, I rarely want to.

Mostly I try to enjoy little pieces of people in small doses (I love Renee, my climbing partner, but can't stand to sit across a table from her), but just haven't found a core of people I actually want to spend time with, rather than feel I Should spend time with.

The Social Shoulds are idiots. If you trade fulfillment for the company of a Should, you've walked into the wrong room. The comment about your spouse is tragic and familiar.

Debra, when was the last time you were thrilled, excited to be in the company of someone? Desired to be with them, next to them, held by them? Fell in love? Your questions go away, then, it seems to me.

Even the pain of love lost is better than the gray concrete of living within an intellectual box where feelings have been replaced by thinking about feelings.

I've been trapped in both places.

When was the last time I fell in love? What an impossible question. Define "love." No, I'm not for a moment trying to squirrel out of having to answer.

Is "love" that amazing high I feel when my body and mind can think of no one else? Where I want to explore everything about him, and share everything about myself? A giddy obsession, an incessant wanting to know more about how and what he thinks and feels, a desire to dive right into his soul...?

Or is "love" sharing an album of life's experiences: the "when we first mets," the babies, the travels, the travails...

Is it love if it's fleeting? If I felt it intensely and deeply and fully, only to lose it to the Black Hole of Love Once Known, is it still "love"? If I felt love's power once with someone, have I experienced "love" with that person, despite it's dissipation? Or must love be permanent?

Does "love" mean just what you wrote, when did I last desire to "be with, be next to, be held by, etc."? That's a pretty low standard! Be prepared for a racy response.

YES! Love is all of those things, even their contradictions... love is not diminished by time or place, it runs and it stays because love does not acknowledge limits, let alone give them respect. Once loved, that person is a love, and even though the smallness of jealousy may lessen one person or both, they do not lessen love. Even if love is a chemical imbalance, it drives poetry and through poetry, love spins small worlds and great stars. By altering perception, love changes the very physics of being!

Being in love is different than loving someone, and your Shoulds are showing. Yes, we want to be in love with the people we love, with the people we are supposed to love. But sometimes, if not oftentimes, that doesn't happen and we feel guilt and anguish that gnaw at our serenity, and cause us to stand just outside ourselves and to question what we know so well: Love is sickness and it is health.

And what of love lost? What great abyss opens under our very feet when we have lost the love of our life, when all we have of her laughter is an echo that sounds distant in chambers of a now-empty heart, where we look down and hope the very earth there is gone, so that we may fall away from the ache of not being in the arms of our love…

… from not knowing if those arms hold another, the memory of a face we needed to make smile, a dog-eared photo that we reach for in moments of melancholy, with tears we hide from curious children to adults we blame allergies, from the color of a riotous sunrise after a drenching rain which leaves us untouched because our love is not beside us to share?

If you are not willing to accept loss, then love is not yours and you lose again.

We're really asking… why is love so unruly, why does it step so defiantly outside all the lines, why does it misbehave and ignore all boundaries…

Because it does.

Yes, the loss. Because for me the ecstasy of love is invariably followed by the bitter-sadness of loss.

Do I love Robert? Of course. Of course not. I care for him, I respect him, I have shared and continue to share our children, our memories. Yet our relationship, for me, is barren of emotional intimacy. I do not long for him, yearn to be with him.

When was the last time... this time last year, when I had an affair and a half (the first time during my marriage). I was a little bit in love with the person in the "half" affair, and not in the least in love with the person in the "full" affair.

And the real "love of my life?" Years ago, before Robert. And I look back and wonder how on earth I could have loved that man so deeply, so earnestly, so passionately. I knew, in my heart, I would always love him. Yet I don't. Is human nature so fickle? Is love that fragile and tenuous?

Love is not fragile. It has supple strength that defies logic and is impatient, anxious, selfish, wanting to take control. Is that the irony, the little cosmic joke? Those who recognize love are so painfully aware when it goes missing? And it goes missing through no fault of those we love, adding to the shame that maybe we just stopped working at it?

I think life, generally, is at once more painful and infinitely richer for those who examine with deep intensity. The proverbial double-edged sword. Maybe we could agree to call this one aspect of the "passion" to which we've both referred.

At this time of life, the late summer storm of a love deep, earnest and passionate becomes even more electric because the days shorten. Memory seeds clouds of hope to feel thunder once again. We are that fickle, we were designed to be.

Does love go, or do we realize it was never really there? Is love a mere temporary state of being, its own microcosm of chemistry? Does our capacity for introspection intrude on those heady, dizzying chemicals, marching them toward an inevitable destruction?

You're playing hide-and-go-seek when you ask if Love was never really there. It does not matter if Love is chemistry.

You've never knowingly seen an endorphin, yet Love has enveloped you. You assert the endorphin you can't see is more real than the Love you have known?

Question at midnight the warmth of sunlight at noon.

Love leaves the room after the loss of respect, a hint of laziness, when selfishness and defenses enter. But Love was there, I remember the compulsion to stand next to Her, I remember her scent, and her laugh.

My "love of life" would not allow me to take her for granted, and she would not stop working at it. I think we were in love for years because of her stubbornness. She would not let me hide even in my worst moments.

It ended because it should never have started, but I miss her desperately still and I feel selfish and small because if I was truly a good man, I could conjure love up at will and share it with the deserving.

Peter, this pain is fresh. Who is she?

For years this woman loved me, before deciding she was no longer willing to share. It changed the course of my life. It was a love that removed my coat in a squalling rain to feel my skin peppered with fat wet drops, it brought the warmth of full skin to a chill crisp dawn, it caused me to put down my spear and then my shield so I could hold her.

The affair ended a year ago. My sadness at losing her is at times still beyond my tolerance. There. You have entered. I'm done with this.

Oh, Peter, I'm sorry. Now I understand. Why don't we have coffee and you can tell me about her.

The Scolds of Port Cedar would love nothing more than a chance to fondle their rumors.

As to public perception, you're in a very different place than I am. I have a notoriously wide range of friendships, spanning gaps in age, education, income and even what is sometimes the "gapiest": gender.

I don't think anyone who knows me... or even knows of me... would bat an eye. (Of course, they don't see Lord Byron under your understated exterior.)

On the other hand, "people" (you know, the Shoulds) might look askance at you befriending me. Do you know how often I've been cast as the dumb blonde (and a badly dyed one, at that)?

A man's motives are always known, even if the man is not. There may be a day when my being seen in intimate conversation with a beautiful younger woman in a public place would not raise an eyebrow. Not in Port Cedar.

I hardly qualify as beautiful, but concede that I am unusual enough to raise eyebrows. I'll henceforth look forward only to occasional clandestine coffees and surreptitious emails. I'll avert my eyes at Safeway. Peter, I simply can't believe social convention is so medieval!

In case you haven't noticed, I'm determined to have your unconditional friendship and offer the same. Implicit in that is the highest degree of confidentiality. Where does she work? Care to share her name?

As to where she works or her name, let's just call her Lover. For reasons I can't articulate, naming her or your "Half" and "Full" affairs would make our sharing more difficult, not less. Let them remain representations.

I appreciate the distinction you made between maintaining an illusion and dispelling one. Yet I wonder whether the whole endeavor is "healthy" for you. I'm sure you know that children of alcoholics (as well as those of abusers) tend toward secretiveness. Whatever the motivation, you are a man of many secrets.

To the extent anyone at our stage in life wishes to "work through issues," honesty (and don't quibble with me about whether you are "honest") and openness might be your version of my "letting go."

Beauty is in the eye of the beholder, I suppose.

If my marriage comes apart it would be the height of irony for the wags to say, "You know, just a couple of weeks ago, I saw him at Martha's Café with Debra Shapiro. They sat together on the ferry…"

Most of the "secrets" superimposed on the Peter Hamilton of Port Cedar aren't really secrets. I simply allow misperceptions to flourish, avoid the effort of clarification.

As to actual secrets, I get to choose my "working through" and with whom I share. Don't avert your eyes.

Garbage Man

Forgive me if I cross a line you tell me isn't there: How does Robert leave his beautiful young wife alone on this island for days at a time?

Does he have stirrings that match your own? Do the two of you talk about what could be construed as your abandonment? Were you ever in love with him as we speak of it here… is this isolation a new fence grown up between you, or has it been there all along?

First, I'm still in Seattle b/c I feel like crap (ran a 1/2 marathon in the rain and waited for friends for 25 minutes afterward, shivering, teeth chattering), so don't expect much in the way of humor, wit or clarity.

Love of My Life and I loved each other beyond belief... well, by your definition. In that place, at that time, we loved each other desperately. The serpent? Love of Life had no moral compass. He wasn't a "bad" man, just a very self-centered only child from wealthy family in Bellevue. He adored me, but there's no doubt in my mind that if we were on a sinking ship he'd be on the first lifeboat.

I knew, in my heart, that I couldn't "really" love a man so lacking in moral fiber. And it didn't help that he wasn't nearly as smart as I am (which isn't very). So we spent two years pushing and pulling and finally broke up the day after the Bar exam (I passed; he didn't). I drove to Olympic National Park after the Bar and took the trip we had planned together... alone. I truly hit rock-bottom. I was going to write "you can't imagine the agonizing pain," but I bet you can.

Robert happened to return from an extended assignment ferrying parts for aircraft around the world just when I broke up with Love of Life. We were both runners, and Robert was training for a marathon, so I agreed to keep him company on some of his long training runs. Runs led to breakfast (at the Rainier Bakery, where I would devour one of those colossal cinnamon rolls), breakfast to river trips...

I "chose" Robert b/c he was safe. Though I had a couple brief flings I told myself had potential, knowing full well they didn't, I thought maybe it would help bolster the ego and ease the pain. He was so much older, I "knew" I'd never lose my heart. And, long story short, I stayed. Details available upon request.

No details necessary. I understand this. We took refuge, you and I. There's much here to think about. Safety. Respect. Selfishness. Passion. Commitment. Sex. You've pulled some cover from my own self-delusions. Now I have to go look. Thank you.

What's next? Where will you be in five years? Trapped and older? In love again? Running toward something or running away? Content with horses in the barn, children graduating from high school, a husband at home? A little travel, a little art…?

Where will I be in five years? Will I continue my pattern of making decisions by default?

Why? Is there inherent virtue in staying married? Is it really so much better for the children? Is the grass really greener?

Perhaps more than any, the last question in this list proves the most central in my lame, passive decision-making process. For I don't think there's greener grass, nor do I think I'll ever be in love again. A cold cynicism. After dinner I'll try to hunker down and convey.

Talk about Robert: What does Robert see? What does he want? Where will HE be?

Robert... Robert loves me, has some degree of respect and admiration for me, wants to keep me.

Actually, he would like to go back to the days before my 1 1/2 affairs, because since then I have been uncharacteristically flat and passionless, at least in my relationship with him.

I know it pains him to see my zest and enthusiasm shared with the kids and my friends. I feel cruel when I feed him a crumb of warmth and he devours it so hungrily. But I can't, or won't, manufacture what isn't there.

We know when the emotional bond has snapped between us and those we love… the craving for crumbs of warmth. That was the genesis of the words you found moving … if I was a good man I could conjure love and share it with the deserving.

I have opened a dialogue with Molly about our marriage. Which may end it. One of the things she told me is that she is jealous of those I share deeply with… people who turn to me, for whatever reason, and I respond. I don't do that with her. The zest and enthusiasm shared with others, with children and friends, but not the spouse.

I feel cruel. I so want to be the good man, the good father, the good husband. I am a good father, I suppose, with obvious but not catastrophic shortcomings. I'm not a good husband. I withhold love. I withhold generosity of spirit, pretend that providing a good home and good life is an adequate substitute. I cannot, as you say, "manufacture what isn't there."

Robert is a wonderful person. He loves me and the children. He has a very strong moral and ethical core, although he tends to see life a bit as a ball game: his team vs. the other team. Black hats vs. white hats. But that's part of his refusing to look deeply at things. This quality is odd in him, because he is extremely intelligent.

Yet I've grown weary about discussing issues with him because he doesn't share my love for unfolding layers of things, and examining the gossamer fibers. He's too ideological, though I share his ideology.

Molly says that even our friends notice that I am distant, that at times I obviously don't want to be there. This is even more cruel, because it puts her on display in my own unflattering reflection. And she is so good, good to the core. I feel often unworthy and so very selfish of wanting more and wishing I could simply find it at home, if I would only work a little harder, open myself a little more.

It's entirely possible that Molly is here through inertia. Habit. Fear. I don't know. But when she cries and tells me she envies women who are looked at by their husbands with love and it doesn't matter what they look like… in those moments I want to reach down my own throat and tear out the first thing that comes to hand.

Your situation, your song, is so familiar to me. A plangent refrain: "Why can't I? Why can't I....." Why can't I return the love of one so worthy?

There is counseling. Robert and I went and received a perfect, nutshell training course in how to deal with one another's hot-button issues, and what behavioral habits we need to teach ourselves, etc. It actually helped, in the sense that Robert gained some understanding of how my needs were not being met. But it ultimately fails because what I want is passion and intimacy, and he's simply not capable of teaching himself those qualities.

"Working" at the marriage, feigning passion's presence, leaves a huge chunk of us lonely and flat, the latter of which is anathema to people who thrive on energy and intensity and sensuality (in the broadest sense of that word).

We could view the issue through the lens of self-preservation. We are who we are. We can modify our behavior, but not our hearts. We have an obligation to ourselves. We deserve to have our own needs met.

I tried this last summer with my 1 1/2 affairs, and realized that swapping Robert for another, however "in love" I feel at the time, is merely swapping one set of disappointments for another. Despite what you say, I can't help continuing to believe that love is little more than self-delusion, masturbation. OK, intensely pleasurable self-delusion and masturbation, but nonetheless...

Another path, and it sounds like we've both chosen this in many ways, is to get and give as much as possible to the marriage, and try to fulfill our need, at least our non-sexual needs, elsewhere. Those friends with whom conversation darts and meanders, soars and dives, provokes and stimulates, but always on a foundation of loyalty and love. Those you can trust, on whom you can "try" ideas, you can show your ugliest, most base and crass self, without fearing rejection or small-minded, simplistic condemnation. I could go on, but I know you know.

The only problem with this is that it doesn't fulfill the sexual needs, and by that, I don't mean just sex. I mean all the passions attendant to sexual love. Once again: I know you know.

I've lied to myself in so many ways, and the rough wool shirt is that I know I'm lying even as I struggle to believe that I'm deserving of passion. Why am I more honest with you than with my own wife?

I show frustration even when Molly wants to laugh, as if I find her laughter not full enough or without abandon and she shrinks and I try to crawl inside my own cruel skin.

Counseling is another lie, an attempt to believe I tried when I know that had I tried but a little harder or freed myself from the arms of distraction, been honest, it could have been successful.

You and I disagree about love. Yes, I can view it too as an intensely pleasurable masturbation. But that is music as notes on a page above keys of a piano. I don't want to read the music. I want to play, I want to be played, to be the music, lost in the melody.

When the music fades, we are left with not even talk, Debra, because the melancholy of melodies lost seals our lips, and there is not even glibness to convince our spouse we are still in the room, let alone part of the conversation. Our arms are blades, we can not even embrace them without causing blood to flow.

Ah, you're more honest with me than with your wife because I was honest with you first. I revealed the tortured, frustrated portion of my soul, and it wasn't so different than yours. Your desire for understanding outweighed the discomfort of laying yourself bare.

But what prompted you to reveal your soul, with very little protection, to a man with whom you'd shared only a few lines of text? I know more about you than your husband, you know more about me than my wife. How very strange, in so many ways.

Well... with all due respect, the garbage man probably knows more about my inner soul than Robert does. And this is merely one aspect of our inner selves, however central.

I have always had at least one "Jerry" in my life, or at least a pale imitation of Jerry. I met Jerry when I just returned to Seattle from New York. I was earning money for law school, and volunteering at the ACLU and an anti-death-penalty campaign. Jerry was in his 2nd(?) yr. at UW Law School, also volunteering at ACLU. I was going out with Ron, his friend. (Yes, I was one of those women who always had a boyfriend.)

Over the years Jerry and I were best friends, lovers, and everything in between. The lovers thing didn't cut it for me, which left him both sad and resentful. I could fill in years of tangled history, but the short version is that he got married after a demoralizing series of relationships. He dumped me.

Almost a decade later I moved here to Port Cedar, and Jerry contacted me. His marriage was in shambles. He was in shambles. We once again became more than just best friend confidantes: we revealed and shared and lived each other's thoughts and fears and hopes. The intimacy we shared was one of the most fulfilling experiences of my life. He often came over to the island for the day when Robert was flying and while the kids were in school. I nursed him through his inevitable divorce, and he ultimately remarried and promptly dumped me again, because his wife couldn't handle our friendship.

Basically I'm always looking for another "Jerry." So when I meet anyone, even the above-mentioned and fictitious garbage man, I take risks. I reach for the Jerry in them, I invite them to cut through the crap and be real. I disarm them by disarming myself.

And I see a lot of Jerry in you. Maybe even a deeper, richer Jerry. Life is far too short (this used to be nothing more than a worn cliche to me, now it rings true with a grave certainty) to yield to the dictates of social convention, to stay inside the lines, wasting this chance for intimacy.

Summer

Performing

Our discourse is going to be interrupted. In Seattle on Wednesday for business, down to Pacific Raceways on Thursday for training, with the hope to cut a second off my best time. Back to Seattle for a meeting first thing Friday morning, catch the 8 p.m. ferry home.

We will have discoursus interruptus?

Precisely. And I will have pent-up conversation and may have to go talk with myself.

Cute. But a break might be good. Despite my brave words about reaching for intimacy, I have to admit I'm having reservations about this secret correspondence.

For reasons I haven't yet determined, I have feelings of guilt when I want to go to my computer to see if you've written. The worst of both worlds: we don't get the heat and passion of an affair, but we're saddled with the guilt of deception. Anyway, in the continuing spirit of candor, there it is.

Well, I've always preferred heat and passion to guilt and deception, but only if I can't have it all and have to choose.

You invited me to your reDoubts, I agreed to be seen at the gate. You set clear boundaries, if not built walls, when you redefined the phrase, "intimate relationship."

But I can fade back to a whisper among the spruce and cedar. Our island is no fortress against an enemy already within. And I'm beginning to suspect you are an adept hunter, if not of men then at least of experience. I struggle with that, if you insist on candor.

You've made too much of an impression to fade whisperingly into the cedars (have you crushed a cedar bud between your fingers? Its mantle of opaque velvety-green mingles with the oils of your fingers, revealing layers of acrid yet lovely aroma).

I suppose you are right about my "hunting." Not for conquests, but to fulfill an appetite for newness? Men are attracted to me and I enjoy that, but I don't lead them on. I just like learning who they are and how they relate to the world. Yes, some do have other expectations, but I disabuse them as soon as I am aware.

I just get frustrated, periodically, with having to adhere to the silly, Victorian conventions of the Shoulds of society, Port Cedar society in particular. Why can't I just be?

Honesty out of context can be intentionally misinterpreted. Perhaps another time I can talk you to dinner in "my" Seattle.

Was that ever a Freudian slip on your part or what?! I can imagine nothing nicer than being "talked" to dinner by you. But I would not, under any circumstance, share my dessert.

Talking is the easy part, though, and I wonder if we, even in the course of a friendship, could find a comfortable silence. Even though we've been communicating for a few months now, spicy snippets of email hardly engender comfortable silences.

The restaurant is busy and the waiter is slow. I don't know if we could share "silence" between courses. You are a different person than I anticipated.

Conversation is seduction, dinner is foreplay; we don't have to be impatient, because it's going to last all night long. We make up biographies with scenes set in this very restaurant. There is always enough dessert, the waiter only a glance away if another Sin Cake or glass of Merlot or an espresso is needed…

… before walking back in the rain along streets that run purple and red with reflected neon, hips bumping in perfect rhythm.

Out of narcissistic (Oooooh, say that word out loud: all those luscious sibilants...) curiosity: what kind of person did you anticipate that I would be? What persona do I present? You are not allowed to respond tactfully. I tend to start second-guessing myself, assessing my "performance," and it is so lovely to bask in the glow of reassurance. Ya know how, after first-time sex, the guy's supposed to send flowers?

You are not "performing," but I'm pleased to reassure. Of course, in the right circumstance, I would send flowers, too.

A warning (just in case): cut flowers would be a mistake. I see little more than dying stalks, artificially jammed in a garish vase.

How about a garish vase of paragraph, stems of sentence topped by flowers of adjective and verb, from a garden where not all is beautiful but every plant surreal? Your velvety-green cedar buds have been planted in moist island loam.

Dignity

Practice in the morning was short. We were on the track for about three laps before it started to rain. But at 4:15 the track was dry and clouds did not threaten.

I asked Kirk if the monster Corvette from California could be beat, and Kirk said "He won't last the weekend."

I raced the guy to the chicane, braking at the last possible moment. He hit the brakes too late and too hard and went into the turn backwards. Later he forced Kirk over the curbing to avoid a wreck.

They finally black-flagged him and sent him home. California's mechanic said they made the decision not to race because they didn't have the "setup" for this track. It wasn't setup the driver lacked.

In the next race, I got to the chicane first and had a clear path through. Kirk launched from 15th, went to the right side and passed 10 cars in the first 400 yards. By the third lap, I was already coming up on slower cars. About midway through the pack, I got stuck behind a very nice man from Arizona who drove his line, which happened to be wherever I needed to get by him.

I tried to slip past on the back straight, but at the last minute Arizona looked in his mirrors and saw Kirk coming up on his right, but not me on his left. He moved over in front of me, I hit the brakes to avoid smacking him and Kirk shot by us both. I swung over and put the hammer down.

Kirk is the wiliest driver I know, but on the next-to-last lap at the end of the back straight, he went up on the curbing in the turn, unsettled his car and spun. During one rotation I saw him looking right at me as I was about to spear right through his door, but he kept going backward out into the grass, and I just missed him.

He gunned it out with rooster tails of dirt and hunted down Arizona, but he couldn't get to me in traffic and I won the race by about a car length.

Wonderful! You've created the perfect sport for this timid non-competitor (which I am for the most part, if we don't include my hunting): I can't help skimming the account rapidly the first time, as though I was in a race in which mere hundredths of seconds counted, too. Then I go back and take in the details —all before my second cup of coffee on a dreary Sunday morning. I tried to look up results, but all they had was the stuff from last year.

It was a successful day. Now I need two more just like it.

That last sentence is a key to me, by the way. Instead of savoring the win, I wished my nemesis Randy Jones would have been here, because I think I would have beat him, too.

If I don't dominate tomorrow and the next day, I will not feel I have raced to my potential. I will remember defeats more than victory. This nature rewards me, then cheats me of appreciation of what I have done.

That is who I am: This was only today.

Oh, I know just what you mean about not being able to rest on laurels, having to prove yourself each day, each race. I was just lamenting my inability to use past victories as evidence of present and future competence... I've got more but Jacob just woke up.

It was very gratifying yesterday having people who know racing talk about the effortlessness. One videographer came up and said, "That was amazing. I was out there filming all day and you were like a machine. Hitting every turn exactly the same way, every shift, and just running away from the field." And it was nice setting a new personal best.

But the euphoria did not last. The rush comes from uncertainty, right, my huntress? If the quarry is too slow, it's just calisthenics. I imagine it's a deformity we share… a need to compete, but unable to relish victory.

Wriggling and struggling, then lithely drifting and ephemeral, the savor of victory allows you to hold her hand, and trace the length of her narrow, willowy fingers with your own, but she pulls away, eluding.

Ah, the curse. Like pursuing love, the reality is no match for the heady desire of longing for.

Trap her, make her yours.

I did not do my best, the competitors were weak, my car dominant, home track, etc., etc. A dopamine-deficient who looks at the victory in hand for only a moment, and then to the horizon wondering if that movement there, or that over there, will offer a decent chase, the true prize, perhaps absolution.

Thanks for understanding. We are alike in as many ways as we are different.

Tell me: When you trap a weak one, do you let them go gently, allowing them to preserve their dignity, if they have any left?

Seriously, Peter, do savor your accomplishment. Send the "Yes, buts" (second cousins, once removed, of the Shoulds) back to their humid, mosquito-infested midwestern home town, and tell them they may not visit you for the summer. It's a fabulous victory.

I'm speaking very much from the heart here. Just today I received a package containing a beautiful plaque for my marathon victory. Though I had already completely forgotten the race, dismissing it b/c there was so little serious competition, etc. etc. etc. (you could fill in the blanks with your own words describing your own dismissal), I smiled with a thrilling bit of pride as I held tangible evidence of my accomplishment.

Jacob got his new, steel-stringed, amp-ready guitar and is upstairs performing his entire repertoire. The kids and I went to the library and feasted. I decided to re-read Stegner, another of my literary heroes. (See, I have "heroes," too, except that I don't believe in heroes.)

You never answered my question about the hunt. I have come to believe that somewhere under your self-protective veneer, there is a girl who secretly hopes there are rainbows, love and heroes. If I assume that, does it become real?

There may be a fate worse than that of a serial tautologist, but would he have to assume that for it to be true? Pardon my lingering fog of exhaustion.

There are worse things than being a serial tautologist. At least I assume that's true.

The hunt: when I trap a weak one, etc? First of all, I wasn't writing about trapping people, I was writing about trapping the savor of victory.

But you must mean men? Do I allow them their dignity? Oh, yes, for by the end I have entirely convinced them of the impossibility, the futility, maybe even some degree of the undesirability, of a relationship with me.

Bereft

Molly and I had another counseling session yesterday. "Dr. Helen" is one of those people who is so "intentional" in everything she says. I imagine it's professional and appropriate, but feels artificial.

About 20 minutes from the end, we were talking about a trip Molly and I plan to take to San Francisco. In truth I'm dreading it. Without a sense of romance, just seeing the urban sights isn't very appealing, and I don't think Molly is interested in seeing hangouts from my college days. But I didn't want to hurt her feelings so I said it would be fun.

Dr. Helen asked if that was what I was really feeling. I said sure. Then Molly said, from my left shoulder, "Why can't you be honest?"

I told her I was looking forward to the trip. Dr. Helen asked me if I said that because I really wanted to go, or if I was afraid of hurting Molly's feelings. "A little of both," I said.

"Which is the first emotion you have when you think of telling Molly you would rather not go?" Dr. Helen asked.

I could not answer. Literally, I could not speak. Molly started to cry and left. Dr. Helen just looked at me with a sad smile.

"We can't manage outcomes, Peter," she said. "If you can't be honest, you can't communicate."

"But it's bad to disappoint other people," I said.

"The person you're protecting may be yourself," she replied.

So that was an hour and $150 wasted, Molly is in tears, and I feel like shit.

That sounds awful, though I don't think you wasted your $150. It sounds to me like that was an important communication between you and Molly. Would you like to go for a walk and talk about it?

I think a walk would do me good, but I don't want to pull you away from your day.

I have chores but I was going to meet Barbara at noon. I will cancel on her and meet you at the bridge instead.

* * *

I waited for 20 minutes, then walked up the trail.

My fault, I was late. Hannah called 20 seconds after I left the house. She was having a difficult morning at her play-date; she's been a little fragile ever since the toxic shock episode.

I had to go bring her home from her friend's house, though she may have just been bored. Cindy isn't the brightest crayon in the box, and not one of Hannah's best friends. Hannah recovered remarkably fast, the little manipulator, and wanted me to play make-believe with her cats as soon as we got back. I headed to the trail but you were nowhere to be seen. I waited then decided you had left, so came home.

No worries. I enjoyed the walk, seeing the river so low and full of pollen. The eddies and whorls spiral with foam like miniature galaxies. Obeying the same math, I suppose.

Galaxies obey math? I thought math described, didn't govern. But never-mind, Mr. Philosophy, I don't want a lesson.

I have to go anyway, Jacob is bringing teammates/friends home after baseball for a romp and maybe a sleepover. At least one doesn't eat salmon, and Hannah said she is tired of chicken. It looks like I'm going to be cooking three different menus!

Sounds like a good night for pizza. Or maybe cook what's available and let them eat what they want. Enjoy your evening.

You sound upset. I think I let you down.

Thank you, but you are not responsible. The comment the counselor made, about trying to protect myself, makes me feel selfish when I was thinking I was doing the right thing.

But it's true: Some of what I do "for" other people is to keep them from moving away from our "connection." I am desperately afraid of loss. I need to know that someone is "there."

After taking all the kids home this morning, I drove to Orcas Bay for a run. As I was sloshing along the beach, I thought of the feeling you were desperately trying to avoid, the feeling leading to your need to have someone "there."

You don't want to feel "bereft." Isn't that a perfect word to capture the raw emotion of wanting someone "there?"

And while I know you'd agree that you can't just trade Lover's "there" for my "there" or anyone's "there," I also think that this collection of "theres" are an attempt to mitigate the loss.

All that on only one cup of coffee.

Good morning.

Your word, "bereft," is the perfect word. I do know that I often get a feeling of "bereft" that is irrational, that I try to exercise "control" out of fear that I'm sure to suffer "loss," and often fear disorder in the life of my partner.

But chastising myself for these weaknesses has not made me a stronger man.

Project

I'm off to Seattle, leaving on the 4 p.m. ferry today to make all connections. Meeting first thing in the morning on a new project, dinner tonight with other players on my "team."

Molly and the twins come over tomorrow, we fly out together to San Francisco in the afternoon, tour The City the next day and Cirque de Soleil on Friday.

I was born in San Francisco. It has always been a special city to me. But in recent years, I have disliked going more and more each time. It has become such a caricature of itself: Fisherman's Wharf a deadly, sterile tourist trap; trollies cliché; even Maiden Lane has department store chains, yes, Gucci or something upscale, but Union Square is no more than a mall.

So, domesticity for me, and urban delights for you. Oh, came across this last night in fiction I'm reading (Penelope Fitzgerald): "Contentment is an unattainable ideal... It's strange, to say the least, that the body is content when it loses itself in its own experience and forgets itself, while the mind is only satisfied while it is absolutely conscious of itself and its own workings." Interesting.

That is a wonderful way to look at it. And the dichotomy can be reversed: "The mind is content when it loses itself, the body only satisfied when it is absolutely conscious."

I played with the words of the quote, too, reversing and substituting and trying them on. Since I couldn't even imagine my mind losing itself (though I can all too clearly imagine losing my mind), I remain, as usual, cursing and worshipping cognition.

How did your meeting go in Seattle?

The Waterfront Lofts project (It has a name — it's becoming more real!) is taking shape. The timing is off for me: I'm stretched already, but there may be too much upside to pass this up.

The price of acquisition is a little steep too, but not out of line for this market. Two years ago, we could have purchased this for about 60% of what they're asking today. We're a ways from making a deal. The meeting this morning was supposed to last two hours. We wanted conditions in the contract about zoning suitability, more time for due diligence. Seller said he was making no guarantees. So we ended up in separate rooms trying to work out strategies to handle the liabilities and not scuttle the deal.

Do you remember the brunette you asked about at the dedication for the new library? She is an attorney working with a firm that might take a small piece of the deal. I sat next to her at lunch, she told me she had a boat in Port Cedar and had followed the library development in the *Port Cedar News*. She came to the dedication that night to see the finished project.

Negotiations went into the afternoon. I had already cut it close meeting Molly and the kids at SeaTac, they made the plane, I wasn't even close. I'm staying over for dinner with the other partners and the lawyer to see how we are going to proceed, and will fly out first thing tomorrow.

San Francisco

The once-great Preston Hotel is not as elegant as I remember. But in about an hour I will be on the streets of S.F. with my children, a boat ride to the Golden Gate, Alcatraz… The City is crowded… then on our way to Cirque du Soleil.

Jacob and I went to the weight room this morning while Hannah had a piano lesson; I can't tell you how I enjoyed it, and on how many levels. First, he's my son, so sharing anything is nice. But beyond that, he's funny, good conversation and an awesome athlete in his own right! I'm so lucky, and I let him know.

We were in San Francisco this time last year, and spent a day doing what you did today. Despite our embarrassment at being the quintessential tourists, we took the Alcatraz tour, which we all loved. The cells were so cold and barren and sinister, and solitary confinement inhumanely so. It was much more dramatic than the Hollywood movie versions: bullet holes in the cafeteria wall, sharks in the surrounding water. The constant echo in the cell blocks alone would drive a man crazy.

It was a sunny, chilly day, and really bitter on the water, but I love being on open water (for dry, limited durations only; do not count on me to visit you ship-side any month other than August) and seeing the city skyline from that vantage.

Then we hit the aquarium; Hannah reminded me just the other day that we "pet" sharks in one of the little artificial pools. Hannah immersed her hand at once, stroking the shark's rough skin. Jacob, my cautious boy, whipped his hand in the pool for a mere millisecond, and only did so after five minutes of cajoling. Robert waited outside and read the newspaper.

It's wonderful having Robert gone. Things go smoothly, we have more fun, it just feels lighter, more upbeat.

I'm about to wake Sam and Abby, get everyone moving in the same slow direction. Odd, how I have to get the ball rolling four hours before we have to be at the airport. Not friction, not stiction, there has to be a word that describes the molasses-like movement, like waiting for honey to pour from the jar, the shampoo to get to the neck of a nearly empty bottle: afflusion? slorified? slorific? I need some help, here.

Viscous. Have a safe trip.

The day started with a viscous frustration, trying to get everyone up and on a plane, the waiting, security warning me it would be ten extra minutes if I did not take off my shoes, Molly forgetting she had scissors in her handbag and having to go out and mail them to herself because the checked luggage was gone and because they were the ones she used to cut her father's hair when he was alive, me running back to get a bag I left by the airport bathroom which was being guarded by airport security…

…every step forward seemed to be walking through honey, viscous and sticky, my shoes wanted to stick to the floor, they pulled away with a crackle...

But we made it out of the awful San Francisco Airport (I do like taking BART from the hotel to the airport, it feels so European), the flight was smooth, and we got both cars at SeaTac and then drove and then got the ferry and were home about nine hours after we left the hotel this morning.

Welcome home.

I'm restless again. Now I know it's exacerbated by the change in weather. Trouble is, the weather keeps changing. Just as I think we will have a spate of beautiful days, the rain descends again.

I ripped out the stinky, cat-peed carpet in the weight room and will lay flooring on Monday. But immediately after ripping out the carpet, pad etc., I knew I just had to paint the playroom, so I stripped the walls and spackled. And then I ran a fence in the horse corral. And so on.

Do you think I have temporary ADD? It's manifesting itself through my reading, too: I'm almost frenetically switching from a book, a magazine and an audio CD. A chapter here, an article there. I can't seem to "sit still," either physically or mentally.

Classic nesting instinct. The weather has me tilted as well, though I have the opposite reaction. I go to bed early and wake tired. I just took a nap and do not feel rested. Lethargic. Head full of sand. Sensitive to light and noise.

Can't read, can't write. A lack of sex has me petulant and feeling sorry for myself.

Biology is driving us toward the cave, but first to gather sticks for the fire and berries for baskets in anticipation of a storm.

Classic signs of depression. Maybe it'll blow over soon. But if it doesn't... you stop that! You know what I'm about to say and you're shaking your head, and have a look of steely determination and defiance and "why does she even bother to broach it?"

AS I was saying before you interrupted with your body language: you might consider TEMPORARY use of anti-depressants. Some are successful for "situational" depression.

Tile or laminate (faux wood) flooring for the weight room? I can't imagine Robert will lift weights again, and if I do (rarely, as that is the one thing for which I use the club) I can have an area rug over the tile in the weight area. The room will have a TV (if you've ever used a stationary bike, you'll understand the degree of desperate boredom that would drive me to a TV).

I can't believe this: I'm asking you Martha Stewart questions, in which I'm sure you don't have an iota of interest. I'm deliberately not deleting this section, just so you can see how my thoughts are strewn across the outer edges of my life today.

I'm going to the gym to lift weights and see if I can get some blood flowing. "Depression" is probably just the unrelenting rain.

Hey, Girlfriend, next time invite me. We could coffee afterward. We could even hot tub... no one is ever there on Sunday.

You're on for the hot tub, as long as I shall not be held responsible for any biologically autonomous reactions to seeing you in a swim suit. Girlfriend.

Very well. But I will hold you fully responsible for any biologically autonomous reactions you DON'T have.

No, that's self control.

Using You

I'm in the middle of a project. Too lazy and cranky to haul a boom box into the bathroom I was painting. I spent much of the time contemplating "trapped," particularly b/c I was, quite literally, trapped amidst narrow walls and drop cloths and drips of paint that take on a life of their own, exploring every surface.

I always end up feeling trapped in a relationship b/c I lose respect. I lose respect not b/c the man is not deserving, as you would say. I lose respect b/c that is what I am compelled to do. As surely as a schizophrenic hears voices, I invariably chase the respect from the relationship.

You seem to think that if I could have a leap of faith, I could allow the one in a thousand to enter my garden. But the inability to make the leap of faith is indelibly etched onto my psyche; it is who I am. If I didn't have this defining characteristic, I think one man in a hundred would probably work for me.

You say here, twice, "that is who I am..."

Is admitting who you are the same as accepting who you are?

Is it who you want to be?

Not being who I want to be causes anxiety, because I don't know how, or if it is even possible to change. Maybe that's why I should take Prozac. So what if it's a short-cut to the person I want to be; if it enables me to get there when nothing else will (and I have no idea whether it would or wouldn't), then what's wrong with Happy Pills? Don't bother answering "they're inauthentic."

Prozac:

(1) There are no short-cuts;

(2) The Prozac path is not a path to the person you want to be;

(3) Nor to the life you want to have, but to a drugged acceptance of the life you've got. Your kids deserve more.

Point of order: Did you address the questions I asked, or brush them off?

Are you ready for your half-marathon this weekend?

A polite fishing expedition when you asked about the marathon this weekend? I realize that, perhaps, you're the real hunter, projected onto me.

And I'm only demonstrating how impossible a task that would be. Off to Home Depot—one final gallon.

Of course I'm a hunter. And if prey, you are elusive; if hunter, your camouflage is nearly perfect.

We are so similar and so very different, life together would have been relentless: fun and pissed off and passionate and sensual and selfish and hurt… had we hours and days we will never have… and I capitulate to the knowledge this is a very good thing.

Cosmic joke… you and I need someone who is not like we are… What we want is not what we need and what we are looking for is of course not outside, not in Lover or Half-Affair or Prozac.

In an alternative world it would have been wonderful to do a battle of lives with you, and exhausting and draining and daunting, but then, not all life is a game to be won.

Ummmm… am I being dismissed?

No, you are being appreciated. I was keying off your "impossible task." I wanted to put you at ease about what you called my "appetites."

Did I say "appetites?" I meant a raw, satiable hunger.

Did you say satiable? Probably not. I hunger for laughter and pain; for the heavy galooping of paint pushing back against a stir stick as each color seeks to stay its own; for silence that embraces voices singing in joy or howling despair; for the space between notes, the quiet between words. I want to hear that.

I did say "satiable," and I beg to differ: it is. It relates to your argument that "love" as you know it doesn't have to be permanent for it to be breathtakingly real. In a similar way, you meet a lovely woman and she becomes your muse. You are, however briefly, satiated. But then you're hungry again. The hunter? Artist searching for muse? A man/woman seeking passion to fill a void?

Another disagreement, by the way. I think you and I, or hypothetical people with the passion/mental energy levels we have, would have no problem with the comfortable silences.

I don't know how I could have forgotten this minor detail, but I'm going to see Mr. Half Affair when I'm in Seattle next week .

You should see ME in Seattle next week. But I don't know if I could handle being Mr. One Fourth.

I can't imagine a man like you as a mere fraction. But meeting you in Seattle would be imbued with far too much meaning... that is, meeting the Seattle You in Seattle. You know: You lock Frivolous and Goofy and Curmudgeon in your walk-in closet in your Port Cedar hide-out, and you pack Debonair and Amorous in a hermetically sealed container in the back of the race car you tow to town, releasing them somewhere on I5 South.

You left out Sensual and Passionate. They ride shotgun.

Hell, they do the driving.

Well, someday if you can slow down enough so we could enjoy the silences between the notes, I will buy you dinner and a glass of Merlot. I like to go fast but don't like to rush. We are racing 9th - 11th, if the car lasts the 4th of July.

I'll be in Seattle 5-8; Hannah has a theater class. I guess our ships will pass in the night... unless...

The near-miss is divine intervention. The ice is too thin. Deep discussion with Molly tonight. I'm not feeling so good about myself.

Oh, Peter, I'm sorry, I was only teasing. I don't know what to tell you. Part of me believes that you can't help what you feel, and that your taking a lover was a matter of survival.

And another part recognizes that this came with a price, and deception is a horrible thing.

Finally, though, you're talking to the wrong person, or maybe the right person: I believe it is something you had to do, and it outweighed the evils, and I would do the same. There are no moral absolutes; it's all a balance.

You don't seem like a very huggable person, but here's a great hug anyway. Don't chastise yourself.

I am in fact a very huggable person. That is how Lover and I started, it was an amazing thing…

…we were acquaintances, she shared with me like you share with me, about her kids and the trouble with her bogus marriage. She had gone to Hawaii with her husband. When she got back, I ran into her in a local store. I asked her how the trip was, I think, whether it was all romance and palm trees.

I told her I was going in a few days. She got this shattered expression on her face and was about to cry. I just instinctively opened my arms and she moved into them. I kissed the top of her head, and our arms just wrapped around each other six or seven times, finding all the right hollows. All of a sudden, everything just stopped. Everything. Just. Stopped.

Then I realized I was holding this woman, not my wife, in the middle of a crowded store just before Christmas and had to let go, which was incredibly difficult.

The next day or the day after that I went into where she worked because I had not been able to think of anything else but how she felt in my arms. I had not been held like that in years, maybe ever like that, and she started to walk toward me. I held up my hand and said, "No, that is really not a good idea."

She got that mischievous look I now know so well and said, "Why? It's just a hug."

We called that the biggest lie.

I went to Hawaii for three weeks with my family and thought of little else but that hug. When we got back, she was gone to Florida for two weeks. She got back around February 7. We made love five days later, then she went to San Diego with her husband on business, but could not stand being with him, and flew back home alone on February 14 to find a Valentine tied to the door of her car in the parking lot at the Port Cedar ferry terminal.

it was just a hug oh god i am so sad.

That was the most touching, romantic story. I reread it once, then stared at the screen, then looked out at the aspen leaves shimmering in the evening sun, a bit battered by the breeze. I tried to think of a clever way of telling you how sorry I am for your loss, and find myself at a loss. But the sentiment is genuine, if the delivery trite. I have been there. The final loss of Love of Life... see, all my men aren't fractions... left me grief-stricken and desolate; I know.

Peter, don't roll those blocks of numbers on a balance sheet. You are feeling a tremendous loss. Now is not the time to make any other significant moves. Put it away. Put Molly away. Just go smoothly right now. Take the kids for a walk on the banks of the river. Go to the gym. Put away your laptop; engage in physical work if you need to work.

I'm trying to top off my physical endurance and strength for the race this weekend. I'm trying not to dwell, trying not to hide, but that brings up that I owe YOU an apology.

You are everything I said: lovely and alluring and engrossing and very thin ice. Please forgive me for trying to use you as an emotional exit strategy. Not intentional, still inexcusable. I'm ashamed, but I know you understand.

I would have done the exact same thing.

Insomnia

We had a birthday party last night for my Abby's friend Sydney, because we missed her party last weekend when we were in Seattle for the Lion King. Molly stayed to care for her mother.

Sydney and Abby have been best friends since before they could walk. Another girl, Elizabeth, came over too.

I brought home pizza. They made brownies that we served with a candle. We watched Star Wars, the three girls in a row on the couch and I in my easy chair, Sam on the floor making snide comments about Wookies. They asked me to make popcorn.

I will cook breakfast as soon as they start to stretch and make sleepy noises leading to giggles, then to laughter. Abby has already been out to scoop up the kitten to take her into the bedroom, and then shut the door.

I will make a batch of home-made pancakes, because I think Abby has used up all the Bisquik making that dough she eats raw. You can imagine the reaction of her carb-phobic father the hypocrite, who plans to poison them with flour and sugar and syrup and then send them home.

Debra, thank you for being there and reading all this and participating in my life in this way. By sharing with you I become more real; by having a friend who knows, the record has more meaning. Thank you, Girlfriend.

I'm printing this and putting it someplace special. I can't imagine where, maybe I will just fold the plain, 8.5 X 11 paper into a little square and tuck it away on my desk somewhere. Thank YOU, girlfriend.

Since you have written about your "mundane," I see so much more humanity in you; whereas before you were very much a silhouette. Life is as much about the pancakes and the pajamas and bad breath as it is the curve of a woman's breast and her lingering sighs.

Abby carries the kitten in her arms into the family room this morning and our boxer, Rogan, starts to twist himself into knots and whine. Rogan wants to be spoken to in the little girl voice. Rogan wants those rubs. Rogan wants that attention.

When the kitten steps across the ottoman to my feet and lies down, Rogan seizes his chance and runs over to Abby and gets his strokes.

The kitten throws a languid glance at the dog and the girl and, with utter indifference, starts to bathe.

Cats don't seem to get jealous. They can have hard lives scrabbling for beetles under the deck, or lay about as a New York diva, demanding food or attention when they want to be rubbed or to be the center of whatever you are doing, often lying aljosif ;ljf oa ;siudfjoj on the computer keyboard. But jealousy does not seem to be their natural affliction.

Dogs are more needy in an unsettlingly human way. Either we have poisoned them within our partnership over these thousands of years, or jealousy is some facet of pack behavior, whether that pack be of dogs, wolves or man and dog scuffling down the driveway to get the Sunday paper.

Cats hunt alone. They seem comfortable there, as long as they have the power to get what they want when they want it.

But cats don't have power, unless it is the power of not wanting. "Power" is a political term, isn't it? Power must be felt, by the holder or the person over whom it is being held, in order for it to exist. And cats aren't distracted by the trappings of power any more than by bittersweet jealousy (bittersweet b/c it burns and sears as viscerally and tragically as grief, but when struck, we know we are alive).

Cats are something we are very much not. They're solely instinct-driven, while creatures like us think and rethink, plan and manipulate, glory and regret. Cats hunt for their needs of the moment and feel what they feel at the moment. Do cats really glory in their victory when they bring the dead bird to the doorstep, or is that merely our anthropomorphization?

If you left Port Cedar, where would you live? If you are a hunter, perhaps you need to be where there is more prey?

I have told you how I need quiet, and time alone. I think that need extends to my physical environment. I chose a calm piece of the earth, the sky looming large and the mountains a far perimeter around the monochromatic sea. A retreat for my senses.

More detail later (crazy day), but you don't even vaguely understand how insomnia has wreaked havoc in my life. I don't consider insomnia a mere inability to get my 8 hrs. I used to go entire nights without a moment's sleep, and have to function the next day. I was completely unable to turn off my mind, no matter how many miles I biked or ran.

It was utterly debilitating. I tried every sleep remedy and relaxation technique known to man: from warm milk to acupressure. When a therapist handed me her revered handout on sleep techniques, I guffawed. That stuff is candy-ass. I'm seriously sick.

Trazadone is entirely different from, for example, SRIs. It's effect is short-acting (about 4 hours) and then it vanishes from my system. Its entire purpose is directed toward one thing: knocking me out. It doesn't "mask" my feelings or emotions the way an SRI does (of course I've dabbled). I'm a happy addict.

In Seattle, or another city, I'd be surrounded by stimulation. I don't think I'd have the grounding I do here, the wherewithal to resist the frenzy of ambition around me, and to stay my own course. And it's tricky enough sifting through expectations and greed and tons of neuroses in an effort to know what my own course is.

I'm probably too much of a coward, too bound by my insecurities, to make a serious effort toward learning new tricks. On the other hand, perhaps I have an obligation to myself to do precisely that.

Have you been an insomniac your entire life? If not, when did it begin? Were you able to spend entire nights with your lovers?

I have a terrible memory, but think insomnia began in law school and got progressively worse. When I was a domestic relations (ha! what a misnomer) lawyer in Seattle, I remember driving to my dad's several times at 4 in the morning, weeping and nearly hysterical. (It was the only time I can remember seeking comfort from my father, and he administered it so tenderly that I remember it well.)

I graduated from law school when I was 23, and that's when I started dating Robert, so (hard as it may be to believe) I haven't exactly had enough lovers since that time to constitute a random sample... Still, your point is a good one. If I were cocooned in the sweet safety of a lover's arms, would it make a difference? I kind of doubt it.

I disagree. Your insomnia began roughly at the time you met the man you married? Am I missing something, here?

You did not answer the first question: Have you ever spent an entire night in the arms of your lover?

My thesis is this: were you free and able to let go and in the safety of arms you trusted and adored, after tender lovemaking and talk of hours duration, you would be able to sleep.

Ah, Dr. Peter, for whom romantic bliss and hot sex are a panacea for all... I promise you I'm not evading. I just don't know the answer to your question. I probably did spend the night spooned next to Love of Life dude. But that was before the insomnia hit badly.

Correlation between husband and insomnia? I'm willing to entertain that idea. I admit I have never connected the two.

Which means your 1.5 affairs did not involve long romantic evenings, dinner and wine and hours of wonderful burrowing under slick hotel sheets in the anonymity of a beloved big city?

Though spooning is bliss, I'm talking about truly tangled, where you can't tell where his skin begins and yours ends, with your head on his chest and your arms bringing the back of his head as close to yours as you can, that you can inhale the scent from his hair, feel his arms around your waist and his hand pressing you to him by the small of your back, held, truly held, and letting go, drifting among the sounds he makes as he breathes, sleep encroaching as tomorrow and yesterday recede from view.

How much detail do you want here?

The "full" affair was with a wealthy man who lives in Seattle. There were many dinners, far too much wine (for him, he never got drunk but drank an alarming quantity), and a bit of very bad lovemaking in his cavernous, skylit bedroom. We had good conversations, though.

The "half" also lives in Seattle. So no hotel sheets. And no lovemaking; that's why he's a "half." And especially no anonymity.

So although "truly tangled" is something familiar to me, it is a distant echo from the past.

Debra, neither qualifies. Letting oneself go, letting the defenses drop, having the faith and the confidence, but above all the trust, to let go, to have not good conversations but wonderful conversations about things that matter, not wine-fueled but love-fueled, not bad lovemaking but great, 4 p.m. on a bright sunny day with the curtains open lovemaking, falling asleep in each other's arms and waking hungry for a 9 p.m. dinner and a chance to love each other again in darkness, yes, cocooned in the sweet safety of a lover's arms.

My god, she has left and I'm dying inside.

Oh, Peter, I am so sorry. These are not empty words, I am viscerally pained for you. I well remember the agony I felt after breaking up with Love of My Life. Even while knowing it was the right thing to do, I wanted him back with all my heart and soul.

I will say one thing, though: if I had a love such as yours with your lover, I would not give it up for a failed marriage and some degree of potential harm to your children.

My children need me at home, today. My lover told me that leaving them would destroy me and if anything happened to them while I was not there, it would without doubt destroy our love, which is why she had to go, because she would not let that happen, our love deserved better…

I have an obligation to the very good woman I married 20 years ago to see if I can be open enough, to see if she can access the man I have hidden from her for so many years. I feel so small, so guilty; it is the right thing to do, though I don't know if I'm strong enough to do it.

I don't mean to argue, but you've adopted a Jewish Friend. That's along the same lines as a Jewish Mother. I won't mail you newspaper clippings, but I will send lots of unsolicited advice your way. So don't be offended, and feel free to send an ethnic "Enough, already!" my way. (No, I didn't grow up speaking Yiddishisms, but when I went to a school full of Jews for college, it just felt right to take on a few of these....)

What I don't understand is why you speak of "leaving" the twins. You could live right next door to your wife. You could have joint custody. You could be almost... yes, I concede almost... as much a part of their daily lives as you are now. More, in some respects. Your time together would be quality time, and not just schlepping them from place to place.

On the other hand, I admire your efforts with your wife. Maybe counseling will enable her to let go and be a freer, more confident person that you can admire. Maybe counseling will enable you to see a more vibrant, sexy woman there. The shared history means so much.

I must make the effort regardless of the loss. That is my commitment to what I think is best for my children and to my wife. She is going to counseling, I am going, we are going.

This mess was our doing, my Lover and I, and it is only right that we bear the brunt of the pain. We were the ones who went into this with our eyes wide open. Putting the pain of abandonment on the innocent is not something I'm prepared to do at this moment.

It remains to be seen if I have the strength to be a good man.

Gilded Cage

Hannah staunchly refused to do anything Robert or I told her today. Complete, outright defiance. Yes, yes, I did the same, but in later years. Classic adolescent behavior.

She spent the entire day in her room, in her pajamas. I'm really at a loss. What do I do after I have talked to her ad nauseum, taken away every privilege for the next 5 years, and left her to stew all day? What if she persists tomorrow?

OK, confession: I feel particularly guilty b/c I let Robert have it this morning. He was being particularly worthless, and I'm particularly resentful that he has devoted his entire life to baseball and professional articles on aircraft that no one reads and he doesn't get paid for. So we exchanged yells.

So now it occurs to me that when Hannah hears me treating Robert with no respect, she imitates the behavior. Does the hypocrite now march upstairs and tell her to "do as I say, not as I do?" Oh, Peter, I feel awful.

If you get back Saturday, the boys will be out of town and you could always stop by here for coffee. Starting next Tuesday, I'm on jury duty, so between that and running enough to have a marathon base, I may be pretty busy. It depends on how jury duty goes.

Hope Hannah has let up on you, and you on yourself. To oversimplify, you now have three to deal with: Hannah, Robert, and you. I think you begin by accepting today. It happened.

Here is my suggestion: go right now into her room and get her. Then the two of you walk into Robert's office. Tell her to stand there or sit there and give her no option. Then look at Robert and say, "I apologize for yelling at you this morning. I was angry and hurt, but that was no excuse for losing my temper or saying all the things I said in the way that I said them."

Give him a 5 or a 10 count to respond in kind if he is likely to, but do not let him use it as an opening to hammer you. Take Hannah back to her room and say, "Hannah, I know you heard Daddy and I fighting this morning, and it made you angry or sad. I apologize to you, too. I should not have done that."

If she does not respond, just walk out and close the door gently.

Part two: "When Hannah hears me treating Robert with no respect..."

Debra, we act this way because we are angry, and we are angry because we are afraid. We are afraid because we feel trapped, but know the trap is of our own making. Then our own behavior makes us feel small and petty. Trapped again.

You are beautiful and smart and have lots of options. One of them is being married to a man because he allows you to be here in Port Cedar while he works in Seattle four days a week while you train for marathons and climb mountains and have horses and raise your children and live a life with room to do things you want to do, straightward and wayward.

Fine. But what's going to come of your frustration and anger that he is who he is and not someone else? You are not going to change him, and I don't think at heart you really want him to take a deep interest in you and the children. You would have no room, then. We get angry when we think that our partner is keeping us FROM happiness, we are mean because we sold our dreams for horses and race cars and a gilded cage we built for ourselves and then lost the key.

Thank you for your pitch-perfect advice about Hannah. I fudged it a bit, did not confront Robert, but went into her room and had that talk. It broke the ice.

Yes, of course you're right about the gilded cage, but everything is a balance. Which choice best satiates our greed? Gilded cage or a long shot for love? The gilded cage always wins for me, b/c I don't believe that the love that you describe would last (for me, at least) longer than a few months. I can't help but believe that familiarity breeds... if not contempt, then at least a passionless boredom.

As to the cage, there is no balance. You bark at Robert, your children suffer. I pretend to be in the moment but am yearning for love, and my children suffer. I want more than a woman I just respect, you don't respect the man you married. One of us is in a state of denial. Available for coffee tomorrow?

I don't think I'm in a state of denial... at least not this evening. I'm beginning to realize how ephemeral my desires are, and how much they're a product of my needs of the moment. Some days I'm desperately starving for love, you know the kind, and Robert can't provide it. Some days I'm arrogant enough to believe I don't need it, and on those days I think I might as well be with Robert. And most days, I want it just enough to be resentful of his keeping me FROM it.

You know, I'd better not meet tomorrow. In the morning I promised Hannah I'd help her make something for Robert for Father's Day, and I'm not sure what time the boys will be home. I also think Hannah might be suspicious. (Did I tell you she met Mr. Half Affair a couple of times?)

If I don't get called for jury duty I'll have the entire week free, since I cleared my calendar in order to perform my civic duty. I have to call in the night before, at 5pm, to see if they need me the following day.

So you are telling me your relationship with Robert is as good as it can ever be for you with anyone? I don't believe that. No hiding now, behind a clever admission of inconsistency.

Enduringly, no, I do not think I could do greatly better with anyone else. This is because my needs, neuroses and insecurities will stand between me and greater happiness. This time I'm talking only about myself, Peter, and not you. I have no reason to think you won't find the love you seek.

There is the wondering that perhaps "this time, well, maybe this time, no it is *this* time" I can prolong the rush of falling in love past the latest sleek woman with a brain and cheekbones. That I'm so shallow reminds me that trying to change, and repeatedly failing, has its own negative consequences.

I put this in context of an article in a science magazine about finding the place where we "fall in love" in the brain, how it is a locus that "lights up" early in a relationship… that is separate from the processes that govern sex or other behaviors. A great premise for a smutty novel about love, lust and addiction and the difficulty in determining the difference.

To you, the idea that there is no "permanent love" is only mildly disconcerting. To me, the realization was devastating. Funny, how far apart we can be.

I do believe your powerful craving for Love is, in large part, a toxic mixture of craving those mysterious "lust chemicals" in the brain and craving an idealized woman. I realize how pessimistic a view this is. But it might be a starting point, as an exercise if nothing else, in examining the real issue: what will fulfill us?

No, I cannot picture a life with Robert. I very consciously (as I have mentioned to him on a number of occasions, hoping that by giving him warnings, my fearsome guilt will somehow be mollified) do not plan a "retirement" with Robert. But, unlike you, I picture a life alone, in a lovely-but-cat-fur-filled house on a hilltop, with just enough guest rooms to accommodate the rare but precious visits from my children and their children and dear old friends.

I'm off to Everett to buy off my Father's Day obligations with a radar detector. Then to Home Depot to buy a new cordless drill to repair the barn door. The work here is endless.

You have a deep need for passion. Robert does not offer it and you plan to leave him and live alone on a hilltop. Which brings up the question: have you picked a date to leave and have you shared it with Robert? If you have an honest, open discussion away from the children, you no longer feel trapped. You could, actually, perhaps even become friends, at least united on the common goal of child welfare.

There is no talking to Robert about this issue. He immediately gets panicked and tells me how difficult he's going to make it for me, which he knows scares me to death. Remember, I'm the one who can't stand conflict. But it isn't telling Robert that is liberating, it's knowing it myself. Have you told Molly you don't want your marriage?

No, I have not, and in many ways am less "authentic" than you, as we used to say, "honest" is more apt. If I am a serial monogamist, if falling in love is more important than comfort, romance as important as sex, then I have to accept that. It is not pretty, but self-reproach for cowardice, or hiding from it, does not make me different.

I'm afraid that Molly and I have grown into two too-different people. Maybe we were always two very different people, and getting married was a "why not" instead of "why."

My drug and alcohol addictions were factors, then the tight focus on financial and professional success, to say nothing of all the baggage from childhood. I just came to believe that I did not deserve love, that I was too ugly to love, or that love itself was an illusion, a temporary state of insanity, and I should just grow up and pretend to be somebody, play golf and hold her bags at the shopping mall.

I don't want to change Molly anymore. Nor, and this is the hard one… nor do I want to make the effort to see if she is different than the taken-for-granted-preconception that she has become for me.

That is incredibly unfair. When we are on vacation and are thrown together, my own anger at being "stuck" makes it impossible for her to "succeed." But she wants to live her life as she wants to live it, and has some pretty strong ideas about what makes her happy.

I know this is wrong and oppressive. We see it in couples back-biting each other at the rental car counter, or him belittling her at the restaurant, or her nagging him in line at Safeway.

It is loss of love and loss of respect, but I don't know which is cause and which is effect.

Interesting, that in this particular way our circumstances are so similar; those might have been my own words.

I got married for a "why not?," too. And I can't bring myself to make the effort to try to discover more in Robert because... because I just think that whatever I did uncover would still be too meager. I want a partner, a companion, someone "there" with me on many levels, not just occupying the same space. Or else I'll just continue to do what I've been doing: fill the voids here and there, and lead a rich and full life... alone.

Respect, equality... I'm beginning to think they're the same. And while I can respect Robert on some levels, it's a left-brained respect, not one I feel viscerally, instinctively. And although by many definitions he's far "superior" to me, he isn't my equal in the ways that are important to me.

Oh, yeah. Good morning.

Respect and equality are not the same. "I respect him" is different than saying "we are equals." It is not hard to define "equal," but nearly impossible to explain respect.

Bitch

Will a wet track await? As I recall, that is your least favorite condition. Enjoy the races, lay yourself bare.

"After all, the field of battle possesses many advantages over the drawing-room. There at least is no room for pretension or excessive ceremony, no shaking of hands or rubbing of noses, which make one doubt your sincerity, but hearty as well as hard hand-play. It at least exhibits one of the faces of humanity, the former only a mask"—Henry David Thoreau.

p.s. Plans changed again. I'm in Seattle through Sat/Sun. duathalon, seeing friends. Do you have my cell number?

It rained. We kept the cars under cover. It would have been nice to go out at least once, especially since a critical turn has been reconfigured. But the real bummer is the forecast for tomorrow is not a whole lot better. Sunday is supposed to clear, we shall see.

You are in Seattle? What a dilemma. Saying you would be here this weekend made my pulse race, though it was likely no more than an invitation for coffee downtown. Debra, I'm sure I have taken your offer of phone number far beyond what was intended— forgive me, please. But I can't. You are too desirable.

I appreciate your candor. I gave you my phone number b/c that is how I can be contacted for the next few days, or so I thought (I don't race my bike in the rain either; I'm not doing the duathalon this morning and Hannah and I are heading home today.) Like an old, married couple I miss our exchanges; I guess I wanted to feel "connected."

And I've told you, no matter how appealing the man, why should I have another affair? While the immediate sexual and emotional gratification is wonderful, it leaves me, on balance, with less than I had when I began (Side note: as I re-read some of the recent exchanges with Mr. 1/2, maybe he is ready to take second best... the affair. But I'm not going there with him, either, for the reasons I have stated.)

So, Peter, what could be safer than a "fully self-contained" woman who doesn't believe in love?

The forecast for this afternoon is good! I'm sorry I can't see your race. I'll be wishing you all kinds of luck. –Debra

If the weather is supposed to be nice, don't go home. Bring your family or friends. I will get you a pit pass. Re: Mr. Half Affair, I can not understand why you would not accept his entreaties. Bring him to the race.

Well, for one thing: he didn't offer any entreaties! And I've told you that, while I don't doubt his respect and affection for me, he is the most self-centered person on earth, as I imagine one needs to be to accomplish what he has in life. Details as you wish.

No details, but thank you. The greatest sleight of hand is to get self-centered satisfaction from giving all to a cause. At least that's what my heros have done. Or would you call that emotional masochism? Talk to you when I have a decent race report.

No hero withstands scrutiny. No passionate love withstands the test of time.

That is a choice. A cynical one, too.

It's not cynical; it's realistic. You stand with your fingers in your ears: "No! Go away, Debra, leave me to my heroes and my loves, my ideals and my fantasies, my dreams and illusions!"

Fine. Fine. I'll leave you to worship Bobby and John Kennedy, nary a whisper of Bay of Pigs and patronage and graft. Khalil Gibran was a prophet, how dare I suggest he was merely a sincerely spiritual guy at the right place at the right time and painted wispy watercolors to echo his catchy prose? And Debra...alluring, intelligent Debra... well, since she's caught Peter Hamilton's eye, she must be a goddess, too, better blind yourself to her ignorance and fear and neuroses and bunions and all that you can't see if you refuse to look.

Well, that's the difference between us: I find enough beauty and passion in life without having to turn a blind eye. And if your idea of "falling in love"... that love you insist that I need for fulfillment... amounts to blinding myself to reality (and don't quibble with me about the definition of reality) then I don't want it.

Whoa! Listen to you! Then you shall not have it. You've described your own despair, not my blindness nor the accuracy of your vision. And that is another difference between us. Passion is not an ideal, Debra, nor self-delusion. It may not be permanent, but it is real. I choose not to hear details of Mr. Half Affair because it is not any of my business.

It's rather patronizing of you, don't you think, to tell me I'm afflicted with despair when I have only noted your idealistic nature as juxtaposed to my own?

Having a bad night. You caught me with my manners down. Apologies.

No, I'm being a bitch, and having a bad night as well. Went out with friends and listened to music. Stirred my untapped passions. I need to get laid.

Only clouds are in tomorrow's forecast, so pull a rabbit out of the hat (as I have every confidence that you can do) and do well in the qualifying round without running in the rain. Poor RacerBoy, you belong on a southern track.

Did you spend the evening alone or find someone to "talk to dinner?"

The Waterfront Lofts partners took me out to dinner. I had declined to participate after our last discussions because of the risk, and it's a bit of a stretch for a developer my size. But they really like what I have done with other restoration projects and they pitched it again pretty hard.

It's an old four-story warehouse on the waterfront with a great view of the Sound. Brick and stone with arched windows; it is really lovely, with restaurants a short walk away. The layout and location are perfect. It would make a tremendous facility for software developers, small-scale chip designers, etc.

But the trouble with buildings of that age in that location is trying to reinforce them to meet current earthquake standards. Some of those old buildings are little more than piles of brick held together with sand. When the soil down there quivers, it turns to soup, like pushing your feet down again and again at the beach. It's best to tear them down and start over, but then, what have you bought and what did you pay for it?

But the other partners showed me engineering that the soils are good and the reinforcing affordable. We'll see, I'm back to considering it.

One of the lawyers on "our side" was the brunette you noticed at the library dedication in Port Cedar. She was at dinner and told hilarious stories about riding her BMW motorcycle by herself from Seattle across Canada to New England, down the East Coast, back across the South to California and up to Seattle.

Ryder

Hardly slept last night. Did you see the moon? The crescent hung red and low on the horizon; When I finally relinquished myself to a fitful slumber, I was awakened by the most aggressive coyotes right in the yard, taunting the dogs, probably chewing on (and closely guarding) a deer. I let my dogs out to chase them away, then had to chase after my dogs as I became worried that the coyote(s?), not backing off one bit, would eat them.

Soon I'll be planning my days around star charts and whether the moon is in retrograde. I can't shake this eerie and uncharacteristic "feeling," but it is probably just something to do with the still air. Plus I'm salty, tired. Just returned from a ride with Joanie.

And why so quiet today? Busy? Still tired, the post-competition fatigue kicking in? Pensive? Just curious. Terminally.

Not neglecting you, but busy and pensive and unsettled as well.

A meeting with finance people I haven't met before, then hopefully the last negotiation on Waterfront Lofts. We may actually sign papers.

The moon plays havoc. It hangs there, while I sleeplessly stare at it, trapped in branches of the tall cedar standing in the middle of the garden, nearly choked with ivy anxieties that writhe gently despite there being no breeze. Something is coming.

Don't say something is coming! For all her bravery on hunting expeditions, this coward is wedded to status quo and the scent of change is disquieting.

Errands all morning: drop the kids off, pick the kids up, go to Sandy's Furnishings where there's no one who is able to take my money for new carpet. But my only-very-occasionally cleaning lady came, and the kids and I took off to hike Santos Mt.

OK, what is up with you? If you tell me you've just been swamped with work, I'll accept it at face value, in the absence of tell-tale trail of body language to the contrary. That's the trouble with e-relationships: How am I to gauge your mood without the indicia of demeanor?

What the fuck is wrong with me? Why can't I just be content at home with a nice wife and wonderful kids and a successful business? Why in the world am I so discontent? Why am I hurting the people I love and who love me? This is insane. I feel like grabbing my passport and disappearing. I am twisted.

If you're once again feeling the ache of loss, I demand that you seek me out for comfort (though I remind you: I am a Jewish mother).

I left something out about my last race. I wasn't trying to hide, as much as figure it out, before I shared.

The woman of the motorcycle? The lawyer on the Waterfront Lofts project? The woman you noted from the library ribbon-cutting? She showed up at the track. She has a friend, a Seattle developer into racing, but different cars in a different class, who I haven't met. She said she came down to see him run and to get away from the city for the weekend, it was the birthday of her brother who had been killed in Afghanistan.

We talked about that and family and of loss and of meaning.

On Sunday we smiled. I raced and won. She gave me a hug and I hugged her back. She gave me her email address. I wrote a quick note. She wrote back. I warned her to "keep a safe distance." She said she would take her chances. I feel deformed.

Oh, my God, Peter, you just can't keep the women away!!! I'm in a rush, and will give your missive the response it deserves later, but for the time being: you must stop berating yourself. True, some men would not reach beyond their dissatisfaction as you have, but who is to say who is the better man? There are many considerations. And you, too, deserve a life. What is her name?

After saying I could not meet you even for coffee in Seattle, though for months there was nothing I had wanted more, all of a sudden this woman appears beside me at a race track and puts her arm around my waist and offers something I've missed deeply. It has to be a trick!

We'll call her Ryder. For all the reasons already stated, I'd rather not give her a name.

Debra, something is moving quietly behind the props and false façades of this world of offices and wives and cars and mountains. Shifting shapes ignore distance, weeks flow in each direction. I'm a caterpillar in a jar tilted one way then the other, up becomes down then changes back again. I'm sad and afraid.

Now I'm rushing off in the other direction, but one thought: perhaps your "problem" is that you keep looking at these women in your life as women, rather than people. Are you able to appreciate all they have to offer without imagining physical passion with them?

I'm suggesting training yourself to create... I dunno... a Chinese wall between yourself and the women. I'm not suggesting all-out repression, but rather a shift in emphasis from the sexual to the platonic. It's easy for me. I have several male friends that, altho I easily could be attracted to, it doesn't even occur to me to pursue (or be pursued) in that way.

Are you creating your own turmoil?

I love you (like a Jewish sister, of course) but that is a bit simplistic. Yes, I'm certain I am creating my own turmoil. Agreed. And your point would be...

...That I just throw the switch? M'kay, you throw the switch that makes you fall back in love with Robert and you and I will blissfully accept our fulfilling lies of domestic bliss.

After you.

I have no relationship with Ryder, nothing physical and only that glancing emotional impact at best. She responded to a hug. She was tempted to steal a kiss, which in honesty I would not have resisted. We email once in a while. Do I tell her romance is too difficult right now?

Am I absolutely insane asking you, of all people, about how NOT to lead someone into an emotional trap?

Oh, no! Don't even consider loving me like you'd love a Jewish sister. First of all, you'd have to swear off me any day now. Second of all, I require you love me far better, far more interestingly, than Jewish sisters (I speak from experience in this matter).

Clarification: I was not invoking the loathsome and pious Shoulds. I was trying to suggest (and I will refine this concept for a later email: I still rush and rush and only intermittently peek at the screen)(but FYI I'll be gone tomorrow afternoon and most, if not all, of Sat—the much-longed-for Mt. Adams climb) that you shift your emphasis, and find a way to experience these women in a way that isn't so harmful to you. Receive all that Ryder (though I think we gotta do better for a name)(and why have I fallen into parentheticals today?) has to offer on every other level.

So much less complicated, yet still so fulfilling (I'm moving far too quickly today for euphemisms)(and I'd ask myself the exact same questions, so don't you dare be offended). How many parentheses? I feel like a twisted cousin of eecummings...

I'm only lightly offended. At one level this seems like such a bizarre oversimplification coming from you. I'm going to mark it down to the fact that you were so rushed, and are such a tease. But I'll love you any way you demand, just don't make me hurry.

Another race this weekend. Then I put the car away and helmet on the rack and focus on my business for a month or two.

Seattle Blues

Okay, you've had enough time to recover from the races. And any other adventure. Tell all. All.

You don't want to know all. Not All. Trust me on that. There are lines. I'll send a race replay.

Dude, you don't think I stick around for your race replays, do you? I want you to be YOU, or else what's the point? Would a diluted friendship satisfy you? At least draw the line closer to the edge, Girlfriend.

Alright, Ms. No Judgment. I showed up at the track on Thursday to set up the car. I was standing in my trailer organizing papers from the last three races when there was a knock at the ramp door. A motorcycle rider in leathers was pulling off a helmet. A mane of dark hair spilled out: Ryder.

Oh my God, Peter. Was her friend racing? And? And!?

No, her friend blew his motor in the last race and didn't have a spare, and there was not enough time for repair.

We talked for a while. She asked if I wanted to go to dinner. I told her it would take a bit to unhook my trailer. She said we should just take her bike. I'm used to speed, but she had me on the edge of her seat. She made decisions in traffic that scared me to death, but knows how to ride. We found a restaurant, had dinner.

And? And!?

Seattle Blues

Ryder pilots us fast from near SeaTac into downtown through traffic. We leave her BMW in plain sight, but chained and alarmed and ticking with heat. We walk to where we guess the restaurant would be.

Behind us, a homeless barrel of a woman pushes the obvious shopping cart; five-foot-ten and two hundred fifty pounds, she stomps heavy on the sidewalk and mutters about s.o.b.'s and assholes. The words steam through clenched teeth as if from a boiler, her tongue a sputtering valve barely holding the pressure.

A frail man in a wheelchair on the corner takes a folded dollar and tells us the club is a block down and across the street.

"What the hell are you saying? You are so stupid!" yells the angry woman, soiled blue sweat pants beneath a red plaid Seattle signature shirt, watching from a point on my shoulder.

"It's right over there," Boiler says and points a hundred feet down the sidewalk behind me. She looks at Ryder's black motorcycle leathers, my jeans and sandals, scornful we can afford to go out to dinner but don't know our way around her corner of this city.

Then she aims more bile at the wheelchair. "You are just a waste of skin."

He looks up at the quivering cheeks spraying hurt into his face. The wheelchair is no defense on this street and he pleads "I didn't mean to..." but clutches the dollar bill tight in his hand.

The signs say "fine dining," but the dirt and broken plank floor in the narrow hall of old industrial red brick suggest the owner is more into music than food. Cover is $8 at the door.

We are early and the band is late, and we get a good table far enough from the stage so we can listen and talk. We talk intensely, cramming experiences we would have if often together into a clear amber distillation of longing and laughing and talking.

"Have any of them been as sophisticated as you?" I ask. She has left men behind who could not keep up, emotionally or physically, others who could not, ironically, let go. She thinks for a moment and says no, and does not offer the obligatory of "Until I met you."

The catfish appetizer tastes of river, Remolade covers it a bit. Ryder orders a gumbo and I an éttouffeé. The food is great but I take it easy, a crucial business meeting early the next morning would be a bad place to learn if the menu was too rich.

We agree being in love at this age is suspending disbelief, leaping the distance from pain to peace. We have each been jealous already of the other's past, and wonder if we share understanding or evasion.

After tuning the piano, the guy in the 40s fedora on stage grabs a microphone that shrieks at his touch. He says the band should finish setting up shortly. Tuning in small riffs, his fingers dance an autonomous melody alive across the keys.

We decide that jealousy does not cower before facts. Facts are bent and woven into explanations of loss that precede cause offered in the moment.

But touch, right now a hand on my arm, gives assurance of presence no words can convey.

"I don't want to talk about Barry any more. I want to be done with that," Ryder says.

"It's all right," I respond about the scab that still hangs from an emotional wound. "I learn more about how to care, what to avoid."

I tell her how I was abandoned as a child and am still a half-man from whom she should flee: "You should run away, you know."

"No," she throws back, "There is too much here."

The music is a soulful blend, more Jazz than Blues, the lead can blow sax and clarinet at the same time. They're from New York, this night in Seattle, the next in Portland

On the wall are drawings of greats from the past, Jazz greats, Blues greats, a photo of Billie Holiday. Blues from the 1940s and 50s that prove Whites cannot know, except from music, the true magnitude of love and loss. We are dilettantes when it comes to sorrow.

An older couple takes to the floor. He is wearing suspenders to hold up jeans, but glides so softly his shoes seem stitched of feathers. This part of the city has collapsed around him, his dancing a glowing ember in a dying fire of what was an elegant era.

His partner is wearing a pink dress and glasses with lenses so thick they bend light like the bottom of Ryder's cheap wine glass. It was silly to think we would find a Pinot Noir. The old woman dances with the love of her life, looking at him with a wistful smile that makes us all wish we could have known them then, and we make their moment ours. When they leave the dance floor, there is polite applause.

Ryder leans against me, her body moves to the music, my hands play upon the fabric of the blouse tightly wrapping her muscular body. She is an athlete with density that is alive.

She sways to the music and I finally lean forward and whisper: "If you are going to ask me to dance, you'd better do it soon because I have a curfew."

She turns and that smile, she has worn it all evening, brightens. I know how she loves to dance. She said Barry judged harshly her love of music.

"Do you mean it?" We get up and dance to the Blues. In her motorcycle leathers, Ryder attracts a lot of eyes. We sit down with a laugh when Jazz reasserts itself, not enough form for feet to find rhythm.

She has a second glass of wine and I drink coffee as she leans back against me and we listen to the band.

We give up our table to the night crowd that has drifted in to stand in the doorway. We walk back past clubs with bright lights strobing behind heavy dark curtains; huge bouncers in club T-shirts stretched across backs ripped with muscle maintain order on narrow sidewalks crowded with 20-somethings fueled by drugs or tequila, talking aggressive to each other and on cell phones.

We talk and hold hands, but Ryder is now the competent lawyer and counsels me how to listen for compromise the next morning, saying I have to visualize what the seller needs as well as what he wants, at what price his fear will trump his ego.

She thanks me for dancing with her, then asks, "Did you dance with me because you wanted to, or because you knew I wanted to?"

"Does it matter?" I reply. She says "Hmmmm."

We walk past a strip club, I glance at a photograph of a stunning brunette with blue eyes and long legs featured on the marquee. "Want to go in?" Ryder asks.

"I was just looking at the picture."

"Watching strippers is licking candy through glass. But maybe we can find one to take back to the hotel," Ryder says. She holds my eyes with hers.

Nervously we wander together closer to the edge. Like standing on top of a dam, or the edge of a canyon, or a cliff above the sea looking down, there is a sense of deep imbalance.

The Blues work well in Seattle, rain-wet loss on the streets, loss of the illusion that one can choose, that character is not fate.

Manipulator

Nice piece. Sorry I haven't written. I've been luxuriating in some of your most evocative writing. I just haven't had the time or mental energy to respond appropriately, so I keep shifting it to the recesses of my "to do" lists. Why did you present it as a "biography"?

I wrote it as a "story" because it's a way of putting you "there" instead of describing about.

I could tell your writing was fairly raw, and it made it more earthy and real than your more polished, synonym-perfected efforts. Very distinct. I love both.

But is it real or not? Because you wrote it as a "biography," I don't know.

Interestingly, the portion about Ryder and Seattle helped me understand the profound differences in how we "define" love. I know, I know, I continue to return to this theme. But I think I can articulate it this time in words that will elucidate rather than confuse.

Hectic day. Hectic week. Did I tell you I spent Sat from 4 p.m. to 6 a.m. at St. Claire Hospital with Jacob, who had something wrong with his neck? But he recovered miraculously. Oy. He's playing baseball as I write. Need to go get him momentarily.

I was hoping where the piece ended up would surprise, turn the story, make it about something else, cause the rest to resolve like focusing a microscope. Glad Jacob is okay.

Your writing was evocative, and enabled me to discern the difference between what we each seek in love, which is something profoundly different for us both.

Your idea of love is what I did with Mr. Half Affair last year. The giddy obsession, the exhilaration, the desire, the wet heat, the drunken glow of endorphins... the vanity and the reassurance of reciprocation. More than anything, the suspension of disbelief.

I had that, at a time when I needed it. But, ultimately it was no more fulfilling than Safeway cake for breakfast.

When I think of having love again, I think of growing with someone. I think of exploring: "intellectual" issues, travel, food, sex, dance lessons, mountain expeditions... exploring together. In a sense, my vision of "love" is as down-to-earth as it gets, while yours is ephemeral and Mount Olympus.

I've got a splitting headache. Screamed, literally, at the kids who have squabbled incessantly for days. I told them I was no longer going to intervene and they could go ahead and tear each other to shreds. They were shocked; I now have a pair of angels.

I don't really turn to you for acceptance, Girlfriend, but when I leave my netherworld and return, no one knows that I have been any place at all. You have become not just a muse but a record, I suppose, of the journey and reflections.

I vehemently disagree that our visions of love are different, but I don't have the energy to go point by point.

Your vision includes a finite, limited version of exploration. So far, with Lover and Ryder, you have loved only in snippets, in sound bites. You have loved in flames, but not in 72 degrees on a Wednesday.

You view love through a filmy lens of romance, and are disappointed that I do not do the same. But in this matter I am stolid. Exploration, at least that of which I speak, is a process, an unfolding, an evolution. A discovery of... too tired.

Don't be stung. Be flattered. Are you mad?

mmmm… noooo… A bit frustrated, I suppose. I had not intended to get into another "debate" about the definition of "love." Don't intend to now. I'll work the piece over a few times and submit for publication. What do you think? A Seattle journal?

Honestly, I don't think it's near your best writing. But I don't have "commercial" taste. Now you're going to be even more pissed. I mean frustrated.

Earlier you said that it was some of my "finest most evocative writing." Do you think the piece could be improved if I made it more surreal?

It's one of your most soulful. The last paragraph stands on its own, from a literary standpoint, but the rest isn't written with graceful metaphor. I think you wrote it while lost in the infinite beauty and soulfulness (is that a word?) of the experience.

I've done that before, just assuming that my words will carry the emotional intensity that I'm trying to convey. Maybe b/c it's a time-worn theme: love and blues in Seattle, that I would think would have to be exceptional to achieve notice.

But, as I said, I don't know diddly about publishing, or even much about literature. I've read my share of the classics, but am not widely connected to the world. I don't know what people like, either literary people or plain folk. You should absolutely try to publish it!

I'm confused. You are all over the map, here. Is it me? Is it you? What's really going on here, Girlfriend?

Despite what you think, Peter, I'm not nearly as smart as you believe, but I am an accomplished manipulator, especially when it comes to men. Yes, my skills are rusty, but I certainly know that I could have made you happy if I had adoringly admired your latest prose.

I'm happy to be your muse, your record, your friend. But I won't humiliate us both by "doing" you, Girlfriend. And yes, I have had literally 1/2 inch of wine and am utterly tossed. A little dehydration, a lack of practice and a lot of Jewish genes... I'm a cheap date if you ever buy me that glass of merlot.

Oh yes, you may have been able to manipulate me. If that is what you were doing with the first words of praise, then I'm disappointed. But I think something else is at work.

Now, go drink some water, get some rest, and the Jewish genes are just delightful, thank you very much, but probably give you a propensity to argue even with the phrase, "Goodnight."

I'm sorry you think I'm argumentative. You're probably right. I need a job.

One other thing to think about, in reading your work and in relating to Ryder this weekend: to me she doesn't sound competitive or confident, she sounds insecure, seeking reassurance rather than dominance. Do ya think?

I don't know. She seems pretty confident to me. There may be conversations I have not written about, haven't shared. Or maybe she's living the life of the lawyer you decided not to be?

I have the life I want. Rode up Filmont Pass then hiked Healy Butte with Barbara today. She mentioned you in connection with the new library. I said I had gotten to know you "a bit," and in a vague, off-hand (as opposed to curiosity sparking inflection) tone in response to her digging for gossip, said that you were far more interesting than what meets the eye, or some innocuous cliché.

Debra, this disturbs me. A whole lot. Please don't break my invisibility. Please. I don't want Barbara or any one else to think I'm anything more than meets their eye. This is for you and for you alone. Be careful. It would take her only a moment to think you and I were having an affair.

You know, that didn't even occur to me, but it certainly should have. I have told her about Mr. Half Affair, though, so she'd probably think (mistakenly, probably) that if I were engaged in intrigue, I'd fill her in.

I'm sorry. I wasn't comfortable hearing her tell me about you and having to pretend that I knew nothing about you. I tried to find a middle ground, where I didn't have to deceive her (at least not completely) but maintained your secrecy. I guess I failed.

Now you stop being mad... I mean, frustrated... this very moment. I miss you and want more than terse one-liners.

I'm heading out this weekend for the too-often-postponed climb of Mt. Adams. This is the last chance Ryan Jones has to make the trip this year, and he is the only one I trust enough to lead the climb. Goodnight.

Crossed the Lines

How was your trek up Mt. Adams?

Terrible. Simply awful. I had to turn back... something that's never happened to me before. I've turned back b/c of weather, but never b/c of anything physical. I was having bizarre heart racing, which was probably exacerbated by the fact we started climbing at 1 am after getting no sleep (the guys got 2 hours, but I couldn't take my sleeping pill so had plenty of opportunity to delight in the dizzying array of stars at almost 7,000').

Hope you're enjoying this perfect day. Jacob had his last baseball game of the season (they lost and he played terribly, poor thing) and I had a good run (altho the sand on Orcas Beach was so hot I had to bring Jazzy home after 1/2 an hour and continue w/o him as his paws were burning!).

Argh, I'm so sorry! Maybe you can take another crack at it. In the meanwhile, I might ask you to take me up Chinook Butte just to get my bearings and see if it is a place to take my own kids.

It is a perfect day, isn't it?

I have climbed Mt. Adams before, so doubt I'll go again this year. It's much more pleasant to head up snowfields and glaciers than to deal with late-season rockfall and scree at lower elevations.

There isn't much poetry in my soul this weekend. Next week Abby and Sam will go with Molly to see her mom for a few days, it will be good to be by myself with the dog.

I don't feel poetic, either. I think I'm too deflated from the aborted climb. Am taking the kids to Seattle for a whirlwind weekend: Friday to Chihuly Museum (have you been?), Fri night to Footloose (did I already tell you this?)(sorry, if so), and on Sun a race in Olympia in which Hannah will run a mile, Jacob a 5k and I'll run a 1/2 marathon. It's small and begins/ends at a park.

I'm debating whether to see Mr. Half Affair on Sat; he's been writing often and intensely. Might be better to leave well enough alone, don't you think?

Your trip sounds like a fun one! Without poetry, what shall we discuss? Religion? Politics? Long conversations on the nature of love?

Actually I'm going to be really busy the next few weeks. Hannah just began a drama program and I'll be dropping her off at 10 and picking her up at 4 each day. Today I dropped Jacob off in Port Cedar, dropped Hannah 20 miles in the other direction, rode up Mt Tamarack and now I'm home, picking up Jacob and driving him to the ortho, haircut etc and picking up Hannah. You gently chastised me once for offering "on the run" comments instead of a thoughtful response, so I'm wary of attempting the latter and achieving only the former! I'll try to write soon.

Fair enough. Write when you can. Careful with Mr. Half Affair, it sounds like he has something (you) on his mind.

I'm seeing him this weekend in Seattle. I'm beginning to think he's the most insecure person I've ever met. Strange as it sounds, he's so oversensitive. But maybe I'll let him take me somewhere public so we can create a stir. Seriously, though, do you care too much about the rumor mill? No one is going to understand any of it anyway. What do you hear from Ryder?

No, I actually don't care about the rumor mill, except how it can hurt the innocent. If Mr. Half takes you somewhere public, I'll enjoy rumblings I imagine would be heard even over here.

I took a left instead of a right last weekend when I went to look at boats. Ryder has a condo in Vancouver B.C. I didn't know she had dual citizenship. Her father is a fisherman out of Anacortes. Her mother, French Canadian/Chinese (explains her looks), died of breast cancer when Ryder was five. She was raised by her mother's family in Vancouver, and keeps a place there because she says it's the only "real city" on the west coast of North America.

We hung out for a couple of days, spent some time with a few of her friends, part of an evening in a hot tub which could have been more comfortable for me—they're younger and drank wine. I think the guys had all been professional hockey players and the women Olympic track and field contenders. I was older, not Canadian, sober and not nearly as fit. A bit of a gulf, but they were gracious; we had some fun.

I bet. Sounds like full-of-fun potential.

I guess I'm accustomed to being grist for the rumor mill altho I, too, try to mitigate where possible. Particularly with Mr. Half, I veto most of his suggested venues as being too public. I forget how zealously you've guarded your privacy and clandestine life.

Yet another clarification: I suggested to Mr. Half that we weight lift, or coffee, and put a damper on his suggestion that I see his "new" (not anymore) house.

Speaking of... I am a very wealthy woman with a very aristocratic voice who has been invited upstairs to a karaoke concert by three lovely little girls who happen to be running a day care center for cats in which my own precious is enrolled. My limousine is about to leave, so I really mustn't dally. I'll check in.

You make a good point about clandestine. Old habits die hard; I suspect my "lives" are not something I'll share with the world.

Abby and Sydney just came in from Sydney's bearing two cans of chowder and some frozen cheese bread, something I would never buy. Give me a loaf of sour dough, soften some butter and soak it into the bread and bake until crispy and top with my favorite sharp white cheddar… take me nearly less time than to buy the frozen crap. But it came from Sydney's.

They make Sam go outside to help them do something. Sydney may like him, "like a boy." You have no idea the deep solace and joy it gives me to see them there, knowing I'm not some outsider in their lives, that they are serene.

"I can't believe school is tomorrow," says Sam.

"You've had three days off," I admonish.

"But it went so fast."

"That means you had a good time."

Back from Seattle. Fun trip, overall. Took the kids to the "Magic" exhibit and show at SMSI, then to "Footloose" at Artists Rep (gotta love the '80s: leg warmers, checkered Chucks, great tunes—almost makes me forget the flip side of the '80s: Reaganomics, Jerry Falwell).

Spent time with Mom and Dad, enjoyable coffee with Mr. Full Affair, (a very lovable scoundrel). This morning got up before 5, drove the kids to a park on the water west of Olympia, and we all ran in a race! The kids ran the 1 mile. Jacob ran a 6:55 mile! I won the 1/2; we all came home with chintzy but priceless hardware.

Unfortunately, I just went out to feed the horses and there's a huge water leak, so I've turned off the main water and am waiting for the flood to subside before attempting triage. Betcha didn't think I could do plumbing.

I would not have thought you could do plumbing, but at this point, we are past surprising each other. Did you see Mr. Half Affair? Was he disappointed if not?

No, Mr. Half had other commitments. Robert is in Phoenix this week visiting his ailing mom (about damn time) and I feel as though the weight of the world has been lifted from my shoulders.

It's been difficult to see the stars this past week through the fog and general angst. Took the kids to Willow Creek yesterday; have you been there? We drove down Henderson Road about 5 miles, then another 5 miles down a dirt road, parking the car on what turned out to be the rim of an amazing and impressive canyon. All I knew was our destination was "Willow Creek," so I had no idea we would have to "hike" a bit to get there. We were wearing Teva sandals.

There were no people, but the hiker's register was sprinkled liberally with whale sightings, which my observant children immediately noted. We were excited as all get out walking (in 85 degree swelter) down into the canyon, which turned out to be a canyon within a canyon where the spring-fed creek meandered on the canyon's floor.

The banks were a verdant oasis, teeming with translucent dragonflies and huge, bright yellow butterflies. Tree branches hung over the water. We waded a long way up and down stream, discovering caves in the canyon walls and tracking frigid mini-flows of water to bubbling springs along the banks. The day was a particularly bright star in the haze.

I have been there, but it has been a few years. It is lovely, a great place to take the kids. Maybe it's some place you and I could go at some point during a day when the rest of our lives are less occupied. The orca pod that lives offshore is a common sight.

Really, Peter, sometimes I don't know if you are as thick-headed as you seem to be, or if you think I am as thick-headed as you seem to be. I doubt a walk down into a secluded canyon is really what you intend. I have a very busy weekend with the kids. I will write next week if I can.

Humdrum

Did you have a good weekend? Are you running the PDX marathon? What is your goal? Hope you are okay.

Yah, but I've missed you. I think I was an insensitive boor.

No, you were not an insensitive boor. But there was another dynamic at work you were not sharing. I missed you. And I do not like it when I have crossed a line with you, even by invitation.

You tried to take some whacks at me, dintchya? You can push me away, but you can't hide from me, Girlfriend.

Honey, those weren't whacks, they were love pats. A mere Category 2 hurricane.

Funny, I always think of myself as such a sensitive person, yet time and again, I see how insensitive I can be with those with whom I am intimate.

Have to go apply make-up; I'm helping in Hannah's class for the first time and she pointedly told me I had to "look respectable" (whose words do you think those are?).

I'm toying with the idea of teaching a class at Port Cedar Community College. Obviously I'm best suited to teach a criminal law class, but it's already offered. Do you think I should present myself as a generalist with a diverse background, suggesting a range of classes I would be well-suited to teach?

I've been chilled since the dark, creeping dampness has moved in. I sit on my hands, blow on them, stuff them between my breasts (purely medicinal: this is no porn email). And it hasn't dropped below 50! I'm beginning to see why old people move south. I can't believe, even with your Viking stock, that you're dreaming of a boat in the chilly, northern waters.

By the way, I really enjoyed your editorial in The Times *about Religion in politics. Of course I thought it was wonderful, but have there been any crosses burned on your lawn? The religious right must be outraged.*

I hear of muttering in the pews, dark words about my godlessness, that I am not of the Chosen and not to be forgiven.

They are frightened. They deny the world because deep in their hearts they are not sure. They have isolated themselves from life and they fear perhaps from God, too. They beat their chests, and and excoriate those who live full, to convince others of their piety, to convince themselves.

Love of man and his imperfection is lost to them. They receive, instead, small solace from thin pages that echo their bigotry out of a book of many contradictions that can and has been used to justify almost everything.

They want to impose on the universe a limit, because the sheer size of being terrifies them. Insignificance is their bogeyman, the deep knowledge that they don't matter in the timeless eyes of God.

Peter, sometimes what you write helps me understand why you are so hungry for passion in all its forms. So much of the world must be monochromatic and bland. You must thirst for things that light your soul and capture your imagination.

Oh, Debra, I'm just a humdrum, everyday house-husband. But thanks.

Funny. But, you know, at some level you are. I just don't know what level that is.

I'm taking off for Seattle on the 1 p.m. ferry after I home-school Jacob this morning (is "home-school" a verb?)—NO kids (extremely unusual). I'm actually looking forward to it; I've rounded up some good friends from law school (last minute, just like everything lately!) and will hang with them tonight, after Thai food, extra spicy.

Tomorrow I fete my sister, beginning with a late morning massage and ending with haute cuisine in Belltown. The next day, the marathon (untrained, hung over and menstruating, in all likelihood, so don't ask me how I did—it'll be nothing short of a miracle if I finish under 4 hrs).

I bet you do great in the marathon. I wish I could be there to send you off and to catch you at the finish, to say nothing of feasting you in Belltown.

BTW, Lover's time was 3:44, not 3:30 as I thought. She was shooting for a 3:40, to qualify for Boston.

Thank you again for your last note. You laid some brick beneath my compulsions.

Have a wonderful time, pace yourself and then let go. Let me know as soon as you can how you did.

We are racing again this weekend at a new track over on the peninsula. It will be fun to see who shows up.

Good luck in your race!

I used to laugh and say anything qualifies for Boston, but now anything in the 3:40s makes me jealous!

Robert is taking care of the kids. I may again try to get together with Mr. Half Affair if we can find a time that works.

Squired

Did Mr. Half Affair squire you around town?

No. And I make a shitty squiree. I don't suffer fools gladly, have even less patience for hypocrites and fools, and he's surrounded by them. Are you ok?

I'm okay. I think it would be great fun squiring you, sleek and dressed-up, watching you misbehave as you made hypocrites and fools suffer more than you suffer by their presence.

You're right, it's irresistible fun! But like a bad drunk, I pay for it afterward. And as I've said before, I'm just not sleek. Not coiffed. Always a bit too sauvage.

Why can't love be rational? Why is love exempt from rules and constraints? Unruly love.

I'm in a post-marathon stupor, so I can't manage much in the way of coherent analysis, and that's probably not what you're looking for right now, anyway.

I don't expect love to be rational. How did you do in the marathon? Were you pleased with your performance? I'm honored actually that you even bothered to respond after such an effort. Please don't apologize.

Thanks for asking: I did really well in the marathon. 3:26, third woman overall, and won the masters (I never give myself much credit for winning the masters, but I will when I am 50!). Best, I felt great. Robert was kind enough to bring the kids and Jacob "ran me in" the last mile (he's FAST!). It was a treat to have someone waiting at the finish.

Debra, good for you!!! Winning the masters is not a trivial accomplishment, nor is third overall! I just got back from the gym, am all disheveled and sweaty. Gotta go shower.

I have to admit, there's worse than being the Other Woman, and it's being the e-Woman! (Not really a complaint, more of a whimper.)

When do you leave for Seattle? Do you have much prep? I'm going to have the house to myself. I couldn't find a house-sitter so I'll drop off Hannah in Seattle and the boys will be in Yakima.

By the way, Robert said last night he thinks I'm having an affair with Ryan Jones. Go figure.

Ryan Jones is a lucky man. Who is he?

I leave for Seattle on Thursday. I think we will be headed back on Sunday. I'm going to wash the race trailer and clean out the truck, organize and run through the check list. Car is ready.

The races head to Portland the following week, again returning on Sunday.

Ryan Jones is a trainer at the gym. The one who led the Mt. Adams climb? I am surprised you don't know him, And I am NOT having an affair with him. He is happily married and has a new baby.

"Happily married" has multiple definitions, as we have discussed. I was just thinking today of how you and I, in our respective dilemmas, would react if shoes were on other feet. Are you in favor of "open" relationships, where the partners can explore outside interests?

In theory or in practice?

Would you be upset if Robert found someone that he wanted to dabble with, or do you just not care that much?

Yes to both. Deeply, searingly, ridiculously. I wouldn't give Robert, or any other mate, ANY room to philander (doesn't that word, "philander," sound like a flower from your garden? A philadendron, a philophilander).

If Robert cheated on me, I would be extremely hurt, though not in the same way, or at the same level, as if Love of Life would have done the same. Not at all the same.

And I'm not sure how much leeway Robert gives me. I've had plenty of opportunity over the years, and have never (ok, not since we were engaged—remind me some time to tell you about Mr. Closing Argument, I was in love with him, too, how could I forget?) cheated until last summer; we've been together for 16 yrs.? It's not as though I have a pattern of cheating, altho I do have a pattern of collecting intimate friends, some of whom are men, and some of whom fall in love with me.

So, dear, are you seeking absolution? Looking to find someone whose standards are even more "flexible" than your own? I'm equally morally corrupt, though in different ways. I'm callous and cruel to Robert b/c of my own insecurities, yet honest. You are kind and, in your way, loving to Molly. Yet you deceive.

Actually no, I'm not trying to find someone whose standards are more flexible, though I would love absolution. I'm just curious where standards fit into your behavior, as well as my own.

It was triggered by Robert's comment about Ryan Jones. At one level, Robert knows you are not "true" to him in any way. So do you. I was curious how you would feel if it went the other way.

I also was exploring my own jealousies. You collect intimate friends. I have a circle of women with whom I have been in love… and for whom I represent a segment of circles of their own.

I would prefer commitment. Above all, trust. Which is laughable, don't you think? I'm in a bit of turmoil. Forgive the scattered thinking.

Then don't think. Put it aside.

You know my response: there is no One. You know, I'm feeling rather guilty for planting the seeds of doubt in your garden. Exterminate them now, or they may overrun your blooms and your blossoms. You're a die-hard romantic.

In fact, I think you've been misplaced. I can see you in so many eras. 1780s-1820s: you'd make (President) Hamilton's Maria Reynolds affair seem infinitely less tawdry with your own colorful escapades (are you a descendant? THAT would make sense!). You'd rival John Adams' wit and cantankerousness. You'd correspond with Jefferson. You wouldn't be a Franklin sycophant; you'd see him for the blustery know-it-all he was.

Or maybe the 1920s. I could see you in Gertrude Stein's salon, holding court. You'd charm the old lesbians as well as the macho he-men Old Rose Is A Rose collected.

But, somehow, your romance seems so sadly out of place in this crude, sexual world. You're a lover, you love with your words and your thoughts and your lips. Sometimes you love, trembling and precarious, from a precipice. And sometimes with superhuman strength and resolution. Your visceral passions seem so incongruous with reality tv.

If you're leaving in the morning: bon voyage, good luck. Try to enjoy the experience, sans all the amorphous distractions of love. Be Hemingway's man and drive with gusto and skill and testosterone. And for God's sake be careful! (If I was my mother's daughter I'd tell you to wear sunscreen.) I'll be looking forward to a full report. I'll prob leave on Monday, returning Tues.

Deflated

We went out at 9:30. I had new brakes and new tires inflated to a pressure I thought would allow them to grow into a good zone. No forecast of rain. Racing in the rain is an altogether higher art.

I started slowly to let all of this work in and had just started to increase my speed when the lead car went off the track and we had a yellow flag. End of qualifying, leaving me in 5th in the third row, two cars in each row.

When the race started at 1:30 I got boxed in and one more car got past, a white Falcon. I caught him down the hill into the hairpin "S" bends. Had a flat tire and had to leave the track. Off soon to see how far I can fight through the pack of cars from last position. Wonderful fun, all combat and little glory.

I have many questions: how do tires inflate? (must have something to do with heat?); There are hills on the track? At the end of the qualifying session you had the worst position? if so, in how much of a disadvantage were you left? You got a flat tire in the middle of the race? Don't you spin out and crash when that happens? Or does a "flat tire" mean it was just under-inflated enough to reduce your speed but not enough to affect driving? I have so many questions.

I'm sorry you sound as deflated as your tires. By the time you get this it'll all be over... for this week. I'm sending you luck for today.

The tire was punctured probably by a piece of debris on the track. It took about 50 seconds from the time I first noticed a softness in my steering to the car being difficult to drive. I was able to get it off the track on an exit road and the race was not affected.

The flat did give me a "dnf" (did not finish) and I had to start the next race from the back of the pack. Though I fought from 35th to 15th today through two yellow flags and a massive mess in turn one, I could not get closer to the leaders. I'm disappointed.

But Sunday's was a great drive: I had made my way up to third when a back marker trying too hard went into the tire wall at the sweeping left turn we call "Big Indy" and they threw the yellow caution flag.

Gary slowed but missed seeing the flagger at the next turn who indicated it was a full race. I saw it and launched, leaving him behind.

Sanderson was still ahead. I stalked him up the hill and around the next left and right, we blew down the straight and right through turn one at about 160 mph. He took an inside line to force me outside of Big Indy. I held off the brakes as long as I could. He held off even longer.

Too long. He was going too fast into the turn. I saw his car bobble and go wide in front of me. I braked hard then dove to the left on the inside, he was still ahead but fighting for control. Later he said his brakes had failed and he thought he was going to have to put it into a spin to avoid sailing off the track.

I posted a time nearly two seconds faster than Reynolds, the next fastest.

Hamilton is in the House! Victory! That's awesome, really. And thanks for the commentary: while it couldn't do the race justice, it did whet my appetite to watch a race.

And the yellow flags: on what basis are the flags flown, safety? And why aren't the "worst" cars given the best positions? Isn't that how it is in track running events? I guess b/c they don't want the cars in one group; they'd prefer to have multiple packs?

Details after you get a good night's sleep; I imagine you won't return home until late.

Voracious

I feel like I have a hangover. Everything aches and I can't wake up. I'm going to the gym for a slow I don't know what. Hope your fatigue wasn't a precursor to the flu that's going around. Where have you been? Long time no hear.

Sorry for being out of touch. Angst battling ennui attacking anomie. Singing business blues with "The Banks."

So, who's winning the battle? Ennui is the most enduring and insidious, angst the most intense, anomie probably, at this point in your relationship with the world, most descriptive.

As to the banks, it seems like everyone is singing the Blues.

Molly and I had an interesting session with the counselor yesterday. Divorce and several variations were discussed. I'm always impressed by Molly's strength. Damn, I wish I was "in love" with her, as opposed to loving her like a sister. Our 20th anniversary approaches, and we each dread the significance.

I also thought about how Ryder, and Lover and others, think about women in your situation. They have self-doubt over the risk of leaving a gray marriage in the hope of finding love and color, giving up security for hope. They especially feel guilty on the impact to their children.

Yet each said they will never "settle," that it was worth it even if they live out their lives alone. But there is a mix of envy and scorn for women who chose safety over romance, whose life is "driving their BMW to Safeway and the gym," as they struggle to pay rent or buy a house.

Life is complicated.

Ironically, my comments about Ryder began b/c I'm troubled that you are "settling." Yet when you turn the "settling" image around on me, I impulsively want to dismiss the idea, invoking my cynical philosophy: "It is all settling. Sooner or later even the most desirable mate becomes less desirable." Out of love. We're back full circle to where we began so long ago.

But, on a cheerier note, your world is ripe with opportunity. You are not the one being left by your spouse, you are the one with a multitude of options and possibility. Life is out there for you.

Cynicism is an admission of failure. You too have options and possibility. Don't dismiss.

It is an amazing thing to sit here and think of my children, small boats afloat that I want to steady with my hands, push gently into the current while at the same time ready to lift them from any eddy or whorl, tumble or splash. The pain and joy and love and loss all wrapped up in this embrace of those wonderful creatures.

But I explore my options every day! I long to travel, to climb more mountains, to have great friends with whom I can share, to continue to marvel at my children as I gently mold their forms. I had options with men, and exercised a couple, remember? No great shakes.

Why can't you stay with Molly and continue to have Lovers? Seattle race weekends, Vancouver weekends, moonlit nights. That way you preserve the family you love, but continue to get your endorphins. Why are you so convinced that gallivanting from port to port on a sailboat, however luxuriously appointed, will satiate your needs? Is this a fantasy, or a well-thought-through plan? Is the grass always greener in your garden?

I'm babbling, not thinking well. I'm bored, and also feeling the ennui. Mom arrived here on Monday telling me she and I were going to India as my birthday present, then left saying she really couldn't plan it b/c... la la la various hypochondriac-related issues. I'm greatly disappointed.

I've been thinking about your 20th anniversary. You know, it really is something to celebrate. The fact is you and Molly have been together as partners, as parents, for decades. You have 20 years of shared memories. You have built a life together. You both deserve congratulations.

Good thoughts. I will schedule an appointment with Molly so we can talk about it. I'm heading to Vancouver B.C. on Friday to look at an apartment project. Shall I bring you something back from "a real European city?"

Oh ho! Vancouver! And since when is Silverthorn Investments an international firm? My thinking is that you head North to view motorcycles, and their Ryders!

It is entirely possible that I will look at boats in the harbor and perhaps a motorcycle or two. And if one has a Ryder, it will be hard not to see.

It will be hard, that much is plain to see! But oh, yes, most definitely bring me something back from Vancouver. Bring me cotton candy tales of lips and caresses, murmurs and nuance. Bring me a ballad of adolescent agony and awkwaorgysrdness how do I look what do I do now. Bring me a poem of moans and moist heat and inside and underside. Bring me a story: a true story, a false story, fiction or non, embellished or straight up (so to speak), factual or poetic license, a suspension of disbelief.

I shall bring you leaves and flowers, vines and fronds; you may find me at your door, unconscious and bleeding from wounds reluctant to close, struck across the back of the head by one of many boughs that swing low in a dancer's rhythm.

I can't believe I'm asking you this, but you are practicing "Safe Love," aren't you?

And I can't believe your last words to me as I venture forth are: "Don't forget your galoshes." A Jewish girlfriend indeed.

OK, this one even made me feel ridiculous. No, I actually have much more to say, but thought you'd had enough "Debra" and figured the rest could wait.

I never get enough. Period.

Au contraire, man of voracious appetites. Your very problem is that you DO get enough, period.

A man of voracious appetites is always hungry.

Nope, a man of voracious appetites is always hungry for something ELSE.

Yesyesyes

I don't suppose it would do any good to ask for the newsflash now and the poetic version later... Check in when you get home, Girlfriend.

Learned a lot about boats, more about the woman, and a bit about myself. You have to wait for the stylized version where walls breathe, cars extend black treads to prowl in a low crouch like cats about to pounce, the waters of Vancouver reflect clouds reflecting streetlights at midnight.

You're not a real Girlfriend. Girlfriends breathlessly describe, the urge to release stronger than that of an adolescent boy.

I just know you would rather have it all than something to compromise your delight. Soon.

Oh, you're right, there's nothing worse than compromised delight. Except maybe delightus interruptus. Very well, take your time. It's good to have you back, nonetheless. Your boat had better be equipped with satellite internet.

Satellite Internet, a cork screw, a coffee pot and large electric blanket. Prebake cakes, or mix? Chocolate chocolate, angel food with fudge?

Nope. You need a duvet with flannel cover. And hope that by the time you lift anchor there is a Safeway at every port.

Almost never chocolate. Carrot, vanilla, hazelnut, spice... and there must always be gobs of lardy frosting, of which I invariably leave a good bit. You see, the hunter in me is irrepressible (or maybe the glutton in me): it's more the power of having all that frosting there than the actual consumption of it.

Far more important to have a library than a cork screw.

Hazelnut carrot cake, with sweet white cream cheese frosting layered three-quarters of an inch thick, a fat triangle of pleasure lying on its side, moist and begging to be molested by a fork.

Criminy, Debra, which of us is the tease?

I'm off to the gym, to lift weights and get a different set of endorphins running, withdrawal is getting to be painful.

YOU are the tease—what withdrawal?

"Hope there's a Safeway in every port?" That's not a tease? Withdrawal from the endorphins splashed in Vancouver.

I'd rather have a Safeway in every port than a sailor. And I'm sure something splashed but I don't believe it's called "endorphins."

One would hope you'd get to port with the sailor. And to starboard, too. Yeah, that splashed too, releasing the aforementioned endorphins. I was trying to be delicate and expressive. Your husband was mentioned in today's *Times*.

Port to starboard, stem to stern, running past all the lines with the sailor. But, of course, you're no sailor, you're one of those motor guys. What are they called? Yachtsmen?—no, too WASPy. Boatsman?—no, sounds like a swarthy Italian gondolier.

Who? Oh, that man who is supposed to be the father of my children? Yes, he stops in now and then. (And if I didn't have a 24" pizza for dinner I'd be really pissed at him.)

I may have to coach Hannah's indoor soccer team. Unbelievably, she actually wants to play. Will you share your playbook, Coach?

My playbook and my book of play are yours, though you should ask Barbara, as her team trounced mine this season.

And "sailor" will work for us guys with windless propulsion too, Love, since seamen gives leeway for far too many puns.

Come ON already. When do I get your story?

When I WRITE it.

I can't wait. I mean it, I can't wait. WRITE.

Have you ever been to a strip club?

No, but I'd love to go. I don't think it'd be much of a turn-on, but what a fabulous study of human nature. Is THAT where you recruited your trois? Oh, God, the diseases, Peter. You can get creepy crawly things just from looking at a stripper. Now, listen to your Jewish Girlfriend and get yourself a nice, classy call girl, right?

And maybe there are things I don't want to know. Or want to know but don't know what I don't want to know.

Oh, sure. Ask, ask again, beg for it, then disappear when the first bit of dribble makes it look like things could get messy.

The only thing that is messy, dear Peter, is this limbo friendship we've established. We dance in a shadowy realm, one in which the play is as intense as conflict. Sometimes, as I tumble and whirl in our words and thoughts, I panic and grasp for solidity. Does he write the truth? Does he live the truth? What are the facts? Does truth matter in the least?

The problem with poetry is that I read the words, and know from the lilting intonation, the mesmerizing cadence, the perfectly chosen adjectives, that here lies terrific power.

Even facts, true as they may be, can be used to distort the "truth." Truth requires context, truth requires background, truth requires an environment, because truth is not one thing separate from all else.

Like the illusion of a chalice between two faces, sometimes truth is just what stands out from the background. But you have to decide what is background and what is subject, truth is brought to the facts as much by the seeker as the sought.

And right now, truth is stalking me. I hear branches bend behind me and in this place, branches rustle without wind and truth may twist within the vines themselves.

Wow. I feel like we've just made love. I read the words again—grapes plucked at Harvest in crisp-but-not-chill Napa air, taut skin barely able to contain delicious fluids—and again, until I am staring at the lines and curves of the letters themselves. I'm denied comprehension.

You send me a gift, but no answer, though I know the gift was meant somehow to assuage. My plaintive questions were meant to convey the jungle in which I find myself. I hack at the vines of your stories, determined to beat a path to your truth, knowing that the truth lies in the vines, themselves.

Imagine what our making love would feel like. Want a snippet? And think before you answer. It continues the Ryder tale. Don't just say yes without consideration, please.

Yesyesyes

Party

The Party

Gorgeous "Brandi," with high-cheekbones and long legs, teased Ryder with a kiss. Then Brandi left the stage to give a private dance, and from the way she drew attention and money from the clientele it was clear it would be longer than I wanted to wait before she might be available to dance for us.

"Let's go," I said to Ryder, she nodded and we headed toward the elevator to make our way down from the saloon that occupied most of the fifth floor of this innocuous office building in a surprisingly nice part of Vancouver.

I hit the button for the lobby but one of three guys in the elevator with us hit "3" and elbowed his friend and said, "You have to see this."

When the doors parted on the third floor, they opened on a twisted dark shadow of what we had left above. The pink and beige curtains gave way to draperies of Red and Black. A man was dressed in a body stocking with the front cut out for his cock and balls. He embraced a woman with a short blond wig and painted circles on her cheeks in a leather maid's outfit and mesh stockings.

"Whoa, you are freaks!" barked the man who had stopped the elevator. The couple looked at the open doors with startled eyes.

"Yes, we're freaks," said the woman, "but we're not hiding it. Or judging it. That's the only way we're not just like you."

Elevator man laughed at them and hit the button to go down.

Before the doors could close, I grabbed Ryder's hand and led her into the small vestibule, where the man in the body stocking asked for $300 and the woman asked us to sign forms that we were not the police and were there of our own free will.

That may have overstated the case, but no one forced us to walk out of the elevator and into those rooms, or watch while self-proclaimed "freaks" put obsessions on display.

"Do you want to see this?" I asked.

"I won't know that I don't until after I have," Ryder said.

I paid and we signed the forms and walked through a curtain into a very different world.

In the first room, curtains around beds were of gauze, and held open anyway by one of a number of men and women who stood as closely as they could, looking in.

One woman sitting at the head of a bed stroked the hair of a woman lying naked, her eyes closed and hips rising in rhythm to meet the mouth of a man between her thighs.

In the next bed, the scene was reversed, it was a man on his back, a small woman slowly lapping at him with her tongue, stroking him with both hands.

In the next room was a large wooden frame in the shape of an "X." Handcuffs locked the wrists of a short-haired woman to the upright arms of the frame, straps held her ankles spread to the bottom. She started fully dressed. A wrist or ankle was unlocked one at a time so each piece of clothing could be removed until finally, her underwear was cut off with a pair of scissors. Men and women from around the room came and touched her, at first eliciting small moans then eventually bringing her to gasping orgasm.

In the next, a man held in iron straps with keyed locks on each hasp was being being slapped with a leather multi-strap whip by a woman wearing latex. At first she seemed to caress him with the scourge, but each swing came a little harder, caused him to flinch a little deeper, made a noise a little sharper. Every once in a while she leaned over and whispered to him, and he said "Yes, please mistress," and she stood back and continued the punishment.

Across the hall, a woman dressed only in a white unbuttoned shirt sat in a black leather swing. Two men held her arms, two held her ankles wide, another stood deep between her thighs. She gasped and arched her back when they changed places.

As we wandered from room to room, an attractive couple sitting along the wall kept looking at us, the woman especially looking at Ryder. I nudged her and said if she wanted to play, there seemed to be interest.

"Yes... No... Yes... No. I don't know if I am ready for this," she said, finally.

We wandered through the warren of sexuality and finally back to the room where the giant X-frame stood against the wall. As we watched, a small, lithe and very athletic woman with curls cascading about her face was leaning back, eyes closed in satiation. Two men, very much alike in tight jeans and crisp white shirts, each with a small pony tail binding thick black hair back from olive skin and beautiful in a softly threatening way, unlocked the wrist and ankle cuffs. The woman stepped unsteadily over to a chair where her clothes were folded and began to dress.

One of the two men approached us.

"Would you like to be next?" he asked Ryder.

Ryder's gaze went from him to his "brother," then to me.

"Do you think it's safe?" she asked.

"Safety is a very relative term," I replied.

"No always means no, even here," said the second man. "You decide what happens, always."

"That's what worries me," said Ryder, not quite under her breath. She handed me her small purse and took the hand of one of the men who led her to the frame and locked her hands and ankles into place. The two men were joined by the younger couple we had seen earlier. The woman walked up and gave Ryder a long kiss on the mouth and started unbuttoning her blouse.

The evening unfolded more slowly than I could have imagined, full of images I wanted to watch but did not want to see. Ryder's voracious appetite was a difficult and compelling fantasy. Eventually we returned to my hotel. "I have lost count," she said at one point.

"I don't keep score," I replied.

"Liar," she said, then fell asleep.

End.

Here we go again.

As a story about you, I'm entranced. As you note, context is everything, and the image of a "regular guy" plunked into a whorehouse of mirrors is ripe with opportunity. But if it is pure fiction, conjured for all, it doesn't stand on its own. And I'm confused when you present it in the form of a "biography" as you do here.

I'm so sorry to seem testy in response to something I crave: your writing. But do I treat this as pure fiction, and critique it as a potential submission for a literary journal? Do I treat it as fact and ask all the questions that it engenders? Do I just close my fingers around the crystal sphere and feel it pulse?How would Ryder react being put on display in your writing?

Of course this does not stand alone. Hold the sphere in your hand. Everything is upside down. Truth? Fiction? There is not an answer that will satisfy you. Ryder liked the piece. She thinks I should send it off to be published.

Peter, I have never said this before and can't believe I am saying it now, but I don't want to know if any of this is "real." I don't want to know that it is fact, and I don't want to know that it is fiction.

When the discomfort it creates overpowers me, I want to be able to say it is fiction. When my anger at being deceived is rising, I want to say it might be real. I know this makes no sense, but do you understand?

I have long regarded "cognitive dissonance" as a survival mechanism. Yes, I understand. I'm so sorry to have caused you such discomfort. Where do we go from here?

The sun was impossibly low in the late afternoon sky. The sunlight and warm air masqueraded as a summer's day, yet a vague chill unveiled October. There are no sounds of Fall, only the last rubbing of cicadas' wings and the final, deep-throated croak of a toad, forlorn remnants of summer.

The trail has been lectured by successive late summer torrents, yet an unruly inch of dust pillows my footsteps as I run, rising weightlessly in the air just inhabited by my ankles.

The Aussie balks as he approaches the lightning-blackened hollow of a man-sized stump, sniffing suspiciously at the charred remains pointing accusatorially toward the heavens. The deadwood's life has been drained by ravages of decay's incessant thirst and I could roll it without much effort. Its surface is smooth, bark and branches devoured by insects and time.

The Aussie plows single-mindedly over bitterbrush and through dry grass, vaulting a fallen tree, chasing movement he no longer sees, following instinct, pure and irreducible.

Very nice, Debra, and I think I understand.

Finding the Lines

Exhausted... haven't slept more than 8 hrs in 3 days. We ate an early dinner and the kids and I watched BBC's "Lion, Witch and Wardrobe," which they needed to see BEFORE the Hollywood version. Interesting, in the BBC version the protagonists are very human: Lucy is downright fat, Edmund has too many freckles, Susan is plain. There are virtually no special effects, it's more like a simple stage set. The story and the acting stand alone. I'm babbling, sorry...

It is good to hear from you, though something in your tone makes me want to hand you a glass of red wine and let you lean back against my chest and tell me what you feel. You asked me to tell all. You wanted to know what I see and feel, right? There are no lines, right?

I now realize there are lines, even if I am usually the last to draw them. I have been struggling to accept you as you are. There are so many things about you that glitter, and I have tasted tempting flavors of a deep and enduring friendship. But your duplicitous nature leaves me cold.

I'm not condemning. But I guess I am judging. What standards can I apply but my own? Abstractly I applaud you for reaching out and plucking juicy fruit from what could be a barren life. I empathize with your succumbing to passions. I justify why all of it is really OK.

But, Peter, I don't like the way it makes me feel. Do you understand what I'm saying?

My behavior is despicable. Please accept my apologies for dragging you through the sleaze.

There are other points of view, but to plead for understanding would be to make excuses, and I have no interest in excuses.

Thank you for being willing to take an occasional walk in the garden. There is a new thicket of faux bamboo the color of a bruise that weeps small droplets of blood-red sap as if stuck by one thousand pins.

A cedar from the north has arrived, a haunting tree. Its bole is surrounded by soft needles, but it's a bad place for naps even on hot days when the sun can't penetrate its drooping branches.

Forget the words. Think of it all as a tale told to entertain, disturb and explore; a short story in a book you will not recommend to friends. Forgive me.

I'm the one who owes the apology. I offered you the safety of unconditional friendship, then began imposing layers of conditions.

You haven't "dragged me through" anything, of course.

As for "understanding," I think on many levels I do understand. As I said, on an abstract, theoretical level I understand. On days when I'm feeling brash and tough and

Colette, I say "fuck it" and admire your brazen audacity. But something lingers in some ephemeral cavity of my being, an uneasy gloom.

There, I've said it. I don't want to end our intimacy; that was not my intention in sharing these feelings with you. But I realize I've been distant lately as I try to smooth my conflicting emotions enough to catch glimpses and wafting scents and cup my hand around errant blossoms from the safety of your garden wall.

If anyone could understand it is you, with your beauty and intelligence, infidelities and passions. If anyone could understand "the hunt," or compulsive search for love, or experience, it is you. But I get it. Through a different lens, it is simply sordid.

So, let's put this on the shelf in your bedroom closet next to love letters from men in your past. Here… take this small box sintered from dark sand of a Vincente Island beach, adorned on the lid with a tip of fern in the shape of an eye closed as if in dream. Each lash is itself another frond, and the lash of each of those is another, even smaller. Lacquered to the lid of the box are the infinitely closed eyes of a woman who will not see.

On top we shall emboss a warning: "The words within are but an act of seduction. There is no such thing as love..."

I continue to maintain that I do understand, but surely you realize it is complicated. And how did you know about the box of old love letters in my closet!?

I completely understand the thrill of personal exploration, mining the depths of love and passion. I do. And I'm jealous beyond belief. I yearn for the drugs of the hunt. I just think there are countervailing considerations that you gloss over, using your soul's poetry to justify. Those considerations carry more weight for me. That doesn't mean I am right and you are wrong. But it is a line that we draw in a different place.

It is hardly my intention to preach, Peter. You would be appalled at my daily interactions with Robert. It would not sit right with you. It would probably distress you to act that way toward Molly. I'm only trying to explain why I'm having difficulty riding shotgun with you on these hunts.

Because we all have a box of old love letters in our closets. Even if the closets are just in our hearts, our minds.

Look, it is obvious that my tale has taken you to a place you do not want to be. I have given you the path back. Take it, please. Before you do both of us damage. There is no place to ride shotgun. There are no hunts. Simply a garden where wild things grow. Believe nothing else.

I've got to go drop Hannah off at drama, so I don't have time to think about this, much less write it in either a cogent or eloquent fashion, but perhaps that's a good thing.

When I think of your deceptions, and the deceptions within deceptions, I wonder how much of my candor has been returned with deception. I guess it isn't enough to be just your muse. I want a real person at the other end of this relationship.

At this point I don't have the vaguest idea what is real and what isn't. And it does matter. What kind of relationship can we have when I question your every word?

The overriding piece of my discomfort lies not in your romances, but in your deceptions, which are legion. I have disclosed so much of myself to you, Peter. I have revealed my insecurities and my humiliations and my fears. OK, you probably haven't seen me without mascara, but I have been real.

Debra, you select what facts make up "the truth." We all do. Sometimes intentionally, most often not. You claim honesty, but are you honest with yourself? You asked me to bring you a story, you asked for "suspension of disbelief."

You and I are each "hunters," or perhaps more accurately "seekers," whether for "falling-in-love chemicals" or validation and self affirmation. We are very much alike for all of our differences.

My only question is whether you are honest with me. I have put great trust in you. I have reached for true candor. I think there need to be clear lines (I know, I know, my words 'there are no lines' will always haunt me) between poetry and reality. And I don't trust you any longer.

Do not tell me of the trust you put in me before you think of the trust I put in you. Do not tell me about reaching for candor then doubt my honesty, until I react with fear when you pull back.

Do not ask for lines between reality and poetry after demanding to share my struggle to believe in poetry and heroes and love, while you claim ownership of what's real.

Do not condemn me for giving you a gate out and back to where cars and plumbing and bloody noses are the "facts" of life.

My hope was that you would decide to jump off the wall and run with me here as I chase dreams through the shadows. I will check back at some later time to see if you are even inclined to perch upon the wall to watch leaves and fronds thrash and tremble, to hear flowers giggle, or sing along with organ notes from the patch of reeds with mouths just above the water line.

Oh, Peter, I sought the secrets of your soul, and told you I wanted to devour them raw and whole, unrefined and unadorned with the condiments of tact or conventions. Then I gagged on the glut of confidences I had ravenously extracted. I balked and drew the line I had previously declared didn't exist.

What can I say? It is just who I am. I act too impulsively. Then I regret.

No judgment.

Fall

Mundane

For too long I have been sneaking into your garden, breathing the heavy, heady fragrance of the lilies at the south end of the pond, just before you reach the footpath lined by cattails.

The other moonlit night, as I stole inside, the wooden gate snapped viciously on its hinges (three rusty devils who had been lying in wait), sending the door rocketing after me.

Though the maple rails have long since worn smooth by your hand's caress, a discontented splinter pierced the skin of my palm, which I had extended to stop the door from banging against me.

Determined to ignore the dull ache, I strode briskly toward the lilies. I extricated myself from the gentle tendrils of the willow, and refused to chat with the sunflowers. I wanted to inhale the fragrance of the lilies. My head swam, as it always does, as I bathe in the ecstasy of your garden. But the twinges of pain from the splinter kept me curiously sober.

Strangely, I began to long for the simple earth that lay beyond the magical confines. I wanted you to scoop a handful of dirt into your hand, with a confidence that assured that some of it would linger beneath your fingernails. I wanted you to mingle that honest earth with the other-worldly soils. I wondered what would happen.

Once I sat in an orchard in Israel where I worked and where yellow globes of grapefruit hung heavy and I dug my fingers into fine dark earth left by the River Jordan that flows from the Golan to the Galilee. I begged God at that moment to absorb me, make of me that dirt, to meld me with the earth, to nourish the trees and their yellow fruit. God said, not now.

Now I ask God to take me or send me forth, to give me knowledge at least of what, if not why. What is it I am supposed to give, what is the song I am supposed to sing, for whom am I singing this song?

Debra, I am coming apart, the pieces are not binding together, all the tools I have gathered over the years to maintain order in the garden, the rakes and hoes and shovels, they have been taken from me and I am on my knees, driving my fingers deep into the earth, feeling the dark warmth, smelling the decay that gives life, knowing my hands shall never be clean, knowing they are not hands at all but roots, knowing I am not a gardner, but the vine.

For once, I can't think of a single thing to say. I wish I had something merely to engage you and keep you here. A pretext for your company.

Instead, I'll turn off my computer. I won't listen for the message alert, or glance at the inbox screen for Peter Hamilton in bold. I'll step out of the garden, and try to shake off the leaves and the blossoms that have blown into my hair.

I'll put on my Hanna Anderson stripey pajamas that I bought myself in the kid's department so I could match the soft, stripey sleepwear of my son nearly ten years ago. I'll nibble on my eclectic assortment of reading material, and lavish my affection on any number of cats. But most... I'm babbling. Too confused, too stimulated.

A boat sits at anchor just out from the channel outside Port Cedar. There is plenty of room for when my kids come to stay, it has hooks for backpacks and coats and a table and they sit there and do their homework while I cook them dinner.

When they're at school or at their mother's I write of oceans of cloud breaking on shore of the High Cascades, of urban prowls in clubs and restaurants with a woman on my arm, we hunt as a pair, then of boats among the orca of the Inland Passage off the fjords of Canada.

I am trapped, Debra. Trapped by this dream, trapped by a life that is melding into this dream, trapped by a libido making of me a marionette, trapped by love for a fine-boned Jewish girl who won't let go of her own chains, trapped by roles I have played since childhood taking care of others and begging to be taken care of, trapped by a need to prove myself to myself, trapped by doubt of my own substance, trapped by the footfalls of old age, trapped by a mind that penetrates and a soul that wanders and heart that seeks and a conscience that guilts me into a daily dirge of routine.

You are trapped by the very things that should free you. So I shall unlock the gate and bring you back to the mundane.

Jacob wakes by himself most mornings, but often burrows deep under his layers and layers of soft blankets waiting for me to give him wake-up kisses. On weekends he reads in bed for an hour before seeking me out, walking stiffly down the stairs in soccer t-shirt and nylon shorts, kissing bad breath onto the side of my face as he folds himself into me as though trying to snuggle back into his blankets.

Tough little Hannah sleeps until the last possible moment. I sit gently next to her, invariably she's wrapped around a cat. I speak sweetly, softly, something I do best in the morning... my time. The moment she wakes she resists, not my tenderness, but rather, the demands of the day.

And I write to you. Good morning. Are you reading the paper? Have you let out the dogs and in the cats? Is your coffee struggling this morning, or merely bubbling playfully?

I like this day because your email was waiting when I moved from the morning paper.

My pair: Abby up and dressed and beating me to the comics. Sam stumbles to the table, he often stares out the window, seeing nothing, in a state between wake and sleep; alertness comes sometime during a breakfast of chicken snacks and milk. Then, he's is awake and ready to really start his day.

Dog accompanies me to the paper box at the end of the driveway, as he does every day. He can be anywhere in the house, and if I say "Newspaper," he bounds to the front door.

You should see my dog when I take out any piece of clothing that has ever been used as running attire. He whines and jumps and runs around the room. I feel cruel on days I'm riding my bike or something else instead. Are you looking forward to the day, or does it belong the Shoulds?

There are pieces on the board to move and counter. There is a "detachment," a serenity-side-benefit enhanced by the honesty that Molly has forced upon me.

And I guess what Dr. Helen asked still has impact. If I stop constantly managing outcomes, then I get to let things be what they will be. That is liberating, in a way.

As usual, you've really made me think. I see my pattern of rushing into sexual relationships to secure my power. I'm insecure, I don't like things 1/2 way (I can't believe I'm saying this but I think it has to do with a psychoanalytic phenomenon called "splitting"... for another conversation), but as soon as I've made the sexual conquer I feel secure. Maybe I don't have enough confidence in my other attributes.

So your "serenity," though it sounds heavenly, is foreign to me.

Does this all go back to the "balance of power" that you claim to not understand? No, no, settle down, its not part of a game or a hunt. But its presence is undeniable in any relationship.

I'm trying to write and listen to the news at the same time; how do people do that? I can't walk and chew gum at the same time. So much for multi-tasking. Sorry this is disjointed. Heavy thoughts but not enough time/focus to hone into anything comprehensible.

The twins helped me make dinner tonight. Last night I asked Molly what she had planned and she said "I have Tortellini for the kids," which left me to forage. I ate pistachios; the night before I don't remember, cheese maybe.

So I bought a package of free-range chicken thighs and called Abby from the car. "Sweetie, I need you to turn the oven on."

When I got home I had Abby clean the chicken while Sam fed the dog, closed up the garage and took out the garbage. Abby and I spiced the chicken with sage and chili powder and put it skin-side-down on a rack after cranking the oven up to 500 degrees.

I had Sam wash a cup of basmati rice and put it on to boil with 14 oz of chicken stock.

We turned the chicken three more times, and the rice was done when the chicken came out of the oven; it was Sam's turn to set the table and we ate as we watched the news. Oklahoma is burning, floods inundate California.

Free-range chicken costs an extra 40¢ a pound but has a cleaner taste, the fat less cloying. The skin was crisp, just as Abby likes it, and now she's not afraid of 500 degrees. Sam now knows how to cook basmati rice. Small accomplishments, but still…

I love, love hearing about you and the twins. I'm not sure why. At first it was b/c it added an unseen dimension to you, but now it's beyond that. I guess they've come alive for me as individuals. I can't wait to have a daughter that age. Yah, I know about adolescence, but to me it seems the perfect age to connect.

Peter, why on earth do you think that separating from Molly would be severing a connection with the twins? Do you really think that? Your relationship with them exists independently of The Family. You are still there, they are still there. The subtleties of the routines may change, but the essential dynamics will remain the same. And I speak with at least the tiniest bit of authority, after a year of divorce law and its aftermath.

Not very articulate today (as you might have noticed). Must be this cold. It's just knocking me out.

You're right, this is the perfect age to connect. I'm doing my best, we are connecting and I'm overwhelmed by guilt that I may break this connection, especially as they enter true adolescence.

My hope is that I will give them an alternative. That their mother will become even stronger and offer an independent role model. And I'm probably making self-serving justifications.

But not sharing the rhythm of life, the newspaper in the morning with my daughter, homework? I gasp with loss.

Oh, Robert. Oh, Molly.

Robert and I have no rhythm, hence no loss, but I am deeply sorry for yours. I also believe new rhythms and routines will replace the old.

Interesting... how different our mood is from last night.

I was going to steal into Seattle today for the sole purpose of seeing the Hesse exhibit. Then I checked the ferry schedule and realized that while I could get there, I'd never see all I wanted to see and be able to get back home.

Just as well. I have a marathon this weekend that I've not trained for and plenty to do here around the house.

Orgeyserms

A 3:33… very well done, Debra.

Yah, thanks, I did do well, better than I deserved. And thanks for troubling to investigate; that pleases me.

When I limped back to my car right after the marathon (I don't hang out), the first thing I saw was that my car window had been smashed. Confession, though: I was secretly happy to have an excuse to stay in Seattle an extra night. Had a lovely weekend, details to follow.

The two weird things: first, my time was to the minute the same time as last year. The other that I was only 24th? or something in my age group, but 124th overall among over 3,900 women! So next time I complain about being an old hag in a young women's world, just remind me of all the 30-year-old women who finished behind me.

How was your weekend?

Molly and I took Sam and Abby to Seattle to see Lion King at McKenna Auditorium. It was a good show. I disappeared the next day, bought a couple pounds of Starbucks and spent a couple of hours perusing Parnassus Books.

I spend hours in Parnassus Books whenever I go to Seattle! What did you buy? What did you think of McKenna? It used to be a show place, I think they have let it go.

For the boat's library I bought Tom Robbins and John Fowles.

You are right about McKenna. What a dismal venue. I remember long ago when Seattle was so proud of it. Was it called the "Civic" then? I'm surprised the McKenna family wants the association. Perhaps they can donate another half-million and get their name off.

Yes, McKenna used to be the Civic, guess you didn't go to Seattle Opera much when you were a bartender at 13 Coins.

I was a waiter, not a bartender.

You don't do obsequious very well for one who was a waiter. I really did miss you, Girlfriend.

And I missed you. We have nearly everything, except sex, emotional vulnerability, and trust. If each of us weren't so self-centered, if I needed less sex or you needed more, this could have been a stunning love affair.

Add "narcissistic" to the list: I theorize that one reason we like and understand each other so well is that we're each a vague reflection of the other... maybe that's another facet of your "chalice or faces" metaphor?

...Hold on a minute. Who says I don't need sex much, or need much sex? Craving sex and indulging in it, however, are two separate things. At least sometimes.

But you're right about emotional vulnerability and trust. Sometimes I still think you sit around your office drinking black coffee (Starbucks: how do you drink that acidic crap?) laughing over my gullibility. I honestly do.

And I don't know if I could ever trust anyone enough to let down my guard and give myself completely. Isn't that heartbreaking? I don't think I ever realized that, until I just wrote it. But it certainly explains my choosing Robert.

It is heartbreaking, Debra. But we chose Robert and Molly because with them we *could* let down our guard.

You were the one who said you don't need much sex. "One orgasm and then I am asleep" or some such. Maybe a couple more would get your attention. You described it much as a bodily function and accused me of romanticizing it (gloriously, happily guilty as charged).

Starbucks: Italian or French roast, ground on #4, and made with about one large scoop per cup of water, about twice as strong as most would recommend, and drunk within 5 minutes.

I guess "not much sex" is relative, and I somehow forgot I was talking to you.

OK, if one, solitary orgasm a night, no matter what quality and quantity of foreplay preceded it, relegates me to near frigidity in your eyes, so be it. How many orgasms are prescribed, Dr. Hamilton?

You should be flattered, in an odd way, that I have difficulty "letting down my guard" with you. All your duplicity aside, my hunter's instinct tells me I have encountered a beast as "powerful" (ouch, hate to use that loaded word) as I, and tells me to be wary.

My mom is coming today. And, by the way, if you ever doubt I have a "job," rest assured that care of my incredibly needy parents is a full-time one.

My experience is that women are biologically capable of between two and five. My theory is that multiple female orgasms potentially add diversity to the species. For the same reason, men are limited to one. And that's why group sex is so erotic.

You and I do not let our guard down because neither of us wants to be disposable. We want to burn our brand into our lover's consciousness, we want to leave at least a mark, if not a scar.

We set nets for each other and laugh and dance about the bait. The irony is that we are each ensnared in our own defenses.

When making love, are you able to lose yourself, truly let go and trust your lover, or do you "stand outside yourself," judging his "performance" and your own?

Snort, snicker. Was it Lover who got you to believe in two to five orgasms??? She's gooood. Ryder is a whole different story.

Re: performing: It's far too easy for you to launch these questions. New rule: I'll answer anything but you must answer anything you ask. How 'bout that?

(Laughing) I don't think Lover was faking, but okay, fair enough.

Almost always self-forgetting, but I will admit it's a fragile state. A lover going through the motions can bring me back with a crash.

Sex can be warmth and holding and soft sounds, luxuriating in each others presence, taking time and then more time. If just between more important moments elsewhere in life, then one partner feels used or recipient of a "mercy fuck." Not so good.

Thats different than the "quickie," 10 minutes of mutual sharing as the two of you rush around doing other stuff… but the quickie too has to exist in context with romance, dinners, and waking up at 3 a.m. in the arms of the other, feeling that is the best place in the world to be.

Busy day, hence the belated response to your question. Do I lose myself? It entirely depends on the circumstance. Robert and I haven't had sex often over the past year, for obvious reasons. But I usually lose myself with him, and always have an orgasm.

With Mr. Whole Affair I was entirely and completely standing outside myself. I was excruciatingly aware of all that was going on. (And he made it even more grotesque by wanting really rough, "dirty" talk...which, if he had been someone I loved and trusted, would have been a fun game, but under the circumstances...yuk.) Why do you ask?

Curious from the comment you made about judging your "performance." It made me wonder if you "analyzed" or "judged" your own performance and that of your lover while making love.

If I had sex for the first time with someone, even someone I knew and felt intimate with, I would not lose myself, or at least not much of myself. I would be self-consciously wondering whether I was adequately providing pleasure.

Side question: with lovers, besides your husband, have you faked orgasm to preserve your lover's ego? Or the opposite: withheld orgasm to knock your lover's ego off kilter and gain some control? In obeying the new rule, (I read it as also requiring you to respond if I do) I will answer: No to both. Though, I have had to resort to a fantasy on occasion. Dammit, I will find those lines.

Yes, of course I've faked it, but not for many years. I haven't had any need. No, I don't judge a man's performance (well…ok, my Jewish lovers have been lousy, and they say the women are worse!). My criticism and hyper-awareness is always directed at myself.

And no, it has never even occurred to me to withhold the Big O as a power grab, although it's a fair question, given what I've acknowledged about hunting and balances of power.

I had a couple of Jewish lovers. I can't say they were bad, but dammit, there are times when I just don't think we should have to TALK about what it is we are doing! But we never disappeared into mutual trust and satisfaction.

I'm surprised you never played the sexual inadequacy card for power and dominance, though it is a bit of a "nuclear option," with fallout global and catastrophic.

It's wonderful you and husband have a successful sexual relationship when you do. I'm surprised, given he can not touch your soul, that he is able to reach you sexually. Your desert is not without oasis. It is odd how that works. There have been beautiful woman in my past with whom I never "clicked," we just never were in sexual harmony. Don't know why, whether chemistry was wrong, trust was missing, or if people are just wired differently and the sexual cues are out of sync.

As much as I agree with you about making love (as opposed to "having sex"), I also think there is an element of Love as Art, or something like that. Sometimes I love the contrivance: setting the stage, candles or... I've got to continue later, the kids are demanding snuggles and dessert.

Setting the stage is part of anticipation, and very different than self-consciousness.

After dinner we share a chocolate tort as I drink espresso and she finishes her second glass of wine... I love taking the fork and creating a swirl of raspberry on the rich dark chocolate, a small smear of whipped cream, everything balanced, and offering it to her as she sits next to me, the full length of our legs touching.

She has one hand holding her glass, the other tucked strategically between my thighs. Her hands are occupied so I create a chocolaty berry creamy promise. She opens her mouth, the tip of her tongue protrudes slightly past her lower lip to catch crumbs or cream or berry juice that might fall. She receives the perfect bite and I can see her eyes close slightly while she drifts back into now.

Her pleasure is erotic for me, not whether I am adequate but whether she is so present that her body has overruled all judgments and inhibitions. Thank god for chocolate and red wine and long nights when it rains.

I love your description of "anticipation." That is precisely the fun of the long, slow dinner, followed by the walk in the mist.

As for the compatibility with husband: it puzzles me, too. For me, sex is so completely mental and emotional. I'm always surprised at the men women find attractive: vapid movie stars or stereotyped hunks. Honestly, I hardly notice. And here I'm so emotionally distant from husband, but have orgasms like Old Faithful.

Maybe it's the security. Maybe it's knowing each other's bodies so well: it's been 16 years... too tired.

"but have orgasms like Old Faithful." Those would be orgeysms, right? Perhaps orgeyserms?

I guess that is what I was unable to convey. Sex, without the deep, magnetic, emotional bond, is not as attractive as it used to be. How strange. How limiting. How liberating. If a day comes when your marriage is truly over, and I have done what it takes to be free, it would be an honor to talk you to dinner.

Funny I chose the embodiment of ejaculation to describe orgeyserisms. I wasn't so much trying to argue about contrivance, or connection, as I was making an observation for your benefit.

Pasting Yourself

I've been busy today. Ok, thats a lie. I mean, it isn't a lie, its actually true, but I haven't been too busy to write.

I think I've broken Rule 1, the one about not being jealous. Not in a conventional sense, but... it occurred to me (I never know how many "c"s and "r"s in that word, no matter how many times I look it up) that you probably copy much of what you write to Ryder to me and vice versa. On the one hand, its efficient and sensible. On the other, I've been increasingly wondering of whom you think when you write.

We all want to be special, but I feel like one of your harem. Silly, I know. But I was startled when you said Ryder thought you should publish that story, "Seattle Blues." I thought you said you had written it for me.

I did write it "for" you. At the same time, I hope one of my stories will be published. I did not want to sell that one without sharing it with Ryder.

Please, Debra, if you are going to break any of your rules of our relationship, don't let it be for THAT reason. You are special, you are unique, and our relationship is not shared. That kind of jealousy is ridiculous.

No, you misunderstand. I'm not jealous of Ryder, I'm disturbed at the idea that you write something and send it to us both. I'm not talking about the stuff you write to publish, but rather our daily correspondence.

As to our personal correspondence, I do not copy what I write to you to anyone. You are my secret, the only one who knows all.

Thank you, I'm somewhat assuaged. Hannah just walked in screaming, first at Jacob then at me. When I said, "Hey, whatever happened, there's no reason to be mad at me," she screamed back, "You had Jacob as a son!" I'm going to feed the horses and pour a glass of wine. Caveat: I'm in a terrible mood, not sure why.

You can be as bitchy with me as you'd like, but thank god for the asbestos of electronic communication. If jealous, you could get too hot to handle.

That isn't hot, its tepid. And, again, I am NOT jealous of Ryder. I'm really not, have never been. I never should have used that word. I was only trying to say that I didn't like the idea that you cut and pasted yourself. Now I'm going to pour that wine.

Copy and pasted myself? Even the thought seems a little weird. Our correspondence is unique, Debra. In my life, no one has ever asked to know all, I have never wanted to share all.

By the way, Ryder has recently said some things that make her kind of scary. Don't ask, please. But it won't last.

My vulnerability to you is total. Tell me that you accept that our correspondence is unique. Though our intercourse has been only written, it has also been exclusive. I don't share it, others would not accept it. Ironies abound. I only have one Girlfriend.

I do. Purr.

And, if I ever get that boat, leaving my multiplicities behind, you are REQUIRED to come spend a week with me. The Inland Passage is anything but boring, especially to a girl that considers herself to be a naturalist, and the boat will be warm.

You'll never leave your multiplicities behind; you are a man of them. But, hopefully, you will leave your duplicities behind.

Reserve for me instead the Mediterranean. I can think of no one with whom I would more enjoy Venice or Rome.

It's a date, then. Rome. Would you mind terribly if we stopped in Paris for three or so weeks? I need to see the museums again; Montmartre, perhaps explore a few castles on the Loire. I've not been to Venice. We should see it before it sinks. I did not spend nearly enough time in Greece, and missed the southern islands completely. Six months ought to do it.

I'll never say "no" to Paris, though it may be hard to reach by boat. I don't know about the Greek Islands. It depends on whether I could see them anew, or whether they would be tainted by memories. But Venice, for sure.

My God, Debra, my marriage is so over, but I feel such guilt, and uncertainty. Despair.

Do we have to leave Europe? Return to despair? Seriously, though, I apologize. I sometimes forget all about Molly. Like Robert, she seems so peripheral, though in reality she is front and center. Your dealings and feelings...

Dubious Morals

Twins and I took the 10 a.m. ferry to the mainland, went to Costco, then Barnes & Noble for a book for Abby, a CD for Sam and a couple of boating magazines for me. Got back to the house at about 7:30, cooked some basmati rice, Molly walked in from a movie with the Wilsons just as the rice was done. Set the table, we had dinner.

How have you been?

Molly goes to movies without you and the kids?

Molly and I decided it's better all the way around for us to establish separate patterns. Besides, work is so slow now, I have more time at home, when I'm at home.

I was struck by a line from a movie today (my whirlwind tour of cinema Francais continues). A beautiful actress (1959) has allowed herself to be "picked up" by a man, who is falling in love with her during the one-night-stand, and is asking penetrating questions (oh, will you stop!) of her.

He asks whether "this" (the pickup) happens to her often. She answers that she is of dubious morals. He asks what it means for her to be of dubious morals. She says, "It means I am dubious of the morals of others." I love that. I'm dubious of other people's morals, too, and very sure of my own.

Do lane bumpers in bowling improve children's learning, or just make it more fun? Do they encourage undisciplined play by removing consequences? Are you and I "immoral" for what we want, or for only what we do? I need another cup of coffee if we're going to have this discussion.

But aren't lane bumpers the Shoulds? Are they some abstract concept that is supposed to be explicit, but is obscure to me?

As applied to us, I can only say you provide something that my life has lacked, that I no longer wish to do without. When I think of my children and their pain in seeing a failed marriage, a broken family unit, I also know they see a more fulfilled mother who has a light in her eyes that's been dim.

I know, the Shoulds would say that since we haven't so much as touched each other physically we're OK, still bound for heaven.

I feel like I've spun straight back to the conversation we had so many months ago about the Shoulds. I can't wrap my mind around this thing, conscience.

You don't believe in God, so you can't believe in Heaven. Where do you turn for your absolutes?

Conscience needs to be discussed within a framework of fear. We do what we "Should" because we're afraid of the consequences, afraid at being cast out by the tribe.

Oh, you are black and grim tonight. I think conscience presumes moral absolutes. But whose moral absolutes? By definition there can't be moral absolutes, because the whole concept of "moral" is subjective.

And what about the dissolute? Don't you find that once you rebel against your conscience, it's easier to do it the second time, and easier still the third? Does that mean we (the dissolute, that is) have worn down that part of our conscience?

I'm a man of dubious morals. Was I at one time a man of better morals now worn down, the drip of small indiscretions eroding the foundation… Or was I a young man of lesser morals, now accreting morality like barnacles, year after year, and just now recognizing my failings?

Are you bailing out on me, or is this just philosophy?

I'm just trying to digest some stuff I've been reading 'cause its been sticking in my throat like a lump of, I dunno, whatever gets stuck in throats. I was just thinking aloud.

Oh Peter, doesn't the relationship with Ryder make you feel awful? I understand the novelty of it, I suppose, and the eroticism, but is that who you are? I just don't see a future for you with her, and you don't seem like a man who just fucks for sport. No judgment there, really, truly. I am curious, is all.

Whoa. Where did that come from? There are things about Ryder I haven't shared that might give her more substance for you. But you made it clear you didn't want to hear any more about all that, so I don't bring it up.

But you're right, too, Ms. Moralist. The answer is yes, I do feel guilty, not only about Ryder but for Ryder. Because I do know there is no future there, and it is only a toxic blend of selfishness and cowardliness that keeps me from ending it.

It wasn't guilt I was thinking about so much. Hah! This from your Jewish Girlfriend! But guilt seems to be related to the Shoulds, and you know I believe we should move out of their neighborhood. It's something else.

You meant shame, I suppose.

Guilt is public, and drives us in the direction of the flock. Shame is private, about violations of who we really are.

Perhaps there is overlap, guilt from knowing how others see us, shame the melding of that judgement into how we see ourselves.

That's why I asked you about Ryder. Don't you see what that really is? Have you really, honestly looked at it, looked at her, looked at yourself?

A man raised with self-loathing is not anxious to find a mirror.

Really? With all of your insight, you won't take a look at what you are doing, who you are becoming?

As if I didn't have enough on my plate with impending divorce and struggling business? I have meetings with banks again tomorrow in Seattle that I have to prepare for… Molly has asked for alone-time with the twins for a couple of days, our anniversary is coming up and I have not thought of a gift that isn't a cliché.

Keep this up and I'll need your Prozac. Life is in session, the math final begins in an hour and I haven't opened the textbook all year long.

Biology

Happy Halloween. Are your kids attired as Star Wars heroes? Do they go to the Port Cedar fire station for the haunted house?

Hannah and I love costume, but Jacob's imagination just doesn't stretch in that direction. He finally agreed to be a vampire (I wouldn't let him be a professional soccer player, saying he'd just end up wearing what he wears every day, and if he wants to ring doorbells and beg for candy he has to offer a show) but moaned and winced when I applied the white face paint. It sounded like an amputation, not cosmetics.

I loved trick-or-treating. Although it was before the day of pre-fab costumes, I loved the scheming months in advance: what would I "be" and how would I create it? One year, I was a robot and covered myself in aluminum foil (before my reincarnation as an environmentalist).

That was seventh grade. I remember b/c I wore the wonderful costume to our first dance, in the school gym. I don't think anyone asked me to dance the whole time, and the Last Dance was "Hey, Jude," which to this day I switch off as soon as I hear it.

I loved the excuse to look inside the neighbors' houses. My parents were The Jews, the eccentric New Yorkers, and didn't mingle much in the patrician neighborhood, and I was always curious about these people who were members of the Country Club and vacationed in Hawaii.

I loved the candy. Like Jacob, the real joy was in the hoarding. I would line up the full-sized candy bars in stacks in a row. They would remind me of wads of Monopoly money: lotsa cash and Boardwalk and Park Place, too.

Darkness never seemed to come, and I wouldn't have dreamed of trick-or-treating before every hint of daylight had been swallowed by darkness. I loved the frigid night air, almost electric with excitement. It never seemed to rain on Halloween in those days, but it was always windy.

The schools do a great job of celebrating Halloween with the kids: parties, parades, sweets. And the fire station is wonderful, esp. for the younger kids. But I don't get the sense that my kids experience Halloween the way I did.

Vicissitudes... Perhaps it's the winds of winter. Perhaps it's the giddy relief I feel at Robert's return to his airplanes 150 miles away for 3 lovely nights with my burden that much lighter.

I know that unsettledness, of course, but I spit and slur when I try to pronounce "Vicissitudes."

Well, the sibilants still sound nicer than the gutturals. And I don't believe a gentleman of your refinement is capable of spitting or slurring. I'm at loose ends. Not depressed, but certainly not elated. I feel as though I need a rest, but I'm restless. I yearn for change, yet long to settle into the comfort of a new routine.

You want the cave, but yearn for a different cave companion. Evolution is demanding new combinations, perhaps a survivor beyond all survivors from your helixed strands. It's biology expressing Her demands without regard for your serenity. Restlessness creates endings that precede new beginnings.

No, I still won't let you take Prozac.

Funny, you always seek that shiny, arousing, beguiling "NEWness" in a person, while I tend to look to activities. I find a new mountain to climb, an audio book to transport me to Liberia in the terror reign of Charles Taylor while I shovel horse poop in the barn.

I don't look for new DNA, and I don't expect to find any, although I'm always open to surprises. I stumbled upon you, didn't I? A multi-faceted snowflake, intimidating yet vulnerable to the faintest ray of sunlight.

I guess that's the human condition: cycles of satisfaction and satiation, then searching and yearning. But my satisfaction with activities is no more sustained than yours with women. Always the cycle. Always grayness, always doors.

I agree with you that there are other ways to ameliorate the "push," the restlessness — a new mountain, a new book — much less destructive than my own. Though Nature easily accepts creative destruction in Her thrust for new combinations.

Satisfaction and satiation then yearning and searching then again and yet again… No mystic causation, simply an imperative. And a source of art, this helplessness in being both human and animal, rational and driven, poetic despair as desire for permanence battles knowing that we do not last.

But I don't think our "restlessness" is a biological imperative for everyone. Think of all those people, most people, who cling to the known, the familiar, people who are lulled into tranquil submission by their own gentle DNA. Does everyone feel the restlessness we do? Are the stirrings more widespread but suppressed? Or are we just more selfish?

We're not all alike, even biologically, and there are good biological reasons we're not all alike.

Don't look at individuals but at the larger set… the tribe. There may be an evolutionary advantage to the tribe for about 10% of its individuals to be restless, even if it's to the detriment of those individuals.

There's a survival advantage to having one gene for sickle cell anemia and a distinct disadvantage if one inherits two. Blue eyes, brown skin, curly hair: who is to say what may be of use when the weather changes?

Or maybe we're just trying to fill the "God" space in our lives, hoping against hope that significance lies around the next bend.

I absolutely AGREE that restlessness, along with everything else, including love and faith, is a result of biology. I only lament that we're cursed with unruly and disruptive DNA, while "Miss Brenda" is content to attribute all to God's will, Donna is content with driving her new Mercedes to the charity ball, and Robert content with his profession, baseball and a shell of a family.

We are not sheep, and I would not give up the garden for a pasture. We are compensated with passion while others get pleasure from "things" or "roles." (Roles was one of the opening salvos we had to this long dialogue. Do you remember?)

I guess the reason I keep inching toward happy pills is the possibility that if I could overcome my own insecurities and impatience and (as you so correctly observed) judgmentalism, maybe I could suspend disbelief, too, just enough...hah! Drug myself into love!

Drugged into love? Ah, Love, a many splendored N-methyl-3-phenyl-3-[(alpha, alpha, alpha-trifluoro-p-tolyl)oxy]propylamine hydrochloride.

Opium felt like the closest thing to love of any of the drugs I have taken. Does it act naturally on dopamine receptors in the Love Cortex? That was many years ago. In Afghanistan. Oh, there's a flashback.

You need to be swept off your feet by a wonderful, intelligent, 40-year-old who can sing opera, make love to you until your 9:30 sleep time and brew you coffee in the morning while teaching your children Socrates, I suppose the Talmud is optional. Keep looking, I think he's out there.

I'm thinking of running off to live on a trawler.

A trawler? Make it a yacht and I'll join you. No, I'm far too much a creature of terra firma, though I do love to sleep on boats (have never made love on a boat — how blissful that would be).

As for the 40 yr. old serenading me with opera, after seven hours of intercourse: You have lost your mind.

First, if any man other than Placido Domingo himself sang opera to me, I'd most coldly demand that he go to the shower and leave me in peace.

And you know better than to think I would choose a 40 yr. old. And I don't think I have the temperament for hours of lovemaking, nor the stamina. I'd have to train long and hard.

Need a stamina coach? I'll leave the "long and hard" comment alone for the time being.

Trawler is what they call all boats that are not sailboats. You might wait until I can tell a bilge from a bowline before joining me, however. I can't do a sailboat. Too much work. That's why God made petroleum.

Ah, your true, resource-extractive, control-freak nature reveals itself at last. The only kind of boat in which I'd have any interest is a sailboat. Silent, sleek and almost a part of the water, the wind and the sky.

I sailed a bit as a youth. Then, just after college, my former roommate and dear friend, Rachel, a hopeless JAP from (where else?) Long Island, came to visit. While in Seattle we decided to rent a boat on Lake Washington. The boat-rental guy told us that in order to rent a boat, we had to know how to rig a mast. Rachel looked at me, I met his eye and said, "Of course."

I don't know when I've laughed so hard in my life, trying to "rig that mast." Somehow I managed, with some lucky concoction of vague recollection, resourcefulness and stubbornness. Of course, we thought we'd be lost at sea.

Hey, your daughter is an awesome soccer player! I guess there was an intramural game at school today. (Though Jacob and his friend Ryan swear the sweet little thing illegally slide-tackled...more power to her if she did and got away with it...)

Did not slide-tackle! Well, maybe. She plays hard.

I have meetings later this week with my bank about the Waterfront Lofts project. They're asking questions about how we calculated seismic suitability. My partners provided that engineering, so I don't have all the answers, yet.

Talk soon.

Existential Blahs

You can tell from my subject heading that I remain uninspired today, yet not as glum as yesterday. I'm also a bit spent: composed a condolence letter to Mr. Half Affair, whose mother died. Three short paragraphs, but so difficult to say something from the heart that doesn't sound Hallmark. Going to Seattle next weekend. Maybe I'll wish him well in person.

The problem with really smart people like you is that you don't like to do nothing. Look for a job. I'm glad you're able to get away. You've been despondent.

The problem with really smart people like you... well, there are really too many to name. But the worst is holding my poor, deformed feet to the proverbial fire.

I'm taking Jacob to guitar, picking up Hannah then deciding whether it's worth it to drive to Port Cedar to lift weights and luxuriate at the club. With a life like mine, how can you even suggest that I look for something as tiresome as employment?

Because, My Love, you're looking for fulfillment you don't currently have raising your wonderful children, running marathons, climbing mountains and musing on morality. I see tears in your eyes from echos you hear when you stop long enough to listen. I know I cannot fill the void, pray that you can.

No, you can't fill the void, because no one person can. But it doesn't make me cherish any less that you're along for the ride. How are you doing?

You've burrowed much deeper than I ever intended, and recently found voids I'd hidden from myself.

I've been better. It is my 20th Anniversary and my wife was uncertain if she wanted to go to lunch.

So I got your glum, girlfriend. I'm off to Seattle for another meeting with bankers with more questions about the financials.

My mom insists that I "play down" holidays and ceremonies. I guess she's right: I eloped instead of having a wedding. Though I secretly love my birthday more than any day of the year, I don't particularly like having it recognized by others. The subconscious perfectionist in me has such high expectations, I refuse to allow myself to get my hopes up, to expect too much; the reality never lives up to my ornate fantasies.

Your 20th wedding anniversary: Don't view it as a Hallmark silver bells affair. View it as an anniversary of a partnership that was successful in significant ways. In all sincerity, Peter, I take my hat off to you and to Molly. I know your sadness that the passionate love has not endured. But think of what has endured! Platonic love, respect, a shared life. You deserve to celebrate.

Drive carefully today. It's raining so hard the puddles are fighting for space on the road. Let me know how it went.

Molly is very sad. I'm very sad. We're coming to a denouement. Molly said it was time that she and I discuss terms of divorce, the possibility of mediation and the timing of telling the children. She said she will keep the house, so I should find some place to live during the divorce. That I should begin throwing things away I don't want to move.

Self-loathing is rising in my gorge like bile. I want to cut small slivers of flesh from my fingers. I feel like a swimmer spun by a wave into the sand and can't get my breath because I don't know which way to lunge for air. I may need some of your sleep drug. I'm now drugged from lack of sleep.

I'm sorry I didn't write last night. I just couldn't do much of anything. Robert and I had a fight, and after the day with Hannah there was nothing left for you, for myself, for anyone but the large black cat who remained purring above me on the rim of the couch as I slumped down below.

Coincidence that we both hit this low at the exact same time. Today I drove home from dropping off Hannah in silence, refusing to turn on NPR. I am so tired of "unhappy" news. I want happy news: "Today the Democrats, led by Senator Peter Hamilton, created a truly fair and equitable system of progressive taxation. Proceeds will be used, pork-free, to support Hamilton's new education system. Hamilton's recall of all troops from Iraq will save the country an estimated 567 billion, earmarked for... And in other news, Safeway has announced it will be adding Prozac to its slices of carrot cake."

I'm at my wits end with Hannah. She is completely defiant. It's as though adolescence has begun in earnest. I'm frustrated and disconsolate, part of the reason I've been miserable last few days.

You should be First Diva, a house in Port Cedar and another in Seattle, running, rocking out. What mischief you could cause, what incredible fun. Of course, I would pursue you with renewed vigor, at least until you told me I was becoming a pest.

A thought on Hannah: She is very much your daughter and is testing her talents with control. She's picked up on your internal (hell, external, too) disharmony. Give her more control over some things, Debra, give her some more responsibility. Ask her for some help with a challenging task. And you, dear love, decide what you are modeling for your sensitive children.

Oh my God. When you and my mom concur that I need to cede more power to Hannah, it must be so. I would relish (what a ridiculous connotation) elaboration. I really would.

So, if I were a celebrity, you'd pursue me? You are a shallow and vain creature indeed.

Actually, I'd pursue you only because you'd have fame and power. I've no interest at all in your perspectives, or your humor, or your insights, or our comradeship and similarities. Nope. None. I'm more shallow than a light rain wetting a busy street.

Don't go falling in love with me, okay?

Angry with Myself

I'm going to the gym. Will not run in this crappy rain, so I'll ride the hamster wheels at the gym for an hour, then lift if I can summon the strength (this damn cold leaves me shaky and weak) and if not I'll treat myself to another soak (in this rain, literally) in the hot tub.

Lori Brenner called and asked whether she could come over on Halloween, so of course I said yes, but now regret it. I don't wanna stay up that late! If I was dressed to the nines at some friend's party in Seattle, it would be fun, but the last thing I want to do is make merry here, in the drear. If she still wants to come, I may create a last-minute party for myself and the kids.

Tomorrow is another discussion with The Bank. Wish me luck.

Molly has asked for a couple of days with Abby and Sam, I think I told you, so I'll probably stay in Seattle.

Ryder called in the middle of the night at the hour of my 3 a.m. birth to tell me happy birthday. I don't remember ever telling her the day I was born, let alone the hour, but she had it dead on. She must have actually looked into the town where I pulled my first breath decades ago.

Who is Lori Brenner again? Not that I have another set of eyes for anyone but you.

Lori is Jacob's friend Paul's mom. She's fantastic. A really capable attorney, very "artsy." Going through divorce. In fact, you and Lori would make a great couple, but I think she's seeing someone.

And Peter: Even if I could accept being the "other woman," I won't be the "other, other woman." That said, I still think Ryder is a whack job and you should reconnect with Lover.

Love, it's clear that I failed to communicate the relationship to Lover. She's a friend who lives out-of-state and is rebuilding her life. I'm sorry for causing you discomfort. As to Ryder, I'm trying to figure out how to end it. Lori sounds like an interesting person, but I'm not looking for more entanglements.

I'm very tired. Goodnight.

Hold your daughter tight. Goodnight. Perhaps I will dream of you. In some ways, I think the chasteness of our relationship deepens it.

You're a dreamer. I'm sure the reality would never measure up.

I think it does. Everything I know, that I see, that we share.

Peter, you fall in love at the flash of a smile, you make up and then believe in what you want to see and fail to see what's real. You don't know what you know. You are a romantic, and not always in the best way.

Where did THAT come from? Why are you angry with me? What have I done?

I am not angry with you, I'm angry with myself.

Goodnight.

Ice Axe

Molly gets back from caring for her mother in Seattle on Wednesday. She'll come in on the same ferry I leave on. I have the fantasy we'll actually sit in the same seat, going opposite directions.

I have a meeting with the bank that promises to be interesting, if not unpleasant. I may see Ryder, though we have had some real difficulty communicating.

Will you take Ryder to the same places you took Lover in Seattle? Too bad you're not going on Monday. I could spy on Ryder! Sometimes a glimpse is worth a thousand words, even a thousand of your words.

You and Molly seem to have come to some sort of understanding, even if it's not explicit.

Yes, Molly and I have agreed that the tension is better if we split up our time at home. In some ways it's not too different than it was, but without the friction, and I actually am getting more time with the kids. She has a little more free time, though she spends much of it with her mother, who is fading.

And you and I have lapsed into formality.

Peter (now that's formality: a real heading, a salutation, forebodes trouble...), I need a break.

Enjoy your love, and don't relinquish it lightly. I know that for you, Don Juan Hamilton, love has been plentiful, but there won't necessarily be anyone better than Ryder around the corner.

I don't think I can be Girlfriend, staying sedately on my side of the Chinese wall, giving you advice (unsolicited, of course, but you know I can hold nothing back, nothing...) about your lovers.

Maybe someday we can find a more comfortable place, our "roles" clearly and comfortably defined. Maybe I'll be able to play passion on the computer with you without wanting, wanting, wanting.

You are precious to me. Your words and thoughts have filled me, filled me, filled me. (I'm beginning to think I'm haunted by Gertrude Stein, Stein, Stein's ghost. Shoot me, already.)

Tile in the Loretto airport was parrot blue and yellow and meant to greet visitors to Mexico with a festival, visual excess blaring like mariachi trumpets. Now they were tawdry, plaster spilled and never mopped, tiles misaligned, a mockery of bright colors masking sorrow.

They had nothing left to say.

They looked at each other, begging the other to conjure magic words, to unfold a paper with a potion inside, a butterfly to bring forgiveness on luminescent wings, something to unlock a future each wanted to believe, that they had seen but could not reach.

Then she would look toward the security gate, and he toward the road outside where a relentless sun assaulted the shade.

Americans returning to San Francisco and Seattle pushed by with woven Mexican bags full of bargain Mexican shirts purchased at a great discount after much haggle to sit in closets until sent directly to secondhand stores or Goodwill in a year without once being worn. The bags would be used longer than the clothes.

"Call the flight, call the flight, call the flight," she muttered.

"Say the words, say the words, say the words," he muttered.

Finally, the words, barely discernible through a crackle of lousy wiring, came over the loudspeaker.

While she did not jump up, she looked up at the speaker, then at him, and he at her.

"That's my plane."

"That's your plane." He stood. He could not tell her to stay. He had nothing left to offer but what he had already given.

If not enough, then it was time to let go.

The hug, when it came, was awkward. They had shared too much, the hug was just an insult to their memories. He quickly let go. But he kissed her, lightly on the cheek, then moved his lips to her ear and said, "Don't forget me."

She tossed her one small backpack to the guard at the table who had been watching the painful goodbye. Unable to speak, she did not turn around. If she had, he would have opened his arms.

Instead, she moved resolutely toward her plane. He turned, not wanting anyone to see the tears streaming down his face, and walked to a street where the sun beat mercilessly at pavement.

Part of the reason you're upset is that I'm not allowing you to have your cake and eat it, too.

You deceive Ryder by sharing your heart with me. I'm saddened by your infidelity to your wife, but that's all. At this point you're married in name only. You both know that. She must know you're having affair(s). But I don't want to participate in the deception and dishonesty to Ryder. And it isn't good for you, either. Doesn't it feel wrong? Doesn't it hurt you, humiliate you?

Someday you'll either be attached to Ryder or you may have found someone else. I may, as well. But there aren't other options for the present. I'll feel the loss deeply, painfully, regularly. But it's better than doing something that feels wrong. I miss you, Peter.

Don't do this to me, even if out of pain. I don't deserve this analysis out of you at this point, the judgments. "Better than doing something that feels wrong?" Please. Yes, my duplicities humiliate me. And worse.

I don't care what you do. I am not judging you. But I care what I do, and I am judging me. And, most importantly, I won't be the other other woman, period. As much as I'd like to be Collette, loving here and there with abandon, I'm not. Once again, you've found my lines.

Debra, you are not "the other woman." You are the one who told me not to fall in love with you. Remember?

I'm sorry I began this game of "biography." I think it substitutes for the "real" world, as you say. It is an illusion, but the illusion is of safety.

He was meeting her, his lover who wasn't me, in Seattle. They would go shopping together.

They would walk through Seattle Square, arm in arm, laughing. I wouldn't be there to tell him to go to the Discovery Store and buy last year's Kick Disc for his soccer kids, or about the radar baseball that clocks how fast it's thrown.

I wouldn't go to Parnassus Books with him, this man who wasn't my lover but hers. We wouldn't say "Meet ya back here in an hour," meeting instead every 15 minutes to show each other the book about sea kayaking in the San Juan islands or Joseph Lelyveld's biography that managed to hook us in a few pages, immersing us in a bygone era.

It wouldn't be the two of us spending two hours instead of one, each of us asking the other whether we minded staying just ten more minutes. It's not us wandering Pike Place Market, stopping to drink frothy coffees and playing Biography, no dragging him to REI while I dreamily compare titanium ice axes.

I didn't want to think of the scarf he would buy her at Saks. I wanted him to go shopping for me. It didn't matter in the least what I ended up with, but I desperately wanted to know what, and more importantly, how, he would choose.

I wanted to spend hours tracing his line of thought, a soul detective sleuthing her way to the secrets of love.

This exploration would reveal what I already knew: that he was beginning to know me better than I knew myself. I wanted him to know me in this way, from the outer perimeter of skin and hair, wry smiles and sullen glares, to the deepest regions of the heart beating deep in my chest.

...The scarf was the wrong shade for the jacket, and the jacket had to be cut just right for her athletic frame, her legs much longer than her torso. The jacket had to be just the right length, and the texture of the scarf had to compliment the jacket, and be a color as deep and rich, not the shallow pastels so popular.

Then he realized, again, he was standing next to the wrong woman, not the one he was trying to fit into cashmere and silk.

Parnassus Books had been a disaster. He browsed novels by Fowles, which he owned and could not quite remember.

"*The Tree?* Have I read *The Tree*?" he asked when the woman who was not the right woman walked up and showed him a book on sex, *40 NEW Ideas to Please Your Lover*.

"We have done 30 of these," she said.

"Perhaps they'll give us a 75 percent discount," he replied, drily and without enough of a smile.

Wrong person, wrong time, wrong rhythm. The emotions came in fits, starts and stops, awkward, with effort. That's what he kept coming back to, this relationship was so much effort: having to decide what she meant and when, placating her insecurities, trying to discover or create something they could take for granted.

Even the sex was too much effort. She was performing for him or for herself when he wanted her to just let go, and experience. He just wanted to make love, to be held, to hold and feel skin.

Deciding where to go for dinner had been a disaster. He was hungry, asked her what cuisine she would prefer. She said it seemed like "you've made up your mind and are just being polite," and would not respond further. When they arrived at the first restaurant he could think of, she complained she wasn't dressed for it and "perhaps next time you will involve me in making the decision."

He started the rest of the conversation with "What the fuck...?" and it went downhill from there.

She asked if he was going to leave the hotel that night, it seemed like he hated her. He had to climb back out of his resentment and into a sharing of what she called "triggers."

Wrong person, wrong time, Wrong Person. The woman who should be beside him was not here, she was at home with her husband and children. She could share with him a paragraph from Fowles. She would delight him with her fantasies about ice climbing in the Yukon as she drug him through REI.

"Love, don't you already have a titanium ice ax with a fuchsia handle? I'm sure I saw one in the barn," he could say to the right woman, and it would earn a playful dig in the ribs.

He would look for a backpack for his son and she could give advice, maybe this summer he and his children would actually walk that trail around Mt. Rainier, he longed to show them the beauty of what it was to be man and woman, to be human, to be vulnerable…

Thank you, thank you. Sometimes I forget that there are shades I can't see, events I don't know about, a process and not just a conclusion. Another facet of my tendency to take a single snapshot and build an entire movie around it.

Going to schlep Mom and Hannah into town... no time... but the absolute weirdest thing? My ice axe, which I've had for 20 years, has a fuchsia handle... make of it what you will.

Happy Halloween

How did your meetings go with the bank?

I've had more pleasant days. Nothing concluded. The banker said he'd be in touch. The details are boring.

Ryder had the day off, and said she wanted a chance to ride her BMW. She asked if I wanted to go, but there was something in her demeanor, as well as our recent rough spots, that made me say no. We met later that evening.

Yes, before you ask, my intent was to break it off. But I chickened out, not wanting to cause the pain, to see the pain, to feel the pain. I told myself it would be wrong to break up with her without warning. So I am not just a coward, but a lying coward, too, lying to her and to myself.

She and I spent the weekend, and I decided that a personal confrontation would not be as good as a lovingly crafted letter. Ah yes, that would be much, much better.

Are you getting the theme, here? I justify cowardice in as many ways as I justify my other selfishness.

After lunch, we went our separate ways with sweet-enough good-byes. I was bound for the 4 p.m. ferry to Vincente Island, she headed back to downtown.

Molly was on her way to Seattle to care for her mother, so I stopped at Zupan's to get something for me and the twins for dinner. I bought meat-balls and potatoes to reheat, enough for the three of us.

I felt someone close-by. Ryder was standing just a couple of feet away in her leathers. She said, "Hi." I said "Hi. What are you doing here?" She said she wanted to get something to eat when she stopped for gas on the ride home. "Corn dogs at gas stations just don't cut it," she laughed. She got a chicken salad, I paid for both, we said our good-byes again.

I was driving toward the ferries and looked into my mirror. There was a motorcycle two cars back. Ryder was following me.

I pulled off at the next exit and stopped on the side of a residential street. She pulled over behind me.

"What are you doing?" I asked.

"Who are you taking lunch to?" she asked.

"I'm taking dinner to my kids. What are you doing?"

"You're taking lunch to your Lover."

"Ryder, I'm taking dinner to my children."

"Really?" she said, and started looking relieved.

"This is crazy," I said. "You were following me down the freeway."

"I needed to see where you were going."

"No, you didn't need any such thing. Were you going to follow me all the way to Port Cedar?"

"No. I would have turned back in a minute. I thought you were meeting her here in Seattle."

But at that moment, what was happening really dawned on me. And what I was doing to her, to Molly, my kids, you, myself. It just all came together.

"Ryder… You need to go home," I said. "This is not good. We're done."

"What do you mean?" she asked.

"We're done. We're through. Its over."

"You can't," she said.

"I can. I am. Please don't contact me again. No emails, no phone calls."

It got a little weird. I expected tears. There were none. She just nodded her head, like she expected this. Of course, I kept trying to soften it, saying what a great person she was, etc., but she just kept repeating that she will respect my wishes not to call or have contact, but that I will likely need her, and her lines are open.

When I asked why she said that, she said because she has experience and insight and is a good listener.

I got in my car and took off. She was still standing by the curb in a bad section of town when I left.

Oh, Peter. Thats awful. I'm so sorry, even if I told you she was a whack job. You know, I bet she'll call Molly.

I did ask if she intended to call Molly. She said she would not, does not seek to hurt my children or my family.

It was odd because she had adopted a very clinical voice, without emotion, as if I should turn to her as a trusted counsellor. She just repeated the refrain. I believe her, that she won't call, but we shall see if she withdraws gracefully.

You should be proud of yourself. You did the right thing.

So will you try to reconcile with Molly?

Ryder wasn't the cause of my problems with Molly. And I don't think Molly wants this marriage any more, either. It's probably time for me to try to reconcile me with myself, whatever that means.

Reconcile with yourself? Deception undermines that security, doesn't it? Perhaps you have finally set foot on a new path.

As you're probably beginning to glean, I'm a person with many facets. Some are disparate and even contradictory. All these facets confuse me sometimes, but each of them is "really and truly" me.

I think that's why I look, perhaps harder than most people, for some sort of anchor, steadfast and sure.

Did you cobble together your Halloween party? Did you have Lori Brenner over?

No, I went to a party. I met a retired (my age) adventure racer who paid a lot of attention to me. I didn't stay late, I rode the high all the way home, then realized it was nothing more than vanity... empty, echoes of the past. I went to sleep before midnight, as did the kids.

I'm glad you got to go to a party. And I am amused at my jealousy about a man paying a lot of attention to you. But you sparkle and shine. Don't discount the opportunity, I suppose.

I'm not the one looking for opportunities, remember?

Do you think there has been another single year in the last twenty in which you have stared down the devil and had blinding moments staring into your soul?And with growth, pain. Islands of elation in a river of loss, uncertainty.

Or am I being needlessly dramatic? "Debra, I'm not being patronizing but perhaps you should gulp your first cup of coffee before taking this on..."

You're mean, but so very charming about it. And so very right.

I don't know, Debra. I'm not thinking big thoughts, I'm clinging to small moments.

The kids are still asleep, the paper is read. Second or third cup of coffee. I may brave the rain and go down to the marina and dream about boats.

I was going to ask you to show me your favorite boat, just waiting for a day of sunshine. Also, I didn't know whether it was invested in symbolism: wanting to have it purely and completely "yours" in every way.

Remind me to tell you about how I mis-read compartmentalization of your children.

I don't know when I've been so stir-crazy my whole life. Between this cough (my mind and body are sloppy in the drugged aftermath of tablespoons of cough syrup) and the rain thats predicted to fall all day, I don't know whether I can bring myself to bike to the other side of Vincente Island, whether to run the five miles to Orcas Beach or what, but I know nothing less (well, at least nothing else immediately available to me) will take the edge off. I need hours of deep lungfulls of fresh air.

Debra, something is wrong between us. Whats going on? You have turned cool and cryptic. Should I make the effort to get through, or let you remain at your chosen distance?

I don't trust you right now.

Why? What have I done?

What I just wrote was true, I don't trust you now, and it hurts, but it wasn't what I wanted to say. I'm sorry we've both withdrawn. It's lonely and I miss you.

You withdrew starting with the crack about not measuring up. I'm completely in the dark, here.

I don't know what it is.

I've made you angry with me. I said something wrong, missed something important, let you down in some way.

No. No, I'm angry with myself. The only way you've let me down is... no editing no thought just say it... the honesty thing. I guess I've lost an ounce of my unfathomably deep respect... but mostly it's me. Anger stems from fear, right? Let's not make mountains out of molehills. I'm just a little bit out to lunch, ok?

Anger does stem from fear. And this is more serious than a molehill. You took a personal swipe at me. That was out of character and out of context, so something is going on. This is an opportunity to get below the surface.

I can't. Not now. I don't know if I want to know what's beneath the surface. Ha! This coming from Ms. Left Brain Analysis, herself.

Look, I am here. You know where that is, and how to reach me. But I will not hammer at you. I am just here.

I don't want to want your emails, phone calls, coffee. I don't want to want.

Contract

I wrote something to you (on the exercise bike, when I finally got home), but haven't sent it b/c its awfully raw. Shall I polish or send you the hunk of meat, sinew fat and blood and hope that its easier to digest than it appears?

I am an omnivore.

Here it is:

Don't go falling in love with me, OK?

A while back I wrote that we should maintain the Great Wall of Girlfriends in order to preserve the relationship we've been able to establish. And, of course, we both have spouses. And we don't have many shared interests, and you want to live in the creeping dampness of a boat along the boring PNW coast, and and and. So I was only articulating what we both already knew. It wasn't a dramatic moment during which I revealed an epiphany.

Even when you begin your life as an Honest Man, you may still be reluctant to open each of your imposing compartments to people. It may remain uncomfortable to grant access not only inside but between each.

Here's my sales pitch: in me, your Girlfriend, you have someone eager to prod, challenge and delve. I'm there to proffer the handkerchief (well, the sleeve of my wicking, moisture-management base layer) when you sob, or bleed.

You can call me from "your" side of the boat when you and your lover (no capital) quarrel. You'll snap at me "Stop giving me your incessant drivel of advice. When are you going to learn to just be sympathetic with your mouth closed?" but you'll consider my advice and be comforted that I was there for you. You'll send me an email the next day, after you and your lover spend a starry night at sea forgiving one another...

"Girlfriend," as we both use the term, implies the safety of an absolute. Its a Chinese Wall, a construct standing firmly between our libidos and our friendship. Oh, how we scheme, brimming with mischief, ego and lust, about ways to evade the barrier, but that's all fun and flights of fancy.

Don't squander our friendship on a reckless gamble, a gambol through that part of the garden blanketed with poppies.

I will respect this… the barrier.

And in return, you agree not to fall in love with me, not to be jealous of lovers "no capital" and other interests. And that you will have no regret turning away from a man who seeks to know you.

You shall remain Girlfriend. Unsquandered, untouched, but not unloved.

Yes to the first and last. No to the second. There will be regrets.

And any first-year contracts student will tell you that, for a contract to be effective, there must be "offer" and "acceptance." Do we have a deal or does my rejection of Regrets void the offer?

Since condition #2 was for me, I can choose to waive it, right?

I shouldn't make light. Peter, it's one thing for us to foray off Vincente Island for discreet liaisons with others, return if not satiated at least with memories. It would be something entirely different to know romance was near, to run into you at the soccer field, and wonder who and what, when. It would disrupt the shelter we've built here in Port Cedar. I don't want to want.

Anyway, good morning. Off to drop Hannah at school.

Contracts are useless in this realm, you know that as well as I. Your warning was to protect yourself as much as protect me. You know now that ultimately I will putter off, on waves real or virtual, and you will remain at the dock, secure but… yeah, I hope with a twinge of regret.

Fear, of the day when the shoulder to cry on will not be offered, forces me to turtle up with a shell to duck into.

We are too different and too similar and above all, you will not let yourself fall in love unconditionally. And for me, your analyses and judgments are entertaining, but at the end of the day there needs to be nonverbal communication, there needs to be love and surrender, not debate.

While I would be easily tempted, "girls make the rules," and you get to choose. In choosing, you set the terms, and the terms are such that we're always safe.

Maybe I should stop examining our relationship, and letting you know when something makes me uncomfortable. Once again, we're beginning to sound like lovers obsessed with their relationship, yet enjoying few of the accompanying benefits. In fact, it's probably a good idea. There. I've just done it again, and you'll "accuse" (too strong a term, I know) me of unilaterally establishing a new rule.

Maybe I should should should should should

Whew! A new rule! A rule about RULES! No WONDER I love this girl! Hey, I thought you were going to pour a glass of wine…

Can we go back to "suffused with happiness," which is how you so often make me feel? Can we go back to making you laugh out loud taking me to the rule shed, debating whether manners are condoms for social intercourse? You talk about passive-aggressive? What about "Maybe I should stop examining our relationship..."

It won't surprise you to hear that I disagree!

I completely acknowledge a high degree of self-protection in everything I do. But in constructing the Great Wall of Plato between us I'm protecting something increasingly dear to me: a long... lifelong?... friendship with you. I want an eternity of mutual shoulder-offering.

We don't have to be very profound to know that a walk down the forbidden garden path (Jeez, we've got Adam, Eve, a garden, whence enters the Snake?) would shake our friendship and probably leave it irreparably without its foundation.

Of course for me, unconditional love is unconditional trust. And there is nothing I yearn for more. I just don't believe in it!

Box of Love Letters

Debra, what do you believe in? What ARE you looking for?

Are you truly dissatisfied or is this a sport that the highly intelligent, very sleek and incredibly desirable Debra plays exceptionally well? Are the men you are attracted to, older men of wealth and power, attractive as lovers or as conquests, a way of exercising your considerable will…?

Does the relationship with your husband really represent a jail or is it a safe haven, a "base" to which you can run quickly when about to be tagged in a game of adult, "hide-and-go-seek?"

If one was to shout "Ollie Ollie Oxen Free," would you come out with a laugh and some relief, thrilled you were not discovered, but happy the game is over? By going here, have I tagged you, or have I strayed again outside the lines, played unfair by climbing the tree from where I can see all the hiding places?

Are you angry with Robert for not knowing you, or because, having won with him, there's no game left? Are you angry there may be another game that you don't control, one he's winning while time flies by? What did you see in him and when did he stop being that, or did he stop?

Do you seek someone who will truly see you, someone who will touch your soul, someone who will KNOW you deeply? Would you be willing to give up at that point, and be vulnerable and commit?

Or is there in you, like there may be in me, always a little kernel of dissatisfaction, a wandering, a wondering if the self-forgetting of all-encompassing love might not instead be in the next pair of adoring eyes?

I ask you because I am asking myself: Am I being honest or just selfish? Or does freedom come from knowing how to want what's best for others? No lines? I guess we'll see.

First, you pose questions that define my existence. I have much to think about as I scrub floors this morning. I really must buy you coffee, you're the best therapist around. Please be patient as I analyze rather than answer. If I don't answer, it's because I can't.

I fear I am too cynical for love. But sometimes I think, like Jacob who envisions the worst-case scenario so he can be pleasantly surprised if something wonderful occurs, I'm hiding from hope. Hope may be another aspect of "letting go." And I've come to understand what I have probably known subconsciously, that when one lets go there are no power plays. I thank you for that understanding.

Men of wealth and power: While my instinct is to say "don't be silly," there sure is an undeniable pattern, isn't there? But it can be explained in many ways. Wealthy and powerful men often become wealthy or powerful because they're smart and spirited. (I don't, however, think I'm attracted to wealth. Most of my boyfriends were paupers, though I married a pilot with a pilot's salary. We'll have another conversation about creature comforts, but suffice it to say that if wealth were the lure, I've foreclosed some capital (bad pun) opportunities...)

Power, though, that's worth considering. And so is the wonderful tag metaphor. But you should know, Peter, that I only like the people who climb trees. And so do you.

I can see my emotional needs that Power would serve. I'm always seeking to define myself, my place. After winning a race, outright, #1 female, I push even harder the next day, thinking that there wasn't much competition, or that I just got lucky. I always look to today, tomorrow, and never rest on the laurels of yesterday.

Robert, of all people, used to say about me, "You have no sense of history." He's exactly right. So, in theory, if I perpetually tried to "conquer" someone of Power (is that like a person of color?), I'd be reassuring myself. I guess that's the essence of insecurity, and the essence of me, huh?

I think Robert is a safe haven from which I can play tag. But far, far more than that, he is my jail and I am angry that he doesn't know me, that we are incapable of sharing intimacy, that I live alone in marriage.

As for you, of course there will always be a kernel of dissatisfaction, of yearning for the next pair of adoring eyes. Your inquisitive and intense nature guarantees that. But I don't think it diminishes your capacity to also have the self-forgetting of all-encompassing love.

I guess that's what I keep trying to convey about the serial nature of relationships. I could believe in a temporary all-encompassing love! Something that begins with a spark, a quickening pulse, shared humor. Blossoms into full-blown passion, near-obsession. Spreads into a broader love, friendship, mutual respect, less intense but merely a redistribution of energy, not a dissipation. But what after that? When he and she grow apart, in different directions? New wants, new needs?

Debra, I don't know if you can fall in love, but I'm convinced that if you did, everything about you would go incandescent and everyone near you would bask in the glow, including your Hannah and Jacob. But you may not let it happen.

I accept your "correlative" argument about wealth and power. I don't think it's the money. I agree it's the dynamics of "smart and spirited" men.

But you're a hunter, you hunt as I hunt when racing, taking stock of weaknesses, then dominating opponents. You take stock of their libido, your mind sparkles with intelligence and education. And you are self-effacing, but so whip-smart it's easy for even those wary of ego inflation to find you alluring.

It doesn't take long for you to see what makes them tick, how they might be bent to your will. At that point, or soon after (probably right about when they think they have conquered you), actually you have won, your victory signaled by you leaving.

You're attracted to men of this sort because… winning over wealthy and powerful men is a drug for those cursed with the addiction or disease of the ego.

Remember our discussion about "balance of power?" Power is the game here, in the closest of close combat: of the heart. If you fall in love, you lose. Only by holding back do you win, but in holding back you can't fall in love, and you lose again.

You may have absolutely no awareness that this is the game. Or it might all be quite quite deliberate and if so, I am in very, very deep over my head.

Peter, you are so wrong this time. Perhaps you were fueled by the success of your earlier email. But while I entertained your theories, aired them, tried them on, and even found some degree of suitability, the hunter is but one of my many, disparate facets.

Many specifics bely your "case."

I'm inexpressibly flattered that you, of all people, think I am smart. Unfortunately (and there isn't an ounce of coy here) you're wrong. I know very little, and may actually have a memory problem that results in my forgetting what I have just learned. (Just the other day I was remembering the pleasure I had in reading a book of Churchill. But when I tried to recall specifics, I came up virtually blank. I read ?500-odd pages about the guy, savoring as I read, and would now be hard pressed to write a fifth-grade page-long essay.)

You confuse some degree of insight and mental agility with intelligence. You have each. I have a small degree of the first two and very little of the last.

So, that myth dispelled, let's move on to the stereotype of "Conquer 'em and Leave 'em" image. My history has been one of "long-term" relationships (meaning years, not months). If conquering was the end, why would I linger for so long afterward?

And you are wrong to reject that I would seek powerful men as a way of receiving reassurance and security, however fleetingly. What I was unsuccessful in conveying is how vital those are to me. You portray me as a woman of confidence.

And, once again, that is one facet of me. Definitely. But just one spin of the gem reveals the opposite, equally authentic facet: the perpetually insecure Debra.

Debra,we are not the best judge of our own selves because people like you and I can be overly harsh with the mirror in the name of "honesty."

The memory issue has several possible causes, none of which proves lesser intelligence. We could start with your sleep meds.

To say you seek out powerful men to conquer them is not to say you don't receive reassurance and security from the endeavor; only that you seek them out not for who they are in themselves. But it can be both.

I don't have the details of your long-term relationships, but imagine you have broken most them off. I doubt you have been "dumped" because you did not bring enough to the table.

I'm sorry to disabuse you of your fantasy of the calculating huntress. From your perspective it would be rather thrilling to "flirt" with the femme fatale of Port Cedar. And now you're merely entertaining a bored housewife. But while I do love the game, and exalt in the chase, the end is clearly the one we all seek at some level: love and acceptance.

Of course I want happily ever after. Duh. I WANT a lover, a partner, who brings a vibrant, rich, dynamic self to the relationship. I WANT someone who loves living THEIR life in their own way, sharing love and humor and emotion with me.

I want the intense physical intimacy that is powered by the emotional intimacy. I want someone whose mind is nimble so there will always be conversation, communication. I want permanence. I want our love to last forever. Just because I haven't found it, and wonder whether it is even possible for me (much less probable) doesn't mean I don't yearn for it with all my heart and soul... hang on, Hannah just came in...

...Something really weird just happened. Just as I was crafting this letter to you, the cats must have knocked down a box of old letters —love letters—from the upper shelf in my closet. Hannah brought a handful to me, explaining what happened. As I was putting them away one caught my eye.

It was from Mr. 1/2 affair, but had been written years ago. "I have tried to reach you by phone probably a dozen different times-but with no success. First to try to arrange to meet you for a day and then to find out when you wanted to get together in August. I took your letter at face value and wanted the dates so I could make time on my calendar. So I guess this was just another part of the 'game,' right? Just so you know, I'm not interested in playing anymore." The rest was just a nice letter, very civilized.

Interesting, no? So much for my vociferous denials. Maybe my perception is not as clear as others—often the case.

I sincerely hope you're as tired as I am and won't notice that I have written all sorts of contradictions. I should probably erase, or at least edit, but my instinct is recklessness at the moment.

Got to tuck Hannah in. Wondering how many love letters she managed to devour before bringing them to me...

In truth, Debra? I don't know which is truly more important to you: the chase that you love, or "love and acceptance." I do think that you can't both "win" and "find love."

We each crave intense intimacy. I fear loss of control, I fear my motives, my reactions, my weaknesses, especially now that I have shared them, and yours. You fear these same things, and, perhaps even more, creating your own disappointment.

I don't believe the crashing of love letters to your closet floor is coincidence.

Proses

I've been wondering whether my presence (such as it is) in your life right now might be a diversion with negative results. It helps ameliorate your loneliness, distracts you...

Although nothing would please me more than to soften the blow of a lost love affair, in this case I find myself not wanting to make it easy for you.

I don't want to talk over and over and over about my lost Love. Let's freshen our dialogue, and move to new topics. Is there anything else you'd like to ask?

C'mon, Peter, I've looked forward to hearing from you all day and this is the best you can do? I need a bouquet of words right now. Okay. Why did that box of love letters fall back into my life? Why did that one have to unfurl, temptingly before my eyes? I bent, picked it up and opened Pandora's box... I don't grieve for the particular men, I grieve for having lost love.

You want a bouquet of words? A spray of Violet Longings, with yellow centers of hope and forgiveness? Forget-Me-Not letters falling from the top shelf, among fern-frond fondness and a shockingly silly, colorful naked promise so easy to see and as easy to ignore? You'd like a box of long-stemmed proses?

A woman making love is at her most beautiful, her face not drawn by thought and concern, but features softened and made timeless by Passion. Sensuality expands this moment and erases all boundaries. The right man can see, if only for the minutes of her surrender, the Woman that lives in all lovely and intelligent women who are able to give themselves with vulnerability and admission, not to a man but to Her.

It was She who stole into your closet and tipped the box of love letters to the floor when you readmitted Her into your life with the lovely incantation: "Just because I haven't found it… doesn't mean I don't yearn for it with all my heart and soul." It was Love you summoned, and Who then tugged out the memory that would hold in bright contrast your contradictions and your confusion.

Your once-lover was not interested in playing the game any more, a game that frightens me to death, a game where you have so many advantages, including the charming belief that it's not the game you're playing.

He didn't walk away from you, he left the game. But men are so easy, he came back again, brought close by the promise that this time, no, this time, actually this time, you might be for real.

It was Love herself that smiled that letter to the floor and guided your daughter's hand to yours at the keyboard. At that moment you were acknowledging Love, but denying that you had held Her hostage. Because you need to hunt well so that you can receive assurance, then reassurance; because there's a void you want to fill; fear that you'll not find, fear that you don't deserve, fear, too, that this one, whichever one, was not The One; fear keeps you from letting go, so Love made the contrast known.

Pull aside the gauzy curtain from which you tease. Give Love the tokens She demands.

Mesmerized

Your gossamer words mesmerize. But instead of casting gentle life-giving light, they blind and sear as they permeate my suppression. I'm sorry to cower, Peter, but that, for the moment, is what I must do. Just for now, dandelions instead of long-stemmed proses?

So I'll retreat to the mundane.

I was at Hannah's play today. The group performed for a half-dozen schools from Port Cedar. I didn't actually get to see because I was stagehand for both shows, but from what I did manage to observe, and from the crowd's reactions, it was well-received. (Still tix on sale for Fri/Sat: I bet your kids would love it. I've taken my kids to several performances and they've all been enjoyable.)

Do parents ever get over being nervous for their children? Is there ever a time when one sighs, leans back and says with satisfaction "Ahhhhh, they're launched. Now they must make their own future."

Or am I fated to second- and third-guess every one of their minor decisions, as I do my own? NOW do you think I should try Prozac?

I accept your withdrawal. But may I say you asked for, in fact demanded, a higher intensity, the juice turned up, the volume set high? You demanded a bouquet of unruly and thorned flowers. Forgive me if one drew a drop of blood.

Peter, don't overreact. I'm not leaving, merely assessing the potential damage of serpent wounds, never mind the thorns. More later. But are you ever NOT intense?

There are many snakes. I knew last night when writing that there was a good chance you would flee. And you should. This place is not safe.

You ask for maximum intensity, I give it, then you ask if I am ever not intense? Whether I have a light side? That was a quick change of direction. Apparently I didn't zig as fast as I should have and recognize how badly you wanted to change the subject.

Now you're gettin' it.

But you're right about every point: I beg to see your intensity, and then whine that its overwhelming. Completely unfair. But I assure you it's more a function of my inability to articulate my... I'm too tired... my reluctance, my hesitance, my cowardice, my temporary withdrawal than a rejection, a shutdown.

And I was genuinely curious about your "lighter" side. In public you have a formal, gracious demeanor. You remind me of a southern gentleman. And I know of your intense, passionate side. But I haven't seen a goofy, frivolous Peter.

Sorry for the disjointed and incoherent phrases. I've been sleeping abysmally, so I'm heading in now to knock myself out with a supersize dose of Trazadone. Had a long... argument? fight? discussion? with Robert this evening. I don't know what to call it with him, since he's so passive he isn't even there.

Yeah, now I'm gettin' it.

Lets see, Goofy and Frivolous, I know they're around here someplace. I saw them just the other day, playing tag among the staplers and pencil jugs and telephones, right here on my desk. You can hear them giggle when they think they're being cute and coy, even though sometimes they're hard to see.

You ask for a bouquet of words, then complain the flowers are too bright and the thorns too sharp. I offered what magic I could, Love herself rustling up softly to a box of letters on the top shelf of your closet. And I believe it to be true, but now that I think about it, perhaps She was sending that message not to you, but to me.

I've finally met someone as high-maintenance as I am. Will you just take a deep breath and chill out for a minute?

I'm not jerking you around, Peter. Quite the contrary. I've struggled to find the courage to proceed with candor. Beyond that, I've searched my soul for painful answers to penetrating questions.

Where are we? Shall I persuade and cajole you or give you an easy out?

Why don't *you* tell me where *you* are? What do you expect from me? The twins, Goofy and Frivolous, have been a little scarce over the last year. They've not liked the damp climate and I don't blame 'em.

But I gave you the best I got. I honestly thought that offering to be someone who could know you emotionally would give you a safe place, not a frightening one. But when presented with the bouquet, you ran. Look, you tell me what level to work at here. To the extent of your willingness and my interest, I can talk about anything with anybody.

Oh, Peter, I read, and re-read and re-re-re read your serenade. I allowed its kiss to brush my cheek. And then I froze.

Do you realize what an intimidating person you are? Is it really so hard to understand why I begged for a respite from the intensity? I didn't mean to change the rules. I just wanted to catch my breath.

No, I don't know that I'm intimidating. This is where I live. But I do know not everyone is comfortable here. Which is why I don't often grant entrance. Do you see?

When you've caught your breath, I'll still be puttering among the long-stemmed proses, daffodils with teeth that must be cut back so they don't nip at the careless, lilies with soft silken skin like the cheek of a woman in love, with hues that change color when you smile.

You've given me dusty green buds of cedar to plant in special island loam, and I've yet to see if I can train my dandelions to shake their yellow manes and roar.

I have caught my breath. But I'm sure I will need to do so again, for nothing is tame, though all is well-tended. The flowers bloom lascivious and grow taller than I. The grass is dense: sometimes I trudge through a witch's field of poppies, other times I barefoot fly.

Yes, I can see why people only rarely gain entrance. Thank you for inviting me. One day I'll tell you of the koi in the pond in your garden.

I have a marathon this weekend in Seattle. I hope you enjoy yours.

Jasmine Tree

Remember when I wrote to you of chocolate and discovered your latent boundaries, your "Victorian prudishness," did you say at the time? Then, of course, there were the long-stemmed proses. Do we ever see another clearly enough to trust? Or must we always be on guard against being hurt, cautious about causing pain?

Do you see me clearly? You often see me as though I am transparent. Often you go beyond that, and see what I even fail to see myself.

Yes, I try to allow others this access. I've told you how I value the simplicity of "being myself." But, with that said, I'm instinctively a chameleon. I have a knack for assessing who it is a person wants to see, and (if I bother at all) that is what I show them. Yes, I KNOW this is contradictory. But I'm full of confusing (to me) contradictions; it's one reason I so desperately search for my "place."

However, although I often try to allow others to see me, few others see me with the clarity you do. Do I want this intimacy? It's very, very unnerving.

An observation: you have your life neatly divided into compartments: family, real estate, cars, lover(s), I imagine there's even a niche for me. My premise is that compartmentalization is what enables you to function so highly. Outside observers don't catch a hint of the emotional and psychological discord this artificial lack of overlap must create. True or False?

Stress over the last year has caused some breakdown of the compartments, which in turn adds to the stress, which causes further breakdown, etc. Keeps me busy building walls, so to speak.

I'm able to hide the discord from most. I choose not to with you. You have a niche, but spill uncontrolled all over the other boxes, as you might imagine. Perhaps that will make sense when you know me better.

I do know you better. Peter, you're a man who has been wrestled to the ground by one of the poppies from your garden. You're a man who longs to be in love. Your heroin, perhaps. But, for many reasons, you're making a mistake to attempt to conveniently create a substitute for the love that's slipping away.

And you're glamorizing me along the way. I'm very flattered, really, really flattered, but encourage you to question your motives. Regardless of whatever else, Peter, I'm quite determined you shall be my friend.

Debra, I don't think Im glamorizing you, but will agree that love is my opium. I'm addicted, I crave, I dance about on its warm burnished wood, then suffer the cold concrete of withdrawal.

It's very interesting to me, this very seductive desire "to be known" (and I don't know who is doing the seducing at this point). I don't know that you are as easily known as you claim.

I like being known by you, but it frightens. The hiding is nearly automatic after all these years, but no longer feels so good. Nor are you easily tricked by my feints.

Being known is being naked, anticipation that something significant and wonderful is about to happen, frightened that the other will find flaws we know about ourselves, or simply reject us because we don't measure up.

Putting down the defenses, not fearing self-created loneliness, a chance to breathe, to just be… one of my fears is never being known again. Afraid of being known, afraid of not being known. How Goofy is that?

No hiding behind Goofy. I know exactly what you mean about fear of never being known again.

Yikes. You do know me better. After decades creating smoke screens and hidey holes where I could dodge and duck into my garden if tagged, here you are.

Well, after decades of boldly asserting "there are no lines," you have me scurrying a bit, too. So you've reassured me and I've reassured you. Why are we both so NOT reassured???

Fear of rejection? Of disappointment? Or, perhaps even more frightening — fear of finding something that could disrupt the comfortable lies we've created for ourselves? Fear of falling, losing control to someone we only think we know? Fear of not thinking it through, or of thinking it to death?

"disrupt the comfortable lies we've created for ourselves?" First, was this a Freudian slip or did you mean to write "lies"?

Yes, I absolutely fear you will reject me. And there is a point in any relationship, friendship to love affair, where the blush fades from the rose. There is no way to duplicate the excitement of newness. The thrill of discovery. The thrill of fear of rejection.

When I was at Home Depot buying landscaping supplies, I treated myself to a little jasmine tree. I guess jasmine is really a bush or a shrub, but something as exotic-sounding as "jasmine" (say it slowly, and softly) shouldn't be demeaned by words so stout and ordinary.

Although its an outdoor plant, and would thrive on my deck (the intended location), I potted it and kept it in my bedroom. Its dizzying fragrance is omnipresent throughout the house.

When I walk in my room, I'm struck anew at the powerful and exotic bouquet. I pause and delight in the moment of pure being. Yet, even as I breathe, my sense of smell is becoming accustomed to the jasmine's perfume, which is becoming... ordinary. And soon enough, the pure white little spring blooms will fall from the stems, leaving a shrub, an ordinary shrub.

When romance and passion fade, lovers become partners, and we are left with ordinary. You and I both fear being ordinary.

But you do not forgo jasmine fragrance because it will fade, either through open window or as anticipation devolves into habit. Is "escape from the ordinary" what drives us from our comfortable lies, or does rational fear prevent one from leaping from one rock to the next over waters rushing below? Is it fear of the thundering approach of cliché? Will you abandon this before it arrives, because you don't believe it will last?

A dodge is not an abandonment. While I sometimes yield to the former, I don't plan to jump off the cliff of the latter.

Debra, at least jump off the wall, come inside the gate. Come play with me here in the garden.

What do you mean? That's a place within you, it's how you look at the world, how you see things. I love that you share it with me, but it's not a place where others can go.

It's more than a place within me. It's a way of seeing, a place to play, and as real as any other. Come play with me there.

Peter, I really don't understand what you're saying, or what you mean. You're not talking about leaving your wife or lovers for me, or asking me to leave Robert, or anything like that... you're talking about our email relationship...?

Yes. Here, where blades of grass whisper to the souls of your sandals, and trees chuckle when asking each other if they wood like to dance.

Even if I agreed, I don't know that I could. I don't know how to enter. But I do know I could not keep up with you.

Don't ask how. Leave that to me. All you have to say is that you want to, that you'll walk through the gate when it opens. I'll take care of the rest. Just say that you want to.

I do want to. And even though I don't believe there's a place to go, or that I could, or that those four words mean anything at all, just typing them sent a shiver of electricity right up my spine, from my poor deformed toes to the top of my head, shoulders to fingertips.

We evolved hiding from tigers. So we jump when the grass rustles, even when it's only the wind.

Yucatan

I hate this cold. I have Reynaud's Syndrome, my fingers are nearly blue. Take me to someplace warm. Puerto Vallarta would be nice.

Going to take Jacob to guitar, then to pick up Mom, then to the gym. I'll write this evening.

Tell you what, I'll get my passport out and we'll go to the OTHER side of Mexico and climb Mayan pyramids, snorkel the warm clear blue of the Caribbean, drift senotés, pet dolphins and eat taquitos.

Then we'll just deal with the consequences when we get home. They'll be fine. Won't even miss us. Though our matching sunburns might give us away.

I have been to Cancun, but have never seen the Mayan ruins. May I read the wooden words from a guidebook to you as you drive the rental car from town? As we draw near, the words will start to take form, and by the time we lay eyes on the ruins we'll see them in full bandwidth.

Yes, please read the wooden words from the guidebook as I drive, holding the book with one hand while you twine the hair above my cotton collar with the other, every once in a while leaning over to whisper how glad you are that we are here, on an adventure. We play a game: You read a paragraph and then we rephrase it, we rewrite the guidebook with sensual words of color and grace. We decide to one day carry a laptop and create our own guide.

Then you put the brakes on that idea, tell me you'd rather live the words and feel scritchy salt on your skin and taste it on mine than spend time thinking about computers, batteries and connection ports.

Whoa… I have, once again, gone over the top. I need to regroup. To bed with me now. I need to spread myself thin in the fog.

Damn, you give good email. "To bed with me now." Is that a Freudian order?

More formally known as the "Freudian Command." Often, in the old country, given without the "to" so it becomes more direct without losing its compelling character: "Bed with me now."

In the new country, "now" is often dropped, as well as the "to," and the phrase morphs into "bed with me," (in California spoken often as an interrogative, "...with me?") lending an informality, but some would say a lack of firmness, to the directive.

Peter, your real problem is that you're a thunder egg on the shore. So many beautiful beachcombers will pass you, walk over you, throw you nonchalantly into the waves. You must hope that one will stop, run her fingers over your craggy surface and feel the jewel within. You'll know.

Debra, over here. We can't see the sky from under the heavy canopy, and can't tell how far it extends. It could be hundreds of yards, it could be hundreds of miles in this jungle of the Maya.

We climb the pyramid and I'm taking a bit of the sweat of exertion off the line of your jaw with a kiss. Once above the flat ocean of foliage, I point to another island/pyramid in the distance, and another even farther. I spin a tale of a race that communicated with amber flashes of light bounced from gold and copper mirrors across the vast expanse, a race that made calendars more sophisticated than our own with months based upon the moon and the annual blessing of a two-week cessation of time itself, a goal I have of these weeks spent with you in the Yucatan.

Now I'm just trying to show off. Thanks for being there. Here.

Don't stop! I'm panting!

At night, at the base of the pyramid, the clearing is lit by torches. In the dark is a randomness and threat that powers life in ways we never acknowledge; the drumbeat of hearts, throb of bodies, thickets of wrist-thick vines, death and sex in the dance of existence, seen at the pyramid all in balance, death and sex, sun and moon, order and chaos, peace and war, ocean and beach, light and dark, you and I.

In the play between them, and especially in the dark, on the torch-lit alter, we come face to face with passion, with a moment, with a present that erases what went before and the illusion that we know what will follow.

You've produced the strangest sensation.

I'm here, in my house, homeschooling Jacob and receiving phone calls every ten minutes from Fed Ex about a mis-shipped package. I'm poised to drive quickly to Port Cedar.

And then I'm taken away, to a place where my heart only quickens in response to the sudden touch on my brown, sun-soaked body, skin tight with too much sun.

The evening of the next day we are at the beach. I have a glass of water sweetened with the rind of lemon and lime. We rake white sand between our toes as we sit in chairs between palapas and waves. It's an evening after a day spent in a warm clear world of blues and corals, where long thin barracuda swim and take fish from the hand of our guide.

We're exhausted but full of laughs about swimming down many feet beneath the waves, about the light-dappled white-sand ocean floor giving up to your hand the perfect shell, sharing laughs about how easy you found using the snorkel and the fins on your powerful legs, laughs about the rhythmic sexual slap of the boat upon the wave, laughs about the younger couple on board that seemed so much older and angry at life they were afraid to seize.

We sit and talk with drinks in hand and then, to make me pause, you run the tip of a nail up my arm from my wrist to the crook of my elbow, and eventually I stop. Time stops when you say, simply, thank you for this, this time that stretches out in all directions, from a beach on the Yucatan.

My senses are dulled; I'm slightly drunk from the sun, the heat and the decrease in tempo after the day in the water. I don't drink alcohol when I'm already depleted and dehydrated, but I treat myself to something, maybe fizzy water from a bottle with a twist of lime in MINE.

I nibble on the lime slice, then cajolingly ask for yours. You decline, but it's clear from your teasing eyes that the matter is open for negotiation.

It's late afternoon and the day is spent. A f t e r n o o n...the "f" casts a shadow over the languorous "o"s, and the "n" drifts drowsily toward evening. We have depleted the day, consumed its bounty.

You helped me off the boat. I was sunburned and slightly queasy. Nonetheless, I glowed with the day's exertions. You paid the boatman, and turned to find me already exploring the little dock, asking the old man the names of the warm-water fish that lie in his pail. You put your hands lightly around my shoulders, and I know it's time to go.

It's only a short walk back to the casita. Our hips bump as we walk much closer together than is sensible. We leave the road and turn onto a path leading toward the casita and the ocean, which fills the horizon.

We both stop to gaze at the just-before-sunset, as though responding to a silent command. I shyly, and almost gravely, thank you for the most wonderful day. You kiss the top of my head, and a moment later, on impulse, lay a lingering kiss on the side of my neck. I catch my breath, then breath slowly out, oh. oh.

From behind me you wrap your ownership arms in front...

Oooooph. I need to remember to breathe. We dance very close to the edge of a chasm broad and deep.

You're right. Our next trip will be to Siberia.

Banal and Mundane

To Siberia. Hours and days on a train, the week felt like a month since we'd left Prague, with enough rough bread and cheese, red wine for you, I was carrying gallons of water, provisions, we had enough books to get to Japan, where in about three months we were to catch a ship back to San Francisco.

They called it a sleeper, but we didn't. There was something in the rhythm of the tracks, the sway of the carriage. After a while we didn't resist being tossed gently into one another, we accepted and then enjoyed each other's presence, each other's mass, the catch of each other's strong momentum.

When you got cold you asked, uncertainly, if you could warm your feet with mine. I laughed and said I'd love that, and then captured your frozen toes between my warm thighs, and lay there on my side, trying to find the color of green or gold in your eyes, and drew a fine line from your ear to your collar bone.

Only you could make me long for the frigid, barren reaches of Siberia! This is torture. I'm reluctantly turning off the computer, and trying not to think of the train. I have to get some sleep. I'm off to Everett tomorrow to give away some kittens.

Hey, you sent us to Siberia. I was just providing the clickety clack for snickersnack. Write tomorrow, I hope. If not, Girlfriend, drive safely, hold your children close, allow your husband peace and dignity, and write me when you can.

blah blah blah I spent a night tossing and turning, wishing I could succumb to dreams of Siberia. And I awake to patter? Oh, my junkie, how can you do this to me? Send me off with mere pleasantries?

I have an appointment to "show" a kitten at 4. It would be nice to unload a couple.

I've turned all the attention to me, recently. Are you doing ok?

Yes, doing ok. But Love, we dance quite close in a room quite crowded. I simply tried to leave the floor, for a moment, to get a breath of air and a glass from a passing waiter. Don't delve too deep, okay? And the holidays are hard. It takes a lot of effort to carry the spirit of the season.

Me? Delve too deeply? How could you suggest such a thing? I understand your need for the glass of water from the passing waiter, but I still can't help hoping that it's spiked with a Mickey Finn.

OK, OK, I'll go to the gym today with Banal and Mundane. We'll shoot you an email: "haya doin'? were fine. Were going to Safeway to buy brussels sprouts."

Banal and Mundane are obviously brothers, strong, fairly good-looking, but ohmygod are they a little thick, great for an evening, a party, a roll if you are into that kind of thing, but good lord, a girl wants to be up and gone before the lunkheads wake, with their morning confusion and sounds and smells and heavy-footed trip to the bathroom.

Goofy and Frivolous tried, they really did, (they're female, here) to find the strong points. But the girls were just too quick, too light, they moved around Banal and Mundane as if the boys were inanimate statues cast of iron.

When together, Goofy would say something to Frivolous and they would giggle, then laugh. When Banal would ask what was the joke, they would howl, not able to explain that it was HIM.

The good thing about the boys, aside from being very attractive ("breeding stock" Frivolous said of them in a whisper) was that they were fairly good-humored. While they may not have had great horsepower, neither did they have that stingy smallness so common of those who dimly thought they were bright.

"It's not going to work. I'm bored.to.death. and just cannot pretend I'm not, anymore," Goofy told Frivolous one winter's afternoon that held the sun's orb low in a gauzy skien of cloud that sucked all warmth from the pale light before it reached ground.

She didn't know what she was looking for, but knew she wouldn't find it in the arms of either Banal or Mundane.

Oh, yes. You have Banal and Mundane perfectly. They are heavy-footed when they tromp to the bathroom, where they spend too much time tending to both bodily functions and gazing in the mirror while they shave.

Wasn't it just yesterday, they think, that I led Pleasant Valley High to victory with that unstoppable play?

But you have Goofy totally wrong. She'd never say that to Frivolous, unless she was just being, well, Goofy.

I loved this piece—thank youthankyou thank you.

I'll try to write later. I'm finishing homeschool and want to make it to the gym by 11.

Venice

We should have had coffee today. Or gone to the gym and given each other a spot. Or had a hot tub. Something significant.

Too close to a hug, m'dear.

Darling, after all the travels we've shared together (on your passport): the Yucatan, Siberia, remember we almost went to Venice, surely a little hug would be ok...

... Ah, Venice. We asked the gondolier not to sing, and asked if he knew of a house or a church to which we could gain entry, some place off the maps, off the tour, unvisited in a century except by waifs and rats, a place that held dark secrets of a Venice that will soon disappear.

He said he didn't know until a $20 bill brought his attention to the challenge. When the butterfly of currency flew from my hand to his, he spun the boat 90 degrees up a street so narrow we could reach out and touch the rough walls on either side.

"A few minutes," he said, in Italian.

For a portion of the day you had put an arm around my waist, or supported yourself in the boat with a hand on my thigh, keeping our hips in rhythm. Comfort, not a promise. Tonight we will share pasta in the small café we passed this morning. Maybe more.

The windows were gone from the urban villa we drifted to now. When we pulled up to the portico, a brand-new lock secured a bright new chain that was bolted to the dilapidated doors. The boatman muttered something under his breath, held out his hands, palm up, to demonstrate he was helpless, that he had done his best.

He didn't offer back the $20. I made a motion suggesting he should, he gave me a shrug as if to ask why I wouldn't compensate his effort. I was hot and tired and pissed but didn't pursue it.

You're cranky with me. Your blood sugar is low. You ate lightly for breakfast, and I led us on a forced march around the city. We were in the ghetto, said to be the oldest in Europe, you asking me laughingly whether this synagogue or that mezuzah on the door was making me feel my Jewish roots.

You laughed even more as I gave a tiny stamp of my foot, insisting that I had no Jewish roots. Oh, we have so little time and want to explore every nook and cranny, like two hungry lovers poring over previously forbidden regions.

We are silent as the vaporetto carries us along the canal. When you asked the boatman to take us someplace "special" in your non-Italian, I was embarrassed. His smile gave me a moment of concern, but I didn't know how to tell you without making it too obvious that I was sensing something wrong. You were disappointed, and maybe embarrassed, you were "taken."

I try to cheer you. Your eyes are so flat I'm hurt. I want my hugs and caresses, my animated words, to bring My You back, but know that only dinner holds the power to do that. I'm jealous of dinner. Now I become cranky, too.

Darkness has just fallen, but the stark silhouette of a dilapidated castle stands bravely against the faint remains of the sunset. I shiver. You pull me close, but that is only instinct, not intimacy. I pull away, very slightly, not enough to announce my peeve, but enough so that I know I am alone, we're not together.

It's a stinging slap when you pull away as I'm trying to make an overture. Yes, it's weak, but with weakness I'm trying to say I'm sorry. I'm tired and hungry and it's so frustrating not being awake, wasting not just this moment but these moments in the magical water-logged city, I want to be awake and alive and feel every lap of water against the foundation.

But my head hurts from a lack of water and coffee and food, a nap would work wonders. You pull away, and it feels like we're not together, now you want to be somewhere else, maybe with someone else who can restore magic to your day.

I want to hug and to hold you. I want to be held. I want to make you laugh. Instead I've been small and sarcastic, hurt and angry. I've not been someone you could trust.

Trust with the precious jewel of vulnerability, of ease, of hope, of wonder. Instead, I dropped these to the ground with a laugh at the wrong time, with an echo of petulance. I'm ashamed, and that diminishes me even more.

Hoping that a hug or a hold would tell you I'm sorry, I have not yet summoned the words. I try to let you know that I'm still here but you pull away, and a small candle is extinguished within me. What was together is now apart, flame cannot exist without wick and wax, now wick is short and wax congeals and flame vanished like a genie into a wisp of lingering, greasy smoke.

I begin to protect myself, become self-sufficient, push you away, soft but formal, solicitous but distanced, alone in a shell of misery. I'll not try to touch you again. Suicide in self-defense.

Why didn't I nestle into your embrace, vanquishing the doubts and mistrust that are rising between us as imposingly as that grave we admired in the Old Quarter today: a smooth, marble monolith, formally inscribed and impeccably tended.

If you would only try again, just this minute: hold me and sigh. I wait for the signal, that unobtrusive gesture, that minuscule reassurance, that you love me, but nothing is forthcoming.

You have replaced My You with a grotesque pantomime of yourself. I want to run, but am prisoner on the vaporetto which putters up the canal. Then I'm angry, because I'm trapped by this man who is not My You. Touch me, touch me, I plead silently.

But I draw even further away and will not touch you. Suicide in self-defense.

Distance is my friend, too. She wants distance? I shall show her distance, oh my god not again, I break the most precious moments of my life again, and again. I am small, not lovable, I prove it to her and to me, I cannot be trusted. She has abandoned me, all I need is a touch, a caress, a word, I need a word, I need to say a word, why can't I say I'm sorry, why won't my mouth open and the right words come out, why do I look at the water flowing past the prow, why can't I even look at her, what is it there I'm so afraid to see, is it scorn?

I am as silent as that marble monolith we saw in the Old Quarter today, smooth and blue-veined white and silent. Is it distance I'm afraid to see in her eyes? I'm afraid to see pity. I'm afraid to see reproach. NO! I'm afraid to see revulsion, disdain. I'm afraid to see in her eyes a reflection of how I see myself!

I'm afraid to see there in her eyes my own view of who I am, I'm afraid of the mirror. I stare into brown water, and I notice the garbage in the water now. I stare into the water because I'm afraid of her, because I'm afraid of rejection, not of her rejection but of all the times I have been rejected, not by her but by past loss, it is not today, it is loss from the past that I feel, I bring all that forward and lay it on her and make her responsible for things that happened years before she knew I was alive.

The boatman is silent, he knows something has broken. Why can't I turn to her and say I'm sorry!? Why can't I open my arms and tell her I need her to just tell me she is glad she is here? Why can't I tell her that I hurt? If I could open my mouth, I know she would make the nightmare end.

I don't say a word, I won't say a word. If she wants silence, I can give her silence. I can be as distant as she, I can put myself beyond contact, beyond words, beyond her touch. I can be somewhere else and yet give her no specific to throw at me. I won't look at her but at the water, at slimed green walls sliding by.

Suicide in self-defense.

We're sinking, you and I and this city of water and light, water and darkness. Venice yields herself infinitesimally slowly to the sea, and we yield ourselves readily to self-protection.

Consumed with hate, I plan my renaissance. I'll leave you tomorrow morning, leave you in Venice. I'll go to Barcelona. I hate your naps: you are old and feeble and I'm young and strong. I hate your low-carb diet: I shall eat bread and pasta and panettoni.

Touch me, hold me, pour reassurance down my throat, my head is tilted back, my eyes are closed, my lips are parted and waiting for your sweet reassurance. If you love me, really love me, you won't let me hate you.

Why have you betrayed my devotion? Why have you barred your heart and jailed me outside? I'm hateful and spiteful and don't deserve to be given another chance. I don't want another chance, please touch me, please say something and invite me back.

Off the boat we walk, a third could walk between us, I don't know if a third has arrived, such a short distance so wide, we walk back to the hotel where we were to change for dinner. Silence, the whole city is silent, we share nothing. I can't stand it. I can't stand this, it's her fault my fault no fault I don't know this.

From a side street, not much more than an alley, runs a boy. He has a handful of tired roses. I reach into my pocket for change, but the look you give me causes me to half-smile and half-grimace and I look at him and shake my head.

He looks at you, and then me, with no small bit of scorn. Not that we won't spend the money, but that we're here and have so much and are so sad. He's but a boy and would not understand.

Then, something odd happens. In the distance I hear a horn, just a car horn. Somewhere behind me, a flock of pigeons takes wing. I hear the thrumming of their flight. The air becomes liquid, I feel myself breathe, the air enters my lungs, then leaves. I don't think about breathing, it happens without my effort, I watch it for a few heartbeats.

All that anger, all that guilt, all that shame, still there but now they belong to somebody else. I listen. There is still a small slap of wave, the creak of rope.

I stand beside my fear and it is not me any longer.

The boy hasn't left and I reach into my pocket and hand him an absurd wad of Lira. I see you look up and away, rolling your eyes, then back at me with disdain at this cliché.

The boy starts to hand me the entire bunch of flowers, but I shake my head and pull two small petals from one, leaving the rest of the blossom behind.

"Terminato," I tell him, "Finito," when he protests. I speak no Italian, and I wave his confused presence away. You look at me, wondering. But at least now you are curious, finally the judgment has left your eyes, you are engaged, you are here, not somewhere else, not hiding within.

I take a petal and I stand before you. For a moment I just look into your eyes. Then, as gently as I can, with the smallest floral touch imaginable, I draw it under your eye, along your cheek, to your throat. You raise your chin and close your eyes to feel the softness of a single petal from a cut blossom.

"I was an ass. Please forgive me," I say, as I take the floral tissue and place it to my lips, taking a bit of your salt from the heat, from the day, perhaps from a tear, from you to me.

I need you to know that I have returned. I just stand there, wondering what you will say, if you will reach for me, or hide behind sarcasm, or flee. We stand in the street, facing one another. What will you do?

All I can do is smile at you, because you now know how I feel, and you own completely the next few moments, the next few days, perhaps the next few years, and you know I know that, too.

Oh, Peter.

I don't know if that's a good or a bad "Oh, Peter."

It's perfect. Absolutely perfect.

That moment when you are distracted by the thrumming of the pigeons wings and are able to detach: I didn't breath as I read it. And the Rose Petal Maneuver: Sheer beauty and soul.

But I have to admit, what most affected me (are all people this self centered? Do we all respond most to things that speak directly to us?) was your complete understanding of Me. The look of scorn and disdain with which I try to wither you when I think you are daring to "use" a cliché upon me. The eye roll, outer and inner.

And then your recapture of me, first my engagement, then my lowering of that formidable drawbridge.

The tragedy is reflected in my August anniversary with Robert. I didn't mark the occasion in any way. My memories of the particular day on which we wed are painful, and hold very little joy. But Robert got me a chocolate cake, with chocolate frosting.

Oh, Peter, you know it isn't about getting something. All I could think about was that I have shared my life with him for all these years, and he doesn't even know that chocolate cake with chocolate frosting is near the bottom of my list. I can't remember when he's seen me eat a chocolate cake. I felt so alienated, so alone. Sharing my life with a stranger.

And you, with whom I've shared only words, you know me deep and true.

Goodnight.

Uglies

Do you know:

I have deformed feet. I eat salad with my fingers (or chopsticks). When I'm home, I wear stretch pants with long underwear underneath and my hair in a very unattractive tight bun on the top of my head.

I can look good in a $3,000 Canali suit and then forget to wear socks that match, or will have a pen burst in the pocket of my white shirt (twice).

I'll say things that I think are funny in a group setting that horrify innocent bystanders. I forget names. A lot. Of people I really should remember.

My children are better souls than I ever was or ever will be. I'm too proud, and too small in spirit, too often. I've made some great friendships with some truly great and significant people you've never heard of, and a few that you have.

I have two large moles on my back from tanning as a young man. I love olive oil on everything. I'm full of insecurities, some of which you are coming to know.

I'm a recovering alcoholic who has not had a drink in 20 years, and is thankful for the disease because it taught me much about humility and God and who I am, and about who I am not but feared that I was.

I'd probably look ok in a $500 outfit, but I've never worn one. In fact, now I'm hard pressed to put anything together that doesn't involve jeans.

I shower only after every two days, even after I've run ten miles in the heat; Americans shower too much. I let my hair dry by itself so its always frizzy.

Not only do I not remember names (anybody's), I never learn them even after introduction, b/c I'm so nervous about the whole hand-shaking, fake-smile, pleased-to-meet-you routine.

I'm an absolute perfectionist who can't meet her own standards, yet I'm lazy as all get out. I get what I want but make sure to want only what I can get.

I want garlic in everything but my coffee. I scorn guys like you who watch their diets; I eat man-sized portions of anything I want, bring it on. I'm terrified of making love for the first time and just want to get it over with.

When at home, I wear floppy sweat pants, a torn gray sweatshirt, and brown leather moccasins.

There are times when my hair goes everywhere. I make rude body noises to make my kids laugh. "Niiiice," they say. I used to have beautiful feet, but they have lived in shoes too long.

I get grumpy and reclusive but can be brought out of my shell with lamb chops and a loving touch to the cheek.

I mostly have blind spots, but have spring showers of a narrow little brilliance. I'm moody and reclusive, but can be brought out of my shell with tenderness and humor.

I haven't eaten red meat in decades, and I don't know if I could stand the scent of it cooking. I don't care much for TV except sci-fi shows, and I wish we got local channels b/c I'd watch MacNeill/Lehrer, which isn't anymore.

I love movies that I love, but won't watch anything that has the remotest possibility of jerking a tear, no animal movies period.

I could lose consciousness when my neck is kissed, or my ear. I won't tolerate rude body noises. I hate caring what people think. I'm generous with money. I've never saved much but I've never had a debt besides the mortgage; I pay my only credit card bill each month, on time.

I pretend that I love being old and kicking young women's butts in races, but really I'd rather be young and lose. I pretend that I love kicking butt on my ancient mountain bike with no suspension, but really I wish I could afford a decent bike. I pretend and I pretend, and wish I had the courage not to.

I don't care much for TV, except the nightly news and good movies on DVD. I'm not a sports fan. I'm gentle except when I am fierce, and when I'm fierce, I'm very scary except for those who love me.

I raised myself, and it shows. I'm in some ways brilliant but God has balanced that with blind-spots just as dark. I feel at times like I'm playing Indian Poker in life, and everyone can see the card on my forehead but me.

I take very good care of those around me and can be inhumanely callous to others on the outside. I'm a better man now than at any time in my life, and my children and an affair are partly responsible for that.

I'm bossy, and full of my own ideas, but am just as happy (if not more) to follow the whimsies of my partner. That's part of my current problem: my partner is whimsy-less. Whimsy-free. Without whimsy. Sounds like something Donald Duck would say.

Whimsy-challenged? Whimsy-weak? Whimsy-wanting? You thought it was a trip to the store in Port Cedar, but then I turn left instead of right and we end up on the ferry and having lunch in Friday Harbor.

Swing dancing, learning to cook Thai food; what was the third class we were supposed to take in college?

Not Thai: Szechuan. The third was massage. One of those Saturday-afternoon classes, byo partner. We'd sit on a gym floor on my (barely used) yoga mat, taking turns, solemnly following the directions of the teacher, trying not to giggle. Stop tickling me! Take this seriously, you're going to be tested when we get home. If you keep this up, I'm not going to let you try the oil I purchased just for the occasion. What kind? Hard to describe, and you wouldn't recognize the name, but it smells of ocean breeze and cinnamon fingers.

In massage class, I would tell you that if you touch me there, like that again, with a hand full of massage oil, even in a gym full of people I'm going to roll over and pull you down on top of me and give you the longest most sensual kiss I can muster.

Damn! Detention! Sent to the Principal's office! Again!

Alienation has nothing to do with age. It never did. It has to do with love and respect and joy and who we are as people.

This is a really bad game. Your idea, right?

Why? Why is it bad when it feels so satisfying?

Because it is getting naked in front of you, and I like it, and that just scares the hell out of me.

Keep going until you don't have a stitch on. I'm going to make dinner while I'm very, very distracted.

For years I thought to be strong meant to be tough. I didn't know the difference between being strong and being brittle.

I'll wear socks with holes in them until I realize how ridiculous that is. I don't like cleaning up cat shit and will put the job onto someone else if I can get away with it. I care more about order than dust, a certain amount of clutter is okay but I don't like filth I can smell.

I love sci-fi, but absolutely cannot watch a movie where a woman is being abused, struck, or damaged by a man. I have walked out of the theater. It is not something I can tolerate. I want to turn the tables on the attacker, damage him as he damages her.

I'm tired of sleeping on the couch, but that is the bed I have made for myself. I love giving and receiving oral sex, maybe giving even more.

My father was one of the most abrasive people anyone who knew him had ever met. And a drunk who abused me and my mother. Water under the bridge.

Physically, I'm somewhat fastidious. I shower nearly every day, and I usually shower before sex. I like coming to bed with with a clean body because it allows me to truly let go.

I eat almonds and macadamia nuts and tonight again had pistachios for dinner.

I have yelled at my children in ways I shouldn't have. I have been impatient when they won't grasp a simple mathematical concept. But I thank God I do not appear to have done permanent damage with my abruptness. Let's credit their mother.

I do not like weakness and indecisiveness in men or women but engender it at the same time in a bad game of gotcha.

Oooooohhhhh, no secrets, this is really really scary, now.

I fall in love with strong women, smart women. I seek a partner not a victim, in all senses, though I do and have rescued. It's hard for me, very hard, to break a connection once established.

I eat meat. I cook meat. I scorch red meat until it is charred then cover it with olive oil. I love pork ribs more than halibut, a salad with crumbled bleu cheese.

In the last two years, I've learned to enjoy moderation in nearly everything. But I make coffee too strong, read the paper every single morning, wake slowly and trundle into the day.

I know all those showers were bad enough, but the Fritos are sure to be a deal-breaker: I can eat a 20 oz bag until my lips bleed from the salt.

I never eat chips, especially Fritos, b/c I know I would never stop. I lick the salt from the rim of a Margarita glass, then pass the Cuervo Gold and ice to someone else.

My body tastes of salt on those days I don't shower, when I defile crisp cotton sheets with dried sweat and sentence my lover to bloating the next day. I'm outraged when I see a man mistreat a woman, but would love to spend a dreary Wednesday afternoon with my lover pinning me down, forceful and j u s t the t i n i e s t bit r o u g h.

There's no point in living in a beautiful home in a beautiful place if it's a mess. I love the clear, clean lines and simple, quiet monochrome of the desert; it calms me. I love feeling infinitesimally small and humble in the shadow of the mountains.

He holds your wrists and is strong and broad of shoulder, but what binds you is that he is looking into your eyes. You see his crevasse blue eyes looking deep into yours and probing for connection, gauging you, trying to find the smallest movement that will make you gasp. Filling you with his eyes, he holds you so that any way you move brings him closer, deeper, his eyes into yours. You wonder if he will release before you.

To have a lover know that she is in control, now on top she wants to guide and use him for her pleasure. She is going to be first because that is the game they play, he is patient, he will wait, his satisfaction depends on hers.

Salt is the key to Fritos. Whole corn and corn oil and salt. Bacon, fried in an iron skillet, crisp and brown. Chocolate less than carrot cake, what is it in cream cheese frosting, that fat glob of tart creamy sweet on the fork barely holding a few orange crumbs to justify the bite?

Loss has always been a huge fear for me. Abandonment from childhood still flows through my caregiving and my jealousies. Oh God, the jealousy, the anger that it can stir up, the withdrawal. I will not let you her reach me because you she hurt me years before I even met you her.

I react as a child then apologize, then withdraw. I'm a better man today, because I give more and demand less, but I know that the demon lurks, the wolf is always pacing.

This is so weird on so many levels, whatever the hell THIS is, “the run-away-closer game,” the “I bet I can pick bigger scabs than you can” game, the “I don’t want to be seen so I will show all” game. My God.

But I’m not running away and I do want to be seen. I want to see you.

You are welcome to walk with me here. Find me as life allows, I’ll open the gate and show off your potted jasmine tree, sprouts of juniper/sage, flowers with scent and others with stink, my thorned proses and Passions that are always fighting Love-me-nots for water.

There’s a new bunch in the middle that have yet no name, and are so blindingly white in the sun, I can’t tell their shape. They murmur among themselves, they’re learning to sing. You owe me a description of the koi, drifting with slow purpose among hanging fronds, in the lily-dappled pond.

There’s only one gate and I can’t leave it open.

But find me, there. We can stand outside the walls too, and talk of schools and politics and the Shoulds of life. We can do that as the sun sets, and for as long as we have time.

Yikes, this is scary. I was trying to talk you out of me. Instead, you’ve talked me into you. How the hell did that just happen?

Yikes, indeed: Foreplay? Confession? Psychotherapy? Suicide?

This? This is the tip of the iceberg.

Winter

Archeology

I rented a storage locker in Port Cedar and am moving bits and pieces now to make the big move easier on everyone when Molly and I tell Sam and Abby about the separation. We are supposed to have THE TALK in a few days.

"Man overboard syndrome," as family, my former life, sail away.

Separation? I thought you were going right to divorce? This has got to be so difficult for you, for many reasons.

We call it separation to make it easier. Denial as survival mechanism.

Molly suggested mediated divorce. It was time, past time, she said; we had been "separated" while living in the same house for too many years; mediation would give us an opportunity to find common ground.

Pulling bags of clothes and drawers of toiletries and personal effects out of a marriage of 20 years is an elbow in the gut that stuns my breathing.

Molly noted that now I have three boxes of "drawer junk." This from the end-of-the-day-habit of dumping the contents of my pockets into a drawer: first in my Bohemian Seattle apartment, then the "Hill House," and now the "Log House," hereafter known as "Molly's House."

Each time we moved, I would dump the drawer into a shoe box, rarely to be opened again except on melancholy Saturday afternoons when I was supposed to be cleaning the garage.

REI receipts from the 1980s. An Indian Rupee from the 1990s. Morphine substitute for kidney stones in 2004.

As I look at this detritus, I feel both weightless and lost. Why can't this trash just be thrown away? It's not my life, it's not me. But the attachment is stronger than simple possession. Without these things, what record is there? Fading memories are footsteps in sand.

"It's the archeology of my life," I told Molly.

I'm worried about you. Did you and Molly have THE TALK?

Molly and I took a drive around the island to discuss how we would tell the children. I suggested over dinner: that's where we do family business. She agreed.

We decided to keep living as we do after we tell the kids, to make the transition seem natural, then actually split over spring break. She will take Sam and Abby to her mother's and I will move the rest of my things out.

She and I talked about where the marriage failed. I made her laugh with the story about being followed down the freeway.

"It's so bizarre to laugh, but it's what we have, I suppose," Molly said.

After dinner I started in a sure, calm voice: "Mom and I are fighting and not getting along. Not in any way your fault. You may call me any time. I'll still be picking you up from school, helping with homework. All rules apply."

They didn't show sorrow. At first my feelings were hurt, then I realized: This is exactly what I wanted, that they would have a sense of normalcy, they trust that this is something that is okay. They did the dishes and I watched the news. Like usual. We sat on the couch and watched Saltimbanco for an hour. They were more quiet than usual, then went to their rooms, as usual, to do homework. I slept, as usual, on the couch.

Good morning. I'm imagining you feel light, the slightly giddy, almost queasy light you feel when you've made a big move and you're riding the adrenaline wave all the way into shore.

You've made major decisions in the last few months, and are living with the consequences instead of trying to re-shape the outcomes in your favor, delaying the inevitable, playing God and needing control. You should be incredibly proud.

I know exactly what you were attempting to convey about weaning yourself away from your former established patterns in a way that isn't threatening to the kids.

Any lightness is weighed down by doubt… that my kids will make it through high school unscathed because I'm not there in the house. Last night at dinner, the twins were talking about two boys kicked off the baseball team for skipping school, and then on to Billy Morris, busted for pot.

Sam said, "I don't want to be that kind of teenager. I don't get why it's supposed to be cool." I was proud he was willing to make an ethical declaration, and scared that I'm giving up influence.

But they trust me, they trust their environment. A wonderful conundrum: How did I give them something I never had?

Because you do have it. You didn't have the experience of it, but you have it because you had the capacity for it, the recognition of it, the desire for it. You are more than the sum of your experiences.

I'm not surprised your kids took it in stride. You have described them (and all objective evidence supports) as solid, well- adjusted kids. Over the years you and Molly have shown your love, respect and devotion to them in countless ways. They're not going to discount any of that b/c you're making a change in the pattern. They don't doubt that your love for them and attachment to them will continue unwavering.

I'm really happy for you.

Trust or faith? I've given it to my children, though I never received it. Because it was never given, I tried to take control of it. I'm more honest with more people now than at any time in my life. I wish I'd come to it sooner, and with less damage.

Had a lovely afternoon with Jacob. We drove into town, listening to The Eagles, both crooning along and munching turkey jerky. Picked up Hannah at her friend's mansion overlooking the harbor — perfect backdrop from the hot tub, indoor pool and outdoor pool. Took the kids to Martha's — their favorite.

Robert comes home tonight and, to his credit, will take the kids hiking tomorrow before he leaves early Monday. This time he won't return for a week and a half. Yay!

Hannah has piano at 9:30, then we'll pick up a friend of Jacob's at his mom's on the other side of the island (interesting: several of Jacob's friend's parents have gotten divorced recently). I'll be home all day. I need to move all the furniture out of the upstairs playroom and rip out the carpet, choose a flooring and install it.

No, maybe I'll paint the walls today while the old carpet is still down. That means two trips to the dreaded hardware store (dreaded for them; I like it). (I love the smell of lumber, too. And adore seeing houses being built, esp. the framing stage.)

Singing with children, a wonderful gift. I'm going to take the kids bowling this afternoon. I'm sorry about whatever it is I'm hearing in your voice. The reserve. I hope it's not there to fend off my non-existent expectations.

The reserve: no, quite the contrary. And you can stop reassuring me that you have no expectations b/c those reassurances serve more to undermine my confidence in your affections than they do to reassure.

But we don't have to talk about all that today, on this day after The Day, when you have quite enough on your plate.

Banker

You have been far too quiet, for far too long, and I'm worried about you.

The Waterfront Lofts project collapsed. It's going to do me some real damage.

Oh Peter, I'm so sorry! What happened?

The bank learned the engineering was done by a subsidiary of my partner's development company. The bank wanted another geology report. Then they demanded another engineering report for independent verification of what would be required to reinforce the building.

Any changes were going to be too expensive, and the economy right now has reduced the return on the project considerably. Especially at the price we're under contract for. My "partners" pulled the plug. It's done.

Ryder worked for them, didn't she? Or their law firm? Do you think she had anything to do with this? Why will you be damaged? If you are damaged, don't your partners get damaged, too?

I don't think Ryder had anything to do with it, though I can't be sure. It doesn't matter. It is what it is.

I'm damaged because I stretched as far as I could just to pay my share of current expenses, and the purchase contract had a very high penalty if the deal didn't go through.

My partners will be stung but not damaged. One, they received some of the cash we put into expenses for the engineering. Secondly, the pull-out option was always there and moots the quality of the engineering, even if there are disputes as to the results. It would be a hideously expensive legal battle. Finally, my "partners" can walk away from their loss. It cripples me.

What will you do?

I don't really know yet. I have a few other assets. There may be enough equity lying around to go a little deeper in debt.

We should be sitting on the couch going over your options. I'm going to tuck in the kids.

I've been doing nothing but "going over the options" for a week. They are few. I made some bad choices; these are the consequences. If we were on the couch, I would rather tell you about the semantics of free will until you looked up at me and said: "blah, blah blah."

No, I wouldn't. That's the problem. I'd be forever pouring you into me, absorbing your knowledge. Yes, I'd give you the "blah, blah blahs" when you got just a little too full of yourself and we needed to get down to a much sillier level, but I could listen to you forever. And what do I have to give in return? There's an essential lack of reciprocity... an inequality, if you will.

Debra, just don't. Let's go back to the Yucatan. Your kids, my kids. But excuse me, I just got hung up on pouring me into you, and am a little distracted.

Ah, well, there is that. OK, sorry, I'm pensive, don't know why.

Well, me too. Though probably for different reasons. I'm going to try to negotiate a quick sale tomorrow of one of my buildings. I still may be able to take some financial pressure off, if the buyers are truly interested. I wonder how this situation with the bank is going to impact the divorce.

Receding

Good morning. Finally got the Christmas lights down yesterday and the tree to recycling. How was your holiday?

Christmas lights? How could you needlessly burn all that electricity? Christmas tree? You plunder the earth. We did Christmas, including the fight over thank-you calls. I need to see if I can return the robe Robert got for me before New Years.

I disagree about "needlessly" burning electricity for Christmas lights. "Joy" is adequate reason to burn electricity; or would you reserve each kilowatt for serious "purpose?"

The tree was grown for the purpose and sucked up its share of carbon dioxide before sacrificing itself. Might as well lament the harvest of corn.

Or is it just Christmas you don't like, Ms. Grinch?

I was teasing about the Christmas stuff. I don't give a rip about farm-raised trees, or the lights, for that matter. Much.

I am off to Everett and check on a tenant improvement project. How have you been?

I'm hanging out, tidying and cooking shrimp to serve cold with a bunch of Mexican sauces and salsas and stuff; Bob and Barbara Conner are coming over later.

Fair enough. You are receding—please don't disappear. Have a good time with Bob and Barbara. I wish I was helping you prepare dinner for them. Write when you can.

I am receding. But I won't disappear. Inexplicably, I woke feeling weak in every way: emotionally, physically. I'm drained. I'm always able to rise to occasions, but a few days later I crash. You should have seen me a few days after a trial. So sorry to lean when I should have been there to bolster.

How fun it would be to have a partner. You'd ask "Have any ideas for what to serve Frivolous (he's a guy, I tell you) and his new girlfriend?" I'd think for a moment, then we'd both blurt a variant of "Chicken stuffed with wild rice from the Mt. Stevens Lodge!" and laugh.

I'd immediately start rifling through the junk drawer, looking for the recipe. Five minutes later, leaving me distraught with a pile of papers and birthday candles and coins and string on the counter, you'd quietly go email the lodge, appearing moments later with your bounty.

I'd fling my arms around your neck in gratitude. I wouldn't be alone in the endeavor. Even if I was the one in the grocery store, even if I was at the stove sautéing the chicken or vacuuming the stairs, I would feel like it was our venture. That's what I miss.

Tell you what: You set the table and get the kids to clean up, tell me what you want to serve, and let me cook. I love the busyness, it lets me be at ease with people. I like folks in the kitchen, but hate not having something to do with my hands. When I serve, you can tell people of my 10 years as a waiter in Seattle at ALL the best restaurants.

Multi-tasker though I am, I can't do anything while I'm talking. Social contact, for me, isn't done lightly. It takes all my energy and concentration. I'd be grateful to have someone in the kitchen heating the veggies I've sliced and the chicken I've marinated, chipping into the conversation here and there.

But the thing I miss more than anything is the post-guest rundown. I'll never forget the first time Robert and I were together socially. We shared good food and conversation with friends. But later that night when I tried to discuss any of it, Robert didn't say a word. In fact, he seemed puzzled. I was so confused. I should have known right then that Robert was not the man for me.

"What did you think of the new girlfriend?" I asked.

"Not my type, but Frivolous seems to love her very much."

"Well, next time I'll be on better behavior. I should not have brought out the coloring books. I knew I was being rude at the time. Did you like the sautéed spinach salad?"

"It made my tongue burn for three hours," you reply.

"Yes, but there are even some advantages to that," I smile, and earn a dig in the ribs.

"Next time I need to crisp the chicken, or should I try a proper Kiev?"

First of all, I can think of only one way you could make my tongue burn, and it has nothing to do with food. I love spice, and heat. Yes, literally and figuratively!

Secondly, I'm afraid if you were to ask me about crisping chicken, you'd receive only a blank look. There are some things for which I can't muster much interest. Reminds me of another reason I've been unsettled lately: I'm ready to start "training" and it's too early and I can't decide what I should do this season.

Last night at dinner, Bob (Barbara's husband...very smart... have you met him?) encouraged me to focus on something and be good, instead of my usual do everything b/c it's there approach. My instincts run toward the dilettante: do everything half-assed and enjoy it.

Hannah's birthday. I'm upstairs making her a cookie (with a candle and the birthday song, of course) for breakfast. I made her have yogurt and a glass of milk first, so don't call the child protection agency. I'll write after I've spoiled her for a bit.

Debra, I think you owe it to yourself to run and win your class in a significant marathon after training like the top professionals do, all the way to an adequate taper, etc, etc. Pick a race, set a goal, achieve it.

I toyed with the idea of an Ironman, but I just don't find joy in swimming. If the joy isn't there, I feel like a hamster running on a wheel. You know what it comes down to? I'm not, at heart, a competitor the way you are. The most fun for me is the doing, the training, the work, then the result.

I love running, I love cycling, I love climbing. I do those without any goal at all. Adding a goal here and there provides a new element of challenge, a game to spice things up (and we've already established my love of spice).

But running a fast marathon... who cares? I'd have to spend more time at the track. I'd have to push faster on the longer training runs, so instead of reveling in the stunning beauty of Johnson Ridge's dips and rises, maple and madrona. I'd have to stare intently at the ground, taking care not to trip on the uneven surface.

And for what? Another plastic medal? A personal best 15 minutes faster than before? Perhaps it's symbolic of my greater "problem": I really don't care if I'm good at anything, as long as I'm living, loving. You should train with me!

Bye. Going to gym for short run, long tub.

You know, telling me I need to train with you, talking of long hot tubs is nearly cruel. Yes, I would have loved to have been part of last night's conversation with YOUR friends, They would not just be YOUR friends had I made them dinner.

I know they would have been "our" friends, that's just the point. When we eventually have that coffee, I'll tell you about the realization I made along these lines. I long thought that the difference in age between Robert and me accounted for much of our alienation, and now I no longer think so.

Children

Question: I know my children would be happy in Madrona Village near their friends after I move out, but I would prefer something a little less tract-like. Do I just suck it up? Or find an old boat to fix up and stay at the marina?

Hmmm....you need to be comfortable, wherever it is. That doesn't mean it has to be luxurious, but I'd nix the boat idea in a heartbeat (besides, you'd have an awfully hard time luring me there for coffee).

If you don't find anyplace that you affirmatively want, someplace that feels right, then you might as well settle for Madrona Village. The kids need to be comfortable, too, and the more enjoyable it is to stay with you, the better. Though Madrona Village is awfully "public," and you're awfully private. I can't imagine a marina wouldn't be more so,.

Have you asked your kids? Is it hard, talking to the twins about these topics? Have they been asking questions? MINE have. About you. Details later, it's ok.

YOURS have? Can't wait to hear. No, conversation is very natural with the twins.

Nothing has to be done immediately about a place to live, but soon. I think I can wait for the right place. I like the idea of Abby and Sam wanting to be there, even if it's to be near their friends.

Jacob told me he had a "confession." Last night when I got up to go to the bathroom, I left my computer unattended. He came looking for me and saw part of an email left open. He said he didn't read it, only saw it was from you. I said we were friends, that you're a little unhappy right now, but that you're a private person and I wasn't free to go into details. I reminded him that I have a lot of male friends, and that you were one.

He immediately said "Does it have something to do with his wife?" I wanted to faint but instead said levelly, "Honey, it's complicated and I don't know all the details. I just know he's a bit down and needed a friend."

I hope that was OK. He would never repeat anything to anyone, he's just not that kind of kid.

The kicker, though, was that then he said "I don't care, but whatever you do, don't tell Hannah." I asked why, and he didn't respond. I said "Hannah doesn't think he's my boyfriend, does she?" and he didn't answer. I am utterly floored. Aside from seeing your name prominently displayed on my email screen, I don't know what she could be picking up on. Busted by my 12 yr. old, who is going on 20. She really is extraordinarily savvy to human nature.

And I am really sorry to have jeopardized your privacy.

Well, that is a bit of a drag.

Not so much because of my situation, Debra, but because of yours: you and Robert. It could be terribly destructive for your children to think that mommy has a "boyfriend."

It would also be very easy for this to hit the circuit of 12-year-olds or 13-year-olds and I want my own kids to be out front on this.

That Jacob said "don't tell Hannah" means that he has a variety of opinions on who or what I am. That he did not answer your question about my being a boyfriend means he didn't believe your denial, but did not want to call you a liar.

So, be careful for you and your family, and for what is left of mine. Don't apologize, though. That you and I get busted for having email is ironic beyond belief. Need to think about getting dinner going.

Tell me that your poor kids don't have to eat pistachios for dinner.

My kids decided they wanted hamburgers when we were in Baily's Market, so I had them pick out all the fixings, we talked about $4.99 / lb. versus $2.99 / lb., and dammit, I forgot the paper bag part of the discussion. I will next time, for sure.

We came home and had snacks, and they worked on English papers. They made dinner. Now they're cleaning the kitchen, laughing about back cracks (the sound, not plumber's), and bringing me their math when they have a question.

God, I could have used you tonight. Jacob had a math assignment that involved making these geometric distinctions that were utterly lost upon me. Then I had to "correct" Hannah's paragraph without making it seem that I was changing anything, which would offend her.

I can't believe your kids clean the kitchen, much less cheerfully. I'm thrilled that my kids clear their plates and load them into the dishwasher.

I had these wonderful red pepper/basil chicken sausages (sp?) from Costco. You'd approve: 4 grams fat/16 grams protein and maybe 1 gram carb. I can't eat enough when I bike ride.

And I've outsmarted myself on the paper bag front: how the hell am I supposed to recycle newspaper without paper bags? They are almost as bad as bottled water!

Transport of recycling uses too much gasoline. Burn the newspapers. It's good for the environment.

When Molly is gone on these trips, I teach Sam and Abby to clean the kitchen, load and run the dishwasher, do laundry. Sam just started practicing guitar.

My theory is that the Asian kids you see working at the corner store in Seattle tend the store because it's expected, it's their environment. It's just what they do. It's the same here, in a white-bread way. The twins clean the kitchen and run the dishwasher and practice their instruments and do their homework. It's just what we do. Fish don't fight the water they swim in.

I would have loved those sausages. I ate my burger without a bun, and with olive oil.

I guess, reluctantly, I agree. My kids know their "job" is to go to school. Implicitly, they know they also need to play music, though they have to be reminded to practice regularly.

I have a strong, and probably misguided, sense that I don't want them to have summer jobs, unless they want to (for personal reasons or for the money). I want them to hang out at the beach, to fall in love, to play tennis. I treasure the time I spent playing backgammon and screwing.

A summer job does not preclude playing backgammon and screwing. Nor falling in love. Nor playing tennis. It does provide an environment of expectations, enforced by adults other than parents. Molly gets back tomorrow. I hope Saturday is warmer; I'd like to take Sam kayaking in the bay.

Discovery

I'm distracted this morning. I've made 17 decisions about what I have to do today, changed them 16 times, and now can't remember the first.

My morning meeting with buyers just got cancelled. I was waiting for the 8 a.m. ferry to the mainland when the rep called and said something had come up, they needed to reschedule. My guess is they smell my blood in the water and are waiting for me to drown. You have time for coffee?

Would you like to stop by on your way back? I could put coffee on now so it would be burnt and bitter by the time you got here.

Rabbitbrush Road, I think you said? I know where that is, I'm about a half-hour away. Text me the address?

Detente

Good morning. Coffee brewing and no more hiding today. I have to go to the office and pretend to be somebody. I don't even want to inventory my list of "to dos."

Some day you'll have to tell me what on earth you actually do all day in your office, so I can be even more intimidated.

What do I do all day? I wait to hear from you.

Really, really unfair.

I wake up, re-boot the stupid CPU four times until I finally get it to start, push the coffee carafe under the spout just right so it won't leak all over the place, start my own inventory of all the little things (almost meaningless by themselves, but in combination they form a day) I need to accomplish, and think "I'll be productive, too busy to think of my secret luxury, the one I take out all too often and run against my cheek, the one with the sparkling facets, the one that is disconcertingly absorbing..." and you send a note like that. It's a missile, you war monger, determined to blast through my resolve.

And your reply was not a cluster bomb, designed to explode into fragments shredding hope I could focus on spreadsheets and databases and concrete and signs and highway access permits?

Instead I spend more than an hour or two thinking of a soft gray sweater with a hole over the heart showing skin and muscle beneath, and a soft mouth wanting passion. Your answer wasn't an incendiary launched at my keep?

We need detente. But detente means both (1) an easing of tensions and (2) a coming together, and it is likely that the second would lead to the first.

hmmm....d'ya think (2) would lead to (1) or only raise the battle to fever pitch? This is a very odd battle indeed. I'm dressed up in armor that melts before your gaze, am equipped with the latest defensive weaponry but leave ammunition behind. My plans for attack quickly fade when I see "Silverthorn" on the screen.

Yes. By the way… gray sweater… wet hair… shield or sword? And don't tell me you didn't calculate the effect.

Who, me?

The sweater is silver in its nature, as I told you I am. And that's why I wore it. Its size indicates that it belonged to someone else: a cast-off. The holes illustrate my nonchalance. It's what I wear to mop the floor, which is what I would have done had you not dropped by. Yet it is pure cashmere, of a fine quality. The gray is not unflattering to my eyes. And "touch me, touch me" the sweater's richness purrs.

I want to bury my face in that sweater, hold it close, inhale its scent, inhale its wearer. I could park next to you at the Baily's Market in Port Cedar and while… Bad idea. I forgot the groceries in the cart while thinking of burying my face in that sweater.

Groceries, what groceries? I was thinking about

There are SOOOOooo many things I should be thinking about besides what I am thinking about. My God, Debra, why aren't you draped on me right now, your fingers in my hair, turning off "Cocteau" and telling me to get to work?

The coast... a mountain cabin in winter... a fire, mugs of coffee, the silence of snow piling to the eves... but right now I'd settle for the cab of a pickup in Anacortes.

Some charming place in La Conner. There's a place in Friday Harbor above the espresso store. But a pickup? Not unless it has a camper. I want to stretch out. And I do prefer romance. You know how old-fashioned I can be.

And I think you tease me again and again. Thank God I had to go pick up the kids. For the time being, you are in email jail. You can talk to me through the bars.

Isn't the place in Friday Harbor great? Did you go to the Grateful Bread for breakfast? They've had marathons there. The running is wonderful. There used to be a great gallery, but it moved. There's still a wonderful glass gallery. Did you go to all of those beach places with Lover?

Email jail? I wanna call my lawyer! At worst a misdemeanor No, Friday Harbor was a family weekend when we went.

Parnassus Books

Made it to the office, though I could delay on a day like this because you would not let me out of bed without at least two "Just one more."

I thought of that. Just another in our "differences" category. The real danger is that I wouldn't let you stop talking to me.

I shall sing for my supper.

What will I do for mine? OK, that's gratuitous taunting. But I couldn't resist.

I am in email jail. She stands there just beyond the bars, showing enough leg to arouse my most base desires, to make me suffer the pain of unsated arousal.

C'mon. At some level, probably not very deep, you're relieved that there are bars between us (see how gracefully I avoided saying which of us was behind the bars?)

I want to take you to Parnassus Books and play among the stacks.

He nudged me. "Listen to this" he said, reading a passage from a John Fowles novel. I listened dispassionately, damning his efforts with an icily polite smile, sans comment, when he finished. Fowles had been around forever. Why couldn't he be interested in something contemporary, something post-modernly cool? I suppressed the realization that I had been standing next to him pouring over Faulkner—circa 1936.

My irritation subsided as we leafed through glossy, bound hardbacks in the "New Fiction" section at the front of the giant old bookstore. We wondered aloud which of the bitey titles had anything to do with the subject of the book, and which had only been created by editors-turned-marketers to catch the interest of the otherwise disinterested.

We left the warmth of the brightly lit bookstore and submitted to Seattle's gloomy late-afternoon-in-the-winter drizzle. He headed for the car.

"I thought we were going for coffee?" my statement was a question.

"Let's go to the car first, and grab the umbrella" he answered.

"You know I hate umbrellas," I said petulantly, accusingly. He had made another wrong move.

"Yes, and I also know you hate getting wet, my little cat," he said reasonably, smiling.

For some reason I wanted to run, but wordlessly followed him to the car instead, following a half-step behind in silent protest, a prisoner marched on a chain.

I knew things would spiral. I would wreck, ruin, alienate. Stop, I pleaded to myself. Stop me, I implored him.

At coffee, he tried to placate me. He spun a tale of star-crossed lovers. One was the willowy brunette working the counter. Flickers of sadness haunted her flawless, milky skin and serene countenance. Her fictitious lover sat alone at a tall, round table talking animatedly on a cell phone, leaning back with his long legs stretched forward confidently. He had the self-assurance of someone who had made it.

The story was impromptu, and it was solid. He used maybe a thousand words. His sketch, the confident, dark lines of an illustrator, evoked the universal.

I burned with jealousy. "OK, your turn," he said, genuinely eager to hear a story from me, unaware that all I could think was that my very best efforts after hours of editing could never accomplish what he had nonchalantly produced for me during lazy afternoon coffee. I blushed, knowing I couldn't utter a coherent sentence. "Are you OK?" he asked, true concern in his gaze.

He would discover the truth: that I am not clever or smart or beautiful. He would lose interest, and discard me. It's the way of the world, I told myself, while silently crying no, no... His crevasse blue eyes peered intensely into mine. He saw. He knew.

He grabbed my hand and pulled me from my chair, leaving our untouched $4 coffees on the table. "What...?" I began, but the end of my question trailed behind. He led me out the door and onto the street. This time, the damp air on my face was invigorating, exhilarating. "Where are we going?" I laughed, asking but not caring. "And aren't you forgetting the umbrella?" I asked, teasingly. He swatted me on the butt with the umbrella. Once again, we were light as air.

Debra, you know this is a dangerous game for me, and I suspect for you…?

"She's elevated tantrum to an art form," he muttered, watching the small storm behind her eyes become darker than Seattle's petulant clouds spattering neon-red reflections in wet city streets.

It was one of those days that he loved in Seattle: soft, gray, wet. Like seeing a loving older couple holding hands, it offered a sweet melancholy, but also an invitation to stay inside, find a fire, a quilt, a lover, a cup of coffee.

What was throwing her off, keeping her from enjoying a day at Parnassus Books, a day they had together where they could do anything and be anywhere?

She had been impatient with Fowles. He had been critical of some of her sloppy, undisciplined modern writers. "Their sentences have no soul. Like Jorge Luis Borges, but without his conceptual genius or Dali-esque bending of space and time."

That was unnecessary on his part. He was showing off, not listening, not sharing. Excluding.

Now she wanted to fight over whether he carried an umbrella. She knew he loved the rain much more than she did! He was really just stalling for time, and wanted to keep her from getting wet and chilled. He wanted to hold the umbrella above her; have his arm around her shoulders.

At coffee he tried to make amends with a game of Biography. The barista was a cute brunette; there was a young man playing at being somebody in the corner. He wove for her a tale of love and anguish between the two, a verbal smoke ring. He tried to show her permanence within their transitions.

He could not reach her. Whatever it was, everything he did pushed her farther away. Everything he said seemed to bore her, make her wish she was someplace else.

He searched her face and saw pain, something cutting at her. While he did not think his Borges gaffe was sufficient, it had to do with him. He looked hard to see if she could meet his eye, if she wanted to love, be loved.

He found what he was looking for. She had lost confidence, and felt small. She wanted to tear down the day, cut it down to her own diminished size. She wanted the world to feel as she felt. He smiled. This was a temporary detour, a blood-sugar dead end. He needed to heed the "No Exit," turn down a different street.

"What...?" she started to ask as he grabbed her hand and pulled her away from the two coffees hot and untouched on the table in front of them. No time for debate, they had wasted enough words.

It would be a brisk walk of five blocks, and he hoped the place was open at this time of day. But he was going to spoon-feed her a half-pound of carrot cake with half-inch frosting. He was going to do it with a fork, with his fingers. He was going to sit so close they could share one chair. He was going to laugh at her for the fact that she had ordered her coffee with artificial sweetener, but was willing to swill sugar and fat with complete abandon if it was piled on cheap cake. He was going to wash it down his own throat with drip coffee made in giant stainless steel urns.

When she started to protest, he was going to twirl words like loops of a lariat, rope her in, tie her down, until everyplace she looked she saw another strand, but also the smile and the love in his eyes. Eventually the sugar and gentleness would take hold. She would speak, and he would show how her words delighted him, which they always did, when he was listening.

He was going to show her that she was as bright as he knew her to be; that she did not have to bend before an onslaught of belittlement from a father far away, from a past that blew dry dust into the present, clouding the image in her mirror.

Then he was going to try to find something fun to watch or experience, a bit of music perhaps, a movie where lovers let go with absolute abandon. He would create an evening out of this renewal, remind her that they were matched in so many ways.

NO FAIR!!!! It's just like in the damn story: mine took days to write, and yours mere minutes!! I hatelovehatelovehatelove you....

In answer to your question about the dangers of Biography, yes. Oh, yes, I appreciate the risks. But I have already learned so much about myself. It's a sort of Freudian dream: safely playing out all the relationship issues that have haunted me all my life.

If nothing else (and there's already been so much else) I'm getting great therapy and you're getting...well, whatever it is you're getting. I guess the trick is to not fall in love with your dance partner.

Sure. Okay. Whatever you say. It's too late for me, but I'll help you avoid that pitfall in any way I can, when we're sitting on the couch (not TOO close) and I look at you curled up like a cat, wanting to do anything I can to make you purr ...

It was too early in the day for the carrot cake. Like any good alcoholic, I don't indulge in my cake until after a carefully planned and rigidly adhered-to time, always after dinner.

But you can always try these wonderful organic thumbprint cookies that look like they're made from bird millet at Whole Foods. In fact, just a trip to Whole Foods usually cheers me up.

We would sample the soups—all of them.

"The cioppino" I said, choosing without hesitation the one we would bring home.

"You always choose the cioppino," he said with a mock groan.

"That's because it's always perfect, and I can look forward to it all the way home."

He suggested that we try the bisque, which was also wonderful... "try it just this once." But he knew I'd accuse him of being reasonable. Good thing he liked cioppino.

At the cheese section, I was dreamily submissive, watching his authority and confidence as he chose.

The checker at the cash register said "Looks like a nice dinner... for two."

He smiled, dropping two forks and two knives and two spoons in the bag, "Then I guess we'd better get two sets of these."

Yah, it may be too late, but I'm putting up a struggle. In the cioppino vignette, I changed from second-person "You" to a safe, distant, vague "He."

At least you are putting up a struggle. Though even I stuck resolutely to the third person. As if that gives me some distance. As if I don't see your eyes when I write about hers, your hand when I take hers. I accept that you keep a safe distance. I admire.

But when I read your words, or write my own, it's YOU who are standing beside me, it's YOU I have my arm around, it's YOUR waist tucked in my arm, YOUR neck I brush with my lips.

Third person. So safe, so distant, so wonderfully effective, especially as a device for fiction.

Yah, ok, but my "He" happens to like John Fowles and have eyes the exact color of an icy blue crevasse. Distance.

Hey! I like John Fowles! My eyes are blue! Maybe your guy knows my Uncle Frank! What's your schedule this week?

Why, are we going to Parnassus Books?

I meet you there, later in the afternoon. I walk in the rain from my hotel; I see you in the Blue room. As I walk forward, you just stand there. I stop 5 feet away. I open my arms, invitation and promise, will she accept either one... ?

ohmygod, the two worlds merge for an instant. But no, back to this one… I was thinking about coffee. A walk to your bridge.

Garlic

The coffee pot makes a sound like it's struggling. As strong as I make coffee, maybe it is. The dog wants out, the cats want in.

I like the first cup in the morning, when the sky is still dark and the house is silent. Rich and dark, it hits palate renewed by hours of sleep, awakened by a new day. Like the morning paper, the first cup is the same but new, like the stories within the paper are the same but new, the year is about to be new, too, but I don't think it will be the same.

In a nearly perfect world, where sits the couch where you would be curled up against me in tights with unattractive bun high on your head, me in Pit Bull pants and scruffy sweatshirt, while you read Conrad and I read… AutoWeek?

Ummm… more confessions. On that couch I'd probably be munching granola or something. I'm a muncher. In law school one time, I was in the library and someone asked me to move b/c my munching was annoying them.

And I hated Conrad. Am I just an unintellectual, or do you think Heart of Darkness is a guy thing? I remember Mr. Half Affair loved him. Couch. Couch. Ouch. Couch.

May I eat granola out of your hand?

How about cookie crumbs from that spot on my neck?

Might take a while. Quite a while.

I've got time.

And as to your Conrad confession, well, too little too late. I already confessed to AutoWeek.

AutoWeek. no garlic no carbs… you're lucky I'm a forgiving person.

I have attributes, you just have to look.

I know your attributes only too well, which is why I have to keep reminding myself: AutoWeek, no garlic, scary, no garlic, exercise induced asthma, no garlic…

"Lions and Tigers and Bears!" Oh my.

The asthma is improving, I eat and cook with garlic: I just suffer, would do so for you, am not that scary to those who love me and have found the key, and the AutoWeek… well, deal with it.

Even challenges can become endearments, at least for a while. Something not to think about while I gently inhale cookie crumbs from the hollow of your neck.

Just for the record, the garlic may be a deal-breaker. Serious stuff. Not cute. Not endearing. Since we had our first lover's quarrel, without being lovers, maybe we should go to mediation over the garlic. Or maybe joint psychotherapy.

You're right about challenges being endearments... when the relationship is fresh. As the relationship progresses they become issues, then impediments, then impossible obstacles. Right?

It's a piece of the "in love" you tell me about, the frontal cortex firing submachine-gun style, and the endorphins racing through the bloodstream. Under the influence, who stops to worry about trifles? The heady brew dissolves the doubts and the barriers and the signals that are right before our smitten eyes.

But reality is still there, lurking beneath.

Pre-relationship counseling? Dealing with "whatifs" before they become "can'tstandits?" There's an idea. So you wouldn't panic at not having "power" in the relationship? So I can love you and be happy not being the love of your life, not even the "now" love of your life?

This is very interesting and complicated, dear Debra. You walk away, but you keep coming back.

I thought about that. I loathe conflict. Several times I really wanted to write you off... no, take that back, I didn't want to, I felt compelled to. Yet, uncomfortable as I was, I wanted to persevere, because, agh, gotta go tuck the kids in. Later.

Wow, was that ever interuptus of whateverthisis.

I wanted to persevere because because because...

because I thought we could. I sensed we could muck through the morass and come out on the other side, tired and muddy but ready to laugh and swat each other playfully with cattails.

because I didn't want us to lose each other, as friends and confidantes, or anything else. We're both incredibly stubborn, and both perfectly capable of surviving without the other, and convincing ourselves we're better off, anyway. Even if we ultimately reconnected, I could see both of us holding out for days weeks months, waiting for the other to say "uncle." I don't want to waste that time on vanity.

because you make me think and feel and laugh. There was something on the other side worth the discomfort.

I think you thought I would just go away, and when I did not, you were compelled to push me away, and that didn't work either, because something was worth the discomfort.

Truthfully, everything is swirling right now... too many emotions today, and I bit the big 1/2 off the sleeping pill at 9.

Love: Yours, mine, The Shoulds'. I've been reconsidering. Maybe you're right.

Choice

It seems months since I have slept a night through. I've put air under the wings of all the demons I feared most in life.

At 3 a.m. I wake too hot from a dream that a vagueness had gotten into a locked chamber, and it was stalking a sleeper hibernating for a long journey. I don't think I was the sleeper and don't think I was the threat, either. The vagueness was locked within the chamber too, and it, too, felt vulnerable.

Awake, a cascade of self-loathing drenches me. What have I done to my children and my long-suffering wife, maybe to you… I lay there for two hours, hoping to drift back off, at the same time not wanting to. Sleep didn't come, didn't come.

Peter, stop beating yourself up. What is, is. Just as you told me about what I was teaching my children, what were you teaching yours? That touching and loving and dialogue aren't necessary in a marriage? One day, they will see you with a woman you love. They will hear the two of you talk, think, joke and explore together. They will see her touch you tenderly, they will see how you look at her, and that will be invaluable to them. They will see both a way they can find happiness, and that their father has found his.

As for Molly... were you really doing her a favor by staying in the "marriage?" Even if you hadn't been cheating, at some level she was as unsatisfied as you were. Maybe this process, granted, most painful, will allow her to grow and understand herself and her buried needs, for they must be there, somewhere, unfulfilled.

As to business, I guess I don't really know enough about what you do to have an opinion. But you have many talents.

What did you mean, what you might be doing to me?

I think of the word you used once to describe my feelings of abandonment: "Bereft." The sense of overwhelming loss. It exists at my core, permeated with pain and fear. I've fought and fled from those feelings, from as far back as forever.

It's time to stop. The pain is real, but from the memory of a wound. The fear is real, but the threat is long past. When I feel these things, I need to sit with them instead of running. They will dissipate without my effort.

I know what takes me closer to serenity, if not happiness. I know, all too well, what leads to pain and anxiety.

Honesty has no emotional color of its own, but it brightens or darkens color on the walls with which I surround myself.

I would like to think about this without responding, or presenting my usual reflexive argument.

Oh, hell, coffee's on, there's work to do. I can't luxuriate in self-examination at 5 a.m. after a sleepless moon hangs cold and pale in the predawn sky.

The kids and I are taking off for the beach on Friday for two days. We are going to go hunt for agates.

Today I went to the Seattle Art Museum. There was an exhibit that included a royal carriage from the collection of King Louis-Philippe.

Oh Peter! I so wish you could have been there! The coachman's footrest was cracked where he had placed his foot for support. It was so amazing to see that, it brought everything to life.

Your exclamation today about the museum cut deep into my reserve. "Oh Peter!" you said, and wanted to share. "Oh Peter!" and I was there with those words, in the museum and then at Parnassus Books and eating Tapas. I'm losing my defenses.

Molly is tending to her dying mother in Seattle. My kids and I finished dinner, beans and rice with cheese, an orange for dessert. Now we watch Cirque du Soleil. Then they go to bed. After we have the popcorn they made me buy at Safeway.

Well, perhaps you were bored but you were with me in the aisles of Trader Joe's this afternoon. The artichoke tapenade or the olive? I asked. Both, you answered. Glutton, I laughed, pushing you away then pulling you close once more.

You enjoyed our early dinner at the trendy new restaurant that billed itself as "Indian," but really was typical Northwest cuisine done Indian-style. I ordered a perfectly seared sturgeon in a light curry. You had laughed when I told you we were meeting at 5:15, but the place was full with a line by 5:30 (just reviewed in The Times*).*

Thank you for stealing some time from your kids. You were stingy with your words earlier, and I wondered whether you were displeased with me, or down in general. I'm happy it's neither.

Game Over

You want proof of God?

On Wednesday, the banker delivers more bad news, and a deadline I can't possibly meet.

According to their appraisals, the value of my real estate has fallen below what I borrowed to buy it. The lovely term is "under water." My rephrase is, "out of oxygen."

They won't refinance the current balance of the loan. Consequently, I need to come up with a considerable amount of cash to make up the difference. Which I don't have.

Are you going to lose some assets, or are you in real trouble? I don't mean to minimize, I am just trying to get a sense of scale.

What will you do? I know some people... I might be able to ask my parents for some money.

That's very sweet, but it would probably be awkward to ask your parents for a couple million in cash so you could… send Hannah to piano lessons? Buy Jacob a new baseball glove? And if they asked Robert why he didn't come up with a paltry $million or two for his own children, he would yell at you for getting your nails done too often, just one massage too many…?

I had no idea.

I'm sorry. I didn't need to be snotty. But you see, that was the day's good news.

As soon as I hang up with the bank, I get a call from Molly.

"We need to talk. Now. In person."

Ryder had called Molly on the landline at home. I have no idea how Ryder got that unlisted number. Apparently Ryder just spewed. About me. My trips. About how I am in love with Ryder and always will be.

Molly said: "I can't believe you put your family at risk with this whack job."

Mediation is off the table. Her lawyer's filing for divorce this afternoon. I'm not to return to the house, we'll schedule visits from the children.

All of which proves that God not only exists, but She has a sense of humor.

Oh Peter! I'm so sorry! I told you Ryder might call Molly.

You were smarter than me. So I called Ryder. "Thought I would hear from you," she said in that flat voice.

I asked her why she needlessly hurt a very good woman.

"Why did you protect her feelings when you knew about mine?" Ryder said. I didn't even come close to having an answer for that bit of crazy.

Ryder blamed this on me, said she was just taking care of loose ends, freeing us up, I think is how she phrased it.

"Freeing us up for what?! We were done!" I said.

She said she just was trying to get us to a point where she could move forward without the "ghosts." My guess is that the ghost she saw in my eyes was you.

I told her never to call me again, to never contact me or my family, and if she did, I would file a restraining order. I said she was broken and I wanted nothing to do with her.

Oh, Peter! I'm so sorry!

It's been a bad day.

We've both had a bad day, but mine got a little better. Hannah's cat disappeared four nights ago. Owls or coyotes, probably. Every morning she woke with tears, and every afternoon she spent hours outside, calling, looking. It broke my heart. I was also afraid she would find something the coyotes left behind.

Right after we got offline this morning I was looking and saw there was beautiful kitten at the Humane Society in Everett. I picked up Hannah at school and showed it to her and she became absolutely ecstatic. So we got on the 11 a.m. ferry. When we got the kitten, we were just consumed. Hannah was so happy and it took so long to get home, I didn't think we were going to make the ferry back at one point.

Why did you think you needed to get the kitten today?

I already told you. Her cat O'Malley disappeared. She was absolutely despondent.

I get that. But what I don't understand is why you felt it was so important to fill that loss so quickly.

Now I don't understand. Why would I leave her in a state of despair if I can fix that?

Grief is a part of life. Didn't you just teach her that loved pets, and maybe loved ones, are easily replaceable?

No, I don't think I did. And I really don't think you're in a position to make judgments about that. She lost a cat, we got her a new cat. I think your own crisis is understandably distorting your point of view..

I really wish you wouldn't replace my explanation of what I'm trying to say with your own explanation of why I am saying it. It's a dishonest way of discussing the issue.

I'm just saying that grief feels catastrophic but often is not. We learn we can manage despite being immersed in it. If you replace the dead cat as quickly as possible to make the grief go away, you teach your daughter she can't manage.

I hardly think you would let your daughter experience grief if you could avoid it. If so, I have seriously misjudged you.

That is another dishonest response: You are changing the subject. But yes, I would let some time go by before my daughter got a new cat. I would want her to grieve for the lost cat while I held her in my arms and let her know I understand how badly she feels, but that the pain will go away.

When it had, with the help maybe of a ceremony, we would look for a new cat for its own sake, not to fill the sense of loss for the animal gone.

Oh! A ceremony! That will fix it! Maybe we should invite God, too, and pretend there's a heaven where O'Malley plays with mice!

I think it's cruel to let a child suffer when it's in your power to prevent that suffering. Why hold the child at all? Wouldn't "allowing her to feel the pain" be even more effective if you let her deal with it alone, under your version of "parenting?"

It's easy to do the wrong thing for all the right reasons. And maybe you're right, maybe I'm applying mechanisms I use to protect myself from pain onto you and your daughter.

Tomorrow I rent the first furnished apartment I come across, then head to the city to get bent over by the bank. This sucks. Everything sucks. Good night.

Shit. I can't believe I'm having a tantrum on such a difficult and monumental day for you. I'm so sorry, Peter.

Boat

You have probably completed your move by now. I wonder if you have found internet. I thought it was everywhere. Or are you in hiding (not just from me, but from the world?) Where did you move? Still on the island?

It's good to hear from you. Yes, I'm still on the island. I have moved onto "Trilogy," a lovely older sailboat owned by friends who spend the wet season on their other boat in Panama. Trilogy needs a bit of attention which I have agreed to give her.

What about your children? Do you rent a place when they are to come visit?

They stay with me here. It's a little crowded compared to what most people are used to, but we all fold up pretty small, and you learn how to stay out of each other's way.

They come down the dock on Friday afternoons, every other week, per the parenting plan. Depending on the weather sometimes we head out to anchor in a cove on Vincente Island, sometimes farther out. We were able to find a place to drop the hook (do I sound nautical?) last weekend on the other side and caught a salmon for dinner. In many ways it's very nice, and gives us a chance to be close.

I'm looking forward to exploring with them next summer, assuming I have found a boat of my own that I can afford. We will be pulling up crab pots, finding special places where the blackberries are fat, and catching crawdads with a forked stick.

That sounds dreadful. Let me rephrase... that sounds like a way to get cold, scratched up and like a lot of work. I doubt my kids would find it fun in any way. But I'm glad yours do.

A boat. I guess that's what you always wanted, and the timing is probably right for you. So when you're not out playing Swiss Family Robinson, you live at the marina? Does Ryder still have a boat there?

Robert is home and I'm off to Seattle to visit friends. I hope to have a fun weekend. Hope you enjoy yours.

I don't know if her boat is still here. I don't even remember what kind of boat she has. I haven't looked, and I don't really care. Enjoy your weekend.

Impact

My dad discovered I was in Seattle (my sister was pissed that once again I flit into town without telling her, and immediately called Dad) so I made the obligatory pilgrimage to what remains of my childhood home in Seattle Heights (Jimmy, nasty WASP, used to call it the Golan Heights).

I drove up, resentful that I was spending my precious time on an unpleasant obligation. I braced myself against his overpowering will. But it was surprisingly pleasant, we listened to opera and avoided politics.

There is something very comforting in the sighs of sleeping children. Abby's friend Sydney is here, which makes this small space even smaller, but it works. Sam has to sleep outside in the cockpit, which he thought was rather funny.

Syd gets straight "As" and does most of her homework at school, not the nightly slog it can be for my own. I worry about Syd, I hope she is given a chance to become all that she can.

I shall fill them with bacon and eggs and send them out in the rain for a couple of hours to play soccer. We'll see if Sam wants to join them, or if three is too complex at this age.

I'm wondering about how your son and daughter manage with Sydney. Girls, especially, with their shifting allegiances and tumultuous moods, seem destined for twos or a gaggle, but not a tricky threesome.

Hannah is having two friends over today. She's looking forward to it, and I'm buried in performance anxiety. What will she do with them? She spends so much time alone, lost in imaginary games. And the "skipping grade" age difference becomes so apparent in situations like this, where she seems to have less social poise than... than she Should.

Oh, God, Debra, will you leave her alone? She's doing fine. Don't micromanage this, it's her play-date. Don't over-think it, let it happen, give her the chance to shape her own life.

The rhythm of your life is a down comforter. Treat three as one. If the three is causing unpleasant noise, don't try to sort… make all responsible. Add food at crucial moments.

A down comforter. Yes, that's it exactly. And (not much time, so I'll throw out this undeveloped thought) that's what I originally meant by our "couch," you know. It had no sexual connotations, well, maybe just amorphous overtones. It was a place to be ourselves together.

Debra, the hunger for scents, for shared melodies… The couch is becoming less and less amorphous for me.

I was speaking about the origins of the concept. Relationships evolve. I'm not sure how effective it is for people like us to try to control the evolution. Ultimately, control is quite beyond either of us. Don't you think?

I may be stuck taking the kids to a 2:15 movie... some cartoon re-make of Red Riding Hood. Sitting through those things are acutely painful for me, bored beyond belief.

I'm taking the twins to an orthodontists appointment at 4:30.

Instead of sleeping last night, I was thinking: What if Molly wanted me back? I don't want to be where my play is always greeted with a blank stare and "it's time to do laundry."

You can't go home again, so to speak. I truly believe, left brain/right brain, from my heart and soul, that whatever your future holds, you're going to be immensely more fulfilled.

Debra, do you see you in that future? Would it make any sense for us to come up with some sort of plan?

Plan? You mean, for the future? I say we fuck a few times and find out if the biological imperative trumps the categorical imperative. If not, maybe we could move on and just be friends.

What a lovely invitation. But I don't want to have an affair with you. I don't want to become more deeply involved and then worry that at any time you will be throwing me away.

Throwing you away? The last thing I remember was gushing at you about Trader Joe's. Throwing you away?

I want to grow old with you. I want life with you. Not an affair. I want something that will endure.

Peter, c'mon. Look at your history. Look at mine. Enduring love is an illusion, at least for people like us.

Robert is one issue, but your children are a factor. Your son is now complicit in our "lie," if that's what we let it become. I don't like that. I don't want to start something, well, okay, it has already started, but get any deeper into something that isn't going to endure. Your son's comments were deeply disturbing, and not because I feared we would get "caught."

Jacob's comment disturbed me, too. And I'm tormented that I cannot return the love and respect of his father, and make everything all right. But whether you're in my life or someone else is in my life, or no one is in my life, that's not going to happen. I also don't attach a huge amount of significance to the comment. Jacob knows that Hannah turns everything into romance, and was just telling me that she's bound to do the same with my relationships with men. He was rolling his eyes as he said it.

You were the one who started a discussion about whether I wasn't humiliated and shamed by my own behavior. You were the one who wanted to talk about morals.

Yes, I began (as I have many times before) an abstract conversation about conscience, because I was struggling through Kant's essay on the same. It was play, it was exercise.

Abstract discussion without personal application is masturbation. Fine as far as it goes, but not far enough. Pain of betrayal will endure for those who love us, who seek to be loved. To each other, you and I bare our souls, share melodies, hunger for scents. In those ways, we do the worst.

But those can be discounted, at least to others. Time on the couch cannot. I love you. I want to know if we have a future.

Peter, not that long ago you were asking if you should find a cheap rental house or move onto a boat. Where's the future in that?

For the record, "stopping" is fine. It would be a relief, in a way. I think we could easily turn down the heat and establish a deep friendship. I think we would learn to honor the bumpers and support each other through life, even each other's love affairs. But... at this point I can't say that is what I choose.

You say that "stopping is fine," but you deny "stopping" in the same breath. At this point, stopping is not what I would choose, but this… this…whateverthisis is something to be approached carefully, with respect, with honor, if you will, if it is to endure.

Endure? Peter, who are we kidding? Ourselves, obviously. We both know nothing endures. Modern relationships don't endure.

Nothing endures? If this is not to endure, what are we doing?

I don't want to have an affair with you. I want more. I want your friendship, I want your respect, I want your love. But I don't want to be trivial, I don't want to be the other man, I don't want to be a man your husband and children loathe, I don't want to be an excuse, and I don't want my children's mother to fear running into you at the store.

If this won't endure, what are doing? What about Hannah and Jacob and Abby and Sam? If we believe nothing endures, then we create their pain for a romp? A lark?

You say that "stopping… would be a relief, in a way." It's not relief I feel when I think of that. But I do need to stop seeking myself in the embrace of women. I want this to be different between you and me. I am diminished when you say "nothing endures." That makes this just another selfishness.

I never suggested, either to you or to myself, a "mere" affair. Peter, the idea of having casual sex with you... the idea of having casual anything with you... is ludicrous. There is nothing casual about either of us, or our relationship together.

I am an adulterer. I don't want to be that man anymore. I do not want to be complicit in further adultery. Perhaps that answers your question whether the dissolute have worn down their conscience.

So here is an irony of world-class proportions: I am now lost to a woman with whom I have only had email and for whom I have done the most honorable thing of my last 20 years.

I hope you will not abandon me, I hope you understand what it means to me when you say your children see a more fulfilled mother who has a light in her eyes that has been dim.

Give me a month or so, then we'll try a friendship. And even then I don't know whether it will work.

I spoke the truth, and you didn't want to hear it. I never said that I didn't want a relationship to endure, I said only that the reality is that it probably won't.

I expressed my cynicism. Though I want to with all my heart, I don't really believe in "happy ever after." People grow, people change, people drift away from their lovers. It's infinitely sad, and deeply frightening. If I were, once again, in a relationship with someone I loved, I would fight with all my heart to keep love strong, but might believe deep in the recesses of my mind that I was delaying the inevitable.

Please, no contact for a while. I won't write again.

Of course there is no such thing as enduring love. There are no heroes.There is no denying it.

Love? Love is just a chemical saturation of the cortex designed to promote behavior advantageous to the species or the perpetuation of certain strands of DNA. Eventually the advantage is realized and the brain quiets and off goes love, replaced by habit, familiarity, and the comfort of routine, which have their own evolutionary attributes.

Love is only "real" to the extent that like being immersed in a good novel or a good film we can "suspend disbelief" and not think of it as just a book, just a movie. But the suspension always fails and "what's real" returns with blasé banality like walking from a cool dark matinee into a hot dusty August afternoon.

Heroes? Heroes are a symptom of need, an affliction, an insecurity, an immaturity, Santa with presents father slips under the tree, the Tooth Fairy with quarters from mother's hand sliding beneath pillows heavy with dream.

There is no such thing as love, there are no heroes. I was blind.

Discord

As I sat here just now, absentmindedly answering some emails, thinking of you, of us, of my marriage, I thought "I need to run this by Peter." I laughed aloud, thinking that you were the last person to whom I could turn for advice, but hey! You're my Girlfriend!

And now, in this moment, I feel that we could be "just friends." Better than nothing. Why take away something that has given us both pleasure just b/c we couldn't turn it into something else?

I'm sorry to violate my own "no contact" rule, but I don't think you'll mind.

I had hoped you would understand that I did not defect and betray, but sought to protect those you love most. I tried to do the honorable thing. If you can simply reclassify what I mean to you, then I meant something different than you meant for me.

Where is the honor in running from the pain of love to take shelter under the somnambulistic skirts of the Shoulds? You purportedly do this to spare others pain, yet your wife won't feel any less distress when she sees me than before. My children will not find their parents happily married any more now than before. My husband will have a wife no more now than before.

If your motives are what you say, then you are patronizing. I question those motives, and wonder whether the person you are protecting is yourself.

I've done that before, but not this time.

Jacob's comment, "Don't tell Hannah," cut me deep. A boy that age should not have to convey the need for dishonesty to his mother to protect his little sister. You initiated a discussion on morality and conscience and consequences, and I went to the pain of innocents. Then you said our relationship would not endure.

I saw you throwing me away, you had warned me often enough, and my kids and your kids buffeted. I loathed the long-term consequences for what you believed would be transitory. And I did not trust my patterns, my past motives; I could not be sure I wasn't just repeating that.

I think I understand your patterns, and some of my own. I demand both advance and retreat. I pull words from you, but not wanting clichés, not wanting my own resolve to waiver, wanting to allow you the dignity of keeping your own resolve intact, I withdraw.

But then who do I tell that I'm lost in "A Winter's Tale," how little iceberg continents float in the melt? Who do I tell that my friend brought me alive for an hour yesterday, as we sang of the human condition, and he shared this quote from the Talmud: "We do not see things as they are, we see things as we are."

And to make matters worse, it's discordant with our closeness. We're in this ghastly parody, this netherworld, and I don't like it. It pains me to say it, but I am who I am, and I'm not one for netherworlds and half-measures.

The loss I staved off with hope yesterday whirls with the futility in a macabre dance. I know. I think what we want right now, or what we need, is quite different. Timing is everything, isn't it?

My need is to live knowing my actions have consequences, and not skulking about.

My need is to understand the extent to which an individual woman is just a need to be filled and when I take rather than give. You "feel" different but I don't know why. Because you are holding out a reserve?

"Oh Peter… the coachman's footrest!" Yucatan. Venice. They overwhelm me. Then your husband comes home on Thursday. Last weekend you met an old lover in Seattle who still has a strong attachment to you.

So I feel like I am in a netherworld, too. Am I to be "exclusive" to you, and wait for emails and off-chance afternoons? I don't think that's going to suffice for me, but don't dare ask for more. Do I have coffee with other women, looking for what I find in you but cannot have? Will you dismiss me if I do?

Yes, all of this is discordant with our closeness. I would not call it a parody, but a cliché.

Your "aloneness" is completely disingenuous when you have me... "here," however tangentially.

You've made your choice. I won't lie and say I will "respect" it, for I don't. It feels unnatural, wrong. I think you give up far more than you stand to gain. But I hope you do find understanding, especially if it comes at as dear a price as you lead me to believe.

I'll miss you terribly, and mourn for the death of our possibility. Perhaps we can write to each other this summer.

"Perhaps we can write to each other this summer." Jesus. You say you mourn the death of possibility. But when I ask what that possibility might be, I am dismissed and told I would have had you "tangentially." Would you allow me to be tangential to you in return? Or are you looking for an exit?

Honestly, I don't understand a thing you're saying here. I don't think you have understood me. Could you ask your questions in another way?

Let me be clear: I do not want an exit. But I'm a nervous wreck trying to reconcile my desires and your needs. I can't do it. You want me here in the wings, waiting for you. You hold me at bay with what can only appear to me as a pantomime of nobility.

Yah, I understand the words. But they make no sense to me. I only know you choose these... principles (for lack of better word, I'm not thinking clearly) above me. I think you're a fool, which is good, I guess: my ego is still going strong, right?

Are you asking me, when you say the "view from here," what I want? I want you to get rid of all the bullshit lines and have the courage to see what will happen. But you've already decided against that. It doesn't leave us with options, I'm afraid.

Debra, no fair. Is this the convenient exit you were hoping I would provide, or does this reflect you being hurt in ways you are not willing to share, this brusqueness a defense mechanism hiding what you feel? Anything else makes me think I was the object of play, that this was a game.

I woke, after a good night's sleep, feeling groggy. The gunk that settles in the corner of my eyes rests, instead, in my heart. The dull ache of a hangover pervades my being.

I stood sentry next to the coffee-maker, and watched numbly while it dripped... water. I had forgotten to put in the grounds. I scrambled for the open bag of beans (good thing I've been buying ground, the grinder is such a mess, isn't it? and I'm not sure I'm enough of a coffee connoisseur to tell the difference), and am now drinking a curious blend of water and rocket fuel.

There. Now that I've "said" it to you, it didn't just happen, it took on meaning. It existed in a way it hadn't before you knew it. All these silly things that we share, the silly things we call "mundane," are, in combination, our daily lives. In other words, "girlfriends," right?

And then there are those thoughts that we share that let Peter and Debra transcend their daily lives and become who we really are, who we want and need to be. How many pages have I dog-eared for you: "Peter would love this!"? How many sights have I dog-eared in my mind, wanting to share? Who else would I tell about watching Luis Bunuel's "L'Age D'Or" from 1930, written by Bunuel and Salvador Dali?

Upon re-reading your last letters, I see that you want to know about the future. How can I answer that? There are so many variables, so many paths. This whole thing could crash and burn, or go gently into the night. It could grow and flourish and I could leave Robert. Or more likely, Romeo, you might fall in love with someone else.

There's only one way to tell what the future holds, and you aren't letting the future unfold right now, and I'm bludgeoning you to capitulate to my greed and impatience.

My coffee is better for being made with you watching. Parnassus Books. Carrot cake and the Yucatan. These I have not been able to share with any other. You even hung in there through "Seattle Blues."

You once said, in your past there have been men with pieces of this, but not the package; not the coachman's footrest and the sensuality and the laughter and the ability to take your hand and lead you out of sulking princesshood.

But then, Debra, you were so willing to say, "talk to you next summer," when I was trying to explain why principles have become important to me, though far too late, and why I was asking "what are we?" Then you said I am asking you to wait in the wings, but isn't that really what you are asking of me?

You demand that I cross my lines and admit you spin lines like a web and I have been caught crossing yours in the past?

I didn't want to wait in the wings. I want us to be real. Yes, Parnassus Books, REI, you, me. Real time.

My fever broke in the night but I will stay with Tylenol for today. I pick up the twins from school and have them for the night, maybe two, if I can rearrange a bit of work. Who would have thought I would spend as much time trying to secure time for my kids as a tryst with you in Seattle?

I just returned from a dazzling run. I had a total allergy attack this morning, and running is the best way to stop it.

Jacob is home again, and probably will not return to school. And Hannah, on the drive to school today, said that her "daughter" (in this case Karma, the cat that purrs me to sleep) would very much like to ride on the back of a gazelle. There are simply no words to describe our children, are there?

Peter, thank God I have you to lead me out of "sulking princesshood" into... humility? Of course I expected you to wait in the wings, that goes without saying. That isn't the issue: the issue is me, me my selfish needs, my impatience, me my me my.

I saw the issue from my vantage only, from the perspective of my needs. I needed to be with you, I needed us to GO somewhere, to test the waters, to taste the meal, to see what was there. I couldn't bear to just...sit.

And you needed, I thought, to NOT be with me. But now I am totally confused, because you seem to be saying you DID want to meet in Seattle, or something, that you also wanted "real time."

You won't let our friendship go but you won't have contact with me. I can do nothing now but surrender to sadness' smothering embrace. I'll let go now, Peter.

Damn it Debra, will you please stop stamping your feet and slamming the door with "That's not the way I want it!"

I have asked for some understanding. I have said that I cannot have an affair with you, and no, you don't need to tell me that you haven't asked.

Blahs

Hannah's birthday is on Thursday. Other than that I have absolutely nothing on the calendar. If my friend Rennee is taking any time off I'm going to try to talk her into a backcountry adventure, but she's probably working.

Honestly, things are horribly tense between Robert and me. I'm really trying to get through the next week until he leaves for DC, and then his school routine starts.

First off, if you can, share a laugh with Robert. Try to take the edge off. Do something nice, not to make the world turn, just to make the evening less unpleasant. If he rebukes you, so it goes. But it might be nice if Hannah could see you make the effort. You don't want to propagate this. Look for peace, serenity.

You do want a bit of peace for me, and a bit of serenity. But this is also your way of putting me at a distance, isn't it? The formality, the reminder (to you? to me?) of my family.

The caldron no longer simmered, it began to very gently boil. We were both throwing in scraps of bat wing and lizard's tail and unicorn horn and love and trust and slender, powerful willow branches of passion.

Temperature climbing, the sensation of opening my arms to you in Parnassus Books, I actually saw you there in the Blue Room five feet away, your indecision followed by the absolute decision to find out, once and for all; I felt you in my arms, you looking up and my arms around you, the smell of your skin… the yes yes yes emotion, and realized that this was what I wanted and this was not what I should be doing and thinking and feeling, not now, at least not yet.

I may not be able to stop my heart and my mind in quiet moments, but I made a commitment to myself that I am not going to do with you what I have done with others.

You may not be there then, you may have reconciled your marriage or be with another and I may be, too, but you need to know that you are not one of many, you are unique.

In the mean time I take a quick step back because the heat was growing intense and there is a point where I lose my resolve. I don't want to do that. Not with you. Not now.

blah blah blah very noble… and I answer in kind of course I respect that… blah blah blah

She dismisses my honor with blah blah blah!? Did she read it out loud, did she know what I felt? Blah blah blah?! Blah blah blah makes me want to rendezvous and take her in my arms and look into her eyes and say, gently, a whisper, really, my lips brushing her ear… "blah blah blah?" A bit feisty tonight?

Hell hath no fury like a woman scorned.

Scorned?! SCORNED??! Oh, love, I don't think so. The man wants to prove the quality of his love, show a bit of nobility, and she takes that as being scorned?

You are a pitiable beast tonight, Mr. Hamilton. You reach for me with your torso of a centaur, drawn to me, swaying to my siren song. Yet you scramble away with the legs of a chicken, running toward the Shoulds in the barnyard. You demean my prowess as a seductress and I will not forgive you. Until you whimper a little.

The day will come when I look into your eyes and dare you to kiss me, to hold me, to look at me while we make love at four in the afternoon with the sun streaming across our bodies. Afterwards your fingers twirl strands of my hair from a spot 2" above the back of my neck. Your prowess as a seductress is unmatched. Unfortunately, I love you, too. And you know that. blah blah blah.

Now, this is interesting. You have mounted a full retreat to the safety of the Shoulds, while I feel like saying "Will ya just fuck me already so I can get some reading done instead of these grippingly dramatic emails?"

AND in the course of this email exchange you shift from third-person nouns to third-person pronouns to first-person.

I'm sure you're right. blah.blah.blah.

...By the time the bill came, they had frosting all over the table, their hands and their faces, they were laughing so hard neither could finish a sentence.

"And then Fowles said to Borges... 'blah, blah blah' "

They descended into giggles.

"The modern writer has a freshness about her work that can only be captured with 'blah, blah blah,' " she snorted.

"I think you are going to blow frosting out your nose," he chortled.

"Like the coffee in your lap!? Très élégant," she shot back.

"How do you say 'blah, blah, blah' in French?" he asked.

"bleaux, bleaux, bleaux," she replied, "but the 'x' is silent."

"Except in Paris, where it is said with a sneer… Oooops. Let me help you clean that up."

You satisfy me.

And you me.

and if I had frosting it would have shot out of my nose.

I want more. I want to taste you, hold you and love you until you enter another dimension. Until you want me as badly as I want you. You are right. To ignore this, even postpone this, would be a crime against nature.

Unforgiven

Are you looking forward to the racing season? If memory serves, this is about when you get your car ready.

That's a funny story, kinda sorta funny, as some would say.

After a very thorough examination of my books, the bank decided that they had rights to the race car. They asked me to bring it to them. I told them I no longer had a vehicle to tow it with, since they had already taken my truck, but they were more than welcome to go get it.

Peter, I am really, really sorry. I know that was an important part of your life.

Thank you. But life moves on. Though I'm a firm believer in the old racer's credo that the faster you drive, the slower you age, I may have gotten away with the risk for as long as possible.

Besides, the story isn't over. I moved out of the house rather quickly. The race car was still in the barn. I gave the bank the address, then called Molly and told her the bank was on their way.

When the bank rep got there, I guess he went right to the barn. Molly comes out and tells him to get off her property. He tells her he is there to pick up bank property. She tells him that the real estate and everything on it is a marital asset under her control and to get the hell off her property.

Good for her! I didn't know she had that kind of steel in her.

She is easily underestimated. Which the bank rep did, because he didn't leave. In fact, he was the one who called the cops after Molly went back into the house and got the K-frame Smith & Wesson .38 Special I had forgotten on my side of the bed.

He was cited for trespassing, and Molly was given a warning for "menacing." I was the owner of the firearm, and the deputies called me to come down and pick it up.

Oh my God! No! Really truly?

My guess is that you will read about it in the Sheriff's Calls when the "Port Cedar Weekly" comes out on Wednesday.

I had no idea she would ever, ever do anything like that. I would have been much more cautious about emailing with you!

Molly would have shot me, not you. Maybe.

So later she calls me. Says the car is still there and might be a topic of negotiation at some point, but she was damned if she was going to let the bank just take it out of whatever agreement we might come to. If the bank takes it afterwards, that's my problem.

She apologized that the deputies had taken the gun, and felt much better when I told her I had gotten it back. Then she told me how shocked she was when the deputy asked her for it, and the first thing he did was take out the bullets.

"I thought it was unloaded!" she said.

I told her there was little value in keeping an unloaded gun for self defense.

"So I am learning," she said to me.

What a story! I'm glad she seems stronger. I told you that might happen. And I'm glad that you might get to keep your race car. But with all of your financial woes, how will she survive after the divorce? Will she move back to Seattle and take the kids? Will she get a job?

Molly's mother passed away 10 days ago. Molly was one of two children, her brother died in a motorcycle accident as a teenager. Her father was a lawyer for Microsoft in the early years. Paid with a lot of stock. I have no worry about my children's security.

All things considered, then, if she avoids being liable for any of your debts, Molly may actually come out ahead on the deal.

I made the mistake of saying something very similar. She was pretty straightforward. I'll paraphrase, but this is pretty close:

"Peter, you betrayed me, your children, your family. I ask myself everyday if the good times between us were real, or if you were just killing time while you were looking forward to being with someone else. I have almost forgiven you for everything else. I will never forgive you for that."

Natural Selection

Good morning. Temperature in the boat was 61 degrees. Flannel sheets and microfiber comforter and soft fleece blanket were a nest. I would be there still but: There. Was. No. Coffee. If I build my own, I will have to put in a heater that starts a half-hour before I do.

Thinking of you, how you feel different, that whateverthisis is, it is not that I need you to be "someone who is there," but love sharing with you "here."

Every bachelor boat should have a little 4-cup coffee maker next to the bed. Yours needs a bedside shower, too.

I'm putting my mother on the 11 a.m. ferry, and then having a coffee with friends at Martha's. I will look down on the marina and see if I can tell which of those ~~trailers~~ boats you are living in.

I wonder if your "desire" for me isn't merely one of your void-filling exercises, but rather an atrociously timed accident. It's ok to have me in your life, b/c I'm not a void filler, I'm just something that happened? Aren't I an exception?

Yes, you absolutely need to get to the bottom of the "there" phenomena. I think it's probably a longstanding pattern that began with your parents. I hope that when we're able to talk, you'll take the journey with me.

Robert brought the kids home and immediately left, saying he'll be home Friday. I am flooded with relief. That means I'll have to find a way to get through next weekend, then (I think it's that weekend) I go to Seattle again for a longer stay. (Mom had kidney cancer two years ago and has her semi-annual scan/meeting with the surgeon, and anticipates potentially bad news. I need to be there for her.)

Then I'm going to theater and will actually go out at NIGHT with friends. Time to cut loose a bit, huh?

Robert just left? No other words, no forewarning? Cut loose a bit? Hmmm. Of course I think of bringing the vorpal blade.

Ok, I'll bite. "Vorpal blade"...Lewis Carroll? Deadly?

I think of you being on the couch, as I make dinner. The kids have practiced their instruments (with the usual protest), and are upstairs, left to their own devices. There are bands of orange across a sky of tepid blue. The other islands become silhouettes as it darkens, the water flattens.

You're reading; I'm flurrying in the kitchen with my own brand of disorganization that is done at such speed and such flair that I appear to be a talented multi-tasker. I'm sipping the tiniest bit of wine, and singing.

But I stop, and put down the pan. Without fanfare, I walk to the couch and interrupt your avid perusal of Nerd Weekly. I lean over, and with tender deliberation, kiss the very center of your forehead. Your crevasse blue eyes meet mine, and I hear you say, "thank you, that was perfect," even though no words left your mouth.

As you pull away, I catch your hand and pull you back. I put one of mine on the back of your neck and gently pull your mouth to mine. "mmmm. Merlot." I say, smile and let you go.

Cab sauv, you neanderthal.

Quel Cuveé? The Chicken Kiev will take 40 minutes at 400 degrees, and we can have it on basmati rice. So simple, it's nearly a TV dinner.

Chicken Kiev? You are worth your weight in gold! And definitely my kind of gourmet. I will preheat the oven like no one has before... you will be truly amazed at my culinary expertise.

Quel Cuvee? Hmmm... sounds suspiciously French. Are you trying to intimidate me? If so, you wash the dishes.

I preheat the oven, as promised. And wonder if I can set the table without another detour to your couch.

If you are going to abuse me because I can't tell a Cab Sauv from a Merlot when tasted from the sweetness of your mouth, I will challenge you to tell me the vintage. Yes, French, though as usual, I gargle the beautiful language." I will wash the dishes, as long as I can have another touch or two over the next ten minutes, or more while you take silverware to the table.

In December ... Or in March of 20XX... Will I rattle around in the kitchen without thinking to give you the kiss? Or will I do so, but only dutifully, and will you fail to pull me toward you? Why, why does everything have to die?

Wait… wait! Are you letting fear of the future deprive you of the present? Again!?!

I thought we agreed in counseling to talk about these things before they occurred, so we could either head them off or or do something different.

The Kiev will be ready in a minute. As soon as the kids get to the table, I am going to take some of the melted cheese and pretend it is something gross until they giggle.

Then I am going to look into your eyes and challenge you: Either get back into the "now," in this kitchen right now, with my fingertips now, or tell me what is so scary about something in the dark, so far beyond the tall windows.

Are you trying to stand between me and my depressed, neurotic Jewish heritage? I thought we agreed in counseling that you wouldn't do that. And here you are, making me giggle at the mere thought of what that oooey gooey cheese might be, without even giving me a chance to bewail my destiny. I love you for not respecting my right to sulk. Hey, wait a minute… We don't go to counseling.

We went to counseling as a first date. You really think I would lie here on your couch without professional reassurance?

I vacuumed the house while you were on the ferry on the way back from your mom's. By the way, if you want a really hot shower after dinner, I will get the kids to do the dishes, "don't even want to HEAR any complaints," and then warm eight oz. of hot massage oil and see if I can loosen any muscles tightened by three hours in the car.

I may see if I can tighten a couple of others in the process, but that will be temporary, I promise.

OK, cut! CUT!

References to massage oil and tight muscles are totally below the belt. I mean, off limits. You are an unscrupulous tease. And I am weak...weak....fading....

I'm thinking about what I wrote earlier, speculating that we, you and I, are different than most people. Do you think that is merely a figment of my vanity and narcissism, a need to attribute to myself significance, uniqueness? I suppose everyone believes they are different.

Well, if you do conclude that we are different, it must necessarily follow that any attraction we might feel is directly attributable to natural selection... a very base but omnipotent drive to perpetuate OUR species... something for which we simply cannot be morally accountable, even to the Shoulds. Who are we to thwart the forces of nature?

You are so right. It is our DUTY to have a relationship, simply as homage to biology. I have suffered in the past from "terminal uniqueness." It is flatulent self-indulgence, but otherwise characterized as an impatience with the direction of the flock.

Hmmm, the problem is: why would I have any more respect for our biology than I do for moral imperatives? Oh, cancel that. I'm an avowed naturalist, and it all seems pretty natural...

You don't want to argue with biology. May I quote you? Who are we to thwart the forces of nature? Still reading Kant?

No, Sigmund Floyd today. Actually some really wonderful passages. I now know I am a classic neurotic (the Jewish stereotype complete): "...a person becomes neurotic because he cannot tolerate the amount of frustration which society imposes on him in the service of its cultural ideals."

We may be wired differently from others but society needs those willing to explore, if just to know what directions are possible. Or perhaps where *not* to go.

Outlaws serve an important function by questioning, rejuvenating, keeping the walls of convention from growing too high or too thick such that society has no escape if the planet wobbles. America was founded by outlaws. Jesus was an outlaw. We see in the outlaw, often solitary, a rejuvenation, a renewal.

So saddle up and gallop along beside me. Let's find a stream where the sun hangs long in the sky, and tightens our skin with late afternoon warmth, and shadows reveal more than they hide.

I'm no outlaw. There's no pioneer in my differentness, no revolutionary zeal, nothing noble. I'm just cranky and cynical and am compelled to call it as I see it, wrapped up sometimes in feathers and lace, sometimes delivered crude and bare.

Nonetheless, I'll follow behind you at a sedate canter. You're the speed freak; I hate to gallop. That stream sounds lovely. I'm parched, you can ladle some cool water between my lips, and we'll rest under the shade of the sycamore.

I'd love to be there. I have respite here, too, and I know a lobby in a Seattle hotel where they serve wine and espresso, just a short walk from Parnassus Books. Someday, maybe. Or you could come over here for coffee. Goodnight. Sleep well.

Grocery Bag

Good morning. Coffee is effortless today, for some reason.

In the night, do you like to snuggle closer, arms and legs tangled and your head on a receptive shoulder for a pillow, or are you a solitary sleeper, roll over and back to your lover?

What a silly question to ask me, someone with virtually no experience (in the last, well, say 14 years) in sleeping with a lover. Robert and I sleep apart, but is that b/c Robert is Robert? because of habit? because of the pillows with which I surround myself (bad back)?

But I can say that Love of Life and I were as you described yourself with Lover: hermetically sealed together.

I was about to write: after all we've disclosed, to ourselves and to each other, d'ya think there'd still be mysteries for us? In playing this game, are we robbing our potential future selves of discovery, a thrilling joint adventure?

And then, without being too philosophical before I've had my statutory 2 mugs of coffee, it came to me: that's what it's all about. "Endurance" in a long-term relationship, that element of a relationship that keeps a couple together, has to do with a couple's ability to continue to discover. Know what I mean?

To discovery and endurance, I will add willingness and effort. You had the willingness and made the effort when most of you wanted to bail out on me and armor up. I made the decision (with some prompting) not to run and hide.

It is when we take it for granted that it grows flat and predictable. If we're going to talk so close so early, I'm going to go brush my teeth.

Don't brush your teeth, I don't mind. We don't have to talk, we can just snuggle!

Too late. Going to take Hannah to school. Tomorrow let's get up early so we can sleep in...

By the way, wonderful response. You are so right about willingness and effort. I think back to Love of Life, and while he had the willingness, he didn't have the brains (the ability) to "work through" anything, and I didn't have the maturity, the perspective into myself and the world. I look at others in my life...go Debra, Hannah's waiting...

I LOVE the idea of waking up early so we can go back to sleep. A day extender. As to brushing, I just feel better nuzzling your neck if I know what you are breathing of me is minty fresh.

I hope you and Hannah are getting this sunrise.

Okay, that's enough out of ME this morning. We are going to just trundle Prof. Windbag right back into his dusky office on the third floor of Semantics University, a small complex at the corner of Stupefying and Leaden, one of the preeminent schools in the State of Confusion.

Oh yeah. Good morning.

I tried to get into Semantics U but my grades weren't good enough. Just as well, I only wanted to get into Prof. Windbag's class, and it was full with a long wait list.

I remember a pretentious line from a short story I wrote in college, describing an enigmatic woman opening a door and finding her lover there: "there stood a vicissitude." Can there be control when life is a series of vicissitudes?

Honey, I know you've only just woken up, but I've been lying here next to you for an entire hour, willing you to open your eyes so I could ask you this. What do you mean no philosophy until 12 or seventeen cups of coffee, whichever comes first?

And you're right, as soon as you respond I'll become intimidated and squirrel away, saying "let's just snuggle. Where are you going? NO! Don't leave to brush your teeth, don't don't."

I'm dropping Hannah off at school, then I'll come home where I'll be for most of the day except when I ride (I'm hoping to bundle up and actually get out on the road) for a couple hours. Oh, yeah! Another "ugly": instead of a pump and patch kit I ride with my cell phone so I can call for help if I get a flat! I'm a bike JAP.

You fell in love with the taste of the word: vicissitude

Love, I am NOT looking for the semantic breakdown until our second cup of coffee. I would much rather just inch over here to pull your body close and find your warmth.

You make your own judgments about whether it is morally better to patch a tire. I am glad you have the phone to call for whatever help you need.

You have RUINED bottled water for me. DAMN IT!

Give me a few weeks, Enviropig, and I'll have you carrying cloth shopping bags into Bailey's Market. Then everyone will think we're having an affair.

May I use the paper ones to burn newspapers in the mean time?

"No," she said icily, "it's not just about disposal, it's about extraction."

"In which case you should see what I bought you for your birthday," he replied. "Diamonds have such a history of oppression, don't you think? Gold mining lays waste to the country. So instead ..."

He reached into a long cloth bag, pulled out tissue paper, "I got you this!"

He pulled out more paper, and more paper, and suggested she fold it for reuse. And more paper. Finally the bag was empty. He handed it to her, with a somewhat pleased look on his face.

"I don't... ?" she said, confused.

"This! Your new grocery bag! Made of cotton grown in the Sudan without the use of nitrates, spun by Egyptian girls making $10 per day each (five times the average wage for similar work).

"The dye is made of berries grown in South America on hillsides otherwise untouched by cultivation. The stitching holding it together is hemp from Mexico. Everything was imported, in a boat powered only by sail, to final assembly in a factory on the Mississippi, where it was put together by out-of-work American textile workers!"

Her face fell, though she tried to put on a brave one.

"Well, that's all very nice, but I was expecting, uh, I don't know, something smaller, maybe more significant?"

"Love, what could be more significant than a $1,275 grocery bag?!?"

You satisfy me.

You have sent me those three simple words before. I imbue them with great significance.

Good. You are supposed to. And with the words is a deep-throated purr. Another thing to consider: let's see just how serene you actually are if and when we ever make it to that couch, which is where we should be having this conversation.

I will hold you and caress you and wrap you up and smile and look deep into your eyes and… and … and…

This is a Girlfriend bucket of cold water: You're a junkie. In order to let go, to let go of so much, so many, you need a new fix.

Maybe that's OK. Maybe that's healthy and constructive. But maybe you need to step back and go cold turkey, and face your aloneness, like you did once before. Just a thought.

"Cold turkey?" Love, what do you think I have done?

Oh, Peter. For someone of your brains you can sure be a dolt. If you're going "cold turkey," then what am I, chopped liver?

I CAN be a dolt. In fact, I take a certain pride in my doltishness. Some would say I have refined doltishness to a level that those of my capabilities rarely achieve. Given that rarity is an attribute, doltishness at this level is singular in level and purity. Of course, purity is precious, and if I am purely a dolt, then the genius is that I appear to be.

You would have made a wonderful 17th Century jester, clever trickster. Reminds me of something from (?I think) Twelfth Night, where the jester asks whether the lady mourns her brother's death: "I fear your brother's soul is in hell, Madonna."

"I know my brother's soul is in heaven, fool."

"The more fool thou art, Madonna, to fear thy brother's soul in heaven."

En Garde! Yours was more literate than mine.

That's because it was Shakespeare, not me. Proof that I'm unintellectual: I'll be on the exercise bike watching Jean Cocteau's "Orpheus" in a few minutes, and I'll need the subtitles.

What I meant by cold turkey may have been different than you meant… I did not think it meant our talks, our closeness. Because I have accepted that your role in my life is as you choose it. In some ways, in the last few days, I have let you go while still loving you. So throw the bucket of cold water if you will, and I will stand here and take it like a man, but save some… for later.

OK, I'm totally confused, and this time I READ THE WHOLE BLOODY EMAIIL, OK? You've "let me go." Does that mean I've been fired? And even though you've paid my feminine wiles no heed, you need a cold shower (or a bucket of water)? Am I on the right track?

No. And you are either being coy or a bit of a dolt yourself.

Well, now that you mention it, I CAN be a dolt. In fact, I take a certain pride in my doltishness. etc.

I cheat on you sometimes with Goofy, you know.

Caviar? Yes or No.

That's alright, I have "Frivolous" tattooed on the inside of my thigh. Caviar? Not so much… Sushi. Which Cocteau movie?

Frivolous is a GUY! I knew you were gay!

It was Orpheus. I told you yesterday. YOU DON't READ MY EMAIL.

I adore sushi, but mostly in the summer. I prefer warm things in winter.

I do read it, every word. I just forgot. Attentive but Amnesiatic. Some believe the Amnesiatic to be a small ocean in Southern Russia, but it's not. It is a spa for the forgetful.

Frivolous is NOT a guy, she took me dancing and we got undressed in my room afterward… though come to think of it, she did turn out the lights when she came out of the bathroom in a towel. EEWWWW.

Did you shower first? xx

I watch shows about science on the discovery channel, on the human brain, consciousness and Quantum Theory. On occasion I do not wipe the bread board after making a sandwich. And I love bleu cheese: Cambozola, Rogue River Creamery, Oregonzola, and a whole variety of cheddar, as long as they are sharp. I snack on almonds and eat vitamins nearly every day, along with Prilosec for my eroded esophagus.

If I was smart enough, and had even a minuscule knowledge of science, I'd watch the discovery channel. I wipe the bread board without fail, but stuff spills on the refrigerator trays and I live with it for months. You forgot Stilton: the sharpest and stinkiest of the bleu, me too. And Brie and chevre and even cheap smoked cheese, and Swiss and Emmenthaler.

I snack on nuts all day, take my vitamins and take Prozac when I feel my confidence needs a boost, even though my doctor laughs at me and says at that dosage it's merely a placebo.

As to the couch at Martha's Café OR a couch at your house, AND your request for clarification, I already clarified: "How about I just sit over here and be me for a while. When you decide if you want me closer or farther away, you just let me know, and I will wait another five minutes just to make sure you are sure."

Closer.

Will you save my spot in that warm place next to you, if I get up to bring us more Stilton and pour you a fresh glass of wine?

No, no more wine, thank you. I sweated on the bike for two hours today; I am a little dehydrated. How about another handful of Triscuts? And for you… even if my favorite cat tries to settle into that warm spot next to me, I'll gently remove him when you come back. Look, I even saved your place in AutoWeek. But, I don't think I'm going to let you read it.

You have no idea how much I would like to share. But I am going to eat the last piece of carrot cake.

I thought of you today when I watched that Cocteau movie. I think it's the best film I've ever seen. 1949. Poetic, innovative, gorgeous. We would've had fun watching it together, on that couch. That elusive couch.

The elusive couch… let's get the Cocteau movie and bring it home, to that couch… And now I have this vision of you facing me, on the couch, with your hands on the back of the couch on either side of my head, looking into my eyes.

Down into those fathomless crevasses… I'm going to fall so deeply that search and rescue will never find me. Time for bed, Mr. Hamilton. I mean, it's time for me to go to bed. XX

Sweet Dreams. I will not be getting much sleep. I have to go to Seattle tomorrow for even more meetings with lawyers who are asking me questions I did not anticipate.

You know what? I'm really not making much sense, or communicating very well. As much as I'd like to share with you tonight, maybe we should lay toe to toe on the couch, reading our own books by the fire. You get up to poke at the embers. I'll read you an amusing anecdote about Teddy R. But maybe it's not a good night to face each other and try to understand.

Toe to toe would work, or you could lie with your head in my lap and I could trace the lovely lines of your jaw and eyes and cat smile with my finger tips. Or with my head in your lap, I drift; building the next project in my mind's eye while you trace my brow with the lightest of nail. Eventually we decide the morning has more to offer than the spent evening. I read a page of magazine and ...

... and this has gotten out of hand. I need to let my defenses down more slowly.

Enjoy Teddy R. I am off to read about motor boats and build my ship of solitude. Good night, Girlfriend.

The reason you need to let your defenses down more slowly has nothing to do with vulnerability or fear. Rather, it is to allow this new infatuation to blossom slowly, so you can savor every exquisite moment, before it leads ineluctably to disillusionment. I'm on to you, Girlfriend.

On to me? Okay. And so what will you do with that? Withdraw? Feint and parry? And if I just sit and laugh and love, without expectation or judgment, what then?

Hope you have 60 seconds to sit with a child and listen to the rain on the roof, a phrase of opera, the beating of your own heart.

Whateverthisis

I awoke to the insistent beat of rain on the skylight in the front entry. "Can't run today, can't run today" it mocked. Defiant, I checked the weather and discovered there is a storm watch with high winds. I thought Port Cedar was in a rain shadow.

I've been with the kids 24/7 since home school Thursday, and was looking forward to "Me" time. Now I'll be at loose ends. I am thinking of taking off next weekend, maybe see Mr. Half Affair while I'm in Seattle.

Yeah, the weather is awful. It's been a long winter.

I've been invited to a kick-off for a special auto racing benefit at the Rainier Club in Seattle. Business or cocktail attire. Is this the type of event to which a man can invite a woman? Girlfriend, this is such a complicated world now.

...are you asking me about who/when/where you should date? Trying to make me jealous?

I was actually trying to invite YOU. But, how can I make you jealous? You're married, have regular if biological sex with your husband, and are planning a rendezvous with a former sorta lover next weekend who desires you greatly and would offer you a small part of his universe… and it's not a small universe!

I am as accepting of "us" as I can be, I love you very much, but I also trust that you would enjoy seeing a smile on my face.

A smile on your face?

Debra Should: Yes, Peter dear, of course I want to see you happy.

Debra Raw: Not unless I bloody well put it there.

No, no regular sex. We hardly speak to one another, how are we supposed to have sex? And he hardly misses the message when after two weeks away, he returns home on the Thursday 5 p.m. ferry and I leave for Seattle on the outbound of same.

As for Mr. Half Affair, the only reason I'm seeing him is that I thought enough time had passed during and we had developed a solid friendship. And I'm entirely certain that he will only have room for himself in his life.

I don't want to be on anyone's periphery, and he's far too self-centered and self-protective for my liking. In fact, he may even be mad at me. I oh-so-gently poked fun at his zealousness the other day, and haven't heard a peep from him. Just as well, the tone of his emails was disconcertingly flirtatious, and I was wondering what I had gotten myself into.

Peter Should: Debra, love, whatever brings you fulfillment, I want to be there for you, Girlfriend, you and your family. I will wait and wait and chastely see others for movies, but only in group settings, and respect any space that you need for whatever needs you have with whomever.

Peter Raw: Let me take you to Seattle and wine you and dine you and make you laugh; and share with you Parnassus Books and the stalking of bakeries for carrot cake and the art museum; and play backgammon with the loser accepting the unbridled attentions of the winner, I shall lose on purpose to run my lips from your nose to your toes.

Mr. Half might be more insecure than me. On the other hand, you are a femme fatale, and successful men bend before your incredible charm.

I don't know, Debra. What we have and what we want are complicated. Gonna take time to sort out.

Shall I tell you which version I prefer?

The idea of me as a femme fatale is laughable! You've quite romanticized me. I'm an unsatisfied housewife with her nose buried in a book. Or I was, now I'm buried in email. I'd love to know of "all" these successful men who bend before my charm. Sounds wonderful.

Mr. Half Affair. Mister Full Affair. Pilot Husband. Me, though I don't belong in such company. Shall I tell you which version I prefer?

Mr. Full is a sleazy jerk who has slept with 1/2 the women in Seattle (oh, yes, I made sure our sex was very safe). Yes, you should.

We should meet at Parnassus Books. Have coffee on the couch at The Edgewater Hotel.

I'm not going to just sleep with you, you know. Believe it or not, despite your impression of me, I'm not that kind of girl. I don't know you, not in that way. So it would be a very expensive excursion for some time on a (or the?) couch.

And why do you believe I wouldn't think that's worth it?

There are less expensive couches in Port Cedar. And it just seems so contrived, almost as far as we could get from the original idea of the "couch." You know: sweat pants and Popular Mechanics... I just... oh my God, am I really saying this?... didn't want you to get the wrong idea.

I can't believe you are saying it either. Didn't I get the cold shoulder for trying to introduce morality into the play?

Debra, no strings. The reason for Seattle is real time and real privacy and a real chance to explore. I would love to have some real time with you, to see if we would lapse into an easy rhythm where neither of us needs to fill silence.

Though, at some point, it would be worthwhile to see if we have physical compatibility, too, if there is fire as well as smoke. But that is not my goal.

INcompatibility. Wouldn't that be a liberating irony? A safe return to sexless Girlfriendhood? Our coffees would be so without sexual nuance that not even anyone in gossipy, conservative Port Cedar would look askance.

I would accompany you through girlfriends, you would mentor me through travails in my life. No pain, no jealousy, no confusion. No heat, no mystery, no being driven wild with anticipation.

What is it in us, meaning you and me in particular, that makes us wring passions out of life? We don't rest gently, despite your outwardly stoic demeanor and my futile attempts at control.

Somehow, I don't think we would find incompatibility, and hope we could let go enough to find out how hot is heat. We wring passions out of life because we must. The alternative is not.

You know, I am the Master of Lines. Or the Master of Getting Caught Between the Lines. or being strangled by her own lines.

I say there must be no lines then chastise you for going beyond them. I draw secret lines and wait for you to cross. I swing the lines like a jump rope, I slither them on the ground, I wrap them around my own neck. Unfamiliar territory here.

It's hard to believe it is unfamiliar territory for you, but perhaps I am glad that it is. Me too, in many ways.

I don't think of myself as desirable or particularly clever, and though I have a presence and am pretty well read, I know people a lot smarter than me. So what do I really have to offer?

Debra, Yucatan was really us. I believe, in many ways, I could enthrall you with tales of the Mayan calendar and how it makes time disappear in the dark of a new moon, and you would hypnotize me with finger-tips playing in the curls above my collar.

But silence... could we last in silence? Would you ever trust me enough to see me smile and wait for me? Would you ever love me enough to give up the fangs of derision?

Would I be able to come out of my shell long enough to pull you in? Yucatan… Venice… we opened ourselves in many ways… you know the wordsmith, but there is more to my life than words I spin into curtains of truth to be parted again and again.

There is no way I would blame you for drawing another line. I tried and you took offense. If you try, I shall not. No strings, I told you that. Time, and silence. I wonder if we could stand it, I wonder if we will ever find out.

I may be your Faustian bargain. At least you seem to have regained your voice.

You are my muse. I have no explanation for it. "~ Most of us go to our grave with our music still inside of us ~"

I'd say most don't have music inside them. Especially these days when media has become The Art, and has drummed uniform messages of sexuality and consumerism into the American soul.

You know, your statement that I am your muse has me wondering how the whole unexplored sexuality aspect of our relationship has impacted us. I'm still me, I still love words and thoughts, and yours in particular, but I wonder whether you would have been driven to produce them in the same way.

It's connected with the idea of "passionate love" I was exploring. Maybe a better word is "inspiration." Historically many artists have had muses, and many of them have been attractive and of the opposite gender.

I'm undisciplined this morning.

I don't know the role of sexuality in particular, but I think vulnerability is needed to open the heart and soul to art. Sexuality has a role in romance, but it may be secondary rather than proximate cause of creativity.

Why are you the muse? Why not Molly? — I don't know. I did not write for her. Ryder… no. Just no. Lover? She got some of this, long ago, but in a much more structured form.

Why me? I can venture a guess. I'm not very smart or very beautiful or very anything, but I do sparkle. I see and feel deeply, and it shows. Some people are just like that. At the same time, you feel so… familiar.

Yucatan… was very dangerous, because it took our relationship to a new place… I fell in love with the you who was traveling with me… So full, so familiar.

Peter, did you mean it or were you just humoring me when you agreed that we felt "familiar"?

Familiar? Like we had known each other for decades. Wrong answer?

Oh, no! Your answer was very much the "right" answer.

My God, Debra, I have this vision of you in a soft silver sweater with a small hole over the heart, I can see your collar bones and your throat, your shoulder, the thin strap of your top underneath, a broach.

I see you look at me and then ask me to stop looking at you. Then you turn and lean against me and hold the arm that is holding you. Your cat's mouth. Your eyes of such a unique greenish gold of exotic slate.

Your mouth as you begin to surrender to the moment, where thinking and talking evaporate into what you are wanting. If I never hold you, I will think of that; if I hold you often, I will remember that.

Your fingers in my hair, my hands on your back, the feeling of my hands each spread wide on your back and holding you close, knowing how close I could hold you, like that, with my hands.

Wait.... wait! Are you letting fear of the future deprive you of the present? Again!? What do you mean, "if" you never hold me? You're doubly cruel tonight, Mr. Peter Five Syllable Hamilton. Whateverthisis, you can't dismiss it that easily.

Whateverthis is, I have fallen in love with you. But why would you love a man of such dubious morals?

But MY dubious morals tell me I have already done the worst. I have shared my soul with you, I have shared wafting melodies of Me with you. We've already done the worst, haven't we?

No, the worst would be falling in love with each other regardless of consequences.

Ferry

Dear Mr. Hamilton,

I seem to have left the fingers of my left hand twirled around thick strands of hair from that spot 2 inches above the back of your neck. Would you be good enough to return them?

I have acquired, for the novice bachelor, various items which include: high-fiber whole-wheat pasta (trust me, at least palatable), olive tapenade, sun-dried tomato bruschetta and various other sundries. Please arrange for a time and place to pick these up at your earliest convenience, and you shall be saved from another week of tuna fish on Triscuits.

That was very sweet of you. May I postpone receiving the bounty? I'm headed to Seattle for a few days to wrestle with lawyers. A trip to Parnassus Books. Maybe a movie or three. At loose ends: the price of freedom.

Me too. I mean, at loose ends. The kids are at my mom's; Robert is in L.A. My friends claim they are busy. Because of the storm (will this pouring rain never stop?), I told my mom I had to get back to Port Cedar to take care of the animals, and would come back for the kids on Sunday.

I could call the house-sitter and come early. Want to get together? I hear there's a couch at your hotel.

Can you make the 3 p.m. ferry? I have a car on the other end. I'd be happy to give you a ride downtown, to the bookstore, to the couch, or anyplace else you might like to go.

I'll see you at Martha's.

* * *

Was that you running toward the gate? I saw someone in a yellow windbreaker waving at the deckhand, just as they closed the gate. She was pointing at the ferry, he was shaking his head. We hadn't departed the dock. I couldn't get a good look because of the heavy rain. I was standing on the second deck, you might have seen me.

Yes! I told him I could be on board in 20 seconds, but he wouldn't open the gate and started quoting the damn rule book to me! It was so close! I thought could see you, too, but it was raining so hard, I couldn't be sure.

Peter, I am so, so sorry! As I was leaving the house, I realized I'd left the downstairs door open. When I went back, two of the cats had gotten out. The house-sitter couldn't come until morning, so I had to get them back in because of the owls. I thought I had time to catch the ferry but just missed it!

You must have been there right at 2:59. I know they are pretty strict, but would think they could let one more "walk-on" board with a minute to spare.

Yes! I kept looking at my watch the whole way. I was so certain I could make it! But with the storm causing everyone to drive so damn slow, and trying to find a place to park, I just missed it!

Why didn't you call? I wondered all the way over if I should wait at the other end, come back, or head on downtown. I tried to call you a half-dozen times. I could have waited until the next ferry. It was only going to be a couple more hours.

I left my phone in the kitchen last night and forgot to charge it. It was dead as could be, and I didn't know until I got in the car to rush to the ferry. Then, when I pulled up and finally found a place to park, I just ran to the ferry. When I saw the gate close, I was just devastated.

I didn't want you to have to wait for me! I knew you would go to all sorts of inconvenience. It wouldn't have been fair to you and would have just ruined our time together. It's better just to reschedule. Can we? The next time you're in Seattle?

Are you angry? You have every right to be!

Debra, the 3 p.m. ferry today was delayed because of wind in the channel. They were letting walk-ons on board until just before departure at 3:45. You had plenty of time. You just didn't show. Everything you wrote here was a lie. What's going on?

So, you just set me up?

Yeah. I was curious what you would have to say. I'm a little taken aback by the elaborate fabrication.

I changed my mind about coming. I didn't want to hurt your feelings.

You couldn't call? You just left me hanging? You lied to keep from hurting my feelings? C'mon.

I didn't call because I didn't want to hear the disappointment in your voice. And I was conflicted. I didn't want you to try to change my mind.

You were conflicted? Wasn't this your idea?

After I said I would meet with you, and shut down my computer, I started getting second thoughts. By the time I was putting my bag together, I realized that meeting you in Seattle was a really, really bad idea. We were just setting ourselves up for heartbreak, or worse. I didn't know how to tell you, so I just bailed out. I'm sorry.

So you just left me hanging out there? That was a really, really shitty thing to do.

It's not like you arranged the trip to Seattle just to see me. You were going anyway. You already had the hotel reservations; you didn't spend any money you weren't going to spend. So we didn't get to spend a few hours on the "couch," or in the bookstore... what's the big deal?

I wanted to see you. Be with you. Make Biography into an actual memory. See if we were compatible in person. See if our dreams could be real. Meeting with you was a big deal for me.

See if our dreams could be real? Peter, you decided to live on a boat, knowing how I feel about boats. You've had to downsize your life to where there is barely room for your own kids, no room for me, let alone my children.

I told you several times that I didn't want to have an affair, and yes, I changed my mind more than once. But an affair with you would be so dangerous, and has many, far too many, potential downsides. I realized, as I was packing, that the whole idea was just insane.

And so you just blew me off with a package of lies.

It's not like you have been a paragon of truth.

Excuse me? What's that supposed to mean? I was on the ferry. Where the hell were you?

Aside from all your very well-documented duplicities, you have been living down there on a boat in that marina for I don't know how long. How is your friend Ryder?

I have no idea how Ryder is. As to my duplicities, yes indeed. Guilty as charged. But a man can change, and I have.

C'mon, Peter. Given your libido, and Ryder's from what you have described, are you really telling me that if you lived within a two-minute walk, you would not have heard from her?

I've not seen her at the marina. She calls once in a while. I don't pick up and she leaves a message. Sometimes she gets through using a number my phone does not recognize. She asks cursory questions about the twins, about Molly, the goddam weather. What's your point? How does this relate to you blowing me off and lying about it?

Why do you talk to her at all? Why can't you simply tell her not to call? Or do you really like this attention? Do you really like having someone pining for you?

I didn't show because I don't trust you, because you can't be trusted. For reasons that maybe I am only again beginning to understand, you seem unable to break it off with Ryder. You aren't that naïve, Peter. You know what you're doing.

Actually, this is very consistent with your pattern, and maybe with your abandonment issues. You always need to know that someone really wants you. It's probably something you should work on.

Whoa! What the hell just happened, here? Are you saying you don't believe I ended the relationship with Ryder?

I'm not sure what to believe. I think you are either trying to fool me, or you have completely fooled yourself. I don't know what's real. Ryder may not have ever had a boat at the marina, but don't tell me you wouldn't know it if she did.

Jesus. I have no idea where this is coming from. You don't know what to believe? For that matter, why believe in any of it? But here is some truth:

Watch out for purple vines… those are Jealousies. They have flowers that smell erotic but never bear fruit, and get their color from rage. Instead of thorns, they have thin-jointed fingers with inch-long nails filed to a point. Step to the right, and you'll be fine.

Ignore the orange toad. Yes, he's the size of a coffee table, but that's just Mimicry. I taught him to speak before I knew he would learn to say words that you imagine, but say them to you using my voice.

He has no teeth, but he sits behind the Jealousies, trying to lure you into their grasp so he can lap spots of blood from your scratches with his outlandish tongue.

Here's the gate… Hannah has just asked you what's for dinner. Jacob plays Spanish guitar in his room. Robert won't be home for days, and I am over here shedding my need for relationships as if it were old skin. Nothing has changed.

Peter, this is just so typical. You live in fantasy. You've made up this absurd "Garden." You say you've seduced all these beautiful women; that they are so special. But that evaporates for you, and devastates them, as soon as you have made a conquest.

You aren't really that good-looking. I'm wondering how much is real, and how much is just your wishful thinking.

Okay. But while you are at it, why believe any of it?

Why believe that there even is a Ryder? Why believe there even is a Lover? You call yourself a bored Jewish Housewife? Maybe I'm just a bored guy with a wild imagination, sitting at his computer, trying to seduce you with tales of licentious living. Maybe it's *all* just made up.

Are you trying to confess? Come clean? What's real, Peter?

What's real? You've had disappointment, so there is no god. Your hero leaves his glass in the sink? There are no heros. A lover's breath is not minty fresh in the morning? How could you fall for someone of such decay? A man shows pain at your mockery? Obviously he is weak and insecure. That's your "real."

You devise tests that support only your cynicism. You discount evidence to the contrary, and you emphasize details that validate your disappointment. You manage outcomes that guarantee your worst expectations. You always devalue instead of value. No man could survive such a process. That's what's real.

Too late. You're trapped. Lawyers love it when they get to ask, "are you lying now or were you lying then?"

Oh, Debra, don't you know your court has no jurisdiction here? Your rules of logic are not valid, here?

Do you remember telling me after "Venice" how wonderful it was being known? After Parnassus Books and carrot cake? How you thought it so wonderful that someone knew "the real you?"

Okay. I'll play: You thought we had discovered "what's real" through fiction? Known fictionally is fictitiously known.

You don't know what's real, here. Any of it. We have written. That is what you know. You never met Lover, or Ryder, you don't even know their names, and you never will. You will never be able to prove if they are real or not.

Yes, you are right, I suppose. What *do* you know? What *can* you really believe? What *is* real? The only sure fact, at this moment, is that you justify your own lies by calling me a liar.

Here's what I believe: You are a poseur. You say you're a great race car driver, but all you do is build an engine bigger than everyone else and drive away.

You lived this expensive life at the same time you were going broke. You go on and on about the accomplishments of your children who are are not popular, according to my kids.

Even your writing is full of purple prose. You think soars, but it often falls flat. You are full of self-delusion and affectation. A fraud. Much less than you appear in your own mind.

Glad you finally got that on the table. But let's take it a step further, shall we?

What's real? As far as you know, you've been writing emails that have been answered by your own cruel husband. Maybe he has his secretary respond, and they all are laughing at you in the pilot's lounge.

What's real? As far as you know, you slip out of bed at night in an Ambien fog, and you write yourself emails from an email address you created in a state of psychotic longing.

What's real? You can't "know" what's real. What's real is a matter of faith. And you reject faith, just as stridently as you reject god, and heroes. I say love takes a leap of faith, and you laugh and say I suffer from delusions.

Tell you what: Your cynicism is the most insidious lie of all, because it validates whatever fear, or anxiety, or trauma that has left you so twisted. There is no proving or disproving the "truth" of what you fear, so it consumes you.

You won't ever know what's real. Cynicism is the smallest cell in the meanest prison of the human soul, because it mangles hope. And you are hopeless. So screw you.

Fuck you. Fuck you.

Wordless

It was a beautiful spring day. Last night's rain left everything refreshed, and lay in puddles on the road. We were in Seattle, of course, on one of those hills off Bell Avenue.

You were seated on the banana seat of the Sting Ray, and I was on the handlebars. We were laughing, playing as we play, losing ourselves in that exhilarating downhill momentum. Suddenly, you hit the brakes. I went flying over the handlebars.

Maybe you saw an obstacle in the distance. Maybe it was my darkly cynical belief that love cannot endure. You left me (for you did, you know) pondering my assertion that friendship can last, but love is fleeting. I've vomited a collection of thoughts over the past few months to help myself articulate a distinction so clear to me:

I do believe relationships can endure. I believe couplings, relationships, marriages can retain their positive, happiness-giving nature. With a "good enough" list of ingredients, and a mutual determination to hang around in the kitchen long after the meal is served, well past the messy clean up, "good enough" marriages (whatever modern equivalent) can last.

But passionate love burns under a death sentence. Many will not know its precious, white-hot desire. So firmly ensconced are they in the limitations of convention: Is she hot, is he rich, SWM seeks SWF w/ sense of humor… it eludes them.

Others may brush against it and discover seared fingers, a shudder of ecstasy, an hour of torrid bliss. The lucky will live inside it: heat feeding heat, a liquid phoenix melting and reforming, it feels insatiable, infinite.

Passionate love is ravenous, we are voracious. I burn and yearn for you, with no restraint and total focus. I am consumed. Call me again. Leave a message. Again and another and another. Hold me tighter, closer, surround me, suffocate me... devour me as I devour you, don't leave a single "I love you" unsaid, the tiniest patch of my skin uncovered by your own. I will know no love like this again, a love like ours will never die...

But passion's death is inevitable. With queasy apprehension, I dread the pain when your passion for me wanes. I dread the foreboding when you don't call in the morning: "Things got busy and I just forgot." I dread your preoccupation when we make love.

But that is nothing next to the anguish I will feel when my love for you begins to diminish, when I am no longer compelled to seek your embrace, yield to your longing, when intimacy becomes a matter for scheduling, a fill-in when time permits, a snack instead of a meal, when annoyances, once endearing, frustrate and draw derision. All too soon I will forget the passion which we were.

So things have probably worked out for the best.

You may remember Adventure Boy? We stayed in touch. He is producing a short film called "Epic Summer." He has invited me to come along on a once-in-a-lifetime trip down the Colorado River, followed by a bike excursion in Moab, then rock climbing in Colorado. Robert has agreed to take the kids for six weeks. I can hardly wait.

I hope you are well.

—Debra

Thanks for your note, sorry it took me so long to respond. The kids and I are exploring the fjords of Canada, on our way to Alaska, aboard *Trilogy.* Her owners have family obligations on the East Coast and graciously allowed us to use her this summer.

Internet is not always available. I usually don't miss it (we have a ton of books on board, and swap with other sailors), though friends have wondered, at times, if I've dropped off the planet.

I also thought hard about how to respond, if I should respond. I finally decided to write, and let things be as they will be. As to passion and friendship: some are lucky to light bright candles of passion, and sometimes those sputter out, leaving a small wisp of smoke, smelling of waxy despair. But those can ignite love, too, if not as bright, then more warm and lasting.

You were right, back when you said my relationship with the twins had more resilience than I knew. I have them for the summer. Molly is enjoying Europe with college friends. I think she told Abby she has "met someone" over there, and I'm glad for her.

We'll remember this trip forever. Forests and mountains erupt from water's edge. Bears of all sizes lumber along creek-fall cascades. We've been traveling with a pod of orca for a couple of days, who seem to like my music. I don't think I'm making that up, but can never be sure.

I always thought of a "trilogy" as three books in sequence. But, as the three of us meander on rushing tides among these islands, on adventures that braid with those of other boats, perhaps a trilogy may be three simultaneous stories, woven together in time.

And I don't have words to describe a sun rising at dawn through sleepy mists lingering among silent cedars, or setting, molten, with a sizzle into the sea; nor for the muscular metallic density of salmon heavy in the net; nor lightning at midnight, flashing huge castles of cloud into existence during strobes of summer squall.

These moments, words just cannot convey.

~Peter

End

Epilogue

While writing "Chalice," I learned many things. One is that we drag reactions that we justify into our relationships, but without having a clue as to where the behavior actually originated. Most often, we have no idea why we do what we do.

It is very difficult to separate the "subjects" of disagreement from the real "issues" underlying unhappiness, especially when deep survival mechanisms kick into gear.

Anger, irrational jealousy, repetitive withdrawal from intimacy, rejection, devaluation, clinginess to the point of suffocation, and controlling behaviors are very destructive. But they are not inevitable and can be mitigated, if not eliminated, with insight, vulnerability, resources, a lot of hard work and possibly the aid of a professional.

This prompted me to start "It's Nobody's Fault," a short book about our need for "connection," the attachment system that develops during early childhood and influences our romantic relationships, and adult attachment disorders. I hope to finish it before 2014.

"It's Nobody's Fault" is not a fix-your-marriage book, and I am not qualified to write that sort of book. At best, I hope to direct anyone who is interested to resources where they may find their own answers. I'd like to broadcast some of the language and concepts I've been given over the last few years to the general discussion.

More information can be found at erikdolson.com.

Erik Dolson

Erik Dolson graduated from Stanford University in 1973 with a degree in Philosophy. He drifted around Europe and Asia for a couple of years, drove a forklift in Israel during one of their frequent wars, hid from soldiers on Cypress while trying to get to Turkey, was treated well by those who eventually became the Taliban, looked for God in India.

Dolson returned home to San Francisco, then waited tables in Portland, Oregon for six years while trying with little success to get published.

For 25 years, Dolson lived in a small Oregon town where he was owner, editor and publisher of the weekly newspaper and helped raise his two wonderful daughters. After the girls were fledged and his ex-wife took over responsibility for the newspaper, he returned to writing fiction.

Dolson currently splits his time between Oregon and the San Juan Islands. In addition to "Chalice," he is working on the fourth draft of "All But Forgotten," a mystery set in the San Juan's and Seattle, and a small book on Adult Attachment Disorder, "It's Nobody's Fault."

More about Erik Dolson, along with his blog and snippets from the books, can be found at erikdolson.com.

CPSIA information can be obtained at www.ICGtesting.com
Printed in the USA
BVOW08s1538040913

330216BV00001B/52/P

9 780989 747912